Irish-American Poets

Songs and Ballads by the Most Gifted Poets of the Emerald Isle

Including Moore, David, Griffin, Lover, Mangan, and Other Popular Irish...

Irish-American Poets

Songs and Ballads by the Most Gifted Poets of the Emerald Isle
Including Moore, David, Griffin, Lover, Mangan, and Other Popular Irish...

ISBN/EAN: 9783744783279

Printed in Europe, USA, Canada, Australia, Japan

Cover: Foto ©Andreas Hilbeck / pixelio.de

More available books at **www.hansebooks.com**

SONGS AND BALLADS

BY THE MOST GIFTED

Poets of the Emerald Isle

INCLUDING

MOORE, DAVIS, GRIFFIN, LOVER, MANGAN,

AND OTHER POPULAR IRISH BARDS,

With Choice Selections from the Most Brilliant

IRISH-AMERICAN POETS.

———•——

NEW YORK:
FRANK TOUSEY, PUBLISHER.
1880.

POPULAR SONGS AND BALLADS

OF THE

EMERALD ISLE.

———o———

CONTENTS.

SUMMARY OF CONTENTS.

WITH SKETCHES OF THE AUTHORS.

CHOICE SELECTIONS FROM THE MOST POPULAR

IRISH AND IRISH-AMERICAN POETS,

EMBRACING

OLIVER GOLDSMITH, CHARLES LEVER, CHARLES GAVAN DUFFY, JOHN K. CASEY, THOMAS FRANCIS MEAGHER, T. D. SULLIVAN, JOHN BOYLE O'REILLY, JOHN LOCKE, STEPHEN J. MEANY, JOHN SAVAGE, D. F. M'CARTHY, WILLIAM P. MULCHINOCK, MICHAEL DOHENY,

AND THE BEST POETS OF OUR DAY,

WILL BE FOUND

FROM PAGE TO PAGE.

THOMAS MOORE.

IRELAND has been described by strangers as pre-eminently a nation of poets and orators. Her claim to the first portion of this title may be disputed by many, and with every appearance of justice. Ireland has not produced a Homer, a Dante, or a Shakespeare. Yet her people are a singularly poetic and imaginative race; and, if from among them no man has yet arisen to take rank with the glorious triad above mentioned, it is undeniable that in poets of a minor order, (all great and beautiful in their own rank), that lovely western island, which is too painfully close to Great Britain, is most prolific.

As a nation of orators, Ireland's title stands unquestioned. Her greatest orators are doubtless as great as those that have arisen in any nation. A true orator is a prose poet; and of all orators, it has been truly said that Ireland's illustrious son, Henry Grattan, is the most poetical.

Now the reasons, when weighed, will be found sufficient, why Ireland should be pre-eminent in oratory, and yet not have produced a poet of the very highest order. No nation subject to another, enslaved and oppressed, though the minstrels that sing her woes may be the sweetest and most melodious, ever produced a Homer or a Dante; it needs the full freedom, power and energy of political nationality for that. On the other hand, it is the desperate struggle of a people whose national sentiments is unconquerable, against a mighty and unscrupulous tyrant, that gives the broadest and most exciting field to the orator.

Hence, poor, suffering, but indomitable Ireland owns a galaxy of orators unequaled in the world: her Grattan, Flood, Plunkett, Curran, Emmet, O'Connell, Shiell, Meagher and O'Gorman.

But if Ireland's time is not yet come to produce a poet of that rank of which none of the great free nations has ever produced more than one, it is a fact of universal acceptance that in poets of the next grade she is unsurpassed.

Let us take, as our first example, the marvelously gifted child of song whose name is placed at the head of this little volume.

And who has not heard of Tom Moore? His songs have traveled far and wide, and have brought solace, and comfort, and joy to half the world. They have cheered the exile in his lonely hut, the sailor on the forecastle has sung them to the storm, around the soldier's bivouac fire their melody has made the long night pass in happiness away—touching every chord of human feeling—sometimes as full of mystic sadness as is the pale moonbeam, again as sportive, gay and gladsome as the summer breeze that toys with the rose and dances on the ripple of the sunlit sea. Translated into every European language, in every nation they have found a home, and they will be sung and listened to with delight by young and by old, in the far-off days to come, when great cities, yet unbuilt, shall rule the destinies of continents whose wilds are yet untrodden and unexplored. Lord Byron said that Moore's songs: "Oh, Blame Not the Bard," "Breathe Not His Name," "When He Who Adores Thee," were worth all the epics that ever were written.

POEMS OF THOMAS MOORE.

BRIAN THE BRAVE.*

AIR:—"*Molly Macalpin.*"

REMEMBER the glories of Brian the brave,
  Tho' the days of the hero are o'er;
Tho' lost to Mononia† and cold in the grave,
  He returns to Kinkora‡ no more.
That star of the field which so often has
      pour'd
  Its beam on the battle, is set;
But enough of its glory remains on each
      sword,
  To light us to victory yet.

Mononia! when Nature embellish'd the tint
  Of thy fields and thy mountains so fair,
Did she ever intend that a tyrant should
      print
  The footstep of slavery there?
No! Freedom, whose smile we shall never
      resign,
  Go tell our invaders, the Danes,
That 'tis sweeter to bleed for an age at thy
      shrine,
  Than to sleep but a moment in chains.

Forget not our wounded companions, who
      stood§
  In the day of distress by our side;

While the moss of the valley grew red with
      their blood,
  They stirr'd not, but conquer'd and died.
That sun which now blesses our arms with
      his light,
Saw them fall upon Ossory's plain;
  Oh! let him not blush, when he leaves us
      to-night,
  To find that they fell there in vain.

* Brian Boromhe, the great monarch of Ireland, who was killed at the battle of Clontarf, in the beginning of the eleventh century, after having defeated the Danes in twenty-five engagements.
† Munster.
‡ The palace of Brian.
§ This alludes to an interesting circumstance related of the Dalgais, the favorite troops of Brian, when they were interrupted in their return from the battle of Clontarf, by Fitzpatrick, Prince of Ossory. The wounded men entreated that they might be allowed to fight with the rest.—"*Let stakes* (they said) *be stuck in the ground, and suffer each of us, tied to and supported by one of these* stakes, to be placed in his rank by the side of a sound man." "Between seven and eight hundred men (adds O'Halloran) pale, emaciated, and supported in this manner, appeared mixed with the foremost of the troops; never was such another sight exhibited."—*History of Ireland,* book 12th, chap. I.

THE HARP THAT ONCE THRO' TARA'S HALLS.

AIR:—"*Gramachree.*"

THE harp that once, thro' Tara's halls,
  The soul of Music shed,
Now hangs as mute on Tara's walls,
  As if that soul were fled:
So sleeps the pride of former days,
  So glory's thrill is o'er;
And hearts, that once beat high for praise,
  Now feel that pulse no more!

No more to chiefs and ladies bright
  The harp of Tara swells;
The chord, alone, that breaks at night,
  Its tale of ruin tells:
Thus Freedom now so seldom wakes,
  The only throb she gives
Is when some heart, indignant, breaks,
  To show that still she lives!

LET ERIN REMEMBER THE DAYS OF OLD.

AIR:—"*The Red Fox.*"

Let Erin remember the days of old,
  Ere her faithless sons betrayed her,
When Malachi wore the collar of gold
  Which he won from her proud invader;
When her kings, with standard of green unfurl'd,
  Led the Red-Branch Knights to danger,
Ere the emerald gem of the western world
Was set in in the crown of a stranger.

On Laugh-Neagh's bank, as the fisherman strays,
  When the clear cold eve's declining,
He sees the round towers of other days
  In the wave beneath him shining!
Thus shall Memory often, in dreams sublime,
  Catch a glimpse of the days that are over;
Thus, sighing, look thro' the waves of Time
For the long-faded glories they cover.

OH, FOR THE SWORDS OF FORMER TIME.

Oh, for the swords of former time!
  Oh, for the men who bore them;
When, arm'd for Right, they stood sublime,
  And tyrants crouch'd before them!
When pure yet, ere courts began
  With honors to enslave him,
The best honors worn by Man
  Were those which virtue gave him.
    Oh, for the swords of former time, etc.

Oh, for the kings who flourish'd then!
  Oh, for the pomp that crown'd them;
When hearts and hands of freeborn men
  Were all the ramparts 'round them.
When, safe built on bosoms true,
  The throne was but the center,
'Round which Love a circle drew,
  That Treason durst not enter.
    Oh, for the kings who flourish'd then, etc.

THE VALLEY LAY SMILING BEFORE ME.

AIR:—"*The Pretty Girl Milking her Cow.*"

[These stanzas are founded upon an event of most melancholy importance to Ireland, if, as we are told by our Irish historians, it gave England the first opportunity of dividing, conquering, and enslaving us. The following are the circumstances, as related by O'Halloran. "The King of Leinster had long conceived a violent affection for Dearbhorgil, daughter to the King of Meath; and though she had been for some time married to O'Ruark, Prince of Breffni, yet could it not restrain his passion. They carried on a private correspondence, and she informed him that O'Ruark intended soon to go on a pilgrimage (an act of piety frequent in those days), and conjured him to embrace that opportunity of conveying her from a husband she detested to a lover she adored. Mac Murchad too punctually obeyed the summons, and had the lady coveyed to his capital of Ferns." The monarch Roderic espoused the cause of O'Ruark, whie Mac Murchad fled to England, and obtained the assistance of Henry II.

"Such," adds Giraldus Cambrensis (as I find him in an old translation), "is the variable and fickle nature of women, by whom all mischiefs in the world (for the most part) do happen and come, as may appear by Marcus Antoninus, and by the destruction of Troy."]

The valley lay smiling before me,
  Where lately I left her behind;
Yet I trembled, and something hung o'er me,
  That sadden'd the joy of my mind.
I look'd for the lamp which she told me
  Should shine, when her Pilgrim return'd,
But, though darkness began to enfold me,
  No lamp from the battlements burn'd!

I flew to her chamber—'twas lonely
  As if the lov'd tenant lay dead—
Ah, would it were death, and death only!
  But no—the young false one had fled.
And there hung the lute, that could soften
  My very worst pains into bliss,
While the hand, that had wak'd it so often,
  Now throbb'd to my proud rival's kiss!

There *was* a time, falsest of women!
  When Breffni's good sword would have sought
That man, through a million of foemen,
  Who dar'd but to doubt thee *in thought!*
While now—oh! degenerate daughter
  Of Erin! how fall'n is thy fame!
And through ages of bondage and slaughter,
  Thy country shall bleed for thy shame.

Already, the curse is upon her,
  And strangers her valleys profane;
They come to divide—to dishonor—
  And tyrants they long will remain!
But, onward!—the green banner rearing,
  Go, flesh ev'ry brand to the hilt;
On *our* side is Virtue and Erin,
  On *theirs* is the Saxon and Guilt.

GO WHERE GLORY WAITS THEE.

Air:—*"Maid of the Valley."*

Go where glory waits thee;
But, while Fame elates thee,
  Oh! still remember me.
When the praise thou meetest
To thine ear is sweetest,
  Oh! then remember me.
Other arms may press thee,
Dearer friends caress thee,
All the joys that bless thee
  Sweeter far may be;
But when friends are nearest,
And when joys are dearest,
  Oh! then remember me.

When, at eve, thou rovest,
By the star thou lovest,
  Oh! then remember me.
Think, when home returning,
Bright we've seen it burning.
  Oh! thus remember me.
Oft, as summer closes,

When thine eye reposes
On its ling'ring roses,
  Once so lov'd by thee,
Think of her who wove them,
Her who made thee love them;
  Oh! then remember me.

When, around thee, dying,
Autumn-leaves are lying,
  Oh! then remember me.
And, at night, when gazing
On the gay hearth blazing,
  Oh! still remember me.
Then should Music, stealing
All the soul of Feeling,
To thy heart appealing,
  Draw one tear from thee;
Then let Mem'ry bring thee
Strains I us'd to sing thee;
  Oh! then remember me.

———o———

THE MINSTREL BOY.

Air:—*" The Moreen."*

The Minstrel Boy to the war is gone,
  In the ranks of death you'll find him;
His father's sword he has girded on,
  And his wild harp slung behind him.
"Land of Song!" said the warrior-bard,
  "Tho' all the world betrays thee,
One sword, at least, thy rights shall guard,
  One faithful harp shall praise thee!"

The Minstrel fell!—but the foeman's chain
  Could not bring that proud soul under;
The harp he lov'd ne'er spoke again,
  For he tore its chords asunder;
And said: "No chains shall sully thee,
  Thou soul of love and bravery!
Thy songs were made for the pure and free,
  They shall never sound in slavery."

———o———

'TIS THE LAST ROSE OF SUMMER.

Air:—*" Groves of Blarney."*

'Tis the last rose of summer,
  Left blooming alone;
All her lovely companions
  Are faded and gone;
No flower of her kindred,
  No rose-bud is nigh,
To reflect back her blushes,
  Or give sigh for sigh!

I'll not leave thee, thou lone one!
  To pine on the stem;
Since the lovely are sleeping,
  Go, sleep thou with them;

Thus kindly I scatter
  Thy leaves o'er the bed,
Where thy mates of the garden
  Lie scentless and dead.

So soon may I follow,
  When friendship's decay,
And from Love's shining circle
  The gems drop away!
When true hearts lie wither'd,
  And fond ones are flown,
Oh, who would inhabit
  This bleak world alone?

———o———

OH! BLAME NOT THE BARD.

AIR—"*Kitty Tyrrel.*"

OH! blame not the Bard, if he fly to the bowers,
  Where pleasure lies carelessly smiling at fame;
He was born for much more, and, in happier hours,
  His soul might have burn'd with a holier flame.
The string that now languishes loose o'er the lyre,
  Might have bent a proud bow to the warrior's dart;
And the lip which now breathes but the song of desire,
  Might have pour'd the full tide of the patriot's heart!

But, alas, for this country! her pride is gone by,
  And that spirit is broken which never would bend;
O'er the ruin her children in secret must sigh,
  For 'tis treason to love her, and death to defend!
Unpriz'd are her sons, till they've learned to betray;
  Undistinguish'd they live, if they shame not their sires,
And the torch that would light them thro' dignity's way,

Must be caught from the pile where their country expires!

Then blame not the Bard, if, in pleasure's soft dream,
  He should try to forget what he never can heal!
Oh! give but a hope—let a vista but gleam
  Thro' the gloom of his country, and mark how he'll feel!
That instant, his heart at her shrine would lay down
  Ev'ry passion it nurs'd, ev'ry bliss it ador'd;
While the myrtle, now idly entwin'd with his crown,
  Like the wreath of Harmodius, should cover his sword.

But, tho' glory be gone, and tho' hope fade away,
  Thy name, loved Erin! shall live in his songs;
Not e'en in the hour when his heart is most gay,
  Will he lose the remembrance of thee and thy wrongs!
The stranger shall hear thy lament on his plains;
  The sigh of thy harp shall be sent o'er the deep,
Till thy masters themselves, as they rivet thy chains,
  Shall pause at the song of their captive, and weep!

——o——

THE MEETING OF THE WATERS.*

AIR:—"*The Old Head of Denis.*"

THERE is not in this wild world a valley so sweet
As that vale in whose bosom the bright waters meet.†
Oh, the last rays of feeling and life must depart
Ere the bloom of that valley shall fade from my heart.

Yet it *was* not that Nature had shed o'er the scene
Her purest of crystal and brightest of green;
'Twas *not* the soft magic of streamlet or hill,
Oh, no—it was something more exquisite still.

'Twas that friends, the beloved of my bosom, were near,

Who made ev'ry dear scene of enchantment more dear;
And who felt how the best charms of nature improve
When we see them reflected from looks that we love.

Sweet vale of Ovoca! how calm could I rest
In thy bosom of shade, with the friends I love best,
Where the storms which we feel in this cold world should cease,
And our hearts, like thy waters, be mingled in peace.

* "The Meeting of the Waters" forms a part of that beautiful scenery which lies between Rathdrum and Arklow, in the county of Wicklow; and these lines were suggested by a visit to this romantic spot, in the summer of the year 1806.
† The rivers of Avon and Ovoca.

OH! THE SHAMROCK.

AIR:—" *Alley Croker.*"

THROUGH Erin's Isle,
To sport awhile
As Love and Valor wander'd,
With Wit, the sprite,
Whose quiver bright,
A thousand arrows squander'd;
Where'er they pass,
A triple grass*
Shoots up, with dew-drops streaming,
As softly green
As emeralds, seen
Through purest crystal gleaming!
Oh, the shamrock, the green, immortal
shamrock!
Chosen leaf
Of Bard and Chief,
Old Erin's native shamrock!

Says Valor: "See,
They spring for me,
Those leafy gems of morning!"
Says Love: "No—no,
For me they grow,
My fragant path adorning!"
But Wit perceives
The triple leaves,
And cries: " Oh! do not sever
A type, that blends
Three godlike friends,
Love, Valor, Wit, forever!"

Oh, the shamrock, the green, immortal
shamrock!
Chosen leaf
Of Bard and Chief,
Old Erin's native shamrock!

So firmly fond
May last the bond
They wove that morn together,
And ne'er may fall
One drop of gall
On Wit's celestial feather!
May Love, as twine
His flowers divine,
Of thorny falsehood weed 'em!
May Valor ne'er
His standard rear
Against the cause of Freedom!
Oh, the shamrock, the green, immortal
shamrock!
Chosen leaf
Of Bard and Chief,
Old Erin's native shamrock!

* Saint Patrick is said to have made use of that species of the trefoil, to which in Ireland we give the name of Shamrock, in explaining the doctrine of the Trinity to the Pagan Irish. I do not know if there be any other reason for our adoption of this plant as a national emblem. Hope, among the ancients, was sometimes represented as a beautiful child, "standing upon tip-toes, and a trefoil or three-colored grass in her hand."

————o————

I SAW FROM THE BEACH.

AIR:—" *Miss Molly.*"

I SAW from the beach, when the morning
was shining,
A bark o'er the waters move gloriously on;
I came, when the sun o'er that beach was
declining,
The bark was still there, but the waters were
gone!

Ah! such is the fate of our life's early
promise,
So passing the spring-tide of joy we have
known;
Each wave that we danc'd on at morning
ebbs from us,
And leaves us, at eve, on the bleak shore
alone.

Ne'er tell me of glories, serenely adorning
The close of our day, the calm eve of our
night—
Give me back—give me back the wild
freshness of morning,
Her clouds and her tears are worth
evening's best light.

Oh, who would not welcome that moment's
returning.
When passion first wak'd a new life thro'
his frame,
And his soul, like the wood, that grows
precious in burning,
Gave out all its sweets to love's exquisite
flame.

————o————

'TIS GONE, AND FOREVER.

AIR:—"*Savournah Deelish.*"

'Tis gone, and for ever, the light we saw
    breaking,
  Like Heaven's first dawn o'er the sleep of
    the dead,
When man, from the slumber of ages
    awaking,
  Look'd upward and blessed the pure ray,
    ere it fled!

'Tis gone, and the gleams it has left of its
    burning,
But deepen the long night of bondage and
    mourning
That dark o'er the kingdoms of earth is
    returning,
  And, darkest of all, hapless Erin, o'er thee.

For high was thy hope, when those glories
    were darting
  Around thee, thro' all the gross clouds of
    the world;
When Truth from her fetters indignantly
    starting,
  At once, like a sun-burst,* her banner
    unfurl'd.

Oh, never shall earth see a moment so splen-
    did!
Then—then, had one Hymn of Deliverance
    blended
The tongues of all nations, how sweet had
    ascended
  The first note of Liberty, Erin, from thee.

But, shame on these tyrants, who envied the
    blessing!
  And shame on the light race, unworthy its
    good,
Who, at Death's reeking altar, like furies
    caressing
  The young hope of Freedom, baptiz'd it in
    blood!

Then vanished for ever that fair, sunny
    vision,
Which, spite of the slavish, the cold heart's
    derision,
Shall long be remember'd, pure, bright, and
    elysian,
  As first it arose, my lost Erin, on thee.

*"The Sun-burst" was the fanciful name given
by the ancient Irish to the Royal Banner.

---o---

SHE IS FAR FROM THE LAND.*

AIR:—"*Open the Door.*"

She is far from the land where her young
    Hero sleeps,
  And lovers are around her sighing;
But coldly she turns from their gaze, and
    weeps,
  For her heart in his grave is lying!

She sings the wild song of her dear native
    plains,
  Every note which he lov'd awaking.—
Ah! little they think, who delight in her
    - strains,
  How the heart of the Minstrel is breaking!

He had liv'd for his love, for his country he
    died,

They were all that to life had entwin'd
    him,
Nor soon shall the tears of his country be
    dried,
  Nor long will his love stay behind him!

Oh! make her a grave where the sunbeams
    rest,
  When they promise a glorious morrow;
They'll shine o'er her sleep, like a smile from
    the west,
  From her own loved Island of sorrow!

* This poem was written on the death of Sarah
Curran, who was engaged to the immortal Emmet.
She died in Italy, of a broken heart, some few years
after her lover was executed.

---o---

BELIEVE ME, IF ALL THOSE ENDEARING YOUNG CHARMS.

AIR:—"*My Lodging is on the cold Ground.*"

Believe me, if all those endearing young
    charms,
  Which I gaze on so fondly to-day,
Were to change by to-morrow, and fleet in
    my arms,
  Like fairy gifts, fading away,

Thou would'st still be ador'd as this moment
    thou art,
  Let thy loveliness fade as it will;
And around the dear ruin each wish of my
    heart
  Would entwine itself verdantly still.

It is not while beauty and youth are thine
    own,
And thy cheeks unprofan'd by a tear,
That the fervor and faith of a soul can be
    known,
    To which time will but make thee more
    dear!

Oh! the heart, that has truly lov'd, never
    forgets,
    But as truly loves on to the close;
As the sunflower turns on her god, when he
    sets,
    The same look which she turn'd when he
    rose!

———o———

REMEMBER THEE.

AIR:—" *Castle Tirowen.*"

Remember thee! yes, while there's life in
    this heart,
It shall never forget thee, all lorn as thou
    art;
More dear in thy sorrow, thy gloom and thy
    showers,
Than the rest of the world in their sunniest
    hours.

Wert thou all that I wish thee, great,
    glorious and free,
First flower of the earth, and first gem of
    the sea;

I might hail thee with prouder, with happier
    brow,
But, oh! could I love thee more deeply than
    now?

No, thy chains as they torture thy blood as
    it runs,
But make thee more painfully dear to thy
    sons—
Whose hearts, like the young of the desert-
    bird's nest,
Drink love in each life-drop that flows from
    thy breast.

———o———

WE MAY ROAM THROUGH THIS WORLD.

AIR:—" *Garyone.*"

We may roam thro' this world like a child
    at a feast,
    Who but sips of a sweet, and then flies to
    the rest,
And, when pleasure begins to grow dull in
    the east,
    We may order our wings, and be off to the
    west;
But if hearts that feel, and eyes that smile,
    Are the dearest gifts that Heaven
    supplies,
We never need leave our own Green Isle
    For sensitive hearts and sun-bright eyes.
Then remember, whenever your goblet is
    crown'd.
    Thro' this world whether eastward or
    westward you roam,
When a cup to the smile of dear woman goes
    'round,
    Oh! remember the smile which adorns her
    at home.

In England the garden of beauty is kept
    By a dragon of prudery, plac'd within call;
But so oft this unamiable dragon has slept,
    That the garden's but carelessly watch'd
    after all.
Oh! they want the wild sweet-hriery fence,
    Which 'round the flowers of Erin dwells,
Which warns the touch, while winning tho
    sense,

Nor charms us the least when it most
    repels.
Then remember, wherever your goblet is
    crown'd,
    Thro' this world whether.eastward or
    westward you roam,
When a cup to the smile of dear woman goes
    'round.
    Oh! remember the smile which adorns her
    at home.

In France, when the heart of a woman sets
    sail,
    On the ocean of wedlock its fortune to try,
Love seldom goes far in a vessel so frail,
    But just pilots her off, and then bids her
    good-by?
While the daughters of Erin keep the boy.
    Ever-smiling beside his faithful oar,
Thro' billows of woe and beams of joy,
    The same as he look'd when he left the
    shore.
Then remember, wherever your goblet is
    crown'd,
Thro' this world whether eastward or
    westward you roam,
    When a cup to the smile of dear woman
    goes 'round,
    Oh! remember the smile which adorns her
    at home.

COME, REST IN THIS BOSOM.

AIR:—"*Lough Sheeling.*"

COME, rest in this bosom, my own stricken
    dear!
Tho' the herd have fled from thee, thy home
    is still here;
Here still is the smile that no cloud can
    o'ercast,
And the heart and the hand all thy own to
    the last!

Oh! what was love made for, if 'tis not the
    same,
Thro' joy and thro' torments, thro' glory
    and shame?

I know not, I ask not if guilt's in that heart,
I but know that I love thee, whatever thou
    art!

Thou hast call'd me thy Angel, in moments
    of bliss,
Still thy Angel I'll be, 'mid the hours of
    this—
Thro' the furnace, unshrinking, thy steps to
    pursue,
And shield thee, and save thee, or perish
    there too.

WHEN THROUGH LIFE UNBLEST WE ROVE.

AIR:—"*Banks of Banna.*"

WHEN through life unblest we rove,
    Losing all that made life dear,
Should some notes, we us'd to love
    In days of boyhood, meet our ear;
Oh! how welcome breathes the strain,
    Wakening thoughts that long have
      slept—
Kindling former smiles again
    In faded eyes, that long have wept!

Like the gale, that sighs along
    Beds of oriental flow'rs,
Is the grateful breath of song,
    That once was heard in happier hours,

Fill'd with balm, the gale sighs on,
    Though the flowers have sunk in death;
So, when pleasure's dream is gone,
    Its memory lives in music's breath!

Music!—Oh! how faint, how weak
    Language fades before thy spell!
Why should feeling ever speak,
    When thou canst breathe her soul so
      well,
Friendship's balmy words may feign,
    Love's are ev'n more false than they;
Oh! 'tis only music's strain
    Can sweetly soothe, and not betray!

LOVE'S YOUNG DREAM.

AIR:—"*The Old Woman.*"

OH! the days are gone, when beauty bright
    My heart's chain wove;
When my dream of life, from morn till
    night,
    Was love, still love!
    New hope may bloom,
    And days may come,
Of milder, calmer beam,
But there's nothing half so sweet in life
    As love's young dream!
Oh! there's nothing half so sweet in life
    As love's young dream!

Tho' the bard to purer fame may soar,
    When wild youth's past;
Tho' he win the wise, who frown'd before,
    To smile at last;
    He'll never meet

    A joy so sweet
    In all his noon of fame,
As when first he sung to woman's ear
    His soul-felt flame:
And, at every close, she blushed to hear
    The one loved name!

Oh! that hallow'd form is ne'er forgot,
    Which First Love trac'd;
Still it lingering haunts the greenest spot
    On Memory's waste!
    'Twas odor fled
    As soon as shed;
    'Twas morning's winged dream!
'Twas a light, that ne'er can shine again
    On life's dull stream!
Oh! 'twas light, that ne'er can shine again
    On life's dull stream!

ARABY'S DAUGHTER.

FAREWELL—farewell to thee, Araby's
    daughter,
  (Thus warbled a Peri beneath the dark
    sea)
No pearl ever lay, under Oman's green
    water,
  More pure in its shell than thy spirit in
    thee.

Oh, fair as the sea-flower close to thee
    growing,
  How light was thy heart till love's
    witchery came,
Like the wind of the south* o'er a summer
    lute blowing,
  And hush'd all its music and wither'd its
    frame!

But long upon Araby's green sunny
    highlands,
  Shall maids and their lovers remember the
    doom
Of her who lies sleeping among the Pearl
    Islands,
  With nought but the sea-star† to light up
    her tomb.

And still, when the merry date season is
    burning,
  And calls to the palm-groves the young
    and the old,
The happiest there, from their pastime
    returning,
  At sunset, will weep when thy story is
    told.

The young village maid, when with flowers
    she dresses
  Her dark-flowing hair for some festive
    day,
Will think of thy fate, till neglecting her
    tresses,
  She mournfully turns from the mirror
    away.

Now shall Iran, belov'd of her hero! forget
    thee?—

Tho' tyrants watch over her tears as they
    start,
Close, close by the side of that hero she'll set
    thee,
  Embalm'd in the innermost shrine of her
    heart.

Farewell!—be it ours to embellish thy pillow
  With every thing beauteous that grows in
    the deep;
Each flower of the rock, and each gem of the
    pillow,
  Shall sweeten thy bed, and illumine thy
    sleep.

Around thee shall glisten the loveliest amber
  That ever the sorrowing sea-bird has
    wept;
With many a shell, in whose hollow-
    wreath'd chamber,
  We Peris of ocean, by moon-light have
    slept.

We'll dive where the gardens of coral lie
    darkling,
  And plant all the rosiest stems at thy
    head;
We'll seek where the sands of the Caspian‡
    are sparkling,
  And gather their gold to strew over thy
    bed.

Farewell—farewell—until Pity's sweet
    fountain
  Is lost in the hearts of the fair and the
    brave,
They'll weep for the chieftain who died on
    that mountain,
  They'll weep for the maiden who sleeps in
    this wave.

---

* "This wind (the Samoor) so softens the strings of lutes, that they can never be tuned while it lasts."—*Stephen's Persia.*
† "One of the greatest curiosities found in the Persian Gulf is a fish which the English call Star fish. It is circular, and at night very luminous, resembling the full moon surrounded by rays"—*Mirza Abu Taleb.*
‡ "The bay Kieselarke, which is otherwise called the Golden Bay; the sand whereof shines of fire."—*Struy.*

———o———

OFT, IN THE STILLY NIGHT.

Scotch air.

OFT, in the stilly night,
  Ere Slumber's chain has bound me,
Fond mem'ry brings the light
  Of other days around me;

    The smiles, the tears
    Of boyhood's years.
The words of love then spoken;
    The eyes that shone,

Now dimm'd and gone,
The cheerful hearts now broken.
Thus in the stilly night,
Ere slumber's chain has bound me,
Sad mem'ry brings the light
Of other days around me.

When I remember all
The friends, so link'd together,
I've seen around me fall,

Like leaves in wintry weather;
I feel like one,
Who treads alone
Some banquet hall deserted,
Whose lights are fled,
Whose garland's dead,
And all, but he, departed!
Thus in the stilly night,
Ere slumber's chain has bound me,
Sad mem'ry brings the light
Of other days around me.

---o---

THO' THE LAST GLIMPSE OF ERIN.

AIR:—*"Coulin."*

THO' the last glimpse of Erin with sorrow I see,
Yet wherever thou art shall seem Erin to me;
In exile thy bosom shall still be my home,
And thine eyes make my climate wherever we roam.

To the gloom of some desert, or cold rocky shore,
Where the eye of the stranger can haunt us no more,

I will fly with my Coulin, and think the rough wind
Less rude than the foes we leave frowning behind.

And I'll gaze on thy gold hair, as graceful it wreathes,
And hang o'er thy soft harp, as wildly it breathes;
Nor dread that the cold-hearted Saxon will tear
One chord from that harp, or one lock from that hair.

---o---

RICH AND RARE WERE THE GEMS SHE WORE.

AIR:—*"The Summer is Coming."*

RICH and rare were the gems she wore,*
And a bright gold ring on her wand she bore;
But, oh! her beauty was far beyond
Her sparkling gems and snow-white wand.

"Lady! dost thou not fear to stray,
So lone and lovely, thro' this bleak way?
Are Erin's sons so good or so cold
As not to be tempted by woman or gold?"

"Sir Knight! I feel not the least alarm;
No son of Erin will offer me harm;
For, tho' they love woman and golden store,
Sir Knight! they love honor and virtue more!"

On she went, and her maiden smile
In safety lighted her 'round the Green Isle;
And bless'd for ever is she who relied
Upon Erin's honor and Erin's pride!

* This ballad is founded upon the following anecdote:—"The people were inspired with such a spirit of honor, virtue, and religion, by the great example of Brian, and by his excellent administration, that, as a proof of it, we are informed that a young lady of great beauty, adorned with jewels, and a costly dress, undertook a journey alone, from one end of the kingdom to the other, with a wand only in her hand, at the top of which was a ring of exceeding great value; and such an impression had the laws and government of this monarch made on the minds of all the people, that no attempt was made upon her honor, nor was she robbed of her clothes or jewels."—*Warner's History of Ireland*, Vol. i, book 10.

---o---

I'D MOURN THE HOPES.

AIR:—*"The Rose Tree,"*

I'D mourn the hopes that leave me,
If thy smiles had left me too;
I'd weep, when friends deceive me,
If thou wert, like them, untrue.

But, while I've thee before me,
With hearts so warm and eyes so bright,
No clouds can linger o'er me,
That smile turns them all to light!

'Tis not in fate to harm me;
　While fate leaves thy love to me;
'Tis not in joy to charm me,
　Unless joy be shar'd with theo.
One minute's dream about thee
　Were worth a long—an endless year
Of waking bliss without thee,
　My own love—my only dear!

And, tho' the hope be gone, love,
　That long sparkled o'er our way,
Oh! we shall journey on, love,
　More safely without its ray.

Far better lights shall win me
　Along the paths I've yet to roam,
The mind that burns within me,
　And pure smiles from thee at home.

Thus, when the lamp that lighted
　The traveler at first goes out,
He feels awhile benighted,
　And looks 'round in fear and doubt.
But soon, the prospect clearing,
　By cloudless starlight on he treads,
And thinks no lamp so cheering
　As that light which Heaven sheds!

THE FAREWELL TO MY HARP.

AIR:—"*New Langolee.*"

DEAR harp of my country in darkness I
　found thee,
The cold chain of silence had hung o'er
　thee long,
When proudly, my own Island Harp! I
　unbound thee,
And gave all my chords to light, freedom,
　and song!
The warm lay of love and the light note of
　gladness
Have waken'd thy fondest, thy liveliest
　thrill;
But so oft hast thou echoed the deep sigh of
　sadness,
That even in thy mirth it will steal from
　me still.

Dear harp of my country! farewell to thy
　numbers,
The sweet wreath of song is the last we
　shall twine;
Go—sleep, with the sunshine of fame on thy
　slumbers,
Till touch'd by some hand less unworthy
　than mine.
If the pulse of the patriot, soldier, or lover,
　Have throbb'd at our lay, 'tis thy glory
　alone;
I was but as the wind, passing heedlessly
　over,
　And all the wild sweetness I wak'd was
　thy own.

AS SLOW OUR SHIP.

AIR:—"*The Girl I Left Behind Me.*"

As slow our ship her foamy track
　Against the wind was cleaving,
Her trembling pennant still look'd back
　To that dear isle 'twas leaving.
So loath we part from all we love,
　From all the links that bind us;
So turn our hearts, where'er we rove,
　To those we've left behind us!

When, 'round the bowl of vanish'd years,
　We talk, with joyous seeming,
And smiles that might as well be tears,
　So faint, so sad their beaming;
While mem'ry brings us back again
　Each early tie that twin'd us,
Oh, sweet's the cup that circles then
　To those we've left behind us!

And, when in other climes we meet
　Some isle or vale enchanting,
Where all looks flow'ry, mild and sweet,
　And nought but love is wanting;
We think how great had been our bliss,
　If Heav'n had but assign'd us
To live and die in scenes like this,
　With some we've left behind us!

As trav'lers oft look back at eve,
　When eastward darkly going,
To gaze upon that light they leave
　Still faint behind them glowing—
So, when the close of pleasure's day
　To gloom hath near consign'd us,
We turn to catch one fading ray
　Of joy that's left behind us.

COME O'ER THE SEA.

AIR:—" *Cuishlih ma Chree.*"

Come o'er the sea,
  Maiden! with me,
Mine thro' sunshine, storm, and snows!
  Seasons may roll,
  But the true soul
Burns the same, where'er it goes.
Let fate frown on, so we love and part not;
'Tis life where *thou* art, 'tis death where thou
      art not!
  Then come o'er the sea,
  Maiden! with me,
Come wherever the wild wind blows;
  Seasons may roll,
  But the true soul
Burns the same, where'er it goes.

Is not the sea
  Made for the free,
Lands for courts and chains alone?
  Here we are slaves;
  But, on the waves,
Love and Liberty's all our own!
No eye to watch, and no tongue to wound us,
All earth forgot, and all Heaven around
      us?
  Then come o'er the sea,
  Maiden! with me,
Come wherever the wild wind blows;
  Seasons may roll,
  But the true soul
Burns the same, where'er it goes.

HAS SORROW THY YOUNG DAYS SHADED.

AIR:—" *Sly Patrick.*"

Has sorrow thy young days shaded,
  As clouds o'er the morning fleet?
Too fast have those young days faded,
  That even in sorrow were sweet?
Does Time with his cold wing wither
  Each feeling that once was dear?—
Come, child of misfortune! come hither,
  I'll weep with thee tear for tear.

Has love to that soul so tender
  Been like our Lagenian mine,
Where sparkles of golden splendor
  All over the surface shine!
But if in pursuit we go deeper,
  Allur'd by the gleam that shone,
Ah! false as the dream of the sleeper,
  Like Love, the bright ore is gone.

Has Hope, like the bird in the story,
  That flitted from tree to tree
With the talisman's glittering glory—
  Has Hope been that bird to thee?
On branch after branch alighting,
  The gem did she still display,
And, when nearest and most inviting,
  Then waft the fair gem away?

If thus the sweet hours have fleeted,
  When Sorrow herself look'd bright,
If thus the fond hope has cheated,
  That led thee along so light;
If thus the unkind world wither
  Each feeling that once was dear;
Come, child of misfortune! come hither,
  I'll weep for thee tear for tear.

NO, NOT MORE WELCOME.

AIR:—" *Luggelaw.*"

No, not more welcome the fairy numbers,
  Of music fall on the sleeper's ear,
When, half-awaking fearful slumbers,
  He thinks the full choir of Heav'n is near.
Then came that voice, when all forsaken,
  This heart long had sleeping laid,
Nor thought its cold pulse would ever waken
  To such benign, bless'd sounds again.

Sweet voice of comfort! 'twas like the stealing

Of summer wind thro' some wreathed
  shell;
Each secret winding, each inmost feeling
  Of all my soul echoed to its spell;
'Twas whisper'd balm—'twas sunshine
  spoken!

I'd live years of grief and pain
To have my long sleep of sorrow broken
  By such benign, bless'd sounds again!

WEEP ON—WEEP ON.

AIR:—" *The Song of Sorrow.*"

WEEP on—weep on, your hour is past,
  Your dreams of pride are o'er;
The fatal chain is 'round you cast,
  And you are men no more.
In vain the hero's heart hath bled;
  The sage's tongue hath warned in vain—
Oh, Freedom, once thy flame hath fled,
  It never lights again.

Weep on; perhaps in after days
  They'll learn to love your name;
And many a deed may wake in praise,
  That long hath slept in blame.

And when they tread the ruin'd isle,
  Where rest, at length, the lord and slave,
They'll wondering ask, how hands so vile
  Could conquer hearts so brave?

" 'Twas fate," they'll say, " a wayward
    fate
  Your web of discord wove;
And while your tyrants join'd in hate,
  You never join'd in love.
But hearts fell off that ought to twine,
  And man profan'd what God had given,
Till some were heard to curse the shrine
  Where others knelt to Heaven."

———o———

OH! 'TIS SWEET TO THINK.

AIR:—" *Thady, you Gander.*"

OH! 'tis sweet to think that, where'er we rove,
  We are sure to find something blissful and dear;
And that when we're far from the lips we love,
  We have but to make love to the lips we are near!
The heart, like a tendril, accustomed to cling,
  Let it grow where it will, cannot flourish alone;
But will lean to the nearest and loveliest thing
  It can twine with itself, and make closely its own.
Then, oh! what pleasure, where'er we rove,
  To be doomed to find something, still, that is dear;
And to know, when far from the lips we love,
  We have but to make love to the lips we are near!

'Twere a shame, when flowers around us rise,
  To make light of the rest if the rose is not there;
And the world so rich in resplendent eyes,
  'Twere a pity to limit one's love to a pair.
Love's wing and the peacock's are nearly alike,
  They are both of them bright, but they're changeable, too;
And, wherever a new beam of beauty can strike,
  It will tincture Love's plume with a different hue!
Then, oh! what pleasure, where'er we rove,
  To be doomed to find something, still, that is dear;
And to know, when far from the lips we love,
  We have but to make love to the lips we are near!

———o———

WHEN TWILIGHT DEWS.

WHEN twilight dews are falling soft
  Upon the rosy sea, love,
I watch the star, whose beam so oft
  Has lighted me to thee, love!
And thou, too, on that orb so clear,
  Ah! dost thou gaze at even,
And think, tho' lost forever here,
  Thou'lt yet be mine in Heaven?

There's not a garden walk I tread,
  There's not a flower I see, love!
But brings to mind some hope that's fled,
  Some joy I've lost with thee, love!
And still I wish that hour was near,
  When, friends and foes forgiven,
The pains, the ills we've wept thro' here,
  May turn to smiles in Heaven!

LESBIA HAS A BEAMING EYE.

AIR:—"*Nora Creina.*"

LESBIA has a beaming eye,
  But no one knows for whom it beameth;
Right and left its arrows fly,
  But what they aim at no one dreameth;
Sweeter 'tis to gaze upon
  My Nora's lid that seldom rises;
Few her looks, but every one
  Like unexpected light surprises.
    Oh, my Nora Creina, dear,
  My gentle, bashful Nora Creina.
    Beauty lies
    In many eyes,
  But love in yours, my Nora Creina.

Lesbia wears a robe of gold,
  But all so close the nymph has lac'd it,
Not a charm of beauty's mould
  Presumes to stay where nature plac'd it;
Oh, my Nora's gown for me,
  That floats as wild as mountain breezes,
Leaving every beauty free
  To sink or swell, as Heaven pleases.
    Yes, my Nora Creina, dear,
  My simple, graceful Nora Creina!
    Nature's dress
    Is loveliness,
  The dress *you* wear, my Nora Creina!

Lesbia has a wit refin'd,
  But when its points are gleaming 'round
    us
Who can tell if they're design'd
  To dazzle merely, or to wound us?
Pillow'd on my Nora's heart,
  In safer slumber love reposes;
Bed of peace! whose roughest part
  Is but the crumpling of the roses!
    Oh, my Nora Creina, dear!
  My mild, my artless Nora Creina!
    Wit, tho' bright,
    Has not the light
  That warms your eyes, my Nora Creina!

OH! BREATHE NOT HIS NAME.

AIR:—"*The Brown Maid.*"

OH! breathe not his name—let it sleep in the shade,
Where cold and unhonor'd his relics are laid!
Sad, silent, and dark be the tears that we shed,
As the night-dew that falls on the grass o'er his head!

But the night-dew that falls, tho' in silence it weeps,
Shall brighten with verdure the grave where he sleeps;
And the tear that we shed, tho' in secret it rolls,
Shall long keep his memory green in our souls.

WHEN IN DEATH I SHALL CALM RECLINE.

AIR.—"*Unknown.*"

WHEN in death I shall calm recline,
  O, bear my heart to my mistress dear;
Tell her it liv'd upon smiles, and wine
  Of the brightest hue, while it linger'd here:
Bid her not shed one tear of sorrow
  To sully a heart so brilliant and light;
But balmy drops of the red grape borrow,
  To bathe the relic from morn to night.

When the light of my song is o'er,
  Then take my harp to your ancient hall;
Hang it up at that friendly door
  Where weary travelers love to call:

Then if some bard, who roams forsaken,
  Revive its soft note in passing along,
Oh! let one thought of its maker waken
  Your warmest smile for the child of so g

Keep this cup, which is now o'erflowing,
  To grace your revel when I'm at rest;
Never, oh! never, its balm bestowing
  On lips that beauty hath seldom blest!
But when some warm, devoted lover
  To her he adores shall bathe its brim,
Oh! then my spirit around shall hover,
  And hallow each drop that foams for him.

THE TIME I'VE LOST IN WOOING.

AIR:—"*Pease upon a Trencher.*"

THE time I've lost in wooing,
In watching and pursuing
    The light that lies
    In woman's eyes,
Has been my heart's undoing.
Tho' Wisdom oft has sought me,
I scorn'd the love she brought me;
    My only books
    Were woman's looks,
And Folly's all they've taught me.

Her smile when Beauty granted,
I hung with gaze enchanted,
    Like him, the Sprite,*
    Whom maids by night
Oft meet in glen that's haunted.

Like him, too, Beauty won me,
But, while her eyes were on me,
    If once their ray
    Was turn'd away,
Oh! winds could not outrun me.

And are those follies going?
And is my proud heart growing
    Too cold or wise
    For brilliant eyes
Again to set it glowing?
No—vain, alas! th' endeavor
From bonds so sweet to sever;
    Poor Wisdom's chance
    Against a glance
Is now as weak as ever!

* This alludes to a kind of Irish fairy, which is to be met with, they say, in the fields, at dusk. As long as you keep your eyes upon him, he is fixed and in your power; but the moment you look away, (and he is ingenious in furnishing some inducement), he vanishes. I had thought that this was the sprite which we call the Leprechaun; but a high authority upon such subjects, Lady Morgan, (in a note upon her national and interesting novel, O'Donuel,) has given a very different account of that goblin.

NIGHT CLOSED AROUND THE CONQUEROR'S WAY.

AIR:—" *Thy Fair Bosom.*"

NIGHT clos'd around the conqueror's way,
    And lightning show'd the distant hill
Where those who lost that dreadful day,
    Stood few and faint, but fearless still!
The soldier's hope, the patriot's zeal,
    Forever dimmed, forever crost—
Oh, who shall say what heroes feel,
    When all but life and honor's lost!

The last sad hour of Freedom's dream,
    And Valor's task, mov'd slowly by,
While mute they watch'd, till morning's beam
    Should rise, and give them light to die!
There is a world where souls are free,
    Where tyrants taint not nature's bliss;
If death that world's bright opening be,
    Oh! who would live a slave in this?

YOU REMEMBER ELLEN.

AIR:—" *Were I a Clerk.*"

YOU remember Ellen, our hamlet's pride,
    How meekly she blessed her lot,
When the stranger, William, has made her his bride,
    And love was the light of their lowly cot.
Together they toiled thro' winds and rains,
    Till William, at length, in sadness, said:
" We must seek our fortune on other plains,"
    Then, sighing, she left her lowly shed.

They roam'd a long and a weary way,
    Nor much was the maiden's heart at ease,
When now, at close of one stormy day,
    They see a proud castle among the trees.
" To-night," said the youth, " we'll shelter there;

The wind blows cold, the hour is late;"
So he blew the horn with a chieftain's air,
    And the porter bow'd as they pass'd the gate.

" Now, welcome, lady!" exclaim'd the youth—
" This castle is thine, and these dark woods all."
She believ'd him wild, but his words were truth,
    For Ellen is lady of Rosna Hall.
And dearly the lord of Rosna loves
    What William, the stranger, woo'd and wed;
And the light of bliss, in the lordly groves,
    Is pure as it shone in the lowly shed.

THOMAS DAVIS.

THOMAS OSBORNE DAVIS was born in Mallow, county Cork, in 1814, and died in September, 1845, in Dublin. In early youth he was distinguished for the ardor and severe discipline with which he pursued his studies, and this closeness of application he steadily continued till the twenty-sixth year of his age, when he had accumulated an amount of knowledge rarely possessed by a man of his years. He finished his education in Trinity College, Dublin, and in 1840 was called to the Irish Bar.

Upon the dismissal of Chancellor Plunket in that year, Davis first directed his mind to politics; he and his friend, John Dillon, becoming contributors to one of the Dublin papers. Some time after, this journal having changed its independent tone (the proprietor was looking for place, which he subsequently obtained), they withdrew their support, and transferred their services to the silent but practical work of the committee of the Repeal Association—of which they were both members. The want of a thoroughly independent and national journal being felt by the young men of the country, Thomas Davis, John Dillon, and Charles Gavan Duffy determined, in 1842, to establish the *Nation* as a political and literary journal, under the editorial management of Mr. Duffy, who had previously conducted the *Belfast Vindicator.* The *Nation's* principal aim was to teach the people that in education and industrial pursuits their true dignity consisted, and to impress upon them the importance of temperance and self reliance as the means best calculated to secure the nationality and independence of the country.

It was then that Davis became a man of great and noble purposes; he threw his whole heart and soul into the new undertaking, and possessing the rare power of imbuing others with his own burning spirit, the *Nation* was supported by a staff of writers never equalled before in Irish journalism. To promote the object for which this journal was established, the editor held it to be indispensable that songs and ballads for the people should form a prominent feature. He knew their stirring and fascinating influence upon the Irish heart. A poet who could produce such national ballads as would find a ready acceptance with the people was required; and though Davis had previously never attempted verse, he did not hesitate in this emergency to undertake to supply this great *desideratum.*

The following vigorous and highly dramatic ballad was his first contribution; this, and his other productions in this volume will amply prove that he did not mistake his vocation. He not only wrote himself, but incited others to do the like, until the *Nation* became the medium of giving to the world some of the finest ballads of modern times. A more earnest or sincere man than Davis never lived. In his total abnegation of self, in his unwearied industry, was "his own parallel."

The characteristics of his nature were a strict love of truth and right, and an exuberant, joyous spirit; and though confident of his power as a poet and essayist, his ambition was to rank beside Owen Roe and Grattan, rather than beside Moore and Goldsmith. He estimatted talents and fame, however brilliant and dazzling, and liberty, however broad and secure, in proportion only as they promoted solid virtue and permanent happiness. Acting upon these principles, he effected, during his short career, more than most others in a life-time could accomplish. His devoted love for Ireland knew no bounds, his fidelity to her interests has rarely been equalled; and he served her with intense zeal, without stint or reserve, for the sole gratification of doing good to his kind. His simplicity and almost womanly tenderness of nature were beautifully blended with the severe integrity of his principles. His masculine understanding, his high enthusiasm, his marvellous energy and unconquerable resolution preëminently fitted him for the achievement of any noble or patriotic enterprise. He bore nature's impress of a great man, and she had marked him as the faithful champion of his country's rights and freedom.

POEMS OF THOMAS DAVIS.

THE DEATH OF OWEN ROE.

[Time—10th Nov., 1649. Scene—Ormond's Camp, County Waterford. Speakers—A Veteran of Owen Roe's clan, and one of the horsemen, just arrived with an account of his death.]

" Did they dare—did they dare, to slay Owen Roe O'Neill?"
" Yes, they slew with poison him they feared to meet with steel."
" May God wither up their hearts. May their blood cease to flow,
May they walk in living death, who poisoned Owen Roe!

Though it break my heart to hear, say again the bitter words."
" From Derry, against Cromwell, he marched to measure swords.
But the weapon ot the Saxon met him on his way,
And he died at Clough-Oughter, upon St. Leonard's day."

" Wail—wail ye for The Mighty One! Wail—wail ye for the Dead;
Quench the hearth, and hold the breath—with ashes strew the head.
How tenderly we loved him! How deeply we deplore!
Holy Saviour! but to think we shall never see him more.

" Sagest in the council was he,—kindest in the hall,
Sure we never won a battle—'twas Owen won them all.
Had he lived—had he lived, our dear country had been free;
But he's dead—but he's dead, and 'tis slaves we'll ever be,

" O'Farrell and Clanrickard, Preston and Red Hugh,
Audley and MacMahon—ye are valiant, wise, and true;
But what—what are ye all to our darling who is gone?
The Rudder of our Ship was he, our Castle's corner stone!

" Wail—wail him through the Island. Weep—weep for our pride!
Would that on the battle-field our gallant chief had died!
Weep the Victor of Benburb—weep him, young man and old;
Weep for him, ye women—your beautiful lies cold!

" We thought you would not die—we were sure you would not go,
And leave us in our utmost need to Cromwell's cruel blow—
Sheep without a shepherd, when the snow shuts out the sky—
Oh! why did you leave us, Owen? Why did you die?

" Soft as a woman's was your voice, O'Neill! bright was your eye.
Oh, why did you leave us, Owen! why did you die?
Your troubles are all over, you're at rest with God on high;
But we're slaves, and we're orphans, Owen!—why did you die?"

------o------

LOVE'S LONGINGS.

To the conqueror his crowning,
   First freedom to the slave,
And air unto the drowning,
   Sunk in the ocean's wave.
And succor to the faithful,
   Who fight their flag above,
Are sweet, but far less grateful
   Than were my lady's love.

I know I am not worthy
   Of one so young and bright;
And yet I would do for thee
   Far more than others might;
I cannot give you pomp or gold,
   If you should be my wife,
But I can give you love untold,
   And true in death or life.

Methinks that there are passions

Within that heaving breast
To scorn their heartless fashions,
   And wed whom you love best.
Methinks you would be prouder
   As the struggling patriot's bride,
Than if rank your home should
      crowd, or
   Cold riches 'round you glide.

Oh! the watcher longs for morning,
   And the infant cries for light,
And the saint for Heaven's warning,
   And the vanquished pray for might;
But their prayer, when lowest
      kneeling,
   And their suppliance most true,
Are cold to the appealing
   Of this longing heart to you.

------o------

THE BOATMAN OF KINSALE.

His kiss is sweet, his word is kind,
   His love is rich to me;
I could not in a palace find
   A truer heart than he.
The eagle shelters not his nest
   From hurricane and hail,
More bravely than he guards my breast—
   The Boatman of Kinsale.

The wind that round the Fastnet sweeps
   Is not a whit more pure;
The goat that down Cnoc Sheehy leaps
   Has not a foot more sure.
No firmer hand nor freer eye
   E'er faced an Autumn gale—
De Courcy's heart is not so high—
   The Boatman of Kinsale.

The brawling squires may heed him not,
   The dainty stranger sneer—
But who will dare to hurt our cot,
   When Myles O'Hea is here?
The scarlet soldiers pass along—
   They'd like, but fear to rail—
His blood is hot, his blow is strong—
   The Boatman of Kinsale.

His hooker's in the Scilly van,
   When seines are in the foam;
But money never made the man,
   Nor wealth a happy home.
So, blest with love and liberty,
   While he can trim a sail,
He'll trust in God, and cling to me—
   The Boatman of Kinsale.

------o------

THE WELCOME.

COME in the evening, or come in the morning,
Come when you're looked for, or come without warning;
Kisses and welcome you'll find here before you,
And the oftener you come here the more I'll adore you.

Light is my heart since the day we were plighted,
Red is my cheek that they told me was blighted;
The green of the trees looks far greener than ever,
And the linnets are singing, "true lovers, don't sever."

I'll pull you sweet flowers, to wear if you choose them;
Or, after you've kissed them, they'll lie on my bosom.
I'll fetch from the mountain its breeze to inspire you;
I'll fetch from my fancy a tale that won't tire you.
  Oh, your step's like the rain to the summer-vex'd farmer,
Or saber and shield to a knight without armor;
I'll sing you sweet songs till the stars 'rise above me,
Then, wandering, I'll wish you, in silence, to love me.

We'll look through the trees at the cliff, and the eyrie,
We'll tread 'round the rath on the track of the fairy,
We'll look on the stars, and we'll list to the river,
Till you ask of your darling what gift you can give her.
  Oh, she'll whisper you: "Love as unchangeably beaming,
And trust, when in secret most tunefully streaming,
Till the starlight of Heaven above us shall quiver,
As our souls flow in one down eternity's river."

So come in the evening, or come in the morning,
Come when you're look'd for, or come without warning,
Kisses and welcome you'll find here before you,
And the oftener you come here the more I'll adore you.
  Light is my heart since the day we were plighted,
Red is my cheek that they told me was blighted;
The green of the trees looks far greener than ever,
And the linnets are singing, "true lovers, don't sever."

MY LAND.

She is a rich and rare land;
Oh! she's a fresh and fair land;
She is a dear and rare land—
  This native land of mine.

No men than hers are braver—
Her women's hearts ne'er waver;
I'd freely die to save her,
  And think my lot divine.

She's not a dull nor cold land—
No! she's a warm and bold land;

Oh! she's a true and old land—
  This native land of mine.

Could beauty ever guard her,
And virtue still reward her,
No foe would cross her border
  No friend within her pine!

Oh, she's a fresh and fair land;
Oh, she's a true and rare land!
Yes, she's a rare and fair land—
  This native land of mine.

THE GERALDINES.

The Geraldines—the Geraldines! 'tis full a thousand years
Since, 'mid the Tuscan vineyards, bright flashed their battle-spears;
When Capet seized the crown of France, their iron shields were known
And their saber-dint struck terror on the banks of the Garonne;
Across the downs of Hastings they spurred hard by William's side,
And the grey sands of Palestine with Moslem blood they dyed;
But never then, nor thence, till now, has falsehood or disgrace
Been seen to soil Fitzgerald's plume, or mantle in his face.

The Geraldines—the Geraldines! 'tis true in Strongbow's van,
By lawless force, as conquerors, their Irish reign began;
And, oh! through many a dark campaign they proved their prowess stern,
In Leinster's plains, and Munster's vales, on king, and chief, and kerne;
But noble was the cheer within the halls so rudely won,
And gen'rous was the steel-gloved hand that had such slaughter done;
How gay their laugh, how proud their mien, you'd ask no herald's sign—
Among a thousand you had known the princely Geraldine.

These Geraldines—these Geraldines! not long our air they breath'd;
Not long they fed on venison, in Irish water seethed;
Not often had their children been by Irish mothers nursed,
When from their full and genial hearts an Irish feeling burst!
The English monarchs strove in vain, by law, and force, and bribe,
To win from Irish thoughts and ways this " more than Irish " tribe;
For still they clung to fosterage, to brehon, cloak, and bard;
What king dare say to Geraldine: " Your Irish wife discard?"

Ye Geraldines—ye Geraldines!—how royally ye reigned
O'er Desmond broad, and rich Kildare, and English arts disdained;
Your sword made knights, your banner waved, free was your bugle call
By Glyn's green slopes, and Dingle's tide, from Barrow's banks to Youghal.
What gorgeous shrines, what brehon lore, what minstrel feats there were
In and around Maynooth's grey keep, and palace-filled Adare!
But not for rite or feast ye stay'd, when friend or kin were press'd;
And foemen fled, when " *Crom abo* " bespoke your lance in rest.

Ye Geraldines—ye Geraldines!—since Silken Thomas flung
King Henry's sword on council board, the English thanes among,
Ye never ceased to battle brave against the English sway,
Though ax and brand and treachery your proudest cut away.
Of Desmond's blood, through woman's veins passed on th' exhausted tide:
His title lives—a Saxon churl usurps the lion's hide;
And, though Kildare tower haughtily, there's ruin at the root,
Else why, since Edward fell to earth, had such a tree no fruit?

True Geraldine! brave Geraldine!—as torrents mould the earth,
You channelled deep old Ireland's heart by constancy and worth;
When Ginckle 'leaguered Limerick, the Irish soldiers gazed
To see if in the setting sun dead Desmond's banner blazed!
And still it is the peasant's hope upon the Curragh's mere,
" They live, who'll see ten thousand men with good Lord Edward here "——
So let them dream till brighter days, when, not by Edward's shade,
But by some leader true as he, their lines shall be arrayed.

These Geraldines—these Geraldines!—rain wears away the rock,
And time may wear away the tribe that stood the battle's shock;
But ever, sure, while one is left of all that honored race,
In front of Ireland's chivalry is that Fitzgerald's place.
And, though the last were dead and gone, how many a field and town,
From Thomas Court to Abbeyfeale, would cherish their renown,
And men would say of valor's rise, or ancient power's decline,
" 'Twill never soar, it never shone, as did the Geraldine."

The Geraldines—the Geraldines!—and are there any fears
Within the sons of conquerors for full a thousand years?
Can treason spring from out a soil bedewed with martyr's blood?
Or has that grown a purling brook, which long rushed down a flood?—
By Desmond swept with sword and fire,—by clan and keep laid low,—
By Silken Thomas and his kin,—by Sainted Edward! No!
The forms of centuries rise up, and in the Irish line
COMMAND THEIR SON TO TAKE THE POST THAT FITS THE GERALDINE!

THE BATTLE OF FONTENOY.

THRICE, at the huts of Fontenoy, the English column failed,
And, twice, the lines of Saint Antoine, the Dutch in vain assailed;
For town and slope were filled with fort and flanking battery,
And well they swept the English ranks, and Dutch auxiliary.
As vainly through De Berri's wood, the British soldiers burst,
The French artillery drove them back, diminished, and dispersed,
The bloody Duke of Cumberland beheld with anxious eye,
And ordered up his last reserve, his latest chance to try.
On Fontenoy—on Fontenoy, how fast his generals ride!
And mustering come his chosen troops, like clouds at eventide.
Six thousand English veterans in stately column tread,
Their cannon blaze in front and flank, Lord Hay is at their head;
Steady they step adown the slope—steady they climb the hill;
Steady they load—steady they fire, moving right onward still,
Betwixt the wood and Fontenoy, as though a furnace blast,
Through rampart, trench, and palisade, and bullets showering fast;
And on the open plain above they 'rose and kept their course,
With ready fire and grim resolve, that mocked at hostile force:
Past Fontenoy—past Fontenoy, while thinner grow their ranks—
They break, as broke the Zuyder Zee through Holland's ocean banks.

More idly than the summer flies, French tirailleurs rush 'round:
As stubble to the lava tide, French squadrons strew the ground;
Bomb-shell and grape, and round-shot tore, still on they marched and fired—
Fast, from each volley, grenadier and voltigeur retired.
"Push on, my household cavalry!" King Louis madly cried;
To death they rush, but rude their shock—not unavenged they died.
On through the camp the column trod—King Louis turns his rein:
"Not yet, my liege," Saxe interposed, "the Irish troops remain!"
And Fontenoy, famed Fontenoy, had been a Waterloo,
Were not these exiles ready then, fresh, vehement, and true.
"Lord Clare," he says, "you have your wish, there are your Saxon foes!"
The marshal almost smiled to see, so furiously he goes!
How fierce the look these exiles wear, who're wont to be so gay,
The treasured wrongs of fifty years are in their hearts to-day—
The treaty broken, ere the ink wherewith 'twas writ, could dry,
Their plundered homes, their ruined shrines, their women's parting cry—
Their priesthood hunted down like wolves, their country overthrown,
Each looks, as if revenge for all were staked on him alone.
On Fontenoy, on Fontenoy, nor ever yet elsewhere,
Rushed on to fight a nobler band than these proud exiles were.

O'Brien's voice is hoarse with joy, as, halting, he commands,
" Fix bay'nets"—"charge,"—like mountain storm, rush on these fiery bands!
Thin is the English column now, and faint their volleys grow,
Yet, must'ring all the strength they have, they make a gallant show.
They dress their ranks upon the hill to face that battle wind—
Their bayonets the breakers' foam; like rocks, the men behind!
One volley crashes from their line, when, through the surging smoke,
With empty guns clutched in their hands, the headlong Irish broke.
On Fontenoy, on Fontenoy, hark to that fierce huzza!
"Revenge! remember Limerick! dash down the Sassenagh!"
Like lions leaping at a fold, when mad with hunger's pang,
Right up against the English line the Irish exiles sprang;
Bright was their steel, 'tis bloody now, their guns are filled with gore;
Through shattered ranks, and severed files, and trampled flags they tore;
The English strove with desperate strength, paused, rallied, staggered, fled—

The green hill-side is matted close with dying and with dead;
Across the plain, and far away passed on that hideous wrack,
While cavalier and fantassin dash in upon their track.
On Fontenoy—on Fontenoy, like eagles in the sun,
With bloody plumes the Irish stand—the field is fought and won!

———o———

THE BRIDE OF MALLOW.

'TWAS dying they thought her,
And kindly they brought her
To the banks of Blackwater,
   Where her forefathers lie;
'Twas the place of her childhood,
And they hoped that its wild wood,
And air soft and mild would
   Soothe her spirit to die.

But she met on its border
A lad who adored her—
No rich man, nor lord, or
   A coward, or slave;
But one who had worn
A green coat, and borne
A pike from Slieve Mourne,
   With the patriots brave.

Oh! the banks of the stream are
Than emeralds greener
And how should they wean her
   From loving the earth?
While the song-birds so sweet,
And the waves at their feet,
And each young pair they meet,
   Are all flushing with mirth.

And she listed his talk,
And he shared in her walk—
And how could she balk
   One so gallant and true?
But why tell the rest?
Her love she confest,
And sunk on his breast
   Like the even tide dew.

Ah! now her cheek glows
With the tint of the rose,
And her healthful blood flows
   Just as fresh as the stream;
And her eye flashes bright,
And her footstep is light,
And sickness and blight
   Fled away like a dream.

And soon by his side
She kneels a sweet bride,
In maidenly pride
   And maidenly fears;
And their children were fair;
And their home knew no care,
Save that all homesteads were
   Not as happy as theirs.

———o———

THE SACK OF BALTIMORE.

[lmore is a small seaport in the barony of Carbery, in South Munster. It grew up around a castle of
coll's, and was, after his ruin, colonized by the English. On the 20th of June, 1631, the crew of two
me galleys landed in the dead of the night, sacked the town, and bore off into slavery all who were
o old, or too young, or too fierce for their purpose. The pirates were steered up the intricate
el by one Hackett, a Dungarvan fisherman, whom they had taken at sea for the purpose. Two years
re was convicted and executed for the crime. Baltimore never recovered this. To the artist, the
ary, and the naturalist, its neighborhood is most interesting.—*See "Smith's Ancient and Present
f the County and City of Cork,"* vol. i. p. 270.]

THE summer sun is falling soft on Carb'ry's hundred isles—
The summer sun is gleaming still through Gabriel's rough defiles—
Old Inisherkin's crumbled fane looks like a moulting bird,
And in a calm and sleepy swell the ocean tide is heard;
The hookers lie upon the beach; the children cease their play;
The gossips leave the little inn; the households kneel to pray—
And full of love, and peace, and rest—its daily labor o'er—
Upon that cosy creek there lay the town of Baltimore.

A deeper rest, a starry trance has come with midnight there;
No sound, except that throbbing wave, in earth, or sea, or air.
The massive capes, and ruined towers, seem conscious of the calm;
The fibrous sod and stunted trees are breathing heavy balm.
So still the night, these two long barks, 'round Dunashad that glide,
Must trust their oars—methinks not few—against the ebbing tide—
Oh! some sweet mission of true love must urge them to the shore—
They bring some lover to his bride, who sighs in Baltimore!

All—all asleep within each roof along that rocky street,
And these must be the lover's friends, with gently gliding feet—
A stifled gasp—a dreamy noise! "The roof is in a flame!"
From out their beds, and to their doors, rush maid, and sire, and dame—
And meet, upon the threshold stone, the gleaming saber's fall,
And o'er each black and bearded face the white or crimson shawl—
The yell of "Allah!" breaks above the pray'r, and shriek, and roar—
Oh, blessed God! the Algerine is lord of Baltimore!

Then flung the youth his naked hand against the shearing sword;
Then sprung the mother on the brand with which her son was gor'd;
Then sunk the grandsire on the floor, his grand-babes clutching wild;
Then fled the maiden, moaning fast, and nestled with the child;
But see, yon pirate strangled lies, and crushed with splashing heel,
While o'er him in an Irish hand there sweeps his Syrian steel—
Though virtue sink, and courage fail, and misers yield their store,
There's *one* hearth well avenged in the sack of Baltimore!

Midsummer morn, in woodland nigh, the birds begin to sing—
They see not now the milking maids—deserted is the spring!
Midsummer day—this gallant rides from distant Bandon's town—
These hookers crossed from stormy Skull, that skiff from Affadown;
They only found the smoking walls, with neighbors' blood besprent,
And on the strewed and trampled beach awhile they wildly went—
Then dashed to sea, and passed Cape Cleir, and saw five leagues before
The pirate galleys vanishing that ravaged Baltimore.

Oh! some must tug the galley's oar, and some must tend the street—
This boy will bear a Scheik's chibouk, and that a Bey's jerreed.
Oh! some are for the arsenals, by beauteous Dardanelles;
And some are in the caravan to Mecca's sandy dells.
The maid that Bandon gallant sought is chosen for the Dey—
She's safe—she's dead—she stabbed him in the midst of his Serai;
And, when to die a death of fire, that noble maid they bore,
She only smiled—O'Driscoll's child—she thought of Baltimore.

'Tis two long years since sunk the town beneath that bloody band,
And all around its trampled hearts a larger concourse stand,
Where, high upon a gallows tree, a yelling wretch is seen—
'Tis Hackett of Dungarvan—he who steered the Algerine!
He fell amid a sullen shout, with scarce a passing pray'r,
For he had slain the kith and kin of many a hundred there—
Some muttered of M'Morrogh, who had brought the Norman o'er—
Some cursed him with Iscariot, that day in Baltimore.

———o———

THE LOST PATH.

Sweet thoughts, bright dreams, my comfort be,
  All comfort else has flown,
For every hope was false to me,
  And here I am, alone.
What thoughts were mine in early youth,
  Like some old Irish song,
Brimful of love, and hope, and truth,
  My spirit gushed along.

I hoped to right my native isle,
  I hoped a soldier's fame,
I hoped to rest in woman's smile,
  And win a minstrel's name.

Oh! little have I served my land—
  No laurels press my brow,
I have no woman's heart or hand,
  Nor minstrel honors now.

But fancy has a magic power,
  It brings me wreath and crown,
And woman's love, the self-same hour
  It smites oppression down.
Sweet thoughts, bright dreams, my comfort be,
  I have no joy beside;
Oh! throng around, and be to me
  Power, country, fame and bride.

OH! THE MARRIAGE.

Oh! the marriage—the marriage,
  With love and *mo buachail* for me,
The ladies that ride in a carriage
  Might envy my marriage to me;
For Owen is straight as a tower,
  And tender and loving and true,
He told me more love in an hour
  Than the squires of the county could do.
        Then, oh! the marriage, etc.

His hair is a shower of soft gold,
  His eye is as clear as the day,
His conscience and vote were unsold
  When others were carried away;
His word is as good as an oath,
  And freely 'twas given to me;
Oh! sure 'twill be happy for both
  The day of the marriage to see.
        Then, oh! the marriage, etc.

His kinsmen are honest and kind,

The neighbors think much of his skill,
  And Owen's the lad to my mind,
Though he owns neither castle nor mill.
But he has a tilloch of land,
  A horse, and a stocking of coin,
A foot for the dance, and a hand
  In the cause of his country to join.
        Then, oh! the marriage, etc.

We meet in market and fair—
  We meet in the morning and night—
He sits on half of my chair,
  And my people are wild with delight.
Yet I long through the winter to skim,
  Though Owen longs more, I can see,
When I will be married to him,
  And he will be married to me.
    Then, Oh! the marriage—the marriage,
      With love and *mo buachail* for me,
    The ladies that ride in a carriage
      Might envy my marriage to me.

THE BURIAL.*

Why rings the knell of the funeral bell from a hundred village shrines?
Through broad Fingall, where hasten all those long and ordered lines?
With tear and sigh they're passing by—the matron and the maid—
Has a hero died—is a nation's pride in that cold coffin laid?
With frown and curse, behind the hearse, dark men go tramping on—
Has a tyrant died, that they cannot hide their wrath till their rites are done?

THE CHANT.

" *Ululu! ululu!* high on the wind,
  There's a home for the slave where no fetters can bind.
  Woe—woe to his slayers"—comes wildly along,
  With the trampling of feet, and the funeral song.

    And now more clear
    It swells on the ear;
    Breathe low, and listen, 'tis solemn to hear.

" *Ululu! ululu!* wail for the dead,
  Green grow the grass of Fingall on his head;
  And spring-flowers blossom, ere elsewhere appearing,
  And shamrocks grow thick on the Martyr for Eriu.
  Ululu! ululu! soft fall the dew
  On the feet and the head of the martyr'd and true."

    For awhile they tread
    In silence dread—
    Then muttering and moaning go the crowd,
    Surging and swaying like mountain cloud,
    And again the wail comes fearfully loud.

" *Ululu! ululu!* kind was his heart!
  Walk slower, walk slower, too soon we shall part.
  The faithful and pious, the Priest of the Lord,

---

* Written on the funeral of the Rev. P. J. Tyrrell, P. P. of Lusk; one of those indicted with O'Connell in the government prosecutions of 1843.

His pilgrimage over, he has his reward.
By the bed of the sick, lowly kneeling,
To God with the raised cross appealing—
He seems still to kneel, and he seems still to pray,
And the sins of the dying seem passing away.

"In the prisoner's cell, and the cabin so dreary,
Our constant consoler, he never grew weary;
But he's gone to his rest,
And he's now with the blest,
Where tyrant and traitor no longer molest—
Ululu! ululu! wail for the dead!
Ululu! ululu! here is his bed."

Short was the ritual, simple the prayer,
Deep was the silence and every head bare;
The Priest alone standing, they knelt all around,
Myriads on myriads, like rocks on the ground.
Kneeling and motionless—"Dust unto dust."
"He died as becometh the faithful and just—
Placing in God his reliance and trust;"

Kneeling and motionless—"ashes to ashes"—
Hollow the clay on the coffin-lid dashes;
Kneeling and motionless, wildly they pray,
But they pray in their souls, for no gesture have they—
Stern and standing, O! look on them now,
Like trees to one tempest the multitude bow;
Like the swell of the ocean is rising their vow:

THE VOW.

"We have bent and borne, though we saw him torn from his home by the tyrant's crew—
And we bent and bore, when he came once more, though suffering had pierced him through:
And now he is laid beyond our aid, because to Ireland true—
A martyr'd man—the tyrant's ban, the pious patriot slew.

"And shall we bear and bend for ever,
And shall no time our bondage sever,
And shall we kneel, but battle never,
          For our own soil?

"And shall our tyrants safely reign
On thrones built up of slaves and slain,
And nought to us and ours remain
          But chains and toil?

"No! 'round this grave our oath we plight,
To watch, and labor, and unite,
Till banded be the nation's might—
          Its spirit steeled.

"And then, collecting all our force,
We'll cross oppression in its course,
And die—or all our rights enforce,
          On battle field."

Like an ebbing sea that will come again,
Slowly retired that host of men;
Methinks they'll keep some other day,
The oath they swore on the martyr's clay.

————o————

THE TRUE IRISH KING.

THE Cæsar of Rome has a wider demesne
And the *Ard-Righ** of France has more clans in his train;
The scepter of Spain is more heavy with gems,
And our crowns cannot vie with the Greek diadems;
But kinglier far, before Heaven and man,
Are the emerald fields and the fiery-eyed clan,
The scepter, and state, and the poets who sing,
And the swords that encircle a True Irish King!

For he must have come from a conquering race—
The heir of their valor, their glory, their grace;
His frame must be stately, his step must be fleet,
His hand must be trained to each warrior feat;
His face, as the harvest moon, steadfast and clear,
A head to enlighten, a spirit to cheer;
While the foremost to rush where the battle-brands ring,
And the last to retreat is a True Irish King.

Yet, not from his courage, his strength or his name,
Can he from the clansmen their fealty claim.
The poorest, and highest, choose freely to-day
The chief, that to-night, they'll as truly obey;
For loyalty springs from a people's consent,
And the knee that is forced had been better unbent—
The Sassenach serfs no such homage can bring
As the Irishman's choice of a True Irish King!

Come, look on the pomp when they "make an O'Neil:
The muster of dynasts—O'Hagan, O'Shiel,
O'Cahan, O'Hanlon, O'Breslen, and all,
From mild Ardes and Orior to rude Donegal.
"St. Patrick's *comharba*," with bishops thirteen,
And Ollaves, and brehons, and minstrels, are seen,
'Round Tulach-Og Rath, like the bees in the spring,
All swarming to honor a True Irish King.

Unsandalled he stands on the foot-dinted rock,
Like a pillar-stone fix'd against every shock.
'Round—'round is the Rath on a far-seeing hill,
Like his blemishless honor and vigilant will.
The grey-beards are telling how chiefs by the score
Have been crowned on "The Rath of the Kings" heretofore,
While, yet crowded, yet ordered, within its green ring,
Are the dynasts and priests around the True Irish King.

The chronicler read him the laws of the clan,
And pledged him to bide by their blessing and ban;
His *skian* and his sword are unbuckled to show
That they only were meant for a foreigner foe;
A white willow wand has been put in his hand—
A type of pure, upright and gentle command—
While hierachs are blessing, the slipper they fling,
And O'Cahan proclaims him a True Irish King.

Thrice looked he to Heaven with thanks and with prayer—
Thrice looked to his borders with sentinel stare—
To the waves of Loch Neagh, the hights of Strabane,
And thrice on his allies, and thrice on his clan—
One clash on their bucklers—one more—they are still—

What means the deep pause on the crest of the hill?
Why gaze they above him? A war-eagle's wing!
" 'Tis an omen! Hurrah for the True Irish King!"

God aid him! God save him and smile on his reign—
The terror of England, the ally of Spain.
May his sword be triumphant o'er Sassenach arts,
Be his throne ever girt by strong hands and true hearts.
May the course of his conquest run on till he see
The flag of Plantagenet sink in the sea!
May minstrels forever his victories sing,
And saints make the bed of the True Irish King.

THE PENAL DAYS.

Oh! when those days, the penal days,
    When Ireland hopelessly complained.
Oh! weep those days, the penal days,
    When godless persecution reigned;
        When, year by year,
        For serf and peer,
    Fresh cruelties were made by law,
        And, filled with hate,
        Our senate sate
    To wield anew each fetter's flaw.
Oh! weep those days, those penal days—
Their mem'ry still on Ireland weighs.

They bribed the flock, they bribed the son,
    To sell the priest and rob the sire;
Their dogs were taught alike to run
    Upon the scent of wolf and friar.
        Among the poor,
        Or on the moor,
    Were hid the pious and the true—
        While traitor knave,
        And recreant slave,
    Had riches, rank, and retinue;
And, exiled in those penal days,
Our banners over Europe blaze.

A stranger held the land and tower
    Of many a noble fugitive;
No popish lord had lordly power,
    The peasant scarce had leave to live;
        Above his head
        A ruined shed,
    No tenure but a tyrant's will—
        Forbid to plead,
        Forbid to read,
    Disarm'd, disfranchised, imbecile—
What wonder if our step betrays
The freedman, born in penal days?

They're gone—they're gone, those penal days!
    All creeds are equal in our isle;
Then grant, oh Lord, thy plenteous grace,
    Our ancient feuds to reconcile.
        Let all atone
        For blood and groan,
    For dark revenge and open wrong;
        Let all unite
        For Ireland's right,
    And drown our grief in freedom's song;
Till time shall veil in twilight haze,
The memory of those penal days.

MY GRAVE.

Shall they bury me in the deep,
Where wind-forgetting waters sleep?
Shall they dig a grave for me
Under the greenwood tree?
Or on the wild heath,
Where the wilder breath
Of the storm doth blow?
Oh, no—oh, no!

Shall they bury me in the Palace Tombs,
Or under the shade of Cathedral domes?
Sweet 'twere to lie on Italy's shore;
Yet not there—nor in Greece, though I love
    it more.
In the wolf or the vulture my grave shall I
    find?
Shall my ashes career on the world-seeing
    wind?

Shall they fling my corpse on the battle
    mound,
Where, coffinless, thousands lie under the
    ground?
Just as they fall they are buried so—
Oh, no—oh, no!

No, on an Irish green hill-side,
On an opening lawn—but not too wide!
For I love the drip of the wetted trees—
I love not the gales, but a gentle breeze,
To freshen the turf—put no tombstone there.
But green sods deck'd with daisies fair,
Nor sods too deep; but so that the dew,
The matted grass-roots may trickle through.
Be my epitaph writ on my country's mind,
"He served his country, and loved his kind"—
Oh, 'twere merry unto the grave to go,
If one were sure to be buried so.

GERALD GRIFFIN.

GERALD GRIFFIN was born in Limerick, on 10th December, 1803. As a poet he is not so well known as he deserves; but as a novelist he takes his place by universal consent in the first rank, beside Banim and Carleton. His father's want of success as a brewer in Limerick, compelled the family to remove to Fairy Lawn near Glin in the county, a distance of thirty miles from the city. Here the family lived for some time, but the parents were persuaded by an elder brother of Gerald's, an officer in the British army, who served in America, to emigrate to that country.

Gerald, who was intended for the medical profession, remained with his brother, Dr. Griffin, who then resided at Adare, about eight miles from the city. With his two sisters who remained in Ireland, Gerald spent much of his time in rambling through the romantic demesne of Lord Dunraven—fishing in the Mague, or watching its waters glide whisperingly along by time-worn walls of the old castles and monastic ruins of that locality. Poetry was his first and greatest inspiration, and if his natural bent had been properly encouraged, he would probably have been the greatest of the Irish poets. He has, however, proved himself equal to any task which he deliberately undertook to perform.

At the age of nineteen he wrote his drama of "Aguire," of which his brother thought so highly, that he consented to Gerald's going to London to seek his fortune as a dramatic writer—without a single friend there to whom he could look for counsel or support. Imbued with the true poetic spirit, and anxious to devote his whole energies to create a name as a poet, he brought misery and ruin upon himself by the pursuit of his darling passion. At the age of twenty he wrote "Gisippus," which has been pronounced to be "the greatest drama of our time." At twenty-five, he wrote "The Collegians," and thence forward till he withdrew from the world, he never ceased to pour forth the rich creations of his fertile and vigorous imagination, in verse and prose.

But the success which he attained was too dearly paid for. His health was undermined by long vigils, by mental toil and blasted hopes. He became sad and heartbroken. His delicate sensibility of feeling forbade all intercourse with even those who were willing and able to help him—and foremost among these were John Banim and Dr. Maginn. Although his distress was most severe—being sometimes without food for three days, he acted firmly upon his resolute determination of trusting solely to his own efforts for success.

As he approached the goal of his ambition, his keen enthusiasm became blunted and subdued by the anxieties and disappointments which met him on every hand. To his sister he says: "I look now upon success as a matter of mere business. As to Fame, if I could accomplish it in any other way, I should scarcely try for its sake alone." He wore away all relish for it in his too eager pursuit. The publishers for whom he wrote "cheated him abominably," he says. They forgot the first rudiments of arithmetic; they never counted his pages correctly! All of them, except Jerdan of the *Literary Gazette*.

At this time he translated a volume and a half of Prevot's works for two guineas. To cheat a man of such hard earned money was to commit the sin of "defrauding the laborer of his wages." At last he says to his brother: "I am tired of this lonely, wasting, dispiriting, caterpillar kind of existence, which I endure, however, in hope of a speedy metamorphosis. It would amaze you to know all I have done, and to no purpose." His mind was deeply tinged with a strong religious sentiment, and in order to live, as it seemed to him, a more perfect life, he joined the Society of Christian Brothers in September, 1838; a society of good and religious men, who, withdrawing from the world and its fleeting pleasures, devote their whole lives to the education of the poor alone.

No one could describe in more felicitous language than Gerald, the new world of beauty and delight which education could open to minds pent up in darkness; and no one could feel more anxious to transplant light and intelligence to where gloom and ignorance previously ruled supreme. It is this ignorance and not their poverty or toil that degrades men. On the 12th June, 1840, he died in the North Monastery of the Christian Brothers in Cork, after having labored for nearly two years in his new vocation. There is a graceful ease and elegance of versification in all his poems; and though they breathe the ardor and warmth of feelings peculiar to youth, they are ever remarkable for their chasteness and purity of thought and expression.

POEMS OF GERALD GRIFFIN.

—o—

THE BRIDAL OF MALAHIDE.

[Of the monuments most worthy of notice in the chapel of Malahide is an altar tomb surmounted with the effigy, in bold relief, of a female habited in the costume of the 14th century, and representing the Honorable Maud Plunket, wife of Sir Richard Talbot. She had been previously married to Mr. Hussey, son to the Baron of Galtrim, who was slain on the day of her nuptials, leaving her the singular celebrity of having been " a maid, wife, and widow on the same day."]

THE joy-bells are ringing in gay Malahide,
The fresh wind is singing along the sea-side;
The maids are assembling with garlands of
    flowers,
And the harpstrings are trembling in all the
    glad bowers.

Swell—swell the gay measure! roll trumpet
    and drum!
'Mid greetings of pleasure in splendor they
    come!
The chancel is ready, the portal stands wide
For the lord and the lady, the bridegroom
    and bride.

What years, ere the latter, of earthly delight
The future shall scatter o'er them in its
    flight!

What blissful caresses shall Fortune bestow,
Ere those dark-flowing tresses fall white as
    the snow!

Before the high altar young Maud stands
    array'd;
With accents that falter her promise is
    made—
From father and mother for ever to part,
For him and no other to treasure her heart.

The words are repeated, the bridal is done,
The rite is completed—the two, they are one;
The vow, it is spoken all pure from the
    heart,
That must not be broken till life shall
    depart,

Hark! 'mid the gay clangor that compass'd
    their ear,
Loud accents in anger come mingling afar!
The foe's on the border, his weapons resound
Where the lines in disorder unguarded are
    found.

As wakes the good shepherd, the watchful
    and bold,
When the ounce or the leopard is seen in the
    fold,
So rises already the chief in his mail,
While the new-married lady looks fainting
    and pale.

"Son, husband, and brother, arise to the
    strife,
For the sister and mother, for children and
    wife!
O'er hill and o'er hollow, o'er mountain and
    plain,
Up, true men, and follow! let dastards
    remain!"

Farrah! to the battle! they form into line—
The shields, how they rattle! the spears, how
    they shine!
Soon—soon shall the foeman his treachery
    rue—
On, burgher and yeoman, to die or to do!

The eve is declining in lone Malahide,
The maidens are twining gay wreaths for the
    bride;
She marks them unheeding—her heart is
    afar,
Where the clansmen are bleeding for her in
    the war.

Hark! loud from the mountain 'tis Victory's
    cry!
O'er woodland and fountain it rings to the
    sky!
The foe has retreated! he flies to the shore;
The spoiler's defeated—the combat is o'er!

With foreheads unruffled the conquerors
    come—
But why have they muffled the lance and the
    drum?
What form do they carry aloft on his shield?
And where does he tarry, the lord of the
    field?

Ye saw him at morning, how gallant and
    gay!
In bridal adorning the star of the day:

Now weep for the lover—his triumph is sped,
His hope it is over! the chieftain is dead!

But O, for the maiden who mourns for that
    chief,
With heart overladen and rending with
    grief!
She sinks on the meadow in one morning-
    tide,
A wife and a widow, a maid and a bride!

Ye maidens attending, forbear to condole!
Your comfort is rending the depths of her
    soul.
True—true, 'twas a story for ages of pride,
He died in his glory—but, O, he *has* died!

The war-cloak she raises all mournfully
    now—
And steadfastly gazes upon the cold brow.
That glance may for ever unaltered remain,
But the Bridegroom will never return it
    again.

The dead-bells are tolling in sad Malahide,
The death-wail is rolling along the sea-side;
The crowds, heavy-hearted, withdraw from
    the green,
For the sun has departed that brighten'd the
    scene!

Ev'n yet in that valley, though years have
    roll'd by,
When through the wild sally the sea-breezes
    sigh,
The peasant, with sorrow, beholds in the
    shade
The tomb where the morrow saw Hussey
    convey'd.

How scant was the warning, how briefly
    reveal'd,
Before on that morning death's chalice was
    fill'd!
The hero who drunk it there moulders in
    gloom,
And the form of Maud Plunket weeps over
    his tomb.

The stranger who wanders along the lone
    vale
Still sighs while he ponders on that heavy
    tale;
"Thus passes each pleasure that earth can
    supply—
Thus joy has its measure—we live but to
    die!"

GILLE MACHREE.

GILLE MACHREE,* sit down by me,
  We now are joined and ne'er shall sever;
This hearth's our own, our hearts are one,
  And peace is ours for ever!

When I was poor, your father's door
  Was closed against your constant lover;
With care and pain, I tried in vain
  My fortunes to recover.
I said: " To other lands I'll roam,
  Where Fate may smile on me, love;"
I said: " Farewell, my own old home!"
  And I said: " Farewell to thee, love!"
    Sing Gille machree, etc.

I might have said, my mountain maid,
  Come live with me, your own true lover;
I know a spot, a silent cot,
  Your friends can ne'er discover;
Where gently flows the waveless tide
  By one small garden only;
Where the heron waves his wings so wide,
  And the linnet sings so lonely!
    Sing Gille machree, etc.

I might have said, my mountain maid,
  A father's right was never given
True hearts to curse with tyrant force,
  That have been blest in Heaven.
But then, I said: " In after years,

When thoughts of home shall find her!
My love may mourn with secret tears
  Her friends thus left behind her."
    Sing Gille machree, etc.

O, no, I said, my own dear maid,
  For me, though all forlorn, for ever,
That heart of thine shall ne'er repine
  O'er slighted duty—never.
From home and thee though wandering far
  A dreary fate be mine, love;
I'd rather live in endless war,
  Than buy my peace with thine, love.
    Sing Gille machree, etc.

Far, far away, by night and day,
  I toiled to win a golden treasure;
And golden gains repaid my pains
  In fair and shining measure.
I sought again my native land,
  Thy father welcomed me, love;
I poured my gold into his hand,
  And my guerdon found in thee, love.
Sing Gille machree, sit down by me,
  We now are joined, and ne'er shall
    sever;
This hearth's our own, our hearts are one,
  And peace is ours for ever.

* Gille machree,—brightener of my heart.

---o---

OLD TIMES.

OLD times—old times! the gay old times!
  When I was young and free,
And heard the merry Easter chimes
  Under the sally tree;
My Sunday palm beside me placed,
  My cross upon my hand,
A heart at rest within my breast,
  And sunshine on the land!
    Old times—old times!

It is not that my fortunes flee,
  Nor that my cheek is pale,
I mourn whene'er I think of thee,
  My darling native vale!
A wiser head I have, I know,
  Then when I loitered there;
But in my wisdom there is woe,
  And in my knowledge, care.
    Old times—old times!

I've lived to know my share of joy,
  To feel my share of pain,
To learn that friendship's self can cloy,
  To love, and love in vain;
To feel a pang and wear a smile,

To tire of other climes,
To like my own unhappy isle,
  And sing the gay old times!
    Old times—old times!

And sure the land is nothing changed,
  The birds are singing still;
The flowers are springing where we
    ranged,
  There's sunshine on the hill;
The sally waving o'er my head,
  Still sweetly shades my frame,
But ah, those happy days are fled,
  And I am not the same!
    Old times—old times!

Oh, come again, ye merry times!
  Sweet, sunny, fresh, and calm;
And let me hear those Easter chimes,
  And wear my Sunday palm.
If I could cry away mine eyes,
  My tears would flow in vain;
If I could waste my heart in sighs,
  They'll never come again!
    Old times—old times!

THE MOTHER'S LAMENT.

My darling—my darling, while silence is on
the moor,
And alone in the sunshine, I sit by our cabin
door:
When evening falls quiet and calm over land
and sea,
My darling—my darling, I think of past
times and thee!

Here, while on this cold shore, I wear out my
lonely hours,
My child in the Heavens is spreading my
bed with flowers,
All weary my bosom is grown of this
friendless clime,
But I long not to leave it; for that were a
shame and crime.

They bear to the churchyard the youth in
their health away,
I know where a fruit hangs more ripe for the
grave than they,
But I wish not for death, for my spirit is all
resigned,
And the hope that stays with me gives peace
to my aged mind.

My darling—my darling, God gave to my
feeble age,
A prop for my faint heart, a stay in my
pilgrimage;
My darling—my darling, God takes back his
gift again—
And my heart may be broken, but ne'er shall
my will complain.

——o——

THE SISTER OF CHARITY.

She once was a lady of honor and wealth,
Bright glowed on her features the roses of
health;
Her vesture was blended of silk and of gold,
And her motion shook perfume from every
fold.
Joy reveled around her—love shone at her
side,
And gay was her smile as the glance of a
bride,
And light was her step in the mirth-sounding
hall,
When she heard of the daughters of Vincent
de Paul.

She felt in her spirit the summons of grace
That called her to live for her suffering race,
And, heedless of pleasure, of comfort, of
home,
'Rose quickly, like Mary, and answered: "I
come."
She put from her person the trapping of
pride,
And passed from her home with the joy of a
bride,
Nor wept at the threshold as onward she
moved,
For her heart was on fire in the cause it
approved.

Lost ever to fashion—to vanity lost
That beauty that once was the song and the
toast,
No more in the ball-room that figure we
meet,
But gliding at dusk to the wretch's retreat.
Forgot in the halls is that high-sounding
name,

For the Sister of Charity blushes at fame;
Forgot are the claims of her riches and birth,
For she barters for Heaven the glory of earth.

Those feet that to music could gracefully
move,
Now bear her alone on her mission of love;
Those hands that once dangled the perfume
and gem
Are tending the helpless, or lifted for them;
That voice that once echoed the song of the
vain,
Now whispers relief to the bosom of pain;
And the hair that was shining with diamond
and pearl
Is wet with the tears of the penitent girl.

Her down-bed a pallet—her trinkets a bead,
Her luster—one taper, that serves her to read,
Her sculpture—the crucifix nailed by her bed,
Her painting—one print of the thorn-
crowned head,
Her cushion—the pavement that wearies her
knees,
Her music—the psalm or the sigh of disease.
The delicate lady lives mortified there,
And the feast is forsaken for fasting and
prayer.

Yet not to the service of heart and of mind
Are the cares of that Heaven-minded virgin
confined;
Like Him whom she loves, to the mansions of
grief,
She hastes with the tidings of joy and relief;
She strengthens the weary, she comforts the
weak,
And soft is her voice in the ear of the sick;

Where want and affliction on mortals attend
The Sister of Charity *there* is a friend.

Unshrinking, where pestilence scatters his
    breath,
Like an angel she moves 'midst the vapors of
    death;
Where rings the loud musket, and flashes
    the sword,
Unfearing she walks, for she follows her
    Lord.
How sweetly she bends o'er each plague-
    tinted face,
With looks that are lighted with holiest
    grace!
How kindly she dresses each suffering limb,

For she sees in the wounded the image of
    Him!

Behold her, ye worldly!—behold her, ye
    vain!
Who shrink from the pathway of virtue
    and pain,
Who yield up to pleasure your nights and
    your days,
Forgetful of service—forgetful of praise.
Ye lazy philosophers, self-seeking men—
Ye fire-side philanthropists, great at the
    pen—
How stand in the balance, your eloquence,
    weighed
With the life and the deeds of that high-born
    maid!

————o————

A PLACE IN THY MEMORY.

"A PLACE in thy memory, dearest,
    Is all that I claim—
To pause and look back when thou hearest
    The sound of my name.
Another may woo thee nearer,
    Another may win and wear;
I care not if he be dearer,
    If I be remembered there.

" Remember me, then, oh! remember
    My calm, light love;
Though bleak as the blast in November
    My life may prove.
That life will, though lonely, be sweet,
    If its brightest enjoyment should be
A smile and a kind word when we meet,
    And a place in thy memory."

————o————

THE PROPHECY.

IN the time of my boyhood I had a strange
    feeling,
    That I was to die ere the noon of my day;
Not quietly into the silent grave stealing,
    But torn, like a blasted oak, sudden away;

That even in the hour when enjoyment was
    keenest,
    My lamp should quench suddenly, hissing
    in gloom;
That even when mine honors were freshest
    and greenest,
    A blight should rush over and scatter their
    bloom.

It might be a fancy—it might be the
    glooming
    Of dark visions, taking the semblance of
    truth;
And it might be the shade of the storm that
    is coming,
    Cast thus in its morn through the
    sunshine of youth.

But be it a dream, or a mystic revealing,
    The bodement has haunted me year after
    year;

And whenever my bosom with rapture was
    filling,
    I paused for the footfall of fate at mine
    ear.

With this feeling upon me, all feverish and
    glowing,
    I rushed up the rugged way panting to
    fame.
I snatched at my laurels while yet they were
    growing,
    And won for my guerdon the half of a
    name.

My triumphs I viewed, from the least to the
    brightest,
    As gay flowers plucked from the fingers of
    death;
And wherever joy's garments flowed richest
    and lightest,
    I looked for the skeleton lurking beneath.

Oh, friend of my heart! if that doom should
    fall on me,
    And thou shouldst live on to remember
    my love,

Come oft to my tomb when the turf lies
    upon me,
  And list to the even wind mourning above.

Lie down by that bank, where the river is
    creeping
  All fearfully under the still autumn tree,
When each leaf in the sunset is silently
    weeping,
  And sigh for departed days, thinking of
    me.

By the smiles ye have looked—by the words
    ye have spoken—
  (Affection's own music, that heal as they
    fall)—
By the balm ye have poured on a spirit half
    broken,
  And, oh! by the pain ye gave—sweeter
    than all;

Remember me, L——, when I am departed,
  Live over those moments when they, too,
    are gone;
Be still to your minstrel the soft and kind-
    hearted,
  And droop o'er the marble where he lies
    alone.

Remember how freely that heart, that to
    others
  Was dark as the tempest-dawn frowning
    above,
Burst open to thine with the zeal of a
    brother's,
  And showed all its hues in the light of thy
    love.

And, oh! in that moment when over him
    sighing,
  Forgive, if his failings should flash on thy
    brain;
Remember, the heart that beneath thee is
    lying,
  Can never awake to offend thee again.

And say, while ye pause on each sweet
    recollection,
  " Let love like mine own on his spirit
    attend;
For to me his heart turned with a poet's
    affection;
  Just less than a lover, and more than a
    friend."

ORANGE AND GREEN.

THE night was falling dreary
  In merry Bandon town,
When, in his cottage, weary,
  An Orangeman lay down.
The summer sun in splendor
  Had set upon the vale,
And shouts of: " No surrender!"
  Arose upon the gale.

Beside the waters laving
  The feet of aged trees,
The Orange banner waving,
  Flew boldly in the breeze—
In mighty chorus meeting,
  A hundred voices joined,
And fife and drum were beating
  The *Battle of the Boyne.*

Ha! tow'rd his cottage hieing,
  What form is speeding now,
From yonder thicket flying,
  With blood upon his brow?
" Hide—hide me, worthy stranger,
  Though green my color be,
And in the day of danger
  May Heaven remember thee!

"In yonder vale contending
  Alone against that crew,
My life and limbs defending,
  An Orangeman I slew.
Hark! hear that fearful warning,
  There's death in every tone—
Oh, save my life till morning,
  And Heaven prolong your own!"

The Orange heart was melted
  In pity to the Green;
He heard the tale, and felt it
  His very soul within.
" Dread not that angry warning
  Though death be in its tone—
I'll save your life till morning,
  Or I will lose my own."

Now, 'round his lowly dwelling
  The angry torrent press'd,
A hundred voices swelling,
  The Orangeman addressed—
" Arise—arise, and follow
  The chase along the plain!
In yonder stony hollow
  Your only son is slain!"

With rising shouts they gather
  Upon the track amain,
And leave the childless father
  Aghast with sudden pain.
He seeks the righted stranger,
  In covert where he lay—
" Arise!" he said, " all danger
  Is gone and past away!

" I had a son—one only,
  One loved as my life,
Thy hand has left me lonely,
  In that accursed strife.
I pledged my word to save thee
  Until the storm should cease.
I kept the pledge I gave thee—
  Arise, and go in peace!"

The stranger soon departed
  From that unhappy vale;
The father, broken hearted,
  Lay brooding o'er the tale.
Full twenty summers after,
  To silver turned his beard;
And yet the sound of laughter
  From him was never heard.

The night was falling dreary
  In merry Wexford town,
When in his cabin, weary,
  A peasant laid him down.
And many a voice was singing
  Along the summer vale,
And Wexford town was ringing
  With shouts of: " Granua Uile."

Beside the waters, laving
  The feet of aged trees,
The green flag, gayly waving,
  Was spread against the breeze—
In mighty chorus meeting,
  Loud voices filled the town,
And fife and drum were beating,
  Down, Orangemen, lie down!"

Hark! 'mid the stirring clangor
  That woke the echoes there,
Loud voices, high in anger,
  Rise on the evening air.
Like billows of the ocean,
  He sees them hurry on—
And, 'mid the wild commotion,
  An Orangeman alone.

" My hair," he said, " is hoary,
  And feeble is my hand,
And I could tell a story
  Would shame your cruel band.
Full twenty years and over
  Have changed my heart and brow,
And I am grown a lover
  Of peace and concord now.

" It was not thus I greeted
  Your brother of the Green;
When, fainting and defeated,
  I freely took him in.
I pledged my word to save him
  From vengeance rushing on,
I kept the pledge I gave him,
  Though he had killed my son."

That aged peasant heard him,
  And knew him as he stood,
Remembrance kindly stirr'd him,
  And tender gratitude.
With gushing tears of pleasure,
  He pierced the listening train—
" I'm here to pay the measure
  Of kindness back again!"

Upon his bosom falling,
  That old man's tears came down;
Deep memory recalling
  The cot and fatal town.
" The hand that would offend thee,
  My being first shall end;
I'm living to defend thee,
  My savior and my friend!"

He said, and slowly turning,
  Address'd the wondering crowd,
With fervent spirit burning,
  He told the tale aloud.
Now pressed the warm beholders,
  Their aged foe to greet;
They raised him on their shoulders
  And chaired him through the street.

As he had saved that stranger
  From peril scowling dim,
So in his day of danger
  Did Heav'n remember him.
By joyous crowds attended,
  The worthy pair were seen,
And their flags that day were blended
  Of Orange and of Green.

————o————

ADDRESS TO FANCY.

THOU rushing spirit, that oft of old
  Hast thrilled my veins at evening lonely,
When musing by some ivied hold,
  Where dwelt the daw or martin only;
That oft has stirred my rising hair,
  When midnight on the heath has found me,
And told me potent things of air
  Were haunting all the waste around me.

Who sweep'st upon the inland breeze,
  By rock and glen in autumn weather,
With fragrance of wild myrtle trees,
  And yellow furze, and mountain heather.
Who sea-ward, on the scented gale,
  To meet the exile coursest fleetly,
When slowly from the ocean-vale,
  His native land arises sweetly.

That oft has thrilled with creeping fear
  My shuddering nerves at ghostly story,
Or sweetly drew the pitying tear,
  At thought of Erin's ruined glory.
A fire that burns—a frost that chills,
  As turns the song to woe or gladness;
Now couched by wisdom's fountain rills,
  And skirting now the wilds of madness.

Oh! spirit of my Island home,
Oh! spirit of my native mountain,
Romantic fancy! quickly come!
  Unseal for me thy sparkling fountain.

If e'er by lone Killarney's wave,
  Or wild Glengariff's evening billow,
My opening soul a welcome gave
  To thee beneath the rustling willow.

Or rather who, in riper days,
  In ruined aisles at solemn even,
My thoughtful bosom wont to raise
  To themes of purity and heaven!
And people all the silent shades
  With saintly forms of days departed,
When holy men and votive maids
  Lived humbly there, and heavenly hearted.

Oh thou, the minstrel's bliss and bane,
  His fellest foe, and highest treasure,
That keep'st him from the heedless train,
  Apart in grief—apart in pleasure.
That chainless as the wandering wind,
  Where'er thou wilt, unbidden blowest,
And o'er the rapt, expectant mind,
  All freely com'st, and freely goest.

Come, breathe along my eager chords,
  And mingle in the rising measure,
Those burning thoughts and tinted words
  That pierce the inmost soul with pleasure.
Possess my tongue—possess my brain,
  Through every nerve, electric thrilling,
That I may pour my ardent strain
  With tuneful force, and fervent feeling.

---o---

HY-BRASAIL—THE ISLE OF THE BLEST.

[From the Isles of Aran and the west continent, often appears visible that enchanted island called O'Brasil, and in Irish Beg-ara, or the Lesser Aran, set down in cards of navigation. Whether it be real and firm land, kept hidden by special ordinauce of God, as the terrestrial paradise, or else some illusion of airy clouds appearing on the surface of the sea, or the craft of evil spirits, is more than our judgments can sound out. There is, westward of Aran, a wild island of huge rocks, (Skira Rocks) the receptacle of a deal of seals thereon yearly slaughtered. These rocks sometimes appear to be a great city far off, full of houses, castles, towers, and chimneys; sometimes full of blazing flames, smoke, and people running to and fro. Another day you would see nothing but a number of ships, with their sails and riggings: then so many great stacks or reeks of corn and turf; and this not only on fair sun-shining days, whereby it might be thought the reflection of the sunbeams on the vapors arising about it, had been the cause, but also on dark and cloudy days.—*O'Flaherty's West Connaught, Irish Archæological Society's Publications,* page 68.

On the ocean that hollows the rocks where ye dwell,
A shadowy land has appeared, as they tell;
Men thought it a region of sunshine and rest,
And they called it *Hy-Brasail*, the isle of the blest;
From year unto year, on the ocean's blue rim,
The beautiful specter showed lovely and dim;
The golden clouds curtained the deep where it lay,
And it looked like an Eden, away, far away!

A peasant who heard of the wonderful tale,
In the breeze of the Orient loosened his sail;
From Ara, the holy, he turned to the west,
For though Ara was holy, *Hy-Brasail* was blest.

He heard not the voices that called from the shore—
He heard not the rising wind's menacing roar;
Home, kindred, and safety, he left on that day,
And he sped to *Hy-Brasail*, away, far away!

Morn rose on the deep, and that shadowy isle,
O'er the faint rim of distance, reflected its smile;
Noon burned on the wave, and that shadowy shore
Seemed lovelily distant, and faint as before;
Lone evening came down on the wanderer's track,
And to Ara again he looked timidly back;
O! far on the verge of the ocean it lay,
Yet the isle of the blest was away, far away!

Rash dreamer, return! O, ye winds of the main,
Bear him back to his own peaceful Ara again.
Rash fool! for a vision of fanciful bliss,
To barter thy calm life of labor and peace.
The warning of reason was spoken in vain;
He never revisited Ara again!
Night fell on the deep, amidst tempest and spray,
And he died on the waters, away, far away!

————o————

FAME.

Why hast thou lured me on, fond muse, to
quit
The path of plain, dull, worldly sense, and
be
A wanderer through the realms of thought
with thee?
While hearts that never knew thy visitings
sweet,
Cold souls that mock thy gentle melan-
choly,
Win their bright way up fortune's glittering
wheel,
And we sit lingering here in darkness still,
Scorned by the bustling sons of wealth and
folly.
Yet still thou whispered in my ear: " The
day,
The day may be at hand when thou and I
(This season of expectant pain gone by)
Shall tread to joy's bright porch a smiling
way,
And rising, not at once, with hurried wing,
To purer skies aspire, and hail a lovelier
spring."

————o————

KNOW YE NOT THAT LOVELY RIVER?

Know ye not that lovely river?
Know ye not that smiling river?
Whose gentle flood,
By cliff and wood,
With wildering sound goes winding ever.
Oh, often yet with feeling strong,
On that dear stream my memory ponders,
And still I prize its murmuring song,
For by my childhood's home it wanders.
Know ye not, etc.

There's music in each wind that blows
Within our native valley breathing;
There's beauty in each flower that grows
Around our native woodland wreathing.

The memory of the brightest joys
In childhood's happy morn that found us,
Is dearer than the richest toys,
The present vainly sheds around us.
Know ye not, etc.

Oh, sister, when 'mid doubts and fears,
That haunt life's onward journey ever,
I turn to those departed years,
And that beloved and lovely river;
With sinking mind and bosom riven,
And heart with lonely anguish aching,
It needs my long-taught hope in Heaven,
To keep that weary heart from breaking.
Know ye not, etc.

————o————

FADED NOW.

FADED now, and slowly chilling,
  Summer leaves the weeping dell,
While, forlorn, and all unwilling,
  Here I come to say farewell.
Spring was green when first I met thee,
  Autumn sees our parting pain.
Never, if my heart forget thee,
  Summer shine for me again.

Fame invites! her summons only
  Is a magic spell to me,
For, when I was sad and lonely,
  - Fame it was that gave me thee.
False she is, her slanderers sing me,
  Wreathing flowers that soonest fade;
But such gifts if Fame can bring me,
  Who will call the nymph a shade!

Hearts that feel not—hearts half broken,
  Deem her reign no more divine;
Vain to them are praises spoken,
  Vain the light that fills her shrine.
But in mine those joys elysian
  Deeply and warmly breathe;
Fame to me has been no vision,
  Friendship's smile embalms her wreath.

Sunny lakes and spired mountains
  Where that friendship sweetly grew—
Ruins hoar, and glancing fountains,
  Scenes of vanish'd joys, adieu!
Oh, where'er my steps may wander,
  While my home-sick bosom heaves,
On those scenes my heart will ponder,
  Silent, oft, in summer eves.

Still, when calm, the sun, down-shining,
  Turns to gold that winding tide,
Lonely on that couch reclining,
  Bid those scenes before thee glide;
Fair Killarney's sunset splendor,
  Broken crag and mountain grey,
And Glengariff's moonlight tender,
  Bosomed on the heaving bay.

Yet, all pleasing rise the measure
  Memory soon shall hymn to thee,
Dull for me no coming pleasure,
  Waste no joy for thought of me.

Oh, I would not leave thee weeping,
　But, when falls our parting day,
See thee hushed, on roses sleeping,
　Sigh unheard, and steal away.

Oh, farewell! those joys are ended—
　Oh, farewell! that day is done;
Palled in clouds, and darkly blended,
　Slowly sinks our wasted sun.
When shall we, with souls united,
　See those rosy tints return,
And, in blameless love united,
　View the past, yet never mourn?

Hues of darker fate assuming,
　Faster change life's summer skies;
In the future, dimly glooming,
　Forms of deadly promise rise.
See a loved home forsaken,
　Sundered ties and tears for thee;
And, by thoughts of terror shaken,
　See an altered soul in me.

Sung in pride and young illusion,
　Then forgive the idle strain;
Now my heart, in low confusion,
　Owns its sanguine promise vain.
Fool of Fame! that earthly vision
　Charms no more thy cheated youth
And those boasted dreams elysian
　Fly the searching dawn of truth.

Never in those tender bowers—
　Never by that reedy stream—
Lull'd on beds of tinted flowers,
　Young Romance again shall dream.
Now his rainbow pinions shaking,
　Oh! he hates the lonesome shore,
Where a funeral voice awaking,
　Bids us rest to joy no more!

Yet, all pleasing rise the measure
　Memory soon shall hymn to thee,
Dull for me no coming pleasure,
　Lose no joy for thought of me.
Oh, I would not leave thee weeping,
　But, when falls our parting day,
See thee hush'd, on roses sleeping,
　Sigh unheard, and steal away.

———o———

SAMUEL LOVER.

FORTY years ago, when Moore was reposing under the shade of the bays which his muse had so gloriously won, the subject of this sketch was at the zenith of his fame. He occupied the ground from which Moore had retired—though his songs bore no more comparison to Moore's than the twitterings of the goldfinch does to the carol of the lark; still, at the time to which we refer, Samuel Lover was (next to Moore) the most popular Irish poet. For Thomas Davis had not as yet become aware of the wealth of that rich vein of poetry which lay hidden in the depth of his loving Irish heart. It is true that Griffin and Banim, so immeasurably Lover's superiors as novelists, also occupied the poetic field at the same time; but their songs never attained the popularity of Lover's, though the latter never wrote anything as full of genuine Irish feeling as "Gille Machree" or "Soggarth Aroon." It is to his comic songs he owes his popularity with the masses of his countrymen, though the "Angel's Whisper," "Fairy Boy," and "Four-leaved Shamrock" are some of the most beautifully-rendered illustrations of those exquisitely poetic legends which take such a hold on an imaginative and simple-hearted people.

Samuel Lover was a native of Dublin, in which city he first saw the light in the year 1797.

He commenced life as a portrait-painter, and soon became so successful in his profession that he received the patronage of some of the leading members of the Irish aristocracy, including the Duke of Leinster, the Marquis of Wellesley, Lord Cloncurry, and a host of other noblemen. In 1828 he was elected an Academician of the Royal Hibernian Society of Arts, of which he subsequently became secretary. When our great national poet, Moore, visited Ireland, and was so splendidly and enthusiastically welcomed in his native city, his young townsman composed a song in his honor, which he sang at the grand banquet given by the Irish Capital to her most gifted son. Moore was highly pleased with the poetry and the music, and passed a flattering though well-merited eulogium on the young aspirant to poetic fame, which at once placed him prominently before the public on the road over which he traveled so steadily and so successfully for the ensuing twenty years.

Poems of Samuel Lover.

———o———

THE FOUR-LEAVED SHAMROCK.

I'll seek a four-leaved shamrock
  In all the fairy dells,
And if I find the charmed leavès,
  Oh, how I'll weave my spells.
I would not waste my magic might
  On diamond, pearl or gold;
For treasures tire the weary sense—
  Such triumph is but cold.
But I would play the enchanter's part
  In casting bliss around:
Oh! not a tear nor aching heart
  Should in the world be found,
      Should in the world be found.

To worth I would give honor,
  I'd dry the mourner's tears;
And to the pallid lip recall
  The smile of happier years;
And hearts that had long been estranged,
  And friends that had grown cold,

Should meet again like parted streams
  And mingle as of old.
Oh! thus I'd play the enchanter's part,
  Thus scatter bliss around;
And not a tear nor aching heart
  Should in the world be found,
      Should in the world be found.

The heart that had been mourning
  O'er vanished dreams of love,
Should see them all returning,
  Like Noah's faithful dove.
And Hope should launch her blessed bark
  On Sorrow's dark'ning sea,
And Mis'ry's children have an Ark,
  And saved from sinking be.
Oh! thus I'd play the enchanter's part;
  Thus scatter bliss around,
And not a tear nor aching heart
  Should in the world be found,
      Should in the world be found.

———o———

THE LAND OF THE WEST.

Oh! come to the West, love—oh! come there
  with me,
'Tis a sweet land of verdure that springs
  from the sea;
Where fair plenty smiles from her emerald
  throne,
Oh, come to the West, and I'll make thee my
  own!
I'll guard thee—I'll tend thee—I'll love thee
  the best,
And you'll say there's no land like the land
  of the West!

The south has its roses, and bright skies of
  blue,
But ours are more sweet with love's own
  changeful hue—
Half sunshine, half tears, like the girl I love
  best—
Oh! what is the South to the beautiful West?
Then come there with me, and the rose on
  thy mouth
Will be sweeter to me than the flowers of
  the South.

The North has its snow-tow'rs of dazzling
  array,
All sparkling with gems in the ne'er setting
  day,
There the storm-king may dwell in the halls
  he loves best,
But the soft-breathing zephyr he plays in the
  West—
Then come to the West where no cold wind
  doth blow,
And thy neck will seem fairer to me than
  the snow!

The sun in the gorgeous East chaseth the
  night,
When he riseth refreshed in his glory and
  might,
But where doth he go when he seeks his
  sweet rest?
Oh! doth he not haste to the beautiful West?
Then come there with me, 'tis the land I
  love best,
'Tis the land of my sires! 'tis my own
  darling West.

———o———

CAROLAN AND BRIDGET CRUISE.

[It is related of Carolan, the Irish bard, that when deprived of sight, and after the lapse of twenty years, he recognized his first love by the touch of her hand. The lady's name was Bridget Cruise; and though not a pretty name, it deserves to be recorded, as belonging to the woman who could inspire such a passion. On his return from a pilgrimage which he made to St. Patrick's Purgatory, in Lough Dearg, he found several persons on shore waiting the arrival of the boat which had conveyed him to the scene of his devotion. In assisting one of these devout travelers to get on board he chanced to take a lady's hand, and his sense of touch and feeling was so acute, that upon taking it he exclaimed: "*Dar Lamh mo cardas Criost* (By the hand of my Gossip,) this is the hand of my first love, Bridget Cruise."]

"TRUE love can ne'er forget;
Fondly as when we met,
Dearest, I love thee yet,
   My darling one!"
Thus sung a minstrel gay
His sweet impassion'd lay,
Down by the ocean's spray
   At set of sun.
But wither'd was the minstrel's sight,
Morn to him was dark as night,
Yet his heart was full of light,
   As he thus his lay begun.

"True love can ne'er forget;
Fondly as when we met,
Dearest I love thee yet,
   My darling one!
Long years are past and o'er,
Since from this fatal shore,
Cold hearts and cold winds bore
   My love from me."
Scarcely the minstrel spoke,
When quick, with flashing stroke,
A boat's light oar the silence broke
   O'er the sea.

Soon upon her native strand
Doth a lovely lady land,
While the minstrel's love-taught hand
   Did o'er his wild harp run:
"True love can ne'er forget;
Fondly as when we met,
Dearest, I love thee yet,
   My darling one!"
Where the minstrel sat alone,
There, that lady fair hath gone.
Within her hand she placed her own,
   The bard dropped on his knee.

From his lips soft blessings came,
He kiss'd her hand with truest flame,
In trembling tones he named—*her* name,
   Though her he could not see;
But, oh!—the touch the bard could tell
Of that dear hand, remember'd well,
Ah!—by many a secret spell
   Can true love find her own!
For true love can ne'er forget;
Fondly as when they met,
He loved his lady yet,
   His darling one.

———o———

THE ANGEL'S WHISPER.

[A superstition of great beauty prevails in Ireland, that, when a child smiles in its sleep, it is "talking with Angels."]

A BABY was sleeping, its mother was weeping,
   For her husband was far on the wild, raging sea,
And the tempest was swelling 'round the fisherman's dwelling—
   And she cried: "Dermot, darling, oh! come back to me!"

Her beads while she number'd, the baby still slumber'd,
   And smiled in her face as she bended her knee;
"Oh! blest be that warning, my child, thy sleep adorning,
   For I know that the angels are whispering with thee.

"And while they are keeping bright watch o'er thy sleeping,
   Oh! pray to them softly, my baby, with me—
And say thou would'st rather they'd watch o'er thy father,
   For I know that the angels are whispering with thee."

The dawn of the morning saw Dermot returning,
   And the wife wept with joy her babe's father to see;
And closely caressing her child with a blessing,
   Said: "I knew that the angels were whispering with thee."

———o———

THE FAIRY BOY.

[When a beautiful child pines and dies, the Irish peasant believes the healthy infant has been stolen by the fairies, and a sickly elf left in its place.]

A MOTHER came, when stars were paling,
  Wailing 'round a lonely spring;
Thus she cried while tears were falling,
  Calling on the Fairy King:

"Why with spells my child caressing,
  Courting him with fairy joy;
Why destroy a mother's blessing,
  Wherefore steal my baby boy?

"O'er the mountain, through the wild wood,
  Where his childhood loved to play;
Where the flowers are freshly springing,
  There I wander, day by day.

"There I wander, growing fonder
  Of the child that made my joy;
On the echoes wildly calling,
  To restore my fairy boy.

"But in vain my plaintive calling,
  Tears are falling all in vain;
He now sports with fairy pleasure,
  He's the treasure of their train!

"Fare thee well, my child, forever,
  In this world I've lost my joy,
But in the *next* we ne'er shall sever,
  Then I'll find my angel boy!"

THE PILGRIM HARPER.

THE night was cold and dreary!—no star was in the sky,
When, travel-tired and weary, the harper raised his cry;
He raised his cry without the gate, his night's repose to win,
And plaintive was the voice that cried: "Ah, won't you let me in?"

The portal soon was opened, for in the land of song,
The minstrel at the outer gate yet never lingered long;·
And inner doors were seldom closed 'gainst wand'rers such as he,
For locks of hearts to open soon, sweet music is the key.

But if gates are oped by melody, so grief can close them fast,
And sorrow o'er that once bright hall its silent spell had cast;
All undisturb'd, the spider there his web might safely spin,
For many a day no festive lay—no harper was let in.

But when this harper entered, and said he came from far,
And bore with him from Palestine the tidings of the war,
And he could tell of all who fell, or glory there did win,
The warder knew his noble dame would let *that* harper in.

They led him to the bower, the lady knelt in prayer;
The harper raised a well-known lay upon the turret stair;
The door was oped with hasty hand, true love its meed did win,
For the lady saw her own true knight, when that harper was let in!

MOLLY BAWN.

OH, Molly Bawn, why leave me pining,
  Lonely waiting here for you;
The stars above are brightly shining,
  Because they've nothing else to do.
The flowers late were open keeping,
  To try a rival blush with you,
But their mother, Nature, set them sleeping,
  With their rosy faces washed with dew,
    Oh, Molly Bawn—Oh, Molly Bawn.

The pretty flowers were made to bloom, dear,
  And the pretty stars were made to shine;
The pretty girls were made for the boys, dear,
  And maybe you were made for mine.
The wicked watch-dog here is snarling,
  He takes me for a thief, you see;
He knows I'd steal you, Molly, darling,
  And then "transported" I would be,
    Oh, Molly Bawn—Oh, Molly Bawn.

MOLLY MULDOON.

[NOTE.—It is generally believed that Lover wrote the following sprightly and humorous poem, though his name did not appear to it. We take the liberty of publishing it in this collection.]

MOLLY MULDOON was an Irish girl,
    And as fine a one
    As you'd look upon,
In the cot of a peasant or hall of an earl.
Her teeth were white, though not of pearl—
And dark was her hair, but it did not curl;
Yet few who gazed on her teeth and her hair,
But owned that a power o' beauty was there.
    Now many a hearty and rattling gorsoon,
    Whose fancy had charmed his heart into tune,
    Would dare to approach fair Molly Muldoon,
        But for *that* in her eye,
        Which made most of them shy
And look quite ashamed, though they couldn't tell why—
Her eyes were large, dark blue and clear,
    And *heart* and *mind* seemed in them blended.
If *intellect* sent you one look severe
    Love instantly leapt in the next to mend it—
    Hers was the eye to check the rude,
    And hers the eye to stir emotion,
    To keep the sense and soul subdued,
    And calm desire into devotion.

        There was Jemmy O'Hare,
        As fine a boy as you'd see in a fair,
And wherever Molly was he was there.
His face was round and his build was square,
        And he sported as rare
        And tight a pair
Of legs, to be sure, as are found anywhere.
        And Jemmy would wear
        His *caubeen* and hair
With such a peculiar and rollicking air,
        That I'd venture to swear
        Not a girl in Kildare
Nor Victoria's self, if she chanced to be there,
Could resist his wild way—called "Devil may care."
Not a boy in the parish could match him for fun,
Nor wrestle, nor leap, nor hurl, nor run
With Jemmy—No gorsoon could equal him—None.
    At wake or at wedding, at feast or at fight,
    At throwing the sledge with such dext'rous sleight,—
He was the envy of men, and the women's delight.

Now Molly Muldoon liked Jemmy O'Hare,
    And in troth Jemmy loved in his heart Miss Muldoon.
I believe in my conscience a purtier pair
    Never danced in a tent at a pattern in June—
        To a bagpipe or fiddle
        On the rough cabin door
        That is placed in the middle—
        Ye may talk as ye will,'
There's a grace in the limbs of the peasantry there
With which People of Quality couldn't compare.
    And Molly and Jemmy were counted the two
    That would keep up the longest, and go the best through
        All the jigs and the reels

That have occupied heels
Since the days of the Murtaghs and Brian Boru.

It was on a long, bright sunny day
　They sat on a green knoll side by side.
But neither just then had much to say;
　Their hearts were so full that they only tried
　　To do anything foolish just to hide
　　What both of them felt, but what Molly denied.
They pluck'd the speckled daisies that grew
Close by their arms—then tore them, too;
And the bright little leaves that they broke from the stalk,
　They threw at each other for want of talk;
　　While the heart-lit look and the sunny smile,
　Reflected pure souls without art or guile,
　　And every time Molly sighed or smiled,
　　Jem felt himself grow as soft as a child;
And he fancied the sky never looked so bright,
The grass so green, the daisies so bright,
Everything looked so gay in his sight
That gladly he'd linger to watch them till night—
　　And Molly herself thought each little bird
　　Whose warbling notes her calm soul stirred,
　　Sang only his lay but by her to be heard.

An Irish courtship's short and sweet,
It's sometimes foolish and indiscreet;
But who is wise when his young heart's heat
Whips the pulse to a galloping beat—
　　Ties up his judgment neck and feet,
　　And makes him the slave of a blind conceit?
Sneer not, therefore, at the loves of the poor,
Though their manners be rude their affections are pure;
They look not by art, and they love not by rule,
For their souls are not tempered in fashion's cold school.
Oh! give me the love that endures no control
But the delicate instinct that springs from the soul,
As the mountain stream gushes its freshness and force,
Yet obedient, wherever it flows, to its source.
Yes, give me the love that but nature has taught,
By rank unallured and by riches unbought;
Whose very simplicity keeps it secure—
The love that illumines the hearts of the poor.
All blushful was Molly, or shy at least,
　　As one week before Lent
　　Jem procured her consent
To go the next Sunday and spake to the priest.

Shrove-Tuesday was named for the wedding to be,
　　And it dawned as bright as they'd wish to see.
And Jemmy was up at the day's first peep,
For the livelong night no wink could he sleep.
　　A bran new coat, with a bright big button
　　He took from a chest and carefully put on—
And brogues as well *lampblacked* as ever went foot on,
Were greased with the fat of *a quare sort of mutton!*
　　Then a tidier *gorsoon* couldn't be seen
　　Treading the Emerald Sod so green—
　　Light was his step and bright was his eye,
　　As he walked through the *slobbery* streets of Athy.
And each girl he passed bid "God bless him" and sighed,
While she wished in her heart that herself was the bride.

Hush! here's the priest—let not the least
Whisper be heard till the father has ceased.
   " Come bridegroom and bride,
    That the knot may be tied,
Which no power upon earth can hereafter divide."
Up rose the bride and the bridegroom, too,
And a passage was made for them both to walk through;
And his Rev'rence stood with a sanctified face,
Which spread its infection around the place.
The bridesmaid bustled and whispered the bride,
Who felt so confused that she almost cried,
But at last bore up and walked forward, where
The father was standing with solemn air;
The bridegroom was following after with pride,
When his piercing eye something awful espied!
   He stopped and sighed,
   Looked 'round and tried
To tell what he saw, but his tongue denied;
   With a spring and a roar
   He jumped to the door,
AND THE BRIDE LAID HER EYES ON THE BRIDEGROOM NO MORE!

   Some years sped on,
   Yet heard no one,
  Of Jemmy O'Hare, or where he had gone.
But since the night of that widow'd feast,
The strength of poor Molly had ever decreas'd;
Till, at length, from earth's sorrow her soul releas'd,
Filed up to be ranked with the saints at least.
And the morning poor Molly to live had ceased,
Just five years after the widow'd feast,
An American letter was brought to the priest,
Telling of Jemmy O'Hare deceas'd!
   Who, ere his death,
   With his latest breath,
To a spiritual father unburdened his breast,
And the cause of his sudden departure confessed—
" Oh. Father!" says he, "I've not long to live,
So I'll freely confess, and hope you'll forgive—

  That same Molly Muldoon, sure I loved her indeed;
  Ay, as well as the Creed
  That was never forsaken by one of my breed;
But I couldn't have married her after I saw—"
  " Saw what?" cried the Father, desirous to hear—
  And the chair that he sat in unconsciously rocking—
"Not in her 'karacter,' yer Rev'rince, a flaw—"
The sick man here dropped a significant tear,
And died as he whispered in the clergyman's ear—
  "But I saw, God forgive her, A HOLE IN HER STOCKING!"

THE MORAL.

  Lady readers, love may be
  Fixed in hearts immovably,
  May be strong and may be pure;
  Faith may lean on faith secure,
  Knowing adverse fate's endeavor
  Makes that faith more firm than ever.
  But the purest love and strongest,
  Love that has endured the longest,
  Braving cross, and blight and trial,

Fortune's bar, or pride's denial,
Would—no matter what its trust—
Be uprooted by DISGUST—
Yes, the love that might for years'
Spring in suffering, grow in tears,
Parents' frigid counsel mocking,
Might be—where's the use in talking?—
Upset by a BROKEN STOCKING!

——o——

WIDOW MACHREE.

WIDOW MACHREE, it's no wonder you
        frown,
    Och, hone! Widow Machree;
Faith it ruins your looks, that same dirty
        black gown,
    Och, hone! Widow Machree.
How altered your air,
With that close cap you wear—
'Tis destroying your hair,
    Which should be flowing free;
Be no longer a churl
Of its black silken curl,
    Och, hone! Widow Machree.

Widow Machree, now the summer is come,
    Och, hone! Widow Machree;
When everything smiles, should a beauty
        look glum?
    Och, hone! Widow Machree.
See the birds go in pairs,
And the rabbits and hares—
Why even the bears
    Now in couples agree;
And the mute little fish,
Though they can't spake, they wish,
    Och, hone! Widow Machree.

Widow Machree, and when winter comes
        in,
    Och, hone! Widow Machree;
To be poking the fire all alone is a sin,
    Och, hone! Widow Machree.
Shure the shovel and tongs
To each other belongs,

And the kettle sings songs,
    Full of family glee;
While alone with your cup,
Like a hermit you sup—
    Och, hone! Widow Machree.

And how do you know, with the comforts
        I've towld,
    Och, hone! Widow Machree;
But you're keeping some poor fellow out in
        the cowld,
    Och, hone! Widow Machree.
With such sins on your head,
Sure your peace would be fled,
Could you sleep in your bed,
    Without thinking to see
Some ghost or some sprite,
That would wake you each night,
    Och, hone! Widow Machree.

Then take my advice, darling Widow
        Machree,
    Och, hone! Widow Machree;
And with my advice, faith I wish you'd
        take me,
    Och, hone! Widow Machree.
You'd have me to desire,
Then to sit by the fire,
And sure hope is no liar,
    In whispering to me,
That the ghosts would depart,
When you'd me near your heart,
    Och, hone! Widow Machree.

——o——

J. C. MANGAN.

JAMES CLARENCE MANGAN was born in Dublin in 1803, and died there in 1849. For a period of more than twenty years he had been a contributor to almost every magazine or periodical published in Ireland during that time. When scarcely fifteen years of age he obtained a situation in a scrivener's office, where he remained for seven years, and then became a solicitor's clerk for three years. Describing this period of his life, he says: "I was obliged to work seven years of the ten from five in the morning, winter and summer, to eleven at night; and, during the three remaining years, nothing but a special providence could have saved me from suicide. The misery of my own mind—my natural tendency to loneliness, poetry, and self-analysis, the disgusting obscenities and horrible blasphemies of those associated with me—the persecutions I was obliged to endure, and which I never avenged but by acts of kindness—the close air of the room, and the perpetual smoke of the chimney—all these destroyed my constitution. No! I am wrong; it was not even all these that destroyed me. In seeking to escape from this misery, I had laid the foundation of that evil habit which has proved to be my ruin."

Alas! It is too true that like many another child of song he drank long and deeply; and in his desire to forget himself—to fly from the actual into the ideal, he became an opium-eater. He became connected with the library of Trinity College, where he acquired that knowledge of languages which he afterwards turned to such good account.

In person Mangan was below the middle size. His face was ashy pale, but when kindled up by the light and brilliancy of his full, blue eye, under the influence of his favorite drug, he was perfectly beautiful. He usually wore a carmelite brown kind of frock coat, tightly buttoned, and occasionally over it a small, blue cloak, in the shape of which the *bias* cut was carefully excluded. His hat, which was high-crowned and battered—and the old umbrella under his arm, even the warmest day in summer, gave the finishing stroke to his quaint and specter-like appearance. And yet there was something deeply but painfully interesting about him. On a friend of his presenting a looking-glass to his face, that he might see the ravages which his wild habits were making, he said: "Yes, I see a skinless skull there—an empty socket where intelligence once beamed; but when I look *within* myself, I behold a sadder vision—the vision of a wasted life."

His existence became like that of Savage and Poe, vagrant and dissipated, till he was taken from a garret in a mean street in Dublin to one of the public hospitals, where he died after a week's illness. His remains repose in Glasnevin cemetery, without a stone to mark the spot.

Among the poets whom Ireland has produced within the last forty years, Clarence Mangan deservedly occupies a high place. As a translator he was inimitable; and he translated from the Irish, the French, the German, the Spanish, the Italian, the Danish, and the Eastern languages, with such a versatile facility as not only to transfuse into his own tongue the substance and sense of his original, but the appropriate graces of style and ornament, and idiomatic expression which are peculiar to the poetry of every country. He frequently surpassed his originals in the freedom and fluency of his language; and many of the poems which he has called translations, are entirely his own. It has been well observed that he was a Dervish among the Turks, a Bursch among the Germans, a Scald among the Danes, an Improvisatore in Italy, and a Senachie in Ireland. His original poems exhibit the vigor of his style and the vividness of his fancy; and embody every form of grace and dignity. in the wondrous flow and charming melody of his versification. The only poems of his which are in a collected form are his translations from the German, which were published in 1845, under the title of: "Anthologia Germanica."

POEMS OF J. C. MANGAN.

HIGHWAY FOR FREEDOM.

"My suffering country SHALL be freed,
   And shine with tenfold glory!"
So spake the gallant Winkelreid,
   Renowned in German story.
"No tyrant, even of kingly grade,
   Shall cross or darken *my* way!"
Out flashed his blade, and so he made
   For freedom's course a highway!

We want a man like this, with power
   To arouse the world by *one* word;
We want a chief to meet the hour,
   And march the masses onward.
But chief or none, through blood and fire,
   My Fatherland lies *thy* way!
The men must fight who dare desire
   For Freedom's course a highway!

Alas! I can but idly gaze
   Around in grief and wonder;
The PEOPLE'S will alone can raise
   The people's shout of thunder.

Too long, my friends, you faint for fear,
   In secret crypt and by-way;
At last be Men! Stand forth and clear
   For Freedom's course a highway!

You intersect wood, lea and lawn,
   With roads for monster wagons,
Wherein you speed like lightning, drawn
   By fiery iron dragons.
So do! Such work is good, no doubt;
   But why not seek some nigh way
For *Mind* as well? Path also out
   For Freedom's course a highway!

Yes! up, and let your weapons be
   Sharp steel and self-reliance!
Why waste your burning energy
   In void and vain defiance,
And phrases fierce and fugitive?
   'Tis deeds, not words, that *I* weigh—
Your swords and guns alone can give
   To Freedom's course a highway!

ELLEN BAWN.

ELLEN BAWN—oh, Ellen Bawn, you darling—darling dear, you,
Sit awhile beside me here, I'll die unless I'm near you!
'Tis for you I'd swim the Suir and breast the Shannon's waters;
For, Ellen dear, you've not your peer in Galway's blooming daughters!

Had I Limerick's gems and gold at will to mete and measure,
Were Loughrea's abundance mine, and all Portumna's treasure,

These might lure me, might insure me many and many a new love,
But oh! no bribe could pay your tribe for one like you, my true love!

Blessings be on Connaught! that's the place for sport and raking!
Blessings, too, my love, on you, a-sleeping and a-waking!
I'd have met you, dearest Ellen, when the sun went under,
But, woe! the flooding Shannon broke across my path in thunder.

Ellen!! I'd give all the deer in Limerick's parks and arbors,
Ay, and all the ships that rode last year in Munster's harbors,
Could I blot from Time the hour I first became your lover,
For, oh! you've given my heart a wound it never can recover!

Would to God that in the sod my corpse to-night were lying,
And the wild birds wheeling o'er it, and the winds a-sighing,
Since your cruel mother and your kindred chose to sever
Two hearts that love would blend in one for ever and for ever!

SOUL AND COUNTRY.

ARISE! my slumbering soul, arise!
And learn what yet remains for thee
To dree or do!
The signs are flaming in the skies
A struggling world would yet be free
And live anew.
The earthquake hath not yet been born
That soon shall rock the lands around
Beneath their base.
Immortal freedom's thunder horn,
As yet, yields but a doleful sound
To Europe's race.

Look around, my soul, and see and say
If these about thee understand
Their mission here;
The will to smite—the power to slay—
Abound in every heart—and hand
Afar, anear.
But, God! must yet the conqueror's sword
Pierce *mind*, as heart, in this proud year?
Oh, dream it not!
It sounds a false, blaspheming word,
Begot and born of moral fear—
And ill-begot!

To leave the world a name is naught;
To leave a name for glorious deeds
And works of love—
A name to waken lightning thought,
And fire the soul of him who reads,
This tells above.
Napoleon sinks to-day before
The ungilded shrine, the *single* soul
Of Washington;
Truth's name alone, shall man adore,
Long as the waves of time shall roll
Henceforward on!

My countrymen! my words are weak,
My health is gone, my soul is dark,
My heart is chill—
Yet would I fain and fondly seek
To see you borne in freedom's bark
O'er ocean still.
Beseech your God, and bide your hour—
He cannot, will not, long be dumb;
Even now his tread
Is heard o'er earth with coming power;
And coming, trust me, it will come,
Else were he dead!

THE WOMAN OF THREE COWS.

(*From the Irish.*)

[This ballad, which is of homely cast, was intended as a rebuke to the saucy pride of a woman in humble life, who assumed airs of consequence from being the possessor of three cows. Its author's name is unknown, but its age can be determined, from the language, as belonging to the early part of the Seventeenth century. That it was formerly very popular in Munster, may be concluded from the fact that the phrase,—Easy, oh, woman of the three cows! has become a saying in that province, on any occasion upon which it is desirable to lower the pretensions of a boastful or consequential person.]

O, WOMAN of Three Cows, agragh! don't let your tongue thus rattle!
O, don't be saucy, don't be stiff, because you may have cattle.
I have seen—and, here's my hand to you, I only say what's true—
A many a one with twice your stock not half so proud as you.

Good luck to you, don't scorn the poor, and don't be their despiser,
For worldly wealth soon melts away, and cheats the very miser,
And Death soon strips the proudest wreath from haughty human brows;
Then don't be stiff, and don't be proud, good Woman of Three Cows!

See where Mononia's heroes lie, proud Owen Moore's descendants,
'Tis they that won the glorious name, and had the grand attendants!
If *they* were forced to bow to Fate, as every mortal bows,
Can *you* be proud, can *you* be stiff, my Woman of Three Cows?

The brave sons of the Lord of Clare, they left the land to mourning;
Morrone! * for they were banished, with no hope of their returning—
Who knows in what abodes of want those youths were driven to house?
Yet *you* can give yourself these airs, O, Woman of Three Cows!

O, think of Donnell of the Ships, the Chief whom nothing daunted—
See how he fell in distant Spain, unchronicled, unchanted!
He sleeps, the great O'Sullivan, where thunder cannot rouse—
Then ask yourself, should *you* be proud, good Woman of Three Cows?

O'Ruark, Maguire, those souls of fire, whose names are shrined in story—
Think how their high achievements once made Erin's greatest glory—
Yet now their bones lie mouldering under weeds and cypress boughs,
And so, for all your pride, will yours, O, Woman of Three Cows!

Th' O'Carrolls also, famed when fame was only for the boldest,
Rest in forgotten sepulchres with Erin's best and oldest;
Yet who so great as they of yore in battle or carouse?
Just think of that, and hide your head, good Woman of Three Cows!

Your neighbor's poor, and you, it seems, are big with vain ideas,
Because, forsooth, you've got three cows, one more, I see, than *she* has;
That tongue of yours wags more at times than Charity allows,
But if you're strong, be merciful, great Woman of Three Cows!

THE SUMMING UP.

Now, there you go! You still, of course, keep up your scornful bearing,
And I'm too poor to hinder you; but, by the cloak I'm wearing,
If I had but four cows myself, even tho' you were my spouse,
I'd thwack you well to cure your pride, my Woman of Three Cows!

* My grief.

---o---

KINKORA.

1015.

[This poem is ascribed to the celebrated poet, Mac Liag, the secretary of the renowned monarch, Brian Boru, who, as is well known, fell at the battle of Clontarf, in 1014, and the subject of it is a lamentation for the fallen condition of Kinkora, the palace of that monarch, consequent on his death. The decease of Mac Liag is recorded in the "Annals of the Four Masters," as having taken place in 1015. A great number of his poems are still in existence, but none of them have obtained a popularity so widely extended as his "Lament." The palace of Kinkora, which was situated on the banks of the Shannon, near Killaloe, is now a heap of ruins.]

Oh, where, Kinkora, is Brian the Great?
  And where is the beauty that once was thine?
Oh, where are the princes and nobles that sate
  At the feast in thy halls, and drank the red wine?
        Where, oh, Kinkora?

Oh, where, Kinkora, are thy valorous lords?

Oh, whither, thou Hospitable, are they gone?
Oh, where are the Dalcassians of the golden swords?*
  And where are the warriors Brian led on?
        Where, oh, Kinkora?

---

* *Colg n-or*, or the Swords *of Gold, i. e.*, of the *Gold-hilted* Swords.

And where is Morrough, the descendant of
  kings:
  The defeater of a hundred—the daringly
    brave—
Who set but slight store by jewels and
    rings—
  Who swam down the torrent and laughed
    at its wave,
            Where, oh, Kinkora?

Aud where is Donogh, King Brian's worthy
  son?
  And where is Conaing, the beautiful chief?
And Kiar and Corc? Alas! they are gone—
  They have left me this night alone with
    my grief!
            Left me, Kinkora!

Aud where are the chiefs with whom Brian
  went forth,
  The never vanquished sons of Erin the
    brave,
The great King of Onaght, renowned for his
    worth,
  And the hosts of Baskinn, from the western
    wave?
            Where, oh, Kinkora?

Oh, where is Duvlann of the Swift-footed
  Steeds?
  And where is Kian, who was son of
    Molloy?
And where is King Lonergan, the fame of
  whose deeds
  In the red battle-field no time can destroy?

            Where, oh, Kinkora?

And where is that youth of majestic hight,

The faith-keeping Prince of the Scots?
        Even he,
As wide as his fame was, as great as was his
    might,
  Was tributary, oh Kinkora, to thee!
            Thee, oh, Kinkora!

They are gone, those heroes of royal birth!
  Who plundered no churches, and broke no
    trust;
'Tis weary for me to be living on earth
  When thee, oh Kinkora, lie low in the
    dust!
            Low, oh, Kinkora!

Oh, never again will princes appear,
  To rival the Dalcassians of the cleaving
    swords;
I can never dream of meeting afar or anear
  In the east or the west, such heroes and
    lords!
            Never, Kinkora!

Oh, dear are the images my memory calls up
  Of Brian Boru!—how he never would miss
To give me at the banquet, the first bright
    cup!
  Ah! why did he heap on me honor like
    this?
            Why, oh, Kinkora?

I am Mac Liag, and my home is on the lake;
  Thither often, to that palace whose beauty
    is fled,
Came Brian, to ask me, and I went for his
    sake,
  Oh, my grief! that I should live, and
    Brian be dead!
            Dead, oh, Kinkora!

————o————

PANEGYRIC ON BLACK THOMAS BUTLER.

EARL OF ORMOND, BETWEEN THE REIGN OF HENRY VIII. AND ELIZABETH.

(From the Irish.)

STRIKE the loud lyre for Dark Thomas, the Roman,
  Roman in Faith, but Hibernian in Soul!
Him, who, the idol of warrior and woman,
  Never feared peril, and never knew dole.
Who is the Man whom I name with such rapture?
  Who but our Ossory's and Ormond's Great Chief—
He whom his foes battled vainly to capture—
  He whom his friends loved beyond all belief!

Him the great Henry* gave rubies and rings to—
  Him the King Edward for fleetness admired;
Even as his body, his spirit had wings, too,
  And defied efforts that death alone tired.

* Henry VIII,

Southwards this morn into deep Tipperary,
  Northward ere night on the shores of the Erne,
Always he showed his contempt of those chary
  Shifts of the soul that no Butler could learn!

Oriel of streams, and Duhallow of Harbors,
  Yielded him shorewards their silver and gold* —
All he despised! as those greenwoods and harbors
  Girdling his towers from the ages of old.
Riches he loved not—his trust and his treasure
  Lay in the midst of his far flaming sword;
War was his pastime and battle his pleasure,
  And his own glory the God he adored!

Thrice, and a fourth time, he humbled Clan Caura; †
  His were the warriors that wasted Dunlo—
How his bands ravaged and fired Glen-na-Maura
  Who thoughout green Inisfail doth not know?
Munster beheld his achievements of wonder,
  Connaught and Ulster his bands left bereaven;
Wrath, like the wrath of his lightning and thunder, .
  Cast into shade the high anger of Heaven!

Woe unto us! This great man has departed!
  Quenched lies his lamp in the dust of the tomb!
He, the land's giant, the great Lion-hearted,
  He, even he, hath succumbed unto Doom!
Rest is his lot for whom Life yielded no rest—
  Darkling and lone is his dwelling to-night—
On the proud thousand-yeared Oak of the Forest
  Hath on a sudden come blastment and blight!

Toll ye his funeral dirge, ye dark waters,
  O'er which so often his fleets held their march!
Mourn for the Earl, thou Ierna of Slaughters;
  Build up his pillar and laurel his arch!
Thy foes were his, and with them he warred only—
  Weep for him, then, from the depths of thy core!
Weep for the Chief who hath left thee thus lonely—
  One like to him thou shalt never see more!

O! for myself, my two eyes are as fountains—
  Flowing, o'erflowing, by night and by morn,
Gloomily roam I on Banba's ‡ grey mountains,
  Feeling all wretched, all stricken and lorn.
Jewels and gold in profusion he gave me—
  Would they, not he, were now under the sod!
I shall soon follow him; these cannot save me—
  Death is my guerdon, but, Glory to God!

Glory to God in the Highest—and Lowest!
  His are the Power and the Glory alone—
Pay Him, O, Man, the high homage thou owest,
  Whether thou rest on a footstool or throne!
Yet may His glory be mirrored in others—
  As in the waves the rich poop of the bark;
And the mean man stands apart from his brothers,
  Who doth not trace it in Thomas the Dark!

---

* Viz:—Their white and yellow fish.
‡ *Banba* (Banva) was one of the ancient names of Ireland.

† The MacCarthies.

CAHAL MOR OF THE WINE-RED HAND.

I WALKED entranced
Through a land of Morn;
The sun, with wondrous excess of light,
Shone down and glanced
Over seas of corn,
And lustrous gardens aleft and right.
Even in the clime
Of resplendent Spain
Beams no such sun upon such a land;
But it was the time,
'Twas in the reign
Of Cahal Mor of the Wine-red Hand.

Anon stood nigh
By my side a man
Of princely aspect and port sublime.
Him queried I:
"Oh, my lord and khan,
What clime is this and what golden time?"

When he: "The clime
Is a clime to praise,
The clime is Erin's, the green and bland;
And it is the time,
These be the days,
Of Cahal Mor of the Wine-Red Hand."

Then I saw thrones,
And circling fires,
And a dome 'rose near me as by a spell,
Whence flowed the tones
Of silver lyres,
And many voices in wreathed swell;
And their thrilling chime
Fell on mine ears
As the heavenly-hymn of an angel band—
"It is now the time,
These be the years,
Of Cahal Mor of the Wine-red Hand."

---o---

THE SIEGE OF MAYNOOTH.

*Crom, Crom-aboo!** The Geraldine rebels from proud Maynooth.
And with Him are leagued four hundred, the flower of Leinster's youth.
Take heart once more, oh, Erin! The great God gives thee hope;
And thro' the mist of Time and Woe thy true Life's portals ope!

Earl Thomas of the Silken Robes!—here doubtless burns thy soul;
Thou beamest here a Living Sun, around which thy planets roll.
Oh! would the Eternal Powers above that this were only so!
Then had our land, now scorned and banned, been saved a world of woe!

No more—no more!—it maddeneth so!—But rampart, keep, and tower,
At least are still—long may they be—a part of Ireland's power!
But—who looks 'mid his warriors from the walls, as gleams a pearl
'Mid meaner stones? 'Tis Parez—foster-brother of the Earl.

Enough!—we shall hear more of him! Amid the hundred shafts
Which campward towards the Saxon host the wind upbears and wafts,
One strikes the earth at Talbot's feet, with somewhat white—a scroll—
Impaled upon its barb—Oh! how exults the leader's soul!

He grasps it—reads: "Now, by St. George, the day at last is ours!
Before to-morrow's sun arise we hold you haughty towers!
The craven traitor!—but, 'tis well!—he *shall* receive his hire,
And somewhat more to boot, God wot, than perchance he may desire!"

---

* The war-cries of the principal Irish septs or families were the following:—The FITZGERALDS', Earls of Kildare, *Crom-aboo! Crom for Ever!* or, *Hurrah for Crom!* This cry has been suggested by their strong-hold of Croom, in the County Limerick. The FITZGERALDS', Knights of Kerry, *Farri-buidhe-aboo!* The *Yellow Troop for Ever!* The O'NEILS', Earls of Tyrone, *Lamh-dearg-aboo!* The *Red Hand for Ever!* The Crest of the family is the Red Hand. The O'BRIENS', *Lamh-laider-aboo! The Strong Hand for Ever!* Crest, a dexter arm holding a naked sword. The M'CARTHYS' and FITZMAURICES' was the same as the BRIENS'. But the M'CARTHYS', Earls of Desmond, took *Sean-ait-aboo! The Old Place for Ever!* The DE BURGOS' or BOURKES', Earls of Clanricarde, *Gail-ruath-aboo! The Red Stranger for Ever!* Richard De Burgo, the second Earl of Ulster, was red-haired, and hence he was called the Red Earl, and his descendants the Red Strangers. The FITZPATRICKS', or MAC-GILLE-PATRICKS', *Geair-laider-aboo! The Sharp and Strong for Ever!* Crest, a Lion and a Dragon. The MAC-SWEENEYS', *Battailah-aboo! The Noble Staff for Ever!*—In allusion to a part of the family arms. The HEFFERNANS', *Ceart-na Suas-aboo! The Right from Above for Ever!* intimating that no justice was to be expected without the aid of Heaven. The HUSKEYS', Barons of Galtrim, *Cair-direach-aboo! Strict Justice for Ever!* These cries mean, Success to the cause of the family! Hurrah for the family! or the family and cause, for ever! Previously to attacking an enemy it was customary among the Irish in former times to cry out: *Farrah—Farrah!* which meant, *Fall on—Fall on!* It is not unusual for the Irish soldiers to-day to shout the cry of *Faug a-ballagh! Clear the way!* Napier, in his *History of the Peninsular War,* says: "Nothing so startled the French soldiery as the wild yell with which the Irish regiments sprang to the charge,"

Alas—alas!—'tis all too true! A thousand marks of gold
In Parez' hands, and Leinster's bands are basely bought and sold!
Earl Thomas loses fair Maynooth and a hundred of his clan—
But, worse! he loses half his hopes, for he loses trust in Man!

The morn is up; the gates lie wide; the foe pour in amain.
Oh! Parez, pride thee in thy plot, and hug thy golden chain!
There are cries of rage from battlements, and mellays beneath in court,
But Leinster's Brave, ere noon blaze high, shall mourn in donjon fort!

"Ho! Master Parez! thou?" So spake in the hall the Saxon chief—
"How hast thou proved this tentless loon? But, come, we will stanch thy grief!
Count these broad pieces over well!" He flung a purse on the ground,
Which in wrathful silence Parez grasped, 'mid the gaze of all around.

"So!—right?" "Yes, right, Sir John! Enough! I now depart for home!"
"*Home!* sayest-thou, Master Parez? Yes, and by my Halidome,
Mayest reach *that* sooner than thou dreamest. But before we part,
I would a brief, blunt parle with thee. Nay, man, why dost thou start?"

"A sudden spasm, Sir John."—"Ay—ay! those sudden spasms *will* shock,
As when, thou knowest, a traitor lays his head upon the block!"
"Sir John!"—"Hush, man, and answer me! Till then thou art in bale—
Till then mine enemy and thrall!" The fallen chief turned pale.

"Say, have I kept good faith with thee?"—"Thou hast—good faith and true!"
"I owe thee nought, then?" "Nought, Sir John; the gold lies here to view."
"Thou art the Earl's own foster brother?"—"Yes, and bosom friend!"
"WHAT?"—"Nay, Sir John, I need those pieces, and ——"—"Come, there's an end!"

"The Earl heaped favors on thee?"—"Never King heaped more on Lord!"
"He loved thee? honored thee?"—"I was his heart, his arm, his sword!"
"He trusted thee?"—"Even as he trusted his own lofty soul!"
"AND THOU BETRAYEST HIM? Base wretch! thou knowest the traitor's goal!

"Ho! Provost-Marshal, hither! Take this losel caitiff hence—
I mark, methinks, a scaffold under yonder stone defense,
Off with his head! By Heaven, the blood within me boils and seethes,
To look on him! So vile a knave pollutes the air he breathes!"

'Twas but four days thereafter, of a stormy evening late,
When a horseman reared his charger in before the castle gate,
And gazing upwards, he descried by the light of the pale moon shed,
Impaled upon an iron stake, a well-known gory head!

"So, Parez! thou hast met thy meed!" he said, and turned away—
"And was it a foe that thus avenged me on that fatal day?
Now, by my troth, albeit I hate the Saxon and his land,
I could, methinks, for one brief moment press the Talbot's hand!"

———o———

IRISH NATIONAL HYMN.

OH, Ireland, ancient Ireland,
  Ancient, yet forever young;
Thou our mother, home and sireland,
  Thou at length hast found a tongue.
  Proudly thou at length,
  Resistest in triumphant strength.
Thy flag of freedom floats unfurled;
  And as that mighty God existeth,

Who giveth victory when and where he
  listeth,
Thou yet shall wake and shake the nations of
  the world.

For this dull world still slumbers,
  Weetless of its wants or loves,
Though, like Galileo, numbers

Cry aloud: "It moves—it moves!"
In a midnight dream,
Drifts it down Time's wreckful
stream—
All march, but few descry the goal.
Oh, Ireland be it thy high duty
To teach the world the might of moral
beauty,
And stamp God's image truly on the strug-
gling soul.

Strong in thy self-reliance,
Not in idle threat or boast,
Hast thou hurled thy fierce defiance
At the haughty Saxon host.
Thou hast claimed, in sight
Of high Heaven, thy long- lost right.
Upon thy hills, along thy plains,
In the green bosom of thy valleys,
The new-born soul of holy freedom rallies,
And calls on thee to trample down in dust
thy chains!

Deep, saith the Eastern story,
Burns in Iran's mines a gem,
For its dazzling hues and glory
Worth a Sultan's diadem.
But from human eyes
Hidden there it ever lies!
The aye-travailing Gnomes alone,

Who toil to form the mountain's treasure,
May gaze and gloat with pleasure without
measure
Upon the lustrous beauty of that wonder
stone.

So is it with a nation
Which would win for its rich dower
That bright pearl, Self-Liberation—
It must labor hour by hour.
Strangers, who travail
To lay bare the gem, shall fail;
Within itself, must grow, must glow—
Within the depths of its own bosom
Must flower in living night, must broadly
blossom,
The hopes that shall be born ere Freedom's
Tree can blow.

Go on, then, all-rejoiceful! •
March on thy career unbowed;
IRELAND! let thy noble, voiceful
Spirit cry to God aloud!
Man will bid thee speed—
God will aid thee in thy need—
The Time, the Hour, the Power are near—
Be sure thou soon shall form the vanguard
Of that illustrious band whom Heaven and
Man guard;
And these words come from *one whom some
have called a Seer.*

THE RUINS OF DONEGAL CASTLE.*

(*From the Irish.*)

O MOURNFUL, O forsaken pile,
What desolation dost thou dree!
How tarnished is the beauty that was thine
ere while,
Thou mansion of chaste melody!

Demolished lie thy towers and halls;
A dark, unsightly, earthen mound
Defaces the pure whiteness of thy shining
walls,
And solitude doth gird thee round.

Fair fort! thine hour has come at length,
Thine older glory has gone by.
Lo! far beyond thy noble battlements of
strength,
Thy corner-stones all scattered lie!

Where now, O rival of the gold
Emania, be thy wine-cups all?
Alas! for these thou now hast nothing but
the cold—
Cold stream that from the Heavens doth
fall!

Thy clay-choked gateways none can trace,

Thou fortress of the once bright doors!
The limestones of thy summit now bestrew
thy base,
Bestrew the outside of thy floors.

Above thy shattered window-sills
The music that to-day breaks forth
Is but the music of the wild winds from the
hills,
The wild winds of the stormy North!

What spell o'ercame thee, mighty fort,
What fatal fit of slumber strange,
O palace of the wine!—O many-gated court!
That thou should'st undergo this change?

Thou wert, O bright-walled, beaming one,
Thou cradle of high deeds and bold,
The Tara of Assemblies to the sons of Con,
Clan-Connell's Council-hall of old!

* This fine old castle of his ancestors was razed to
the ground by Hugh Roe O'Donnell, previously to
his journey to Spain, lest it should fall into the
hands of the English.

Thou wert a new Emania, thou!
  A northern Cruachan in thy might—
A dome like that which stands by Boyne's
    broad water now,
Thou Erin's Rome of all delight!

In thee were Ulster's tributes stored,
  And lavished like the flowers in May;
And into thee were Connaught's thousand
    treasures poured,
  Deserted though thou art to-day!

How often from thy turrets high,
  Thy purple turrets, have we seen
Long lines of glittering ships, when summer
    time drew nigh,
  With masts and sails of snow-white sheen!

How often seen, when gazing 'round,
  From thy tall towers, the hunting trains,
The blood-enlivening chase, the horseman and
    the hound,
  The fastness of a hundred plains!

How often to thy banquets bright
  We have seen the strong-armed Gaels re-
    pair,
And when the feast was over, once again
    unite
  For battle, in thy bass-court fair!

Alas, for thee, thou fort forlorn!
  Alas, for thy low, lost estate!
It is my woe of woes, this melancholy
    morn,
  To see thee left thus desolate!

O! there hath come of Connell's race
  A many and many a gallant chief,
Who, if he saw thee now, thou of the once
    glad face!
  Could not dissemble his deep grief.

Could Manus of the lofty soul
  Behold thee as this day thou art,
Thou of the regal towers! what bitter—
    bitter dole,
  What agony would rend his heart!

Could Hugh Mac Hugh's imaginings
  Portray for him thy rueful plight,
What anguish, O, thou palace of the
    northern kings,
  Were his through many a sleepless night!

Could even the mighty Prince whose choice
  It was to o'erthrow thee—could Hugh Roe
But view thee now, methink he would not
    much rejoice
  That he had laid thy turrets low!

Oh! who could dream that one like him,
  One sprung of such a line as his, .

Thou of the embellished walls, would be the
    man to dim
  Thy glories by a deed like this?

From Hugh O'Donnell, thine own brave,
  And far-famed sovereign came the blow?
By him, thou lonely castle o'er the Esky's
    wave,
  By him was wrough thine overthrow.

Yet not because he wished thee ill,
  Left he thee thus bereaven and void;
The prince of the victorious tribe of Dalach
    still
  Loved thee, yea, thee whom he destroyed!

He brought upon thee all his woe,
  Thou of the fair-proportioned walls,
Lest thou shouldst ever yield a shelter to the
    foe—
  Shouldst house the black, ferocious Galls!

Shouldst yet become, in saddest truth,
  A *Dun-a-Gall* *—the stranger's own.
For this cause only, stronghold of the Gaelic
    youth,
  Lie thy majestic towers o'erthrown.

It is a drear, a dismal sight,
  This of thy ruin and decay,
Now that our kings, and bards, and men of
    mark and might
  Are nameless exiles far away!

Yet, better thou shouldst fall, meseems,
  By thine own king of many thrones,
Than that the truculent Galls should rear
    around thy streams
  Dry mounds and circles of great stones.

As doth in many a desperate case
  The surgeon by the malady,
So hath, oh shield and bulwark of great
    Coffey's race,
  Thy royal master done by thee!

The surgeon, if he be but wise,
  Examines till he learns and sees
Where lies the fountain of his patient's
    health, where lies
  The germ and root of his disease.

Then cuts away the gangrened part,
  That so the sounder may be freed
Ere the disease hath power to reach the
    sufferer's heart,
  And so bring death without remead.

Now thou hast held the patient's place,
  And thy disease hath been the foe;

---

          * Fort of the foreigner.

So he, thy surgeon, oh, proud house of
    Dalach's race,
Who should he be if not Hugh Roe?

But he, thus fated to destroy
    Thy shining walls, will yet restore
And raise thee up anew in beauty and in joy,
    So that thou shalt not sorrow more.

By God's help, he who wrought thy fall

Will reinstate thee yet in pride;
Thy variegated halls shall be rebuilded, all
    Thy lofty courts, thy chambers wide.

Yes; thou shalt live again, and see
    Thine youth renewed. Thou shalt outshine
Thy former self by far, and Hugh shall reign
    in thee,
The Tirconnellian's king and thine!

---o---

LAMENT FOR THE PRINCES OF TYRONE AND TYRCONNELL.

(From the Irish.)

[This is an Elegy on the death of the princes of Tyrone and Tyrconnell, who having fled with others from Ireland in the year 1607, and afterwards dying at Rome, were interred on St. Peter's Hill, in one grave. The poem is the production of O'Donnell's bard, Owen Roe Mac an Bhaird, or Ward, who accompanied the family in their exile, and is addressed to Nuala, O'Donnell's sister, who was also one of the fugitives. As the circumstances connected with the flight of the Northern Earls, which led to the subsequent confiscation of the six Ulster Counties by James I., may not be immediately in the recollection of many of our readers, it may be proper briefly to state, that it was caused by the discovery of a letter directed to Sir William Ussher, Clerk of the Council, dropped in the Council-chamber on the 7th of May, and which accused the Northern chieftains generally of a conspiracy to overthrow the government. The charge is now totally disbelieved. As an illustration of the poem, and as an interesting piece of hitherto unpublished literature in itself, we extract the account of the flight as recorded in the Annals of the Four Masters, and translated by Mr. O'Donovan: "Maguire (Cuconnaught) and Donogh, son of Mahon, who was son of the Bishop O'Brien, sailed in a ship to Ireland, and put in at the harbor of Swilly. They then took with them from Ireland the Earl O'Neill (Hugh, son of Fedoragh) and the Earl O'Donnell (Rory, son of Hugh, who was son of Magnus) and many others of the nobles of the province of Ulster. These are the persons who went with O'Neill, namely, his Countess Catherina, daughter of Magennis, and her three sons; Hugh, the Baron, John, and Brian; Art Oge, son of Cormac, who was son of the Baron; Ferdoragh, son of Con, who was son of O'Neill; Hugh Oge, son of Brian, who was son of Art O'Neill; and many others of his most intimate friends. These were they who went with the Earl O'Donnell, namely, Caffer, his brother, with his sister Nuala; Hugh, the Earl's child, wanting three weeks of being one year old; Rose, daughter of O'Doherty and wife of Caffer, with her son Hugh, aged two years and three months; his (Rory's) brother's son Donnell Oge, son of Donnell, Naghtan son of Calvach, who was son of Donogh Cairbreach O'Donnell, and many others of his intimate friends. They embarked on the Festival of the Holy Cross in autumn. This was a distinguished company; and it is certain that the sea has not borne and the wind has not wafted in modern times a number of persons in one ship more eminent, illustrious, or noble in point of genealogy, heroic deeds, valor, feats of arms, and brave achievements than they. Would that God had but permitted them to remain in their patrimonial inheritance until the children should arrive at the age of manhood! Woe to the heart that meditated, woe to the mind that conceived, woe to the council that recommended the project of this expedition, without knowing whether they should, to the end of their lives, be able to return to their native principalities or patrimonies." The Earl of Tyrone was the illustrious Hugh O'Neill, the Irish leader in the wars against Elizabeth.]

"The Saturday before the flight, the Earl of Tyrone was with the lord-deputy at Slane, where he had spoken with his lordship of his journey into England, and told him he would be there about the beginning of Michaelmas term, according to his Majesty's directions. He took leave of the lord-deputy in a more sad and passionate manner than was usual with him. From thence he went to Mellifont and Garret Moore's house, where he wept abundantly when he took his leave, giving a solemn farewell to every child and every servant in the house, which made them all marvel, because in general it was not his manner to use such compliments. On Monday he went to Dungarvan, where he rested two whole days, and on Wednesday night they say he travelled all night. It is likewise reported that the countess, his wife, being exceedingly weary, slipped down from her horse, and weeping, said: 'She could go no further.' Whereupon the earl drew his sword, and swore a great oath that 'he would kill her on the spot if she would not pass on with him, and put on a more cheerful countenance.' When the party, which consisted (men, women and children) of fifty or sixty persons, arrived at Loch Foyle, it was found that their journey had not been so secret but that the governor there had notice of it, and sent to invite Tyrone and his son to dinner. Their haste, however, was such that they accepted not his courtesy, but hastened on to Rathmulla, a town on the west side of Lough Swilly, where the Earl of Tyrconnell and his company met with them. From thence the whole party embarked, and landing on the coast of Normandy, proceeded through France to Brussels. Davies concludes his curious narrative with a few pregnant words, in which the difficulties that England had to contend with in conquering Tyrone are thus acknowledged with all the frankness of a generous foe:—'As for us that are here,' he says, 'we are glad to see the day wherein the countenance and majesty of the law and civil government hath banished Tyrone out of Ireland, which the best army in Europe, and the expense of two millions of sterling pounds had not been able to bring to pass.'"—*Moore's Ireland.*

O, WOMAN of the Piercing Wail,
    Who mournest o'er yon mound of clay
        With sigh and groan,
Would God thou wert among the Gael!
    Thou wouldst not then from day to day
        Weep thus alone.

'Twere long before, around a grave
    In green Tirconnell, one could find
        This loneliness;
Near where Beann-Boirche's banners wave
    Such grief as thine could ne'er have pined
        Companionless.

Beside the wave, in Donegal,
  In Antrim's glens, or fair Dromore,
    Or Killilee,
Or where the sunny waters fall,
  At Assaroe, near Erna's shore,
    This could not be.
On Derry's plains—in rich Drumclieff—
  Throughout Armagh the Great, renowned
    In olden years,
No day could pass but woman's grief
  Would rain upon the burial ground
    Fresh floods of tears!

Oh, no—from Shannon, Boyne, and Suir,
  From high Dunluce's castle-walls,
    From Lissadill,
Would flock alike both rich and poor,
  One wail would rise from Cruachan's halls
    To Tara's hill;
And some would come from Barrow-side,
  And many a maid would leave her home
    On Leitrim's plains,
And by melodious Banna's tide,
  And by the Mourne and Erne, to come
    And swell thy strains!

Oh, horses' hoofs would trample down
  The Mount whereon the martyr-saint*
    Was crucified.
From glen and hill, from plain and town,
  One loud lament, one thrilling plaint,
    Would echo wide.
There would not soon be found, I ween,
  One foot of ground among those bands
    For museful thought,
So many shriekers of the *keen*†
  Would cry aloud, and clap their hands,
    All woe-distraught!

Two princes of the line of Conn
  Sleep in their cells of clay beside
    O'Donnell Roe;
Three royal youths, alas! are gone,
  Who lived for Erin's weal, but died
    For Erin's woe!
Ah! could the men of Ireland read
  The names these noteless burial stones
    Display to view,
Their wounded hearts afresh would bleed,
  Their tears gush forth again, their groans
    Resound anew!

The youths whose relics moulder here
  Were sprung from Hugh, high Prince and Lord
    Of Aileach's lands;

Thy noble brothers, justly dear,
  Thy nephew, long to be deplored
    By Ulster's bands.
Theirs were not souls wherein dull Time
  Could domicile Decay or house
    Decrepitude!
They passed from Earth ere Manhood's prime,
  Ere years had power to dim their brows
    Or chill their blood.

And who can marvel o'er thy grief,
  Or who can blame thy flowing tears,
    That knows their source?
O'Donnell, Dunnasava's chief,
  Cut off amid his vernal years,
    Lies here a corse
Beside his brother Cathbar, whom
  Tirconnell of the Helmets mourns
    In deep despair—
For valor, truth, and comely bloom,
  For all that greatens and adorns,
    A peerless pair.

Oh, had these twain, and he, the third,
  The Lord of Mourne, O'Niall's son,
    Their mate in death—
A prince in look, in deed and word—
  Had these three heroes yielded on
    The field their breath,
Oh, had they fallen on Criffan's plain,
  There would not be a town or clan
    From shore to sea,
But would with shrieks bewail the Slain,
  Or chant aloud the exulting *rann**
    Of jubilee!

When high the shout of battle rose,
  On fields where freedom's torch still burned
    Through Erin's gloom,
If one, if barely one of those
  Were slain, all Ulster would have mourned
    The hero's doom!
If at Athboy, where hosts of brave
  Ulidian horsemen sank beneath
    The shock of spears,
Young Hugh O'Niell had found a grave,
  Long must the north have wept his death
    With heart-wrung tears!

If on the day of Ballachmyre
  The Lord of Mourne had met, thus young,
    A warrior's fate,
In vain would such as thou desire
  To mourn, alone, the champion sprung
    From Niall the Great!
No marvel this—for all the Dead,

---

* St. Peter. This passage is not exactly a blunder, though at first it may seem one; the poet supposes the grave itself transferred to Ireland, and he naturally includes in the transference the whole of the immediate locality around the grave.—Tr.

† *Keen*, or *Caoine*, the funeral-wail.

* Song.

Heaped on the field, pile over pile,
   At Mullach-brack.
Were scarce an *eric** for his head,
  If Death had stayed his footsteps while
    On victory's track!

If on the Day of Hostages
  The fruit had from the parent bough
    Been rudely torn
In sight of Muster's bands—Mac-Nee's—
  Such blow the blood of Conn, I trow,
    Could ill have borne.
If on the day of Ballock-boy
  Some arm had laid, by foul surprise,
    The chieftain low,
Even our victorious shouts of joy
  Would soon give place to rueful cries
    And groans of woe!

If on the day the Saxon host
  Were forced to fly—a day so great
    For Ashanee†—
The chief had been untimely lost,
  Our conquering troops should moderate
    Their mirthful glee.
There would not lack on Lifford's day,
  From Galway, from the glens of Boyle,
    From Limerick's towers,
A marshalled file, a long array,
  Of mourners to bedew the soil
    With tears in showers!

If on the day a sterner fate
  Compelled his flight from Athenree,
    His blood had flowed,
What numbers all disconsolate
  Would come unasked, and share with thee
    Affliction's load!
If Derry's crimson field had seen
  His life-blood offered up, though 'twere
    On Victory's shrine,
A thousand cries would swell the *keen*,
  A thousand voices of despair
    Would echo thine!

O, had the fierce Dalcassian swarm
  That bloody night on Fergus' banks
    But slain our chief,
When arose his camp in wild alarm—
  How would the triumph of his ranks
    Be dashed with grief!
How would the troops of Murback mourn
  If on the Curlew Mountains' day,
    Which England rued,
Some Saxon hand had left them lorn,

By shedding there, amid the fray,
    Their prince's blood!

Red would have been our warrior's eyes
  Had Roderick found on Sligo's field
    A gory grave,
No Northern Chief would soon arise
  So sage to guide, so strong to shield,
    So swift to save.
Long would Leith-Cuinn have wept if Hugh
  Had met the death he oft had dealt
    Among the foe:
But, had our Roderick fallen too,
  All Erin must, alas! have felt
    The deadly blow!

What do I say? Ah, woe is me!
  Already we bewail in vain
    The fatal fall!
And Erin, once the Great and Free,
  Now vainly mourns her breakless chain,
    And iron thrall!
Then, daughter of O'Donnell, dry
  Thine overflowing eyes, and turn
    Thy heart aside,
For Adam's race is born to die,
  And sternly the sepulchral urn
    Mocks human pride!

Look not, nor sigh, for earthly throne,
  Nor place thy trust in arm of clay,
    But on thy knees
Uplift thy soul to God alone,
  For all things go their destined way
    As He decrees.
Embrace the faithful Crucifix,
  And seek the path of pain and prayer
    Thy Saviour trod;
Nor let thy spirit intermix
  With earthly hope and worldly care
    Its groans to God!

And Thou, Oh mighty Lord! whose ways
  Are far above our feeble minds
    To understand,
Sustain us in these doleful days,
  And render light the chain that binds
    Our fallen land!
Look down upon our dreary state,
  And through the ages that may still
    Roll sadly on,
Watch thou o'er hapless Erin's fate,
  And shield at least from darker ill
    The blood of Conn!

* A compensation or fine,
† Ballyshannon,

THE POET'S PREACHING.

(From the German of Salis Seewis.)

SEE how the day beameth brightly before us!
  Blue is the firmament—green is the earth—
Grief hath no voice in the universe-chorus—
  Nature is ringing with Music and Mirth.
Lift up the looks that are sinking in Sadness—
  Gaze! and if Beauty can capture thy soul,
Virtue herself will allure thee to Gladness—
  Gladness, Philosophy's guerdon and goal.

Enter the treasuries Pleasure uncloses—
  List! how she trills in the nightingale's lay!
Breathe! she is wafting thee sweets from the roses;
  Feel! she is cool in the rivulet's play;
Taste! from the grape and the nectarine gushing
  Flows the red rill in the beams of the sun—
Green in the hills, in the flower groves blushing,
  Look! she is always and everywhere one.

Banish, then, mourner, the tears that are trickling
  Over the cheeks that should rosily bloom;
Why should a man, like a girl or a sickling,
  Suffer his lamp to be quenched in the tomb.
Still may we battle for Goodness and Beauty;
  Still hath Philanthropy much to essay;
Glory rewards the fulfilment of Duty;
  Rest will pavilion the end of our way.

What, though corroding and multiplied sorrows,
  Legion-like, darken this planet of ours,
Hope is a balsam the wounded heart borrows
  Ever when Anguish hath palsied its powers:
Wherefore, though Fate play the part of a traitor,
  Soar o'er the stars on the pinions of Hope,
Fearlessly certain that sooner or later
  Over the stars thy desires shall have scope.

Look 'round about on the face of Creation!
  Still is GOD'S Earth undistorted and bright.
Comfort the captives to long tribulation,
  Thus shalt thou reap the more perfect delight.
Love!—but if Love be a hallowed emotion,
  Purity only its rapture should share;
Love, then, with willing and deathless emotion,
  All that is just and exalted and fair.

Act!—for in Action are Wisdom and Glory,
  Fame, Immortality—these are its crown:
Wouldst thou illumine the tablets of story,

Build on achievements thy dome of Renown.
Honor and Feeling were given thee to cherish;
  Cherish them, then, though all else should decay:
Landmarks be those that are never to perish,
  Stars that will shine on thy duskiest day.

Courage!—Disaster and Peril once over,
  Freshen the spirit as showers the grove:
O'er the dim groans that the cypresses cover
  Soon the Forget-me-not rises in love.
Courage, then, friends! Though the universe crumble,
  Innocence, dreadless of danger beneath,
Patient and trustful and joyous and humble,
  Smiles through the ruin on Darkness and Death.

THE TIME OF THE BARMECIDES.

(From the Arabic.)

My eyes are filmed, my beard is grey,
  I am bowed with the weight of years;
I would I were stretched in my bed of clay,
  With my long-lost youth's compeers!
For back to the past, though the thought brings woe,
  My memory ever glides
To the old—old time, long—long ago,
  The time of the Barmecides.
To the old—old time, long—long ago,
  The time of the Barmecides.

Then youth was mine, and a fierce wild will,
  And an iron arm in war,
And a fleet foot high upon Ishkar's hill,
  When the watch-lights glimmered afar;
And a barb as fiery as any I know
  That Khoord or Beddaween rides,
Ere my friends lay low, long—long ago,
  In the time of the Barmecides.
Ere my friends lay low, long—long ago,
  In the time of the Barmecides.

One golden goblet illumed my board,
  One silver dish was there;
At hand my tried Karamanian sword
  Lay always bright and bare;
For those were the days when the angry blow
  Supplanted the word that chides,
When hearts could glow, long—long ago,
  In the time of the Barmecides.
When hearts could glow, long—long ago,
  In the time of the Barmecides

Through city and desert my mates and I
  Were free to rove and roam,
Our diapered canopy the deep of the sky,
  Or the roof of the palace-dome—
Oh, ours was that vivid life to and fro
  Which only sloth derides—
Men spent life so, long—long ago,
  In the time of the Barmecides,
Men spent life so, long—long ago,
  In the time of the Barmecides!

I see rich Bagdad once again,
  With its turrets of Moorish mould,
And the Khalif's twice five hundred men
  Whose binishes flamed with gold;
I call up many a gorgeous show
  Which the Pall of Oblivion hides—
All passed like snow, long—long ago,
  With the time of the Barmecides;
All passed like snow, long—long ago,
  With the time of the Barmecides!

But mine eye is dim, and my beard is grey,
  And I bend with the weight of years—
May I soon go down to the House of Clay
  Where slumber my youth's compeers!
For with them and the past, though the thought wakes woe,
  My memory ever abides,
And I mourn for the time gone long ago,
  For the time of the Barmecides!
I mourn for the time gone long ago,
  For the time of the Barmecides!

———o———

EDWARD WALSH.

EDWARD WALSH was born in Londonderry in the year 1805, and died in Cork on the 6th of August, 1850, in the forty-fifth year of his age. Of the number of poets which Ireland has produced during the last fifty years, there was none more Irish than our author. It was his boast that he belonged to an old Sept which was settled on the borders of Cork and Kerry ages before the English invasion; and it would be rare to meet a man of purer heart or more sterling sentiment. His father, who was a small farmer in the county of Cork, eloped with a young lady much above his own position in life. Shortly after marriage his difficulties increased, and to avoid them, he enlisted in the militia, and was quartered in Londonderry when his son was born.

The poet having received a good education, in early life became a private tutor. Some time after he taught school in Millstreet, county Cork, from which he removed in 1837, and went to teach in Toureen, where he first began to write for the magazines. After some time he went up to Dublin, where he soon became disappointed, and was at last elected schoolmaster to the convict station at Spike Island.

In a year or two he left this place and became teacher at the Workhouse in Cork, where he remained till his death. He married early, and has left a wife and family to mourn his loss. Two volumes of his poetical translations from the Irish have been published, with the *original* text on the opposite page. He was a great proficient in the fairy and legendary lore of the country; indeed, second only to Crofton Croker himself. His contributions to Irish literature have been both considerable and creditable; there is a singular beauty and fascinating melody in his verse which cheers and charms the ear and heart.

His translations preserve all the peculiarities of the old tongue, which he knew and spoke with graceful fluency. His ballads are the most literal and characteristic which we possess. His "Jacobite Relics of Ireland," published by that persevering and spirited promoter of Irish literature, John O'Daly of Dublin, contains some of the best specimens of his muse.

POEMS OF EDWARD WALSH.

A MUNSTER KEEN.

On Monday morning, the flowers were gayly springing,
The skylark's hymn in middle air was singing,
When, grief of griefs! my wedded husband left me,
And since that hour of hope and health bereft me.
Ulla gulla, gulla g'one! etc., etc.*

Above the board, where thou art low reclining,
Have parish priest and horsemen high been dining,
And wine and usquebaugh, while they were able,
They quaffed with thee—the soul of all the table.
Ulla gulla, gulla g'one! etc., etc.

Why didst thou die? Could wedded wife adore thee,
With purer love than that my bosom bore thee?
Thy children's cheeks were peaches ripe and mellow,
And threads of gold, their tresses long and yellow.
Ulla gulla, gulla g'one! etc., etc.

In vain for me are pregnant heifers lowing;
In vain for me are yellow harvests growing;
Or thy nine gifts of love in beauty blooming—
Tears blind my eyes, and grief my heart's consuming!
Ulla gulla, gulla g'one! etc., etc.

Pity her plaints whose wailing voice is broken,
Whose finger holds our early wedding token,
The torrents of whose tears have drain'd their fountain,
Whose piled-up grief on grief is past recounting.
Ulla gulla, gulla g'one! etc., etc.

I still might hope, did I not thus behold thee,
That high Knockferin's airy peak might hold thee,
Or Crohan's fairy halls, or Corrin's towers,
Or Lene's bright caves, or Cleana's magic bowers.†
Ulla gulla, gulla g'one! etc., etc.

But, oh, my black despair! when thou wert dying,
O'er thee no tear was wept, no heart was sighing—
No breath of prayer did waft thy soul to glory;
But lonely thou didst lie, all maim'd and gory!
Ulla gulla, gulla g'one! etc., etc.

---

* The keener alone sings the extempore death-song; the burden of the ullagone, or chorus, is taken up by all the females present.

† Places celebrated in fairy topography.

Oh! may your dove-like soul, on whitest pinions,
Pursue her upward flight to God's dominions,
Where saints' and martyrs' hands shall gifts provide thee—
And, oh, my grief! that I am not beside thee!

Ulla gulla, gulla g'one! etc., etc.

———o———

MO CRAOIBHIN CNO.*

My heart is far from Liffey's tide
   And Dublin town;
It stays beyond the Southern side
   Of Cnoc-Maol-Donn,†
Where Cappoquin‡ hath woodlands green,
   Where Amhan-Mhor's§ waters flow,
Where dwells unsung, unsought, unseen,
   Mo craoibhin cno,
Low clustering in her leafy screen,
   Mo craoibhin cno!

The high-bred dames of Dublin town
   Are rich and fair,
With wavy plume, and silken gown,
   And stately air;
Can plumes compare thy dark brown hair?
   Can silks thy neck of snow?
Or measur'd pace, thine artless grace,
   Mo craoibhin cno,
When harebells scarcely show thy trace,
   Mo craoibhin cno?

I've heard the songs by Liffey's wave
   The maidens sung—
They sung their land the Saxon's slave,
   In Saxon tongue—
Oh! bring me here that Gaelic dear
   Which cursed the Saxon foe,

When thou didst charm my raptured ear,
   Mo craoibhin cno!
And none but God's good angels near,
   Mo craoibhin cno!

I've wandered by the rolling Lee!
   And Lene's green bowers—
I've seen the Shannon's wide-spread sea,
   And Limerick's towers—
And Liffey's tide, where hills of pride
   Frown o'er the flood below;
My wild heart strays to Amhan-Mhor's
    side,
   Mo craoibhin cno!
With love and thee for aye to hide,
   Mo craoibhin cno!

* *Mo craoibhin cno* literally means *my cluster of nuts;* but it figuratively signifies *my nut brown maid.* It is pronounced *Ma Creevin Kno.*
† *Cnoc-maol-Donn—The Brown bare hill.* A lofty mountain between the county of Tipperary and that of Waterford, commanding a glorious prospect of unrivaled scenery.
‡ *Cappoquin.* A romantically situated town on the Blackwater, in the county of Waterford. The Irish name denotes *The Head of the Tribe of Conn.*
§ *Amhan-Mhor—The Great River.* The Blackwater, which flows into the sea at Youghal. The Irish name is uttered in two sounds, *Oan Vore.*

———o———

O'DONOVAN'S DAUGHTER.

One midsummer's eve, when the Bel-fires were lighted,
And the bag-piper's tone call'd the maidens delighted,
I joined a gay group by the Araglin's water,
And danced till the dawn with O'Donovan's daughter.

Have you seen the ripe monadan glisten in Kerry?
Have you mark'd on the Galteys the black whortleberry?
Or ceanaban wave by the wells of Blackwater?
They're the cheek, eye and neck of O'Donovan's Daughter!

Have you seen a gay kidling on Claragh's round mountain?
The swan's arching glory on Sheeling's blue fountain?
Heard a weird woman chant what the fairy choir taught her?
They've the step, grace and tone of O'Donovan's Daughter!

Have you mark'd in its flight the black wing of the raven?
The rose-buds that breathe in the summer-breeze waven?

The pearls that lie hid under Lene's magic water?
They're the teeth, lip and hair of O'Donovan's Daughter!

Ere the Bel-fire was dimm'd, or the dancers departed,
I taught her a song of some maid broken-hearted;
And that group, and that dance, and that love-song I taught her,
Haunt my slumbers at night with O'Donovan's Daughter!

God grant 'tis no fay from Cnoc-Firinn that wooes me,
God grant 'tis not Cliodhna the queen that pursues me,
That my soul lost and lone has no witchery wrought her,
While I dream of dark groves and O'Donovan's Daughter!

If, spell-bound, I pine with an airy disorder,
Saint Gobnate has sway over Musgry's wide border;
She'll scare from my couch, when with prayer I've besought her,
That bright airy sprite like O'Donovan's Daughter.

———o———

AN IRISH WAR SONG.

BRIGHT sun, before whose glorious ray
  Our pagan fathers bent the knee,
Whose Pillar-Altars yet can say,
  When time was young our sires were free;
Who saw our latter-days' decree,
Our matron's tears, our patriot's gore,
  We swear before high Heaven and thee,
The Saxon holds us slaves no more!

Our *clairsach* wild, whose trembling string
  Hath long the song of sorrow spoke,
Shall bid the "*Ros-g Catha*" sing
  The curse and crime of Saxon yoke,
  And by each heart its bondage broke,
Each exile's sigh on distant shore,
  Each martyr 'neath the headsman's stroke,
The Saxon holds us slaves no more!

Our Sunburst on the Roman foe
  Flashed vengeance once on foreign field,
On Clontarf's plain lay scattered low
  What power the Sea-kings fierce could
    wield;
  Benburb can say whose cloven shield
'Neath bloody hoofs was trampled o'er,
  And by these memories high we yield
Our limbs to Saxon chains no more!

Send your loud war-cry o'er the main,
  Your Sunburst to the breezes spread;
That slogan rends the Heavens in twain,
  The earth reels back beneath your tread;
  Ye Saxon despots hear and dread,
Your march o'er patriots' hearts is o'er;
  That shout hath told, that tramp hath said,
Our country's sons are slaves no more.

———o———

BATTLE OF CREDRAN.

1257.

[A brilliant battle was fought by Geoffrey O'Donnell, Lord of Tirconnell, against the Lord Justice of Ireland, Maurice Fitzgerald, and the English of Connaught, at Credran Cille, Roseede, in the territory of Carburry, north of Sligo, in defense of his principality. A fierce and terrible conflict took place, in which bodies were hacked, heroes disabled, and the strength of both sides exhausted. The men of Tirconnell maintained their ground, and completely overthrew the English forces in the engagement, and defeated them with great slaughter; but Geoffrey himself was severely wounded, having encountered in the fight Maurice Fitzgerald, in single combat, in which they mortally wounded each other.—*Annals of the Four Masters.*]

FROM the glens of his fathers O'Donnell comes forth,
With all Cinel-Conall,* fierce septs of the North—
O'Boyle and O'Daly, O'Dugan, and they,
That own, by the wild waves, O'Doherty's sway.

* *Cinel-Conall.*—The descendants of Conall-Gulban, the son of Niall of the Nine Hostages, Monarch of Ireland in the Fourth century. The principality was named Tir Chonaile, or Tyrconnell, which included the county Donegal, and its chiefs were the O'Donnells.

Clan Connor, brave sons of the diademed Niall,
Has poured the tall clansmen from mountain and vale—
M'Sweeny's sharp axes, to battle oft bore,
Flash bright in the sunlight by high Dunamore.

Through Inis–Mac-Durin,* through Derry's dark brakes,
Glentocher of tempests, Slieve-snacht of the lakes,
Bundoran of dark spells, Loch-Swilly's rich glen,
The red deer rush wild at the war-shout of men!

Oh! why through Tir-Conall, from Cuil-dubh's dark steep,
To Samer's † green border the fierce masses sweep,
Living torrents o'er-leaping their own river shore,
In the red sea of battle to mingle their roar?

Stretch thy vision far southward, and seek for reply
Where blaze of the hamlets glare red on the sky—
Where the shrieks of the hopeless rise high to their God—
Where the foot of the Sassenach spoiler has trod!

Sweeping on like a tempest, the Gall-Oglach‡ stern
Contends for the van with the swift-footed kern—
There's blood for that burning, and joy for that wail—
The avenger is hot on the spoiler's red trail!

The Saxon had gathered on Credran's far hights,
His groves of long lances, the flower of his knights—
His awful cross-bowmen, whose loud iron hail
Finds through Cota§ and Sciath, the bare heart of the Gael!

The long lance is brittle—the mailed ranks reel
Where the Gall-Oglach's ax hews the harness of steel;
And truer to its aim in the breast of a foeman,
Is the pike of a Kern than the shaft of a bowman.

One prayer to St. Columb ‖—the battle steel clashes—
The tide of fierce conflict tumultuously dashes;
Surging onward, high-heaving its billow of blood,
While war-shout and death-groan swell high o'er the flood!

As meets the wild billows the deep-centered rock,
Met glorious Clan-Conall the fierce Saxon's shock;
As the wrath of the clouds flashed the ax of Clan-Conell,
Till the Saxon lay strewn 'neath the might of O'Donnell!

One warrior alone holds the wide bloody field,

---

* Districts in Donegal.
† *Samer.*—The ancient name of Loch Earne.
‡ *Gall-Oglach* or *Gallowglass.*—The heavy armed foot soldier. *Kern* or *Ceithernach.*—The light armed soldier.
§ *Cota.*—The saffron-dyed shirt of the Kern, consisting of many yards of yellow linen, thickly plaited. *Sciath.*—The wicker shield, as its name imports.
‖ *St. Colum,* or *Colum-Cille, the dove of the Church.*—The patron saint of Tyrconnell, descended from Conall Gulban.

With barbed black charger and long lance and shield—
Grim, savage, and gory he meets their advance,
His broad shield uplifting, and couching his lance.

Then forth to the van of that fierce rushing throng
Rode a chieftain of tall spear and battle-ax strong,
His *bracca,** and *geochal*, and *cochal's* red fold,
And war-horse's housings, were radiant in gold!

Say, who is this chief spurring forth to the fray,
The wave of whose spear holds yon armed array?
And he who stands scorning the thousands that sweep,
An army of wolves over shepherdless sheep?

The shield of his nation, brave Geoffrey O'Donnell,
(Clar-Fodhla's firm prop is the proud race of Conall)
And Maurice Fitzgerald, the scorner of danger,
The scourge of the Gael, and the strength of the stranger.

The launched spear hath torn through target and mail—
The couched lance hath borne to his crupper the Gael—
The steeds driven backwards all helplessly reel;
But the lance that lies broken hath blood on its steel!

And now, fierce O'Donnell, thy battle-ax wield—
The broadsword is shivered, and cloven the shield,
The keen steel sweeps grinding through proud crest and crown—
Clar-Fodhla hath triumphed—the Saxon is down!

---

* *Bracca.*—So called, from being striped with various colors, was the tight-fitting Truis. It covered the ankles, legs, and thighs, rising as high as the loins, and fitted so close to the limbs as to discover every muscle and motion of the parts which it covered. *Geochal.*—The jacket made of gilded leather, and which was sometimes embroidered with silk. *Cochal.*—A sort of cloak with a large hanging collar of different colors. This garment reached to the middle of the thigh, and was fringed with a border like shagged hair, and being brought over the shoulders, was fastened on the breast by a clasp, buckle, or brooch of silver or gold. In battle, they wrapped the Cochal several times around the left arm as a shield.—*Walker's Dress and Armor of the Irish.*

———o———

AILEEN THE HUNTRESS.

[The incident related in the following ballad happened about the year 1731. Aileen, or Ellen, was daughter of M'Cartie of Clidane, an estate originally bestowed upon this respectable branch of the family of M'Cartie More, by James, the seventh Earl of Desmond, and which, passing safe through the confiscation of Elizabeth, Cromwell, and William, remained in their possession until the beginning of the present century. Aileen, who is celebrated in the traditions of the people for her love of hunting, was the wife of James O'Connor, of Cluain-Tairbh, grandson of David, the founder of the *Siol-t-Da*, a well-known sept at this day in Kerry. This David was grandson to Thomas MacTeige O'Connor, of Ahalahanna, head of the second house of O'Connor Kerry, who, forfeiting in 1666, escaped destruction by taking shelter among his relations, the Nagles of Monanimy.]

Fair Aileen M'Cartie, O'Connor's young bride,
Forsakes her chaste pillow with matronly pride,
And calls forth her maidens (their number was nine)
To the bawn of her mansion, a-milking the kine.
They came at her bidding, in kirtle and gown,
And braided hair, jetty, and golden, and brown,

And form like the palm-tree, and step like the fawn,
And bloom like the wild rose that circled the bawn.

As the Guebre's round tower o'er the fane of Ardfert—
As the white hind of Brandon by young roes begirt—
As the moon in her glory 'mid bright stars outhung—
Stood Aileen M'Cartie her maidens among.
Beneath the rich 'kerchief, which matrons may wear,
Strayed ringleted tresses of beautiful hair;
They wav'd on her fair neck, as darkly as though
'Twere the raven's wing shining o'er Mangerton's snow!

A circlet of pearls o'er her white bosom lay,
Erst worn by thy proud queen, O'Connor the gay,
And now to the beautiful Aileen come down
The rarest that ever shed light in the Laune.
The many-fringed *faluinn* that floated behind,
Gave its hues to the sunlight, its folds to the wind—
The brooch that retain'd it, some forefather bold
Had torn from a sea-king in battle-field old.

Around her went bounding two wolf-dogs of speed,
So tall in their stature, so pure in their breed;
While the maidens awoke to the new-milk's soft fall,
A song of O'Connor in Carraig's proud hall.
As the milk came outpouring, and the song came outsung,
O'er the wall 'mid the maidens a red deer outsprung—
Then cheer'd the fair lady—then rush'd the mad hound—
And away with the wild stag in air-lifted bound.

The gem-fastened *faluinn* is dashed on the bawn—
One spring o'er the tall fence—and Aileen is gone!
But morning's rous'd echoes to the deep dells proclaim
The course of that wild stag, the dogs, and the dame!
By Cluain Tairbh's green border, o'er moorland and hight,
The red-deer shapes downward the rush of his flight—
In sun-light his antlers all-gloriously flash,
And onward the wolf-dogs and fair huntress dash!

By Sliabh-Mis now winding (rare hunting I ween)!
He gains the dark valley of Scota the queen
Who found in its bosom a cairn-lifted grave,
When Sliabh-Mis first flow'd with the blood of the brave!
By Coill-Cuaigh's green shelter, the hollow rocks ring—
Coill-Cuaigh, of the cuckoo's first song in the spring,
Coill-Cuaigh of the tall oak, and gale-scenting spray—
God's curse on the tyrants that wrought the decay!

Now Maing's lovely border is gloriously won,
Now the towers of the island gleam bright in the sun,
And now Ceall-an Amanach's portals are pass'd,

Where headless the Desmond found refuge at last!
By Ard-na-greach mountain, and Avonmore's head,
To the earl's proud pavilion the panting deer fled—
Where Desmond's tall clansmen spread banners of pride,
And rush'd to the battle, and gloriously died!

The huntress is coming, slow, breathless, and pale,
Her raven locks streaming all wild in the gale:
She stops—and the breezes bring balm to her brow—
But wolf-dog and wild deer, oh, where are they now?
On Reidhlan-Tigh-an-Earla, by Avonmore's well,
His bounding heart broken, the hunted deer fell,
And o'er him the brave hounds all gallantly died,
In death still victorious—their fangs in his side.

'Tis evening—the breezes beat cold on her breast,
And Aileen must seek her far home in the west;
Yet weeping, she lingers where the mist-wreaths are chill,
O'er the red-deer and tall dogs that lie on the hill!
Whose harp at the banquet told distant and wide,
This feat of fair Aileen, O'Connor's young bride?
O'Daly's—whose guerdon tradition had told,
Was a purple-crown'd wine-cup of beautiful gold?

———o———

J. J. CALLANAN.

———

JEREMIAH JOSEPH CALLANAN was born in Cork in 1795. He was educated for the priesthood, but the delicate state of his health, and the restless spirit, which afterwards became the bane of his existence, and which frequently led him to abandon real good for some vain and shadowy prospect, impelled him, after a residence of two years, to quit Maynooth, and to relinquish all his future prospects in the clerical profession. In 1820 he entered Trinity College as an out-pensioner, with the intention of studying for the bar; but, like his previous choice, he renounced this also after a two years' trial. In 1823 he became an assistant in the school of Dr. Maginn in Cork, where he remained only a few month's—but through Maginn's introduction he became a contributor to " Blackwood's Magazine."

During these six years, and up to 1829, he spent his time in rambling through the country, collecting the old Irish ballads and legends, and in giving them a new dress in a new tongue. Early in 1829 he became a tutor in the family of an Irish gentleman in Lisbon, and on the 19th of September of the same year, he died there, in the 34th year of his age.

His " Recluse of Inchidony," in the Spenserian metre, is his longest poem,—but his verses on " Gougaune Barra " have attained the widest popularity in the south of Ireland.

The Lake of Gougaune Barra—*i. e.*, the hollow, or recess of Saint Finn Barr, in the rugged territory of Ibh-Laoghaire, (the O'Learys' country), in the west end of the county of Cork, is the parent of the river Lee. Its waters embrace a small but verdant island, of about half an acre in extent, which approaches its eastern shore. The lake, as its name implies, is situate in a deep hollow, surrounded on every side, (save the east, where its superabundant waters are discharged), by vast and almost perpendicular mountains, whose dark inverted shadows are gloomily reflected in its still waters beneath. The names of those mountains are *Dereen*, (the little oak wood), where not a tree now remains; *Maolagh*, which signifies a country—a region—a map, perhaps so called from the wide prospect which it affords; *Nad an uillar*, the eagle's nest, and *Faoilte na Gougaune*—*i. e.*, the cliffs of Gougaune, with its steep and frowning precipices, the home of a hundred echoes.

POEMS OF J. J. CALLANAN.

---o---

GOUGAUNE BARRA.

THERE is a green island in lone Gougaune Barra,
Where Allua of songs rushes forth as an arrow;
In deep-valleyed Desmond—a thousand wild fountains
Come down to that lake, from their home in the mountains.
There grows the wild ash, and a time-stricken willow
Looks chidingly down on the mirth of the billow;
As, like some gay child that sad monitor scorning,
It lightly laughs back to the laugh of the morning.

And its zone of dark hills—oh, to see them bright'ning,
When the tempest flings out its red banner of lightning,
And the waters rush down, 'mid the thunder's deep rattle,
Like clans from the hills at the voice of the battle;
And brightly the fire-crested billows are gleaming,
And wildly from Mullagh the eagles are screaming,
Oh, where is the dwelling in valley, or highland,
So meet for a bard as this lone little island?

How oft when the summer sun rested on Clara,
And lit the dark heath on the hills of Ivera,
Have I sought thee, sweet spot, from my home by the ocean,
And trod all thy wilds with a minstrel's devotion,
And thought of thy bards, when assembling together,
In the cleft of thy rocks, or the depth of thy heather,
They fled from the Saxon's dark bondage and slaughter,
And waked their last song by the rush of thy water!

High sons of the lyre, oh, how proud was the feeling,
To think while alone through that solitude stealing,
Though loftier minstrels green Erin can number,
I only awoke your wild harp from its slumber,
And mingled once more with the voice of those fountains
The songs even echo forgot on her mountains;
And gleaned each grey legend, that darkly was sleeping
Where the mist and the rain o'er their beauty were creeping.

Least bard of the hills! were it mine to inherit
The fire of thy harp, and the wing of thy spirit,
With the wrongs which like thee to our country has bound me,
Did your mantle of song fling its radiance around me,
Still—still in those wilds might young liberty rally,
And send her strong shout over mountain and valley;
The star of the west might yet rise in its glory,
And the land that was darkest be brightest in story.

I, too, shall be gone—but my name shall be spoken
When Erin awakes, and her fetters are broken;
Some minstrel will come, in the summer eve's gleaming,
When freedom's young light on his spirit is beaming,
And bend o'er my grave with a tear of emotion,
Where calm Avon-Buee seeks the kisses of ocean,
Or plant a wild wreath, from the banks of that river,
O'er the heart, and the harp, that are weeping forever.

———o———

DIRGE OF O'SULLIVAN BEARE.

[The following dirge for O'Sullivan, translated from the Irish by J. J. Callanan, is unsurpassed in the vehemence of its maledictions by anything in the language.]

THE sun on Ivera
    No longer shines brightly;
The voice of her music
    No longer is sprightly;
No more to her maidens
    The light dance is dear,
Since the death of our darling,
    O'Sullivan Beare.

Scully! thou false one,
    You basely betrayed him,
In his strong hour of need,
    When thy right hand should aid him.
He fed thee—he clad thee—
    You had all could delight thee;
You left him—you sold him—
    May Heaven requite thee!

Scully! may all kinds
    Of evil attend thee!
On thy dark road of life
    May no kind one befriend thee!
May fevers long burn thee,
    And agues long freeze thee!
May the strong hand of God
    In his red anger seize thee!

Had he died calmly,
    I would not deplore him;
Or if the wild strife
    Of the sea-war closed o'er him:
But with ropes 'round his white limbs
    Through oceans to trail him,
Like a fish after slaughter,
    'Tis therefore I wail him.

Long may the curse
    Of his people pursue them;
Scully, that sold him,
    And soldiers that slew him!
One glimpse of Heaven's light
    May they see never!
May the hearth-stone of hell
    Be their best bed forever!

In the hole which the vile hands
    Of soldiers had made thee;
Unhonored, unshrouded,
    And headless they laid thee.
No sigh to regret thee,
    No eye to rain o'er thee,
No dirge to lament thee,
    No friend to deplore thee!

Dear head of my darling,
    How gory and pale
These aged eyes see thee,
    High spiked on their jail!
That cheek in the summer sun
    Ne'er shall grow warm;
Nor that eye e'er catch light,
    But the flash of the storm!

A curse, blessed ocean,
    Is on thy green water,
From the haven of Cork,
    To Ivera of slaughter:
Since the billows were dyed
    With the red wounds of fear
Of Muiertach Oge,
    Our O'Sullivan O'Beare!

—— ——o———

JOHN BANIM.

JOHN BANIM, author of "Tales of the O'Hara Family," was born in the city of Kilkenny, and received his education in its college. About 1813 he went to Dublin to study under an able master, but manifesting no strong desire for the profession of an artist, he returned to his native city, where he became a drawing-master. He did not long bear the fatigue and drudgery of this calling, for he soon had recourse to literature as his chosen profession. As a novelist, his character stands deservedly very high; second, indeed, to no one. The records of departed genius truly show, that the track of gifted individuals is like that of a meteor—brilliant to excess, but equally transient. His burning love of religion and country was traced by him in letters of fire, and his indignant sincerity gave him a power which few possessed before him. His temperament was sensitive and gloomy; hence he depicted the darker passions and more sullen traits of the character of his countrymen. His novels are strong, and full of fire; replete with powerful and striking imagery, both moral and physical—equally indicative of tenderness and strength. His ballads are very national—full of natural feeling, and of true fidelity to Irish character. He returned to Dublin, after the burial of his only son in Paris, quite broken-hearted. Death soon placed him beyond the reach of this world's sympathy, after having attained the high honor of being one of Ireland's greatest novelists.

POEMS OF JOHN BANIM.

AILLEEN.

'TIS not for love of gold I go,
  'Tis not for love of fame;
Tho' fortune should her smile bestow,
  And I may win a name,
             Ailleen,
  And I may win a name.

And yet it is for gold I go,
  And yet it is for fame,
That they may deck another brow,
  And bless another name,
             Ailleen,
  And bless another name.

For this, but this, I go—for this
  I lose thy love a while;
And all the soft and quiet bliss
  Of thy young, faithful smile,
             Ailleen,
  Of thy young, faithful smile.

And I go to brave a world I hate,
  And woo it o'er and o'er,
And tempt a wave, and try a fate
  Upon a stranger shore,
             Ailleen
  Upon a stranger shore.

O! when the bays are all my own,
  I know a heart will care!
O! when the gold is wooed and won,
  I know a brow shall wear,
                    . Ailleen,
I know a brow shall wear!

And when with both returned again,
  My native land to see,
I know a smile will meet me there,
  And a hand will welcome me,
                    Ailleen,
And a hand will welcome me!

————o————

THE RECONCILIATION.

[The facts of this ballad occurred in a little mountain-chapel, in the county of Clare, at the time efforts
were made to put an end to faction-fighting among the peasantry.]

THE old man he knelt at the altar,
  His enemy's hand to take,
And at first his weak voice did falter,
  And his feeble limbs did shake;
For his only brave boy, his glory,
  Had been stretched at the old man's feet
A corpse, all so haggard and gory,
  By the hand which he now must greet.

And soon the old man stopped speaking,
  And rage, which had not gone by,
From under his brows came breaking
  Up into his enemy's eye—

And now his limbs were not shaking,
  But his clinch'd hands his bosom cross'd
And he looked a fierce wish to be taking
  Revenge for the boy he had lost.

But the old man he looked around him,
  And thought of the place he was in,
And thought of the promise which bound
      him,
  And thought that revenge was sin—
And then, crying tears, like a woman,
  "Your hand!" he said—"ay, that hand!
And I do forgive you, foeman,
  For the sake of our bleeding land!"

————o————

THE PARLEY.

OURS is no quarrel that will not be ended,
  Ours are not hearts to hate on to the last—
The foe still devoted, the foe still intended,
  To him, and him only, our challenge we
      cast—
And him—even him—let him now but awake
  To the love he should own for our desolate
      land,
        And his hand we will take,
        And his hand we will shake,
Though the blood of her children be fresh on
      that hand!

And oh! toiling sleeper, when—when wilt
      thou break up
  The fierce haggard dream of thy feverish
      heart,
And from its delusions of tumult awake up
  To know what a dupe and a raver thou
      art?

Wake—wake, in the fair names of manhood
      and mind!
  Of wisdom, of charity, mercy and truth!
        By the love thou dost find
        On thy soul to its kind!
  By its nature! its yearnings eternal for truth!

In the dear name of country we cannot
      adjure thee—
  Thou lone one! no country at present thou
      hast;
But, up at our bidding! and we will ensure
      thee
  A country, and lover of country, at last!
Ay! in lieu of the rage-thirst thou'rt panting
      to slake,
  Up—up, in the name of this desecrate land,
        And your hand we will take,
        And your hand we will shake,
Though the blood of her children be fresh on
      that hand.

————o————

CHARLES J. KICKHAM.

CHARLES J. KICKHAM was born about fifty years ago in the village of Mullinahone, in the county of Tipperary. He came from a noble stock. His father, John Kickham, was a man blessed by Providence with a considerable share of this world's goods, and by the manner in which he dispensed them, he not only "laid up treasures in Heaven," but gained the respect and love of his poor neighbors for miles around. He was, besides, a patriot of the purest mold, and both by precept and example instilled the love of country and kind into the youthful hearts of his children. John Kickham's wife was an O'Mahony, a lady of noble soul, charitable heart and elegant figure. As became the race from which she sprang, she was eminently patriotic.

Blessed with such parents, and gifted by nature with an affectionate heart and the germs of a superior intellect, no wonder this gentle, thoughtful boy developed into the earnest, unselfish patriot and gifted scholar—beloved and honored by all who knew him either personally or by his works.

He was educated in his father's house under the supervision of that fond parent, who provided an excellent tutor for the purpose. He progressed rapidly, bidding fair to fulfill his father's dearest expectations, when a sad incident occurred which marred the hopes of his parents, and threw a cloud over all his future life. When he was about thirteen years of age, he came across a powder-flask which had been incautiously left in his way: going to the fire to drop a few grains in, the whole exploded with a dreadful shock, and the distracted father rushed into the room to find his darling boy, the pride of his parent's heart, apparently dead on the floor. He, however, slowly recovered, but he remained near-sighted and partially deaf ever since. As he could no longer avail himself of his teacher's instructions, he turned his thoughts to self-culture, became a great reader, and spent a great part of his time communing with nature and his own soul in the romantic scenery of his neighborhood.

Charles Kickham has given to the world some excellent novels of Irish life; and as a poet he is particularly happy in expressing the genial feelings and hopes of the people he loves so dearly.

He will ever be remembered as a pure and devoted patriot, as a kind friend, and as a genial gentleman.

Poems of Charles J. Kickham.

———o———

RORY OF THE HILLS.

"That rake up near the rafters,
　Why leave it there so long?
The handle, of the best of ash,
　Is smooth, and straight, and strong;
And, mother, will you tell me,
　Why did my father frown,
When to make the hay in summer time
　I climbed to take it down?"
She looked into her husband's eyes,
　While her own with light did fill;
"You'll shortly know the reason, boy!"
　Said Rory of the Hill.

The midnight moon is lighting up
　The slopes of Sliev-na-mon—
Whose foot affrights the startled hares
　So long before the dawn?
He stopped just where the Anner's stream
　Winds up the woods anear,
Then whistled low, and looked around
　To see the coast was clear.
A sheeling door flew open—
　In he stepped with right good will—
"God save all here, and bless your work,"
　Said Rory of the Hill.

Right hearty was the welcome
　That greeted him, I ween,
For years gone by he fully proved
　How well he loved the Green;
And there was one among them
　Who grasped him by the hand—
One who, through all that weary time,
　Roamed on a foreign strand—
He brought them news from gallant friends
　That made their heart-strings thrill;
"My sowl! I never doubted them!"
　Said Rory of the Hill.

They sat around the humble board
　Till dawning of the day,
And yet not song or shout I heard—
　No revellers were they;
Some brows flushed red with gladness,
　While some were grimly pale;

But pale or red, from out those eyes
　Flashed souls that never quail!
"And sing us now about the vow,
　They swore for to fulfill—"
"Ye'll read it yet in history,"
　Said Rory of the Hill.

Next day the ashen handle,
　He took down from where it hung,
The toothed rake, full scornfully,
　Into the fire he flung,
And in its stead a shining blade
　Is gleaming once again,
(Oh! for a hundred thousand of
　Such weapons and such men!)
Right soldierly he wielded it,
　And going through his drill—
"Attention"—"charge"—"front point"—
　"advance!"
　Cried Rory of the Hill.

She looked at him with woman's pride,
　With pride and woman's fears;
She flew to him, she clung to him,
　And dried away her tears;
He feels her pulse beat truly,
　While her arms around him twine—
"Now God be praised for your stout heart,
　Brave little wife of mine."
He swung his first-born in the air,
　While joy his heart did fill—
"You'll be a Freeman yet, my boy,"
　Said Rory of the Hill.

Oh! knowledge is a wondrous power,
　And stronger than the wind;
And thrones shall fall and despots bow
　Before the might of mind;
The poet and the orator
　The heart of man can sway,
And would to the kind Heavens
　That Wolfe Tone were here to-day!
Yet trust me, friends, dear Ireland's strength,
　Her truest strength, is still,
The rough-and-ready roving boys,
　Like Rory of the Hill.

———o———

SONG OF THE IRISH EXILE.

ALONE, all alone, by the wave-washed
    strand,
And alone in the crowded hall!
The hall it is gay, and the waves are grand,
    But my heart is not there, at all.
It flies far away, by night and by day,
    To the time and the place that are gone—
Oh, I never can forget the maiden I met
    In the valley near Slibebh na m-ban!

It was not the grace of her queenly air,
    Nor her cheek like the rose's glow,
Nor was it the wave of her braided hair,
    Nor the gleam of her lily white brow;

'Twas the soul of truth, and the melting ruth,
    And the eye like the summer dawn,
That stole my heart away, one mild day,
    In the valley near Sliebh na m-ban!

Alone, all alone, by the wave-washed shore,
    My restless spirit cries—
My love, oh, my love, will I never see you
    more?
    And my land! will you ever uprise?
By night and by day I ever pray,
    While lonelily the time rolls on,
To see our flag unrolled and my true love to
    unfold
    In that valley near Sliebh na m-ban!

---o---

THE IRISH PEASANT GIRL.

SHE lived beside the Anner,
    At the foot of Sliv-na-mon,
A gentle peasant girl,
    With mild eyes like the dawn;
Her lips were dewy rose-buds,
    Her teeth, of pearls so rare,
And a snow-drift 'neath a beechen bough,
    Her neck and nut-brown hair.

How pleasant 'twas to meet her
    On Sunday, when the bell
Was filling with its mellow tones,
    Lone wood and grassy dell;
And when at eve young maidens
    Strayed the river bank along.
The widow's brown-haired daughter
    Was the loveliest of the throng.

Oh, brave—brave Irish girls—
    We well may call you brave—
Sure the least of all your perils
    Is the stormy ocean wave;

When you leave our quiet valleys,
    And cross the Atlantic's foam,
To hoard your hard-won earnings
    For the helpless ones at home.

" Write word to my own dear mother—
    Say we'll meet with God above,
And tell my little brothers
    I send them all my love;
May the angels ever guard them,
    Is their dying sister's prayer—"
And folded in the letter
    Was a braid of nut-brown hair.

Ah, cold and well-nigh callous,
    This weary heart has grown,
For thy helpless fate, dear Ireland,
    And for sorrows of my own:
Yet a tear my eye will moisten,
    When by Anner side I stray
For the lily of the mountain foot,
    That withered far away.

FRANCIS DAVIS.

(*The Belfast Man.*)

THIS poet of exquisite lyric gifts and attainments, was born in Belfast. At an early age he was apprenticed to the muslin weaving, a branch of business then superior to most trades even in that thrifty quarter of the country.

' The workshop where Francis Davis plied his trade, and which witnessed his first poetic flights of fancy, was situated in an Orange quarter, known as Brown's Square. Three others occupied the "shop" with himself; these were called the Brothers May. They were members of the choir belonging to St. Patrick's Church, Belfast, and we have the evidence of Dr. Stewart, of Dublin, who was one of the shining lights at the great musical jubilee at Boston, that the choir, organ, and organist of St. Patrick's, Belfast, was among the best in Ireland. The Brothers May were not a little proud of their connection with the choir, and, accordingly, they invited Davis to pay it a visit. The poet did so; and often drew his inspiration from the part-singing of his companions, the Mays.

We think it was in 1844 Davis' first piece was produced. It was entitled: "The Lovely Forsaken," and appeared in the Belfast *Vindicator*, then under the able management of McDevitt and McConvery, the former shortly after becoming editor-in-chief of the Dublin *Freeman*, and who, till his death, remained the firm friend of the Belfast man.

Shortly after this Francis Davis began to contribute to the *Nation* newspaper, then a light and a guide to the great awakening spirit of Ireland's nationality. The constant perusal of the *Nation*, the personal friendship of Charles Gavan Duffy, but above all the young national spirit which surrounded Davis in Belfast, gave a national tone to his mind, and caused those splendid outpourings which, in no respect whatever, are inferior to his great *confrere*, Tom Davis.

Some of the earliest and best compositions of Davis were composed during his daily toil, which, although pretty constant, was of a light character, and not wanting in poetic surroundings.

Poems of Francis Davis.

NANNY.

Oh! for an hour when the day is breaking
Down by the shore, when the tide is making!
Fair as a white cloud, thou, love, near me,
None but the waves and thyself to hear me.
Oh, to my breast how these arms would
    press thee;
Wildly my heart in its joy would bless thee;
Oh, how the soul thou hast won would woo
    thee,
Girl of the snow-neck! closer to me.

Oh, for an hour as the day advances,
(Out where the breeze on the broom-bush
    dances),
Watching the lark, with the sun-ray o'er us,
Winging the notes of his heaven-taught
    chorus!
Oh, to be there and my love before me,
Soft as a sunbeam smiling o'er me;
Thou wouldst but love, and I would woo
    thee,
Girl of the dark eye! closer to me.

Oh, for an hour where the sun first saw us,
(Out in the eve with its red sheets 'round us),
Brushing the dew from the gale's soft
    winglets,
Pearly and sweet with thy long, dark
    ringlets;
Oh, to be there on the sward beside thee.
Telling my tale, though I know you'd chide
    me;
Sweet were thy voice, though it should undo
    me,
Girl of the dark locks! closer to me.

Oh, for an hour, by night or by day, love,
Just as the Heavens and thou might say,
    love;
Far from the stare of the cold-eyed many,
Bound in the breath of my dove-souled
    Nanny!
Oh, for the pure chains that have bound me,
Warm from thy red lips circling 'round me!
Oh, in my soul, as the light above me,
Queen of the pure hearts! do I love thee.

KATHLEEN BAN ADAIR.

THE battle blood of Antrim had not dried on freedom's shroud,
And the rosy ray of morning was but struggling thro' the cloud;
When, with lightning foot and deathly cheek, and wildly waving hair,
O'er grass and dew, scarce breathing, flew young Kathleen ban Adair.

Behind, her native Antrim in a reeking ruin lies;
Before her, like a silvery path, Kell's sleeping waters rise;
And many a pointed shrub has pierc'd those feet so white and bare,
But, oh! thy heart is deeper rent, young Kathleen ban Adair.

And Kathleen's heart but one week since was like a harvest morn;
When hope and joy are kneeling 'round the sheaf of yellow corn;
But where's the bloom then made her cheek so ripe, so richly fair?
Thy stricken heart hath fed on it, young Kathleen ban Adair.

And now she gains a thicket, where the slee and hazel rise;
But why those shrieking whispers, like a rush of worded sighs?
Ah, low and lonely bleeding lies a wounded patriot there,
And every pang of his is thine, young Kathleen ban Adair.

"I see them, oh! I see them, in a fearful red array;
The yeomen, love! the yeomen come—ah, Heaven! away—away!
I know—I know they mean to track my lion to his lair;
Ah! save thy life—ah! save it for thy Kathleen ban Adair."

"May Heaven shield thee, Kathleen! when my soul has gone to rest;
May comfort rear her temple in thy pure and faithful breast;
But to fly them—oh! to fly them, like a bleeding, hunted hare;
No! not to purchase Heaven, with my Kathleen ban Adair.

"I loved, I love thee, Kathleen, in my bosom's warmest core;
And Erin, injured Erin, oh! I loved thee even more;
And death, I feared him little when I drove him thro' their square,
Nor now, though eating at my heart, my Kathleen ban Adair."

With feeble hand his blade he grasp'd, yet dark with spoilers' blood;
And then, as though with dying bound, once more erect he stood;
But scarcely had he kiss'd the cheek, so pale, so purely fair,
When flash'd their bayonets 'round him and his Kathleen ban Adair!

Then up arose his trembling, yet his dreaded hero's hand,
And up arose, in struggling sounds, his cheers for motherland;
A thrust—a rush—their foremost falls; but, ah! good God! see there—
Thy lover's quivering at thy feet, young Kathleen ban Adair!

But, Heavens! men, what recked he then your heartless taunts and blows,
When from his lacerated heart ten dripping bayonets rose?
And, maiden, thou with frantic hands, what boots it kneeling there?
The winds heed not thy yellow locks, young Kathleen ban Adair.

Oh! what were tears, or shrieks, or swoons, but shadows of the rest,
When torn was frantic Kathleen from the slaughtered hero's breast?
And hardly had his last-heaved sigh grown cold upon the air,
When, oh! of all but life they robb'd young Kathleen ban Adair!

But whither now shall Kathleen fly?—already is she gone;
The water, Kells, is tempting fair, and thither speeds she on;
A moment on its blooming banks she kneels in hurried prayer—
Now in its wave she finds a grave, poor Kathleen ban Adair!

————o————

MY BETROTHED.

OH, come, my betrothed, to thine anxious bride,
Too long have they kept thee from my side;
Sure I sought thee by meadow and mountain, *asthore*,
And I watch'd and I wept till my heart was sore,
　　While the false to the false did say:
We will lead her away by the mound and the rath,
And we'll nourish her heart in its worse than death,
Till her tears shall have traced a pearly path,
　　For the work of a future day.

Ah! little they knew what their guile could do—
It has won me a host of the stern and true,
Who have sworn by the eye of the yellow sun,
That my home is their hearts till thy hand be won;
　　And they've gathered my tears and sighs;
And they've woven them into a cloudy frown,
That shall gird my brow like an ebony crown,
Till these feet, in thy wrath shall have trampled down,
.　And, all that betwixt us rise.

Then come, my betrothed, to thine anxious bride!
Thou art dear to my breast as my heart's red tide;
And a wonder it is you can tarry so long,
And your soul so proud, and your arm so strong,
　　And your limb without a chain;
And your feet in their flight like the midnight wind,
When he laughs at the flash he leaves behind;
And your heart so warm, and your look so kind—
　　Oh, come to my arms again!

Oh, my dearest has eyes like the noontide sun,
So bright that my own dare scarce look on;
And the clouds of a thousand years gone by,
Brought back, and again on the crowded sky,
　　Heaped haughtily pile o'er pile,
Then all in a boundless blaze outspread,
Rent, shaken, and tossed o'er their flaming bed,
Till each heart by the light of the Heavens was read,
　　Were as nought to his softest smile!

And to hear my love in his wild mirth sing,
To the flap of the battle-god's fiery wing!
How his chorus shrieks through the iron tones
Of crashing towers and creaking thrones,
　　And the crumbling of bastions strong!
Yet sweet to my ear as the sigh that slips
From the nervous dance of a maiden's lips,
When the eye first wanes in its love eclipse,
　　Is his soul-creating song!

Then come, my betrothed, to thine anxious bride!
Thou hast tarried too long, but I may not chide;
For the prop and the hope of my home thou art,
Ay, the vein that suckles my growing heart,
　　Oh, I'd frown on the world for thee!
And it is not a dull, cold, soulless clod,
With a lip in the dust at a tyrant nod,
Unworthy one glance of the patriots' God,
　　That you ever shall find in me!

————o————

CHOICE SELECTIONS

FROM THE

IRISH AND IRISH-AMERICAN POETS.

ERIN'S FLAG.

BY REV. ABRAM J. RYAN.

UNROLL Erin's flag! fling its folds to the breeze,
Let it float o'er the land, let it flash o'er the seas;
Lift it out of the dust—let it wave as of yore,
When its chiefs with their clans stood around it and swore
That never—no—never! while God gave them life,
And they had an arm and a sword for the strife,
That never—no—never! that banner should yield
As long as the heart of a Celt was its shield;
While the hand of a Celt had a weapon to wield,
And his last drop of blood was unshed on the field.

Lift it up! wave it high!—'tis as bright as of old!
Not a stain on its green, not a spot on its gold,
Tho' the woes and the wrongs of three hundred long years
Have drenched Erin's sunburst with blood and with tears!
Though the clouds of oppression enshroud it in gloom,
And 'round it the thunders of tyranny boom.
Look aloft—look aloft! lo! the clouds drifting by,
There's a gleam through the gloom, there's a light in the sky
'Tis the sunburst resplendent—far, flashing on high!
Erin's dark night is waning; her day dawn is nigh.

Lift it up—lift it up! the old Banner of Green!
The blood of its sons has but brightened its sheen;
What!—though the tyrant has trampled it down,
Are its folds not emblazoned with deeds of renown?
What!—though for ages it droops in the dust,
Shall it droop thus forever?—no—no! God is just!
Take it up—take it up, from the tyrant's foul tread.
Let him tear the Green Flag—we will snatch its last shred.
And beneath it we'll bleed as our forefathers bled,
And we'll vow by the dust in the graves of our dead.

And we swear by the blood which the Briton has shed—
And we'll vow by the wrecks which through Erin he spread—
And we'll swear by the thousands who, famished, unfed,
Died down in the ditches—wild howling for bread.
And we'll vow by our heroes, whose spirits have fled,
And we'll swear by the bones in each coffinless bed,
That we'll battle the Briton through danger and dread;
That we'll cling to the cause which we glory to wed,
Till the gleam of our steel and the shock of our lead
Shall prove to our foe that we meant what we said—
That we'll lift up the Green, and we'll tear down the Red.

Lift up the Green Flag! oh! it wants to go home;
Full long has its lot been to wander and roam:
It has followed the fate of its sons o'er the world,
But its folds, like their hopes, are not faded nor furled;
Like a weary-winged bird, to the east and the west,
It has flitted and fled—but it never shall rest,
'Till pluming its pinions, it sweeps o'er the main,
And speeds to the shores of its old home again,
Where its fetterless folds, o'er each mountain and plain,
Shall wave with a glory that never shall wane.

Take it up—take it up! bear it back from afar—
That banner must blaze 'mid the lightnings of war;
Lay your hands on its folds, lift your gaze to the sky
And swear that you'll bear it triumphant or die!
And shout to the clans scattered far o'er the earth,
To join in the march to the land of their birth;
And wherever the exiles, 'neath Heaven's broad dome,
Have been fated to suffer to sorrow and roam,
They'll bound to the sea, and away o'er the foam,
They'll sail to the music of " Home, Sweet Home!"

———o———

MAN'S MISSION.

BY SPERANZA (MRS. W. R. WILDE.)

HUMAN lives are silent teaching—
  Be they earnest, mild, and true—
Noble deeds are noblest preaching
  From the consecrated few.
Poet-priests their anthems singing,
Hero-swords on corslet ringing,
  When truth's banner is unfurled;
Youthful preachers, genius-gifted,
Pouring forth their souls uplifted,
  Till their preaching stirs the world.

Each must work as God has given
  Hero hand or poet soul—
Work is duty while we live in
  This weird world of sin and dole.
Gentle spirits, lowly kneeling,
Lift their white hands up, appealing
  To the throne of Heaven's king—
Stronger natures culminating,

In great actions incarnating,
  What another can but sing.

Pure and meek-eyed, as an angel,
  We must strive—must agonize;
We must preach the saint's evangel
  Ere we claim the saintly prize—
Work for all—for work is holy—
We fulfil our mission solely
  When, like Heaven's arch above,
Blend our souls in one emblazon,
And the social diapason
  Sounds the perfect chord of love.

Life is combat, life is striving,
  Such our destiny below—
Like a scythed chariot driving
  Through an onward pressing foe.
Deepest sorrow, scorn and trial

Will but teach us self-denial;
  Like the alchemists of old,
Pass the ore through cleansing fire
If our spirits would aspire
  To be God's refined gold.

We are struggling in the morning
  With the spirit of the night,
But we trample on its scorning—
  Lo! the eastern sky is bright.
We must watch. The day is breaking;
Seen, like Memnon's statue waking
  With the sunrise into sound,
We shall raise our voice to Heaven,

Chant a hymn for conquest given,
  Seize the palm, nor heed the wound.

We must bend our thoughts to earnest,
  Would we strike the idols down;
With a purpose of the sternest
  Take the Cross, and wait the Crown.
Sufferings human life can hallow,
Sufferings lead to God's Valhalla—
  Meekly bear, but nobly try,
Like a man with soft tears flowing,
Like a God with conquest glowing,
  So to love, and work, and die!

A LAY SERMON.

BY CHARLES GAVAN DUFFY.

BROTHER, do you love your brother?
  Brother, are you all you seem?
Do you live for more than living?
  Has your Life a law, and scheme?
Are you prompt to bear its duties,
  As a brave man may beseem?

Brother, shun the mist exhaling
  From the fen of pride and doubt,
Neither seek the house of bondage
  Walling straitened souls about;
Bats! who, from their narrow spy-hole,
  Cannot see a world without.

Anchor in no stagnant shallow—
  Trust the wide and wondrous sea,
Where the tides are fresh forever,
  And the mighty currents free;
There, perchance, O! young Columbus,
  Your New World of truth may be.

Favor will not make deserving—
  (Can the sunshine brighten clay?)
Slowly must it grow to blossom,
  Fed by labor and delay,
And the fairest bud of promise
  Bears the taint of quick decay.

You must strive for better guerdons;
  Strive to *be* the thing you'd seem;
Be the thing that God hath made you,
  Channel for no borrowed stream;
He hath lent you mind and conscience;
  See you travel in their beam!

See you scale life's misty highlands
  By this light of living truth!
And with bosom braced for labor,
  Breast them in your manly youth;
So when age and care have found you,
  Shall your downward path be smooth.

Fear not, on that rugged highway,
  Life may want its lawful zest;
Sunny glens are in the mountain,
  Where the weary feet may rest,
Cooled in streams that gush forever
  From a loving mother's breast.

"Simple heart and simple pleasures,"
  So they write life's golden rule;
Honor won by supple baseness,
  State that crowns a cankered fool,
Gleam as gleam the gold and purple
  On a hot and rancid pool.

Wear no show of wit or science,
  But the gems you've won, and weighed;
Thefts, like ivy on a ruin,
  Make the rifts they seem to shade:
Are you not a thief and beggar
  In the rarest spoils arrayed?

Shadows deck a sunny landscape,
  Making brighter all the bright:
So, my brother! care and danger
  On a loving nature light,
Bringing all its latent beauties
  Out upon the common sight.

Love the things that God created,
  Make your brother's need your care;
Scorn and hate repel God's blessings,
  But where love is, *they* are there;
As the moonbeams light the waters,
  Leaving rock and sand-bank bare.

Thus, my brother, grow and flourish,
  Fearing none and loving all;
For the true man needs no patron,
  He shall climb and never crawl;
Two things fashion their own channel—
  The strong man and the waterfall

IRELAND.

BY J. BOYLE O'REILLY.

OH, land of sad fate! like a desolate queen,
  Who remembers in sorrow the crown of her glory,
The love of thy children not strangely is seen—
  For humanity weeps at thy heart-touching story.

Strong heart in affliction! that draweth thy foes
  'Till they love thee more dear than thine own generation;
Thy strength is increased as thy life-current flows—
  What were death to another is Ireland's salvation!

Her sons scatter wide like the seeds on the lea,
  And they root where they fall, be it mountain or furrow;
They come to remain and remember; and she
  In their growth will rejoice in a blissful to-morrow!

They sing in strange lands the sweet songs of their home,
  Their emerald Zion enthroned on the billows;
To work, not to weep by the rivers they come;
  Their harps are not hung in despair on the willows.

The hope of the mother beats youthful and strong,
  Responsive and true to her children's pulsations,
No petrified heart has she saved from the wrong—
  Our Niobe lives for her place 'mong the nations!

Then work, all her sons—be they Keltic or Danish,
  Or Norman, or Saxon—one mantle was o'er us;
Let race lines, and creed lines, and every line, vanish—
  We'll work as the *Gael:* "For the mother that bore us!"

---o---

CAOCH THE PIPER.

BY J. KEEGAN.

ONE winter's day, long—long ago,
  When I was a little fellow,
A piper wandered to our door,
  Grey-headed, blind, and yellow—
And oh, how glad was my young heart,
  Though earth and sky looked dreary—
To see the stranger and his dog—
  Poor "Pinch" and Caoch O'Leary.

And when he stowed away his "bag,"
  Cross-barred with green and yellow,
I thought and said: "In Ireland's ground
  There's not so fine a fellow."
And Fineen Burk and Shane Magee,
  And Eily, Kate, and Mary,
Rushed in, with frantic haste to "see"
  And "welcome" Caoch O'Leary.

Oh, God be with those happy times,
  Oh, God be with my childhood,

When I, bare-headed, roamed all day
  Bird-nesting in the wild-wood—
I'll not forget those sunny hours,
  However years may vary;
I'll not forget my early friends,
  Nor honest Caoch O'Leary.

Poor Caoch and "Pinch" slept well that
    night,
  And in the morning early
He called me up to hear him play
  "The wind that shakes the barley."
And then he stroked my flaxen hair,
  And cried: "God mark my deary."
And how he wept when he said: "Farewell,
  And think of Caoch O'Leary."

And seasons came and went, and still
  Old Caoch was not forgotten,
Although I thought him "dead and gone,"
  And in the cold clay rotten,

And often when I walked and danced
 With Eily, Kate, and Mary,
We spoke of childhood's rosy hours,
 And prayed for Caoch O'Leary.

Well—twenty summers had gone past,
 And June's red sun was sinking,
When I, a man, sat by my door,
 Of twenty sad things thinking.
A little dog came up the way,
 His gait was slow and weary,
And at his tail a lame man limped—
 'Twas " Pinch " and Caoch O'Leary.

Old Caoch! but oh! how woe-begone!
 His form is bowed and bending,
His fleshless hands are stiff and wan,
 Ay—Time is even blending
The colors on his threadbare " bag "—
 And " Pinch " is twice as hairy
And " thin-spare " as when first I saw
 Himself and Caoch O'Leary.

" God's blessing here," the wanderer cried,
 " Far—far be hell's black viper;
Does anybody hereabouts
 Remember Caoch the Piper?"
With swelling heart I grasped his hand;
 The old man murmured: " Deary!

Are you the silky-headed child
 That loved poor Caoch O'Leary?"

" Yes—yes," I said—the wanderer wept
 As if his heart was breaking—
" And where, *a vhic machree*,"* he sobbed,
 " Is all the merry-making
I found here twenty years ago?"—
 " My tale," I sighed, " might weary,
Enough to say—there's none but me
 To welcome Caoch O'Leary."

" Vo—Vo—Vo!" the old man cried,
 And wrung his hands in sorrow,
" Pray lead me in, *asthore machree*,
 And I'll *go home* to-morrow.
My ' peace is made '—I'll calmly leave
 This world so cold and dreary,
And you shall keep my pipes and dog,
 And pray for Caoch O'Leary."

With " Pinch," I watched his bed that night,
 Next day, his wish was granted;
He died—and Father James was brought,
 And the Requiem mass was chanted—
The neighbors came; we dug his grave,
 Near Eily, Kate and Mary,
And there he sleeps his last sweet sleep;
 God rest you! Caoch O'Leary.

*Son of my heart.

TO ERIN.

BY THOMAS DEVIN REILLY.

My country!—too long, like the mist on thy mountains,
 The cloud of affliction hath sadden'd thy brow:
Too long hath the blood-rain empurpled thy fountains,
 And Pity been deaf to thy cries—until now.

Thou wert doom'd for a season in darkness to languish,
 While others around thee were basking in light;
Scarce a sunbeam e'er lighten'd the gloom of thy anguish
 In the "Island of Saints," it seem'd still to be night.

Of thy children, alas! some in sorrow forsook thee,
 They could not endure to behold thee distress'd;
In " the land of the stranger " did others o'erlook thee,
 Unworthy the life-stream they drew from thy breast.

And the song of the minstrel was hushed in thy bowers;
 For Discord's dire trump, thy lov'd harp was thrown by;
While, strong as the ivy that strangled thy towers,
 The gripe of oppression scarce left thee a sigh!

That is past—and for aye let its memory perish;
  The day-spring arises, while heaviness ends;
Wake, Erin! forbear thy dark bodings to cherish—
  The wheel hath revolv'd and thy fortune ascends!

Yes—thy cause hath been heard—men have wept at thy story—
  Alas! that a land of such beauty should mourn!
Have thy children ne'er grac'd the high niches of glory?
  Was kindness ne'er known in their bosoms to burn?

Yes, rich as the mines which thy teeming hills nourish,
  Are the stores of their genius which nature imparts;
And sweet as the flow'rs in thy valleys that flourish,
  The fragrance of feeling that breathes from their hearts!

When stung to despair, in their wildness what wonder
  If sometimes their souls from affection might rove;
That frenzy subsiding, their feelings the fonder
  Will seek their own halcyon channel of love!

Let the past be forgotten! Yet shall thou, fair Erin,
  Fling off the base spells which thy spirit enslave;
Thou shalt, like the sea-bird, awhile disappearing,
  Emerge with thy plumage more bright from the wave.

Once more 'mong the verdure and dew of thy mountains
  The shamrock shall ope its wet eye to the sun,
While fondly the muse shall recline by thy fountains,
  And warble her strains to the rills as they run.

And plenty shall smile on thy beautiful valleys,
  And peace shall return, the long wandering dove;
And religion, no longer a cover for malice,
  Shall spread out her wings o'er an Eden of love.

Then tuning thy mild harp, whose melody slumbers,
  As high on the willow it waves in the breeze;
Let poesy lend thee her liveliest numbers,
  To sound thy reveille, thy anthem of praise.

And say unto those that have left thee forsaken—
  "Return, oh, return, to your lone mother's arms!
Other lands in their sons can a fondness awaken;
  Shall Erin alone for her race have no charms?

"Oh, blush as ye wander, that it e'er should be taunted,
  That strangers have felt what my own could not feel;
That, when Britons stood forth in my trial undaunted,
  My children slunk back unconcerned in my weal.

"Oh, if yet in your bosom one last spark ye treasure
  Of love for the land of your sires—of your birth—
Return! and indulge in the soul-thrilling pleasure,
  Of hailing that land 'mong the brightest on earth!"

Then joy to thee, Erin! thy better day breaketh;
  The long polar night of thy woe speeds away;
And, as o'er thy chill breast the warm sunlight awaketh,
  Each bud of refinement evolves in the ray.

Yet remember—the blossom is barren and fleeting,
  As long as the canker of strife, unsubdued,
With its poisonous tooth at the core remains eating—
  If e'er thou art *glorious*, thou first must be *good*.

———o———

THEY ARE DYING.

BY DENIS FLORENCE M'CARTHY.

HEY are dying—they are dying! where the
    golden corn is growing;
hey are dying—they are dying! where the
    crowded herds are lowing;
hey are gasping for existence where the
    streams of life are flowing;
nd they perish of the plague where the
    breeze of health is blowing.

God of justice! God of power!
  Do we dream? Can it be,
In this land, at this hour,
  With the blossom on the tree,
In the gladsome month of May,
When the young lambs play,
  When nature looks around
On her waking children now,
  The seed within the ground,
The bud upon the bough?
  Is it right, is it fair,
  That we perish of despair
In this land, on this soil,
  Where our destiny is set,
Which we cultured with our toil
And watered with our sweat?

We have ploughed, we have sown,
But the crop was not our own;
  We have reaped, but harpy hands
  Swept the harvest from our lands;
We were perishing for food,
When lo! in pitying mood,
  Our kindly rulers gave
  The fat fluid of the slave,
While our corn filled the manger
Of the war-horse of the stranger!

God of mercy! must this last?
Is this land preordained,
For the present and the past
  And the future, to be chained—
To be ravaged, to be spoiled,
  To be hushed, to be whipt,

Its soaring pinions clipt,
And its every effort foiled?

Do our numbers multiply
But to perish and to die?
  Is this all our destiny below,
  That our bodies as they rot,
  May fertilize the spot
    Where the harvests of the stranger
      grow?
If this be, indeed, our fate,
Far—far better now, though late,
That we seek some other land and try some
    other zone;
  The coldest, bleakest shore
  Will surely yield us more
Than the storehouse of the stranger that we
    dare not call our own.

Kindly brothers of the west,
  Who from liberty's full breast
Have fed us, who are orphans beneath a step-
    dame's frown,
  Behold our happy state,
  And weep your wretched fate
That you share not in the splendors of our
    empire and our crown.

Kindly brothers of the east—
  Thou great tiara'd priest,
Thou sanctified Rienzi of Rome and of the
    earth;
  Or thou who bear'st control
  Over golden Istambol,
Who felt for our misfortunes and helped us
    in our dearth.

Turn here your wondering eyes,
  Call your wisest of the wise,
Your muftis and your ministers, your men
    of deepest lore;
  Let the sagest of your sages
  Ope our island's mystic pages,

And explain unto your highness the wonders
of our shore.

A fruitful, teeming soil,
Where the patient peasants toil
Beneath the summer's sun and the watery
winter sky;
Where they tend the golden grain
Till it bends upon the plain,
Then reap it for the stranger, and turn aside
to die.

Where they watch their folds increase,
And store the snowy fleece

Till they send it to their masters to be woven
o'er the waves;
Where having sent their meat
For the foreigner to eat,
Their mission is fulfilled and they creep into
their graves.

'Tis for this they are dying where the golden
corn is growing,
'Tis for this they are dying where the crowded herds are lowing,
'Tis for this they are dying where the streams
of life are flowing,
And they perish of the plague where the
breeze of health is blowing.

————o————

THE EMPTY SADDLE.

BY STEPHEN J. MEANY.

"He comes—he comes!" cried the Lady
May—
"My Lord returns betimes—
He hath been away the livelong day,
And is back ere the the vesper chimes.
Oh! I knew that his manly heart would
yearn
For the loving heart at home,
That the joys of the chase could ne'er
replace
The joys of his hearth—I come!"

'Twas thus the loving, fair young wife
Exclaimed, in girlish glee,
"I come—I come, my life of life,
Thou'rt back to thy home and me."
For the echo of hoof was heard below,
And the mastiff's welcoming whine—
Nor dreamt she, I trow, of grief or woe,
As she hailed the watched-for sign.

One bound to the casement—one step
without—
One heart-whole cry of love;
One vacant stare, as she asked: "Oh, where
Is that form all forms above?
Ah, I know—I know—a glad surprise
He means for his loving May!"
And with strained eyes and anxious sighs,
She watches and waits that day.

But no clank of spur in the castle hall—
No step on the old oak stair—
And silent all the answering call
To the loving welcomes there.
"Oh, where is he hiding—my life and light?
Why tarries he from my side?
Come forth, Sir Knight, and glad the sight

Of your May—your little bride!"

Oh, woe for the bride! and alas, for her lord!
No playful lord was there;
No pulse was stirred by the joyous word,
As she asked in her grief: "Oh, where?"
But she saw beneath with eye of fire—
'Twas a crushing of heart indeed—
The anguish dire of the faithful squire
And her brave Knight's sorrowing steed.

Ay, sorrowing steed!—It had borne him long
In the battle's rush and roar—
And proud and strong in the hostile throng,
It hath carried him safely o'er—
But now in the peaceful hour of chase,
One stumble—its master dead!
And its grief we trace in the lagging pace,
And the bowed and bending head.

It needed no word to the Lady May
To tell she was widowed now—
It boots not to say how the shock that day
Called the death chill to her brow—
A desolate hearth—a vacant chair—
A breaking heart—no more!
But oft in despair comes the cry: "Oh, where
Stays my lord, when the chase is o'er."

In the early blush of the bright Spring morn,
The Knight had gone forth in glee;
No omen to warn, as the hunter's horn
Rang out right merrily!
And he kissed good-by to the fair young
face,
As he rode from his lordly hall;
But ne'er from the race did his steps retrace,
"The empty saddle" was all!

————o————

MORNING ON THE IRISH COAST.

BY JOHN LOCKE.

[The incident which prompted the writing of the following lines was related to me by a friend who visited Ireland during the summer. On the voyage eastward my friend made the acquaintance of an old man, who, in his frank and candid way, told him he had been thirty years residing in "the States," and that he was then going home to spend the evening of his life in the Old Land, amid the scenes of his youth-hood. His anxiety to see Ireland once more was so deep and fervid, that my friend took a special interest in him. The night before the ship reached the Irish shore they remained on deck, and as the dawning broke, they were rewarded for their weary vigil by beholding the dim outlines of the Irish coast. The sight awakened all the old man's slumbering enthusiasm, and his first impassioned exclamation was: "The top o' the mornin' to you, Ireland, alanna!"]

Th' anam au Dhia! but there it is,
  The dawn on the hills of Ireland!
God's angels lifting the night's black veil
  From the fair, sweet face of my sireland!
Oh, Ireland, isn't it grand you look,
  Like a bride in her rich adornin',
And with all the pent up love of my heart,
  I bid you the top o' the mornin'.

This one short hour pays lavishly back
  For many a year of mourning;
I'd almost venture another flight,
  There's so much joy in returning—
Watching out for the hallowed shore,
  All other attractions scorning';
Oh, Ireland, don't you hear me shout?
  I bid you the top o' the mornin'.

Ho—ho! upon Cleena's shelving strand,
  The surges are grandly beating,
And Kerry is pushing her headlands out
  To give us the kindly greeting;
Into the shore the sea-birds fly
  On pinions that know no drooping,
And out from the cliffs, with welcomes
    charged,
  A million of waves come trooping.

Oh, kindly, generous Irish land,
  So leal and fair and loving,
No wonder the wandering Celt should think
  And dream of you in his roving!
The alien home may have gems and gold—
  Shadows may never have gloomed it;
But the heart will sigh for the absent land,
  Where the love-light first illumed it.

And doesn't old Cove look charming there,
  Watching the wild waves' motion,
Leaning her back up against the hills,
  And the tip of her toes on the ocean?
I wonder I don't hear Shandon's bells,
  Ah, maybe their chiming's over,
For it's many a year since I began
  The life of a Western rover.

For thirty summers, astore machree,
  Those hills I now feast my eyes on,
Ne'er met my vision, save when they rose,
  Over Memory's dim horizon.
E'en so, 'twas grand and fair they seemed
  In the landscape spread before me;
But dreams are dreams, and my eyes would
    ope
  To see Texas' sky still o'er me.

Ah! oft upon the Texan plains,
  When the day and the chase were over,
My thoughts would fly o'er the weary wave,
  And around this coast-line hover;
And the prayer would rise, that some future
    day
  All danger and doubtings scornin',
I'd help to win my native land
  The light of young liberty's mornin'.

Now fuller and truer the shore-line shows—
  Was ever a scene so splendid?
I feel the breath of the Munster breeze,
  Thank God that my exile's ended.
Old scenes, old songs, old friends again,
  The vale and cot I was born in!
Oh, Ireland, up from my heart of hearts,
  I bid you the top of the mornin'.

———o———

THE IRISH EXILES.

BY MARTIN MAC DERMOTT.

When 'round the festive Christmas board, or by the Christmas hearth,
That glorious mingled draught is poured—wine, melody and mirth!
When friends long absent tell, low-toned, their joys and sorrows o'er,
And hand grasps hand, and eyelids fill, and lips meet lips once more—
Oh! in that hour 'twere kindly done, some woman's voice would say—
"Forget not those who're sad to-night—poor exiles, far away!"

Alas, for them! this morning's sun saw many a moist eye pour
Its gushing love, with longings vain, the waste Atlantic o'er.
And when he turned his lion-eye this ev'ning from the west,
The Indian shores were lined with those who watched his couched crest;
But not to share his glory, then, or gladden in his ray,
They bent their gaze upon his path—those exiles far away!

It was—oh! how the heart will cheat! because they thought, beyond
His glowing couch lay that Green Isle of which their hearts were fond;
And fancy brought old scenes of home into each welling eye,
And through each breast pour'd many a thought that filled it like a sigh!
'Twas then—'twas then, all warm with love, they knelt them down to pray
For Irish homes and kith and kin—poor exiles, far away!

And then the mother bless'd her son, the lover bless'd the maid,
And then the soldier was a child, and wept the while he prayed;
And then the student's pallid cheek flushed red as summer rose,
And patriot souls forgot their grief to weep for Erin's woes;
And oh! but then warm vows were breathed, that come what might or may,
They'd right the suffering isle they loved—those exiles, far away!

And some there were around the board, like loving brothers met,
The few and fond and joyous hearts that never can forget;
They pledged: "The girls we left at home, God bless them!" and they gave
" The memory of our absent friends, the tender and the brave!"
Then up, erect, with nine times nine—hip—hip—hip—hurrah!
Drank: "Erin *slantha gal go bragh!*" those exiles far away.

Then, oh! to hear the sweet old strains of Irish music rise,
Like gushing memories of home, beneath far foreign skies;
Beneath the spreading calabash, beneath the trellised vine,
The bright Italian myrtle bower, or dark Canadian pine—
Oh! don't those old familiar tones—so sad, and now so gay—
Speak out your very—very hearts—poor exiles, far away!

But, Heavens! how many sleep afar, all heedless of these strains,
Tired wanderers! who sought repose through Europe's battle-plains—
In strong, fierce, headlong fight they fell—as ships go down in storms—
They fell—and *human* whirlwinds swept across their shattered forms!
No shroud, but glory, wrapped them 'round; nor prayer nor tear had they—
Save the wandering winds and the heavy clouds—poor exiles, far away!

And might the singer claim a sigh, he, too, could tell how tost
Upon the stranger's dreary shore his heart's best hopes were lost;
How he, too, pined to hear the tones of friendship greet his ear,
And pined to walk the river-side to youthful musing dear,
And pined with yearning silent love among *his own* to stay—
Alas! it is so sad to be an exile far away!

Then, O! when 'round the Christmas board, or by the Christmas hearth,
That glorious mingled draught is poured—wine, melody and mirth!
When friends long absent tell, low-toned, their joys and sorrows o'er,
And hand grasps hand, and eyelids fill, and lips meet lips once more—
In that bright hour, perhaps—perhaps, some woman's voice would say—
" Think—think on those who weep to-night, poor exiles, far away!"

———o———

DONAL KENNY.

BY JOHN K. CASEY.

" Come, piper, play the 'Shaskan Reel,'
  Or else the 'Lasses on the heather,'
And Mary, lay aside your wheel
  Until we dance once more together.
At fair and pattern oft before
  Of reels and jigs we've tripped full many;
But ne'er again this loved old floor
  Will feel the foot of Donal Kenny."

Softly she arose and took his hand,
  And softly glided through the measure,
While, clustering 'round, the village band
  Looked half in sorrow, half in pleasure.
Warm blessings flowed from every lip
  As ceased the dancers' airy motion;
Oh, Blessed Virgin guide the ship
  Which bears bold Donal o'er the ocean!

" Now God be with you all!" he sighed,
  Adown his face the bright tears flowing—
" God guard you well, *avic*," they cried,
  " Upon the strange path you are going."
So full his breast, he scarce could speak,
  With burning grasp the stretched hands
    taking,
He pressed a kiss on every cheek,
  And sobbed as if his heart was breaking.

" Boys, don't forget me when I'm gone,
  For sake of all the days passed over,
The days you spent on heath and bawn,
  With *Donal Ruadh*, the rattlin' rover.
Mary, *agra*, your soft brown eye
  Has willed my fate " (he whispered
    lowly);
" Another holds thy heart; good-by!
  Heaven grant you both its blessings holy!"

A kiss upon her brow of snow,
  A rush across the moonlit meadow,
Whose brown-clad hazels, trembling slow,
  The mossy boreen wrapped in shadow;
Away o'er Tully's bounding rill,
  And far beyond the Inny river;
One cheer on Carrick's rocky hill,
  And Donal Kenny's gone forever.

*   *   *   *   *

The breezes whistled through the sails,
  O'er Galway Bay the ship was heaving,
And smothered groans and bursting wails
  Told all the grief and pain of leaving.
One form among that exiled band
  Of parting sorrow gave no token,
Still was his breath and cold his hand;
  For Donal Kenny's heart was broken.

SHAUN'S HEAD.

BY JOHN SAVAGE.

Scene:—*Before Dublin Castle*—Night—a clansman of Shaun O'Neill discovers his chief's head on a pole.

God's wrath upon the Saxon; may they never know the pride
Of dying on the battle-field, their broken spear beside;
When victory gilds the gory shroud of every fallen brave,
Or death no tales of conquered clans can whisper to his grave.
May every light from cross of Christ that saves the heart of man,
Be hid in clouds of blood before it reach the Saxon clan;
For sure, oh, God, and You know all! whose thought for all sufficed,
To expiate these Saxon sins, they'd want another Christ.

Is it thus, oh, Shaun, the haughty! Shaun, the valiant, that we meet?
Have my eyes been lit by Heaven but to guide me to defeat?
Have I no chief, or you no clan, to give us both defense?
Or must I, too, be statued here with thy cold eloquence?
Thy ghastly head grins scorn upon old Dublin's Castle tower,
Thy shaggy hair is wind-tossed, and thy brow seems rough with power;
Thy wrathful lips, like sentinels, by foulest treachery stung,
Look rage upon the world of wrong, but chain thy fiery tongue.

That tongue whose Ulster accent woke the ghost of Columbkill,
Whose warrior words fenced 'round with spears the oaks of Derry Hill;
Whose reckless tones gave life and death to vassals and to knaves,
And hunted hordes of Saxons into holy Irish graves.

The Scotch marauders whitened when his war-cry met their ears,
And the death-bird, like a vengeance, poised above his stormy cheers;
Ay, Shaun, across the thundering sea, out-chanting it your tongue,
Flung wild un-Saxon war-whoopings the Saxon Court among.

Just think, O Shaun! the same moon shines on Liffey as on Foyle,
And lights the ruthless knaves on both, our kinsman to despoil;
And you the hope, voice, battle-ax, the shield of us and ours,
A murdered, trunkless, blinding sight above these Dublin towers.
Thy face is paler than the moon, my heart is paler still—
My heart? I had no heart—'twas yours—*'twas* yours! to keep or kill.
And you kept it safe for Ireland, chief—your life, your soul, your pride—
But they sought it in thy bosom, Shaun—with proud O'Neill it died.
You were turbulent and haughty, proud and keen as Spanish steel;
But who had right of these, if not our Ulster's chief—O'Neill?

Who reared aloft the " Bloody Hand" until it paled the sun,
And shed such glory on Tyrone, as chief had never done?
He was "turbulent" with traitors—he was "naughty" with the foe—
He was "cruel," say ye Saxons! Ah! he dealt ye blow for blow!
He was "rough" and "wild," and who's not wild to see his hearthstone razed?
He was "merciless as fire"—ah, ye kindled him—he blazed!
He was "proud!" yes, proud of birthright, and because he flung away
Your Saxon stars of princedome, as the rock does mocking spray,
He was wild, insane for vengeance—ay! and preached it till Tyrone
Was ruddy, ready, wild, too, with " Red Hands" to clutch their own.

" The Scots are on the border, Shaun!"—ye saints, he makes no breath—
I remember when that cry would wake him up almost from death:
Art truly dead and cold? O, chief! art thou to Ulster lost?
"Dost hear—*dost hear?* By Randolph led, the troops the Foyle have crossed!"
He's truly dead! he must be dead! nor is his ghost about—
And yet no tomb could hold his spirit tame to such a shout!
The pale face droopeth northward—ah! his soul must loom up there,
By old Armagh, or Antrim's glynns, Lough Foyle, or Bann the fair!
I'll speed me Ulster-wards, your ghost must wander there, proud Shaun,
In search of some O'Neill, through whom to throb its hate again.

———o———

A LOVE SONG TO MY WIFE.

BY JOSEPH BRENAN.

COME to me, darling one, nearer and
      nearer—
Time only renders you dearer and dearer;
Grief has no chill for the love that is
      truthful;
Years as they roll find it brilliantly
      youthful—
Steadfastly scorning a moment of ranging—
Changes around, find affection unchanging;
Brightly it silvers the clouds which are o'er
      us;
Nightly it lights up the pathway before us.

See you that calm and majestical river,
Stealing on tranquilly, ever and ever—
Beautiful always, in sunshine or shadow,
Breasting the tempest, or kissing the
      meadow—

Bountiful, too, in its musical flowing—
Source of the green which beside it is
      glowing;
Soul of the woods which so verdantly bound
      it;
Seed of the flowers which are laughing
      around it.

Dear; as that river flows onward and
      onward,
Forcing the seeds of fertility sunward,
So has the current of love for you glided;
Brightening the years which are gathered
      beside it—
Clothing their forms with a raiment of
      purple;
Gracing their hands with the laurel and
      myrtle;

Making each hour, which in quiet reposes,
Break into beauty and blush into roses.

Surely that stream has a lesson for lovers,
O'er it a silver-clad sisterhood hovers.
Birds which, illuming the proximate
        grasses,
Peck into dimples the wave as it passes;
Birds that fulfil their predestinate duty.
Lending their hues to the completion of
        beauty,
Bright in the morning, or dark in the even,
Ultimate tints in the landscape of Heaven.

Thus, as our Love hurries on to its ending,
Beautiful things with its beauties are
        blending,
Fancies which rest in the years by it,
        dreaming
Silver-clad thoughts which are constantly
        gleaming,
Griefs which, at evening, the shadow
        enhances,
Breaking to joys as the morning advances,
Hope for the future, and fond recollection,
Golden-hued guardians of human affection.

What if some casual wing of ill-omen
Glides o'er the wave like the shade of the
        Gnomon,

What if the song-birds at times have been
        wearied,
What if the sunshine has not been unvaried?
What if the buds of our Spring, which
        departed,
Left us in solitude, weak and sad-hearted,
What if we sometimes have moments of
        weeping
Over the little ones death has set sleeping?

Let them sleep on; there are dreams in their
        slumbers,
Soothed by the angels' most musical
        numbers;
Lit by the light of a greatness supernal,
Blest by the bliss which alone is eternal,
Let them sleep on; they are happy above us,
Death cannot make them unable to love us;
Weep not for babes which are benisons o'er
        us;
Grieve not because they are happy before us!

Come to me, darling one, nearer and nearer—
Time only renders you dearer and dearer;
Grief has no chill for the love which is
        truthful,
Years, as they roll, find it brilliantly
        youthful—
Steadfastly scorning a moment of ranging—
Changes around leave affection unchanging:
Brightly it silvers the clouds which are o'er
        us,
Nightly it lights up the pathway before us!

———o———

"THE GLEN OF THE LAKES."

BY REV. T. AMBROSE BUTLER.

GLEN of the Lake! I hail thee with emotion,
    Long sighed-for object of the poet's soul—
A pilgrim-bard presents his heart's devotion
    Beside the hills where Avon's waters roll.
Now sweetly o'er me steals a happy feeling,
    That thou art one I oft beheld before;
The hazy curtains seem to rise, revealing
    The long-sought beauties of thy magic shore.

The silv'ry lakes! what solemn awe around them,
    Embosom'd safely mid the mountains brown;
The heathy cliffs, the waving forests bound them,
    Lugduff, the giant, proudly looketh down.
The summer sun at midday softly peepeth
    Adown the heather, o'er the shadow'd streams;
The gloomy brook awhile in silence sleepeth,
    Then wakes and smiles amid the sunny beams.

So grand, so solemn seems the silence reigning
    Across the Glen in summer's brightest hour,
That nature wearied here in peace remaining,
    Seems slave awhile to slumber's mighty pow'r.

She scarcely breathes beside the streamlet sighing,
　Beneath the pines that guard the sobbing lake;
Till autumn leaves beside the waters lying,
　With rustling voices bid the sleepers wake!

A home was here for sainted hermit glowing,
　With sacred love and wondrous faith divine!
A calm retreat for youth in virtue growing
　Where nature's God could have a fitting shrine.
And so the lakes, through brightest golden ages
　Reflected forms of Erin's sainted men;
And while their names illume historic pages,
　Saint Kevin's works shall speak amid the glen!

They stand majestic—ruined churches lowly,
　Whose mold'ring porches creeping-ivy climbs;
The princes, prelates, hermits meek and holy
　Rest 'neath the cross that tells of better times.
And, grandest sight! "the pillar-tow'r" that telleth
　Of glories gone amid the glooms of time;
For though no more the Abbey-bell out swelleth,
　The voiceless ruins tell their tale sublime!

Unnumbered legends, quaint, and sweet, and tender,
　Are still preserv'd and heard beside the glen
Of holy Kevin, peasants' kind defender—
　The friend and father dear to suffering men.
One summer day, alas! it soon departed,
　When seated nigh the lake with friends most dear,
I heard of Kevin, kind and tender-hearted,
　And felt I then had kindred spirits near!

————o————

THE BELLS OF SHANDON.

BY FATHER PROUT.

WITH deep affection and recollection
　I often think of those Shandon bells,
Whose sounds so wild would, in days of
　　childhood,
　Fling 'round my cradle their magic spells.
On this I ponder, where'er I wander,
And thus grow fonder, sweet Cork, of thee;
　　With thy bells of Shandon
　　That sound so grand on
The pleasant waters of the river Lee.

I've heard bells chiming full many clime in,
　Tolling sublime in cathedral shrine;
While at a glib rate brass tongues would
　　vibrate,
　But all their music spoke naught like thine;
For memory dwelling on each proud
　　swelling
　Of thy belfry knelling its bold notes free,
　　Made the bells of Shandon
　　Sound far more grand on
The pleasant waters of the river Lee.

I've heard bells tolling "old Adrian's Mole"
　in,
　Their thunder rolling from the Vatican,
And cymbals glorious, swinging uproarious
　In the gorgeous turrets of Notre Dame;
But thy sounds were sweeter than the dome
　　of Peter
　Flings o'er the Tiber, pealing solemnly.
　　Oh! the bells of Shandon
　　Sound far more grand on
The pleasant waters of the river Lee.

There's a bell in Moscow, while on tower and
　kiosko
　In St. Sophia the Turkman gets,
And loud in air, calls men to prayer
　From the tapering summit of tall minarets.
Such empty phantom, I freely grant them,
　But there's an anthem more dear to me;
　　'Tis the bells of Shandon
　　That sound so grand on
The pleasant waters of the river Lee.

————o————

THE RIGHTS OF MAN.

BY DR. ROBERT DWYER JOYCE.

THOUGH he was born to till the soil
Or ply the busy trade,
To pamper tyrants by his toil
The poor man ne'er was made;
That wondrous flame, the soul's the same
In poor or noble clay,
And the self-same laws will try its cause
On the final Judgment Day.
 Then here's the son of poverty,
  Who bravely fills his can,
 And drink with me to liberty,
  And the God-made rights of man.

The reckless despot on his throne,
Who gave him right to sway?
To make the suffering millions groan
In bondage day by day?
Is he a god that with his rod
Can fill unnumbered graves?
No! Blood and bone, he still must own,
He's mortal like his slaves!
 Then here's the son of poverty,
  Who fearless fills his can,
 To pledge with me bright liberty,
  And the God-made rights of man.

When delved great Adam's progeny,
And our primal mothers' span,
There was no difference of degree
E'er seen twixt man and man;
But the human might, ambition's flight,
 Have set up tyrants' rule.

A lesson stern the nations learn
In hard misfortune's school.
 So here's the son of poverty,
  Who stoutly fills his can,
 And works with me for liberty,
  And the God-made rights of man.

There never was a law divine
To make the poor bow down
To mortal man, whate'er his line,
However bright his crown;
The poor man's blood is warm and good,
And red as his who reigns,
And why should he bend neck or knee—
 Bow silent down in chains?
 So here's the son of poverty
  Who fills a brimming can,
 And prays with me for liberty,
  And the God-made rights of man.

On many a plain with fire and steel,
The poor man's cause was tried,
And many a deed of noble zeal
That great cause sanctified;
For that good cause, for righteous laws,
Arise, prepare, and be
Brave patriots all, to stand or fall,
Soldiers of Liberty.
 And here's the son of poverty,
  Who clinks with mine his can—
 Who'll strike with me for liberty,
  And the God-made rights of man.

————o————

WE'LL NOT GIVE UP THE OLD LAND.

BY BARTHOLOMEW DOWLING.

FILL high, my gallant comrades, ere we join the bloody fray,
Ere the sword-flash and the sunlight greet the op'ning eye of day;
Here's to home and homeland thro' every weal and woe—
And we'll not give up the Old Land without another blow.

Pledge me fondly, pledge me truly, cross your arms upon your breast,
Pledge your faith to holy Ireland, "island of the blest,"
That wherever exile sends us, or how far away we go,
We won't give up the Old Land without another blow.

No, we won't give up the Old Land, we won't lie down to die—
We won't cringe down to Moloch with yelping whine or sigh;
But we'll stand our rights defending, like the stout pine 'neath the snow,
We can't give up the Old Land without another blow.

Is she worth our love and honor—is she worth our blood and life?
And the price we set upon her, and the straining and the strife?
Yes, she's worth this world all over and worlds we'll never know;
So we won't give up our Own Land without another blow.

Then fill high, my gallant comrades, ere we join the bloody fray,
Ere the swordflash and the sunlight greet the op'ning eye of day;
And as we strike for *freedom* and the friends we can't forget,
We have Ireland, Home and Beauty to claim our prowess yet.

———o———

THOUGHTS ON A DEAD WOMAN.

BY ROBERT WHITE.

(Written in memory of his wife, Alice White, who died November 26, 1875.)

"She should have died hereafter."—MACBETH.

A DEAD Woman! Only a dead woman.
In the floodtide of our soul-stricken grief
Why will the mind, fully formed and fixed
With sentiment soft as in youth immature,
Dream and rave, and feed its thoughts
On the memory of only a dead woman?

The poet prates of the dead past.
Poets are dreamers and makers of
  metaphors.
Figures of speech are the food of their
  faculties.
There is no dead past.
If there is, why not mentally bury
Our memory of only a dead woman?

The priest—God's priest;
The Sainted Sister, the Virgin Spouse of
  Christ.
These ethereal spirits, 'twixt Heaven and
  earth,
Revere, praise and pray for the dead,
And memory of the dead,
And salvation of only a dead woman.

We labor by muscle and fiber of thought;
We rebel 'gainst blessings that God's wisdom
  gives;

We feed upon sin; we revel in vanity;
We crave for more luxury: forgetting the
  while
We are sons of only a dead woman.

The dead past. Why will it not die?
The dead past has live brain-ghosts
That haunt our humanity;
Sleeping and waking—sometimes to sweeten,
But oft, ay! God makes more bitter
Our quickened love of only a dead woman.

The grave, the clay, the cold slab,
The frosty blast, the sweet fragrant flowers,
Entomb, enshrine, enthrone,
And with golden-laced shroud and snow-
  garnished coverlet,
Bury away our youth's impassioned love
With only a dead woman.

Our children grow up, learn and play,
Read, sing, romp and be merry;
Labor, dress, dance and be cheery;
Wonder and grieve at our sadness and
  sorrow—
Forgetting we are living on the thoughts
Of their dead mother—only a dead woman.

———o———

ERIN.

BY DR. DRENNAN.

WHEN Erin first rose from the dark swelling flood,
God bless'd the green island, and saw it was good;
The em'rald of Europe, it sparkled and shone,
In the ring of the world, the most precious stone.
In her sun, in her soil, in her station thrice blest,
With her back towards Britain, her face to the West,
Erin stands proudly insular, on her steep shore,
And strikes her high harp 'mid the ocean's deep roar.

But when its soft tones seem to mourn and to weep,
The dark chain of silence is thrown o'er the deep;
At the thought of the past the tears gush from her eyes,
And the pulse of her heart makes her white bosom rise.
O! sons of green Erin, lament o'er the time,
When religion was war, and our country a crime,

When man, in God's image, inverted his plan,
And moulded his God in the image of man.

When the int'rest of state wrought the general woe,
The stranger a friend, and the native a foe;
While the mother rejoic'd o'er her children oppressed,
And clasped the invader more close to her breast.
When with pale for the body and pale for the soul
Church and state joined in compact to conquer the whole;
And as Shannon was stained with Milesian blood,
Ey'd each other askance and pronounced it was good.

By the groans that ascend from your forefathers' grave,
For the country thus left to the brute and the slave,
Drive the Demon of Bigotry home to his den,
And where Britain made brutes now let Erin make men.
Let my sons like the leaves of the shamrock unite,
A partition of sects from one footstalk of right,
Give each his full share of the earth and the sky,
Nor fatten the slave where the serpent would die.

Alas! for poor Erin that some are still seen,
Who would dye the grass red from their hatred to Green;
Yet, oh! when you're up and they're down, let them live,
Then yield them that mercy which they would not give.
Arm of Erin, be strong! but be gentle as brave!
And uplifted to strike, be still ready to save!
Let no feeling of vengeance presume to defile
The cause of, or men of, the Emerald Isle.

The cause it is good, and the men they are true,
And the Green shall outlive both the Orange and Blue!
And the triumphs of Erin her daughters shall share,
With the full swelling chest, and the fair flowing hair.
Their bosom heaves high for the worthy and brave,
But no coward shall rest in that soft-swelling wave;
Men of Erin! awake, and make haste to the blest,
Rise—Arch of the Ocean and Queen of the West!

———o———

A REMONSTRANCE.

BY T. D. SULLIVAN.

[In 1865 the Hon. Thomas D'Arcy M'Gee visited Ireland, and in a speech at Wexford, poured a malignant tide of abuse on the Irish-American patriots who were prominent in preparing to assist their brethren in Ireland in the contemplated revolution of that exciting period. The following lightning reply flashed out from the columns of the Dublin *Nation*, of which the author was then associate editor.]

'Twas badly done, 'twas badly done,
To come o'er miles of land and sea,
When years of exile past had run,
And speak the words you spoke, M'Gee;
To turn unto the dear old home,
By millions lov'd, where'er they roam,
And, standing in the ancient place,
Before your people, face to face,
To add your words to those that fling
Dishonor on your country's name,
And echo taunts and jibes that bring
To brave men's cheeks a crimson flame.

Better you stayed far—far away,
Content beside your new-made hearth,
Than come with words like these to say
To this green land that gave you birth:
Better you stayed in fortune's smile,
Than sought this sad, yet proud old isle,
To swell the chorus of the foes
Who mock her hopes and slight her woes.
Their scoffs and strokes are hard to bear;
But deeper than her heart is wrung,
When one whose name she long held dear,
Turns on her cause a faithless tongue.

And you, too, speak in scornful tone
Of men who love that sacred cause!
What voice more loudly than your own
Inveighed against the tyrant's laws?
What bolder deeds than those were planned
To which you vowed to set your hand?
What weightier words of sterner rage
Or who in sweeter, fiercer songs,
Has sung the dear isle's deathless charms,
Or told her rosary of wrongs,
To rouse her kindling youth to arms?

And when, an outlaw'd man, you fled,
And joined our exiles o'er the main,
What voice in firmer accents said
The old green flag should rise again?
Told them what hearts so brave and true
For Ireland's freedom yet could do,
And bade them nurse their deadly hate
To crush her wronger soon or late?
Still bleeds and weeps the suffering isle—
Her banner moulders in the dust—
How are those hopes so vain or vile,
You swore so long were true and just?

And what may be their sudden crime,
Those banished millions of our race,
To change them in a little time
From brave and good to false and base?
Ah, Ireland knows those exiles well,
And little heeds the tale you tell;
Each day across the ocean foam
Their loving words come speeding home,
With gifts that make sad hearts rejoice,
And ease awhile their sore distress—
What wonder that the nation's voice
Speaks of them but to cheer and bless.

Ah well, we thought to see once more
The Irish hills—to breathe anew
The air in which you sung before—
Would win a kindlier strain from you—
But let it pass. If traitor swords
Could kill her cause, or bitter words
Could make it folly, crime or shame,
'Twere dead before your wisdom came.
'Tis living still. It will not die
Till foreign rule from hence is hurled.
And Ireland stands a nation high
Amongst the nations of the world.

A PRISON LAY.

BY THOMAS FRANCIS MEAGHER.

I LOVE, I love these grey old walls!
Although a chilling shadow falls
Along the iron-gated halls,
    And in the silent, narrow cells,
    Brooding darkly, ever dwells.

Oh! still I love them—for the hours
Within them spent are set with flowers
That blossom, spite of wind and showers,
    And through that shadow, dull and cold,
    Emit their sparks of blue and gold.

Bright flowers of mirth!—that wildly spring
From fresh, young hearts, and o'er them
       fling,
Like Indian birds with sparkling wing,
    Seeds of sweetness, grains all glowing,
    Sun-gilt leaves, with dew-drop flowing.

And hopes as bright, that softly gleam,
Like stars which o'er the church-yard stream
A beauty on each faded dream—
    Mingling the light they purely shed
    With other hopes, whose light has fled.

Fond mem'ries, too, undimmed with sighs,
Whose fragrant sunshine never dies,
Whose summer song-bird never flies—
    These, too, are chasing hour by hour,
    The clouds which 'round this prison
       lower,

And thus, from hour to hour, I've grown
To love these walls, though dark and lone,
And fondly prize each grey old stone,
    Which flings the shadow, deep and chill,
    Across my fettered footsteps still.

Yet, let these mem'ries flow and flow
Within my heart, like waves that glow
Unseen in spangled caves below
    The foam which frets, the mists which
       sweep
    The changeful surface of the deep.

Not so the many hopes that bloom
Amid this voiceless waste and gloom,
Strewing my path-way to the tomb
    As though it were a bridal bed,
    And not the prison of the dead.

I would those hopes were traced in fire,
Beyond these walls—above that spire—
Amid yon blue and starry choir,
    Whose sounds play 'round us with the
       streams
    Which glitter in the white moon's beams.

I'd twine those hopes above our Isle,
Above the rath and ruined pile,
Above each glen and rough defile,
    The holy well—the Druid's shrine—
    Above them all, those hopes I'd twine,

So should I triumph o'er my fate,
And teach this poor, desponding State,
In signs of tenderness, not hate,
 Still to think of her old story,
 Still to hope for future glory.

Within these walls, those hopes have been
The music sweet, the light serene
Which softly o'er this silent scene,

Have like the autum streamlets flowed,
 And like the autumn sunshine glowed.

And thus, from hour to hour, I've grown
To love these walls, though dark and lone,
And fondly prize each grey old stone,
 That flings the shadow, deep and chill,
 Across my fettered footsteps still.

---o---

WHAT WILL YOU DO, LOVE?

BY SAMUEL LOVER.

WHAT will you do, love, when I am going,
 With white sail flowing,
  To seas beyond?
What will you do, love, when waves divide us,
 And friends may chide us,
  For being fond?
Though waves divide us, and friends be chiding,
 In faith abiding,
  I'll still be true.
And I'll pray for thee on stormy ocean,
 In deep devotion—
  That's what I'll do!

What would you do, love, if distant tidings,
 Thy fond confidings
  Should undermine;
And I abiding 'neath sultry skies,
 Should think other eyes,
  Were as bright as thine?

Oh, name it not, though guilt and shame
 Were on thy name,
  I'd still be true;
But that heart of thine, should another share
 it,
  I could not bear it—
   What would I do?

What would you do, when home returning,
 With hopes high burning,
  With wealth for you—
If my bark, that bounded o'er foreign foam,
 Should be lost near home—
  Ah, what would you do?
So thou wert spared, I'd bless the morrow,
 In want and sorrow,
  That left me you;
And I'd welcome thee from the wasting
 billow,
  My heart thy pillow!
   That's what I'd do.

---o---

TONE'S GRAVE.

BY THOMAS DAVIS.

IN Bodenstown Churchyard there is a green grave,
And wildly along it the winter winds rave;
Small shelter, I ween, are the ruined walls there,
When the storm sweeps down on the plains of Kildare.

Once I lay on that sod—it lies over Wolfe Tone—
And thought how he perished in prison alone,
His friends unavenged, and his country unfreed—
"Oh, bitter," I said, "is a patriot's meed.

"For in him the heart of a woman combined
With a heroic life, and a governing mind—
A martyr for Ireland—his grave has no stone,
His name seldom named, and his virtues unknown."

I was woke from my dream by the voices and tread
Of a band, who came into the home of the dead;
They carried no corpse, and they carried no stone,
And they stopped when they came to the grave of Wolfe Tone.

There were students and peasants, the wise and the brave,
And an old man who knew him from cradle to grave,
And the children who thought me hard-hearted; for they,
On that sanctified soil were forbidden to play.

But the old man, who saw I was mourning there, said:
"We come, sir, to weep where young Wolfe Tone is laid,
And we're going to raise him a monument, too—
A plain one, yet fit for the simple and true."

My heart overflowed, and I clasped his old hand,
And I blessed him, and blessed everyone of his band;
"Sweet! Sweet! 'tis to find that such faith can remain
To the cause, and the man so long vanquished and slain."

In the Bodenstown Churchyard there is a green grave,
And freely around it let winter winds rave—
Far better they suit him—the ruin and gloom—
Till Ireland, a Nation, can build him a tomb.

————o————

THE IRISH WIFE.

BY T. D. M'GEE.

I would not give my Irish wife
  For all the dames of the Saxon land—
I would not give my Irish wife
  For the Queen of France's hand.
For she to me is dearer
  Than castles strong, or lands or life—
An outlaw—so I'm near her
  To love till death my Irish wife.

O, what would be this home of mine—
  A ruined, hermit-haunted place,
But for the light that nightly shines
  Upon its walls from Kathleen's face!
What comfort is a mine of gold—
  What pleasure in a royal life,
If the heart within lay dead and cold,
  If I could not wed my Irish wife.

I knew the law forbade the banns—
  I knew my King abhorred her race—
Who never bent before their clans,
  Must bow before their ladies' grace.

Take all my forfeited domain,
  I cannot wage with kinsmen strife—
Take knightly gear and noble name,
  And I will keep my Irish wife.

My Irish wife has clear blue eyes,
  My Heaven by day, my stars by
    night—
And twinlike truth and fondness lie
  Within her swelling bosom white.
My Irish wife has golden hair—
  Apollo's harp had once such strings—
Apollo's self might pause to hear
  Her bird-like carol when she sings.

I would not give my Irish wife
  For all the dames of the Saxon land —
I would not give my Irish wife
  For the Queen of France's hand.
For she to me is dearer
  Than castles strong, or lands, or life—
In death I would lie near her,
  And rise beside my Irish wife.

————o————

TIPPERARY.

BY FIONULA.

Were you ever in sweet Tipperary, where the fields are so sunny and green,
And the heath-brown Slieve-bloom and the Galtees look down with so proud a mein?
'Tis there you would see more beauty than is on all Irish ground—
God bless you, my sweet Tipperary, for where could your match be found?

They say that your hand is fearful, that darkness is in your eye:
But I'll not let them dare to talk so black and bitter a lie.
Oh! no *macushla storin!* bright, bright, and warm are you,
With hearts as bold as the men of old, to yourself and your country true.

And when there is gloom upon you, bid them think who has brought it there—
Sure a frown or a word of hatred was not made for your face so fair;
You've a hand for the grasp of friendship—another to made them quake,
And they're welcome to whichsoever it pleases them most to take.

Shall our homes, like the huts of Connaught, be crumbled before our eyes?
Shall we fly, like a flock of wild geese, from all that we love and prize?
No! by those who were here before us, no churl shall our tyrant be;
Our land it is theirs by plunder, but, by Brigid, ourselves are free.

No! we do not forget that greatness did once to sweet Erin belong;
No treason or craven spirit was ever our race among;
And no frown or no word of hatred we give—but to pay them back;
In evil we only follow our enemies' darksome track.

Oh! come for a while among us, and give us the friendly hand:
And you'll see that old Tipperary is a loving and gladsome land;
From Upper to Lower Ormond, bright welcomes and smiles will spring;
On the plains of Tipperary the stranger is like a king.

———o———

EMMET'S DEATH.

BY S. F. C.

"He dies to-day," said the heartless judge,
  Whilst he sate him down to the feast,
And a smile was upon his ashy lip
  As he uttered a ribald jest;
For a demon dwelt where his heart should be,
  That lived upon blood and sin,
And oft as that vile judge gave him food
  The demon throbbed within.

"He dies to-day," said the jailer grim,
  While a tear was in his eye;
"But why should I feel so grieved for *him?*
  Sure I've seen many die!
Last night I went to his stony cell,
  With the scanty prison fare—
He was sitting at a table rude,

Plaiting a lock of hair!
And he look'd so mild, with his pale—pale face,
  And he spoke in so kind a way,
That my old breast heav'd with a smothering feel,
  And I knew not what to say!"

"He dies to-day," thought a fair, sweet girl—
  She lacked the life to speak,
For sorrow had almost frozen her blood,
  And white were her lip and cheek—
Despair had drank up her last wild tear,
  And her brow was damp and chill,
And they often felt at her heart with fear,
  For its ebb was all but still.

———o———

THE PATRIOT MOTHER.

BY CARROLL MALONE.

"Come, tell us the name of the rebelly crew
That lifted the pike on the Curragh with you;
Come, tell us their treason and then you'll be free,
Or, by Heaven! you'll swing on you high gallows-tree!"
"*A lanniv! a lanniv!* the shadow of shame
Has never yet fall'n upon one of your name;
And, oh! may the blood from my bosom you drew
In your veins turn to poison when you turn untrue!

" The foul words—oh! let them not blacken your tongue,
That would do to yourself and your country such wrong;
Or the curse of a mother, so bitter and dread,
With the wrath of your God, may they fall on your head!
I have no one but you in this whole world wide;
Yet, false to your pledge, you'll ne'er stand by my side.
If a traitor you lived, you'd be further away
From my heart than if, *true*, you were wrapt in the clay!

" Deeper and darker my mourning would be
For your falsehood so base than your death, proud and free;
Dearer, far dearer than ever, to me,
My darling, you'd be on the high gallows-tree!
'Tis holy, *agra!* with the bravest and best—
Go, go, from my heart, and be joined with the rest:
A lana machree! oh, *a lana machree!*
Sure, a *stag* and a traitor you never will be?"

There's no look of a traitor upon that young brow
That is raised to the tempter so haughtily now;
No traitor e'er held up the firm head so high;
No traitor e'er showed such a proud, flashing eye!
On the high gallows-tree, on the brave gallows-tree,
Where bloomed leaves and blossoms, a sad doom met he;
But it never bore blossom so pure and so fair
As the heart of the martyr that hung from it there!

---o---

KATE OF GARNAVILLA.

BY EDWARD LYSAGHT.

HAVE you been at Garnavilla?
  Have you seen at Garnavilla
Beauty's train trip o'er the plain
  With lovely Kate of Garnavilla?
Oh! she's pure as virgin snows
  Ere they light on woodland hill;
Sweet as dew-drop on wild rose
  Is lovely Kate of Garnavilla!

Philomel, I've listened oft
  To the lay, nigh weeping willow;
Oh, the strains, more sweet, more soft,
  That flows from Kate of Garnavilla!
      Have you been, etc.

As a noble ship I've seen
  Sailing o'er the swelling billow,
So I've marked the graceful mien
  Of lovely Kate of Garnavilla!
      Have you been, etc.

If poet's prayers can' banish cares,
  No cares shall come to Garnavilla;
Joy's bright rays shall gild her days,
  And dove-like peace perch on her
        pillow,
Charming maid of Garnavilla!
Lovely maid of Garnavilla!
Beauty, grace and virtue wait
On lovely Kate of Garnavilla!

---o---

SONG OF THE EJECTED TENANT.

BY WILLIAM PEMBROKE MULCHINOCK.

I LEAVE thee on the morrow, my old accustomed home,
In sadness and in sorrow the hollow world to roam,
Too bold to be a ranger, with heart too full of pride
To crouch unto the stranger whom I have oft defied.
'Tis hard links should be riven that time and friendship wove,
'Tis hard power should be given to hearts that know not love;
'Tis hard when death is near me with certain step, though slow—
When naught is left to cheer me, 'tis hard from home to go.

I leave the chimney-corner, the old familiar chair,
To lay before the scorner my aged bosom bare,
To stand at every dwelling, to catch the rich man's eye,
And with a heart high swelling, for some small pittance sigh.
My hope of joy is broken, my happiness is o'er,
The words of fate are spoken—"beg thou for evermore."
Would that my life were over, my weary life of pain!
Would that the green grave's cover my aged form might gain!

With eye and ear delighted, my only child beside,
I heard her young vow plighted—I saw her made a bride.
In joy we knelt around her; but ere a year went by,
The demon, sickness, found her—she sought her bed to die.
When spring's night stars were paling, our *ululu* was loud,
With woman's bitter wailing, we wound her in her shroud.
She left her child behind her—I reared him on my knee;
Alas! if man was kinder he need not beg with me.

Over the mighty mountain, and by the lone sea shore,
By ice-bound stream and fountain we'll wander evermore;
To us, like a lamb that ranges along a bleak hill-side,
From all the season's changes a shelter is denied.
I will not wish disaster to him that did me wrong,
I leave him to a Master that's merciful as strong;
And when the dawn is breaking upon the land and sea,
I'll say, with bosom aching: "Farewell, old home, to thee."

---o---

HURLING ON THE GREEN.

BY DENNIS HOLLAND.

'Twas night. On Antietam's hight
  The weary warriors lay,
Tired, where the long and bloody fight
  Had tried their worth that day.
Darkness had stilled the strife's alarm,
Though streams of life-blood yet were warm,
  Where the drowsy out-post sank,
And shook his sleeping comrade's arm:
  "You're surely dreaming, Frank."

The startled sleeper gazed toward
  The camp-fire's waning glow;
"Where are we?" "Here on the sloping
  sward;
  And the beaten foe below."
"Thunder! I dreamed of Ireland, lad,
  And a hurling-match." "Well, our foes
  have had
  Full plenty of that I ween."
"But *I* dreamed we tossed the ball like mad
  On a fair broad Irish green."

"Ah, Frank, full many a ball we've hurled,
  And many a head to-day.
The game we've played with our flag unfurled
  Is the game *I* love to play;
When that glorious flag at our front floats
  out,

And with rifle clubbed, and with ringing
  shout,
  We spring 'neath its emerald sheen,
And scatter the foes like a rabble-rout,
  On the crimson-dappled green!"

"Shall we ever again see Ireland, Frank,
  And play upon Irish ground,
This glorious game, where our brethen sank
  In the death of the starved hound?
On our side Erinn,* our island mother,
  Each hurler true as a sworn brother:
  Blither game had ne'er been seen
Than I hope to play some day or other
  To the goal of an Irish green!"

The foe was gone with the morning's light;
  And the flag of emerald hue
Waved proudly above the wooded hight,
  Begemmed with the morning's dew.
And o'er many a fight did that banner wave,
And o'er many an Irish warrior's grave
  Its mourning folds were seen;—
But how many of all that phalanx brave
  Will again see an Irish green?

*Eiro ar fuev-ne; a frequent cry at Irish hurling
matches.

NORA OF CAHIRCIVEEN.

BY MICHAEL SCANLAN.

OH, Nora, dear Nora, you're going to leave us,
    To better your fortune you tempt the rough main,
But think, O mavourneen, how sadly 'twill grieve us,
    To feel we may never behold thee again.
Oh, blame me not, then, that my hot tears are starting,
    Already in fancy the sea rolls between,
And the light of our home, like a dream, is departing,
    And may never come back to old Cahirciveen.

When the bright summer moon thro' the old oak is shining,
    And the note of the harp calls the young and the gay;
When the swains of the village of love-wreaths are twining,
    I'll think of my darling who's far—far away.
When the lads to the dance will lead each village maiden,
    I'll think of the foot that tripped light o'er the green;
I'll turn from their mirth, for my spirit, o'erladen,
    Will weep for the beauty of Cahirciveen.

Oh, flatter me not with your speedy returning,
    Few—few that come back from the far happy shore;
Keep the star of your land in your inmost soul burning,
    But kiss the green hills, for you'll see them no more.
Let me fold you once more to my poor heart that's broken;
    God guard you; remember the days that have been;
From the far distant land send a sign or a token
    That you'll never forget us in Cahirciveen.

Woe—woe to the mother! alas! for the daughter,
    And the dreams that were twined for the bright days to come;
A token of love has come over the water,
    A wreath of green laurel from poor Nora's tomb.
On the wild hills of Kerry the mother is weeping,
    While the lads and the lasses still dance on the green;
'Neath the wild western prairie poor Nora is sleeping,
    Far away from the village of Cahirciveen.

———◇———

"GOD SAVE OLD IRELAND!"

BY THE REV. T. AMBROSE BUTLER.

How fondly now, how proudly now, the exiles' bosoms swell
With thoughts of scenes of loveliness by lake and hill and dell!—
With mem'ries of the sunny hours that faded soon away,
Like golden light that gleams awhile at dawning hour of day!
And tear-drops glisten in the eyes of gallant men and true—
The forest-oak, like fragile flow'r, oft bears the morning dew—
Oh! native isle!—the heart distills such tribute-tears for thee!—
God save Old Ireland!—struggling Ireland!—Ireland o'er the sea!
God save Old Ireland!—struggling Ireland!—Ireland o'er the sea!

How bravely now, how nobly now, the few and fearless stand—
The struggling sons in Freedom's van who work for mother-land!
Who dare the dungeon;—face the steel;—and mount the scaffold high,
Ay!—ready now, like men of old, to bravely fight or die—
Oh! truly shall their mem'ries live—their gallant deeds be told,
And Allen's name shine through the years a burnish'd lamp of gold!

And Celtic mothers pray to Heav'n their sons as brave may be!
God save Old Ireland!—struggling Ireland!—Ireland o'er the sea!
God save Old Ireland!—struggling Ireland!—Ireland o'er the sea!

Oh! may the swan-like dying notes of Erin's martyr'd braves
Be wafted far and move the hearts of those beyond the waves—
The scattered Celts whose discord dire has dimm'd our glorious green—
May all unite in Larkins' name—let women chant his *caione!*.
Oh! let those hands that brush aside the noble soldier's tear
Be stretch'd to those who vow revenge beside O'Brien's bier!
Swear—swear you'll struggle side by side to make your country free!
God save Old Ireland!—struggling Ireland!—Ireland o'er the sea!
God save Old Ireland!—struggling Ireland!—Ireland o'er the sea!

* Pronounced keen.

———o———

THE SHAMROCK AND LAUREL.

BY REV. WILLIAM M'CLURE.

There's a lofty love abounding
In the emblem of a land;
There's fellowship confounding
The evil mind and hand;
In the token of a nation,
In the flow'ret of a race;
And a multiform oblation
Is uplifted by the grace
And patriotism of millions—
To the hearthstones and hamlets
Where gush the native fountains;
To the valleys and the streamlets,
The cities and the mountains—
With a pride as high as Ilion's!

As the lily was the glory
Of the olden flag of France;
As the rose illumes the story
Of the Albion's advance—
In the shamrock is communion
Of all Irish faith and love;
And the laurel crows the union

Of grandeurs interwove
'Round the temple of the chainless
To the laurel fill libations,
The cup with shamrocks wreathing;
And before the monarch-nations
Raise the symbol, breathing:
" Equal Rights "—to lordings gainless!

Interweave the lowly shamrock,
Freedom's laurel to endow;
Ay! unite with Ireland's shamrock
Columbia's laurel-bough—
For there's hope and help unchary
Columbia's skies beneath,
And from every cliff and prairie,
To Erin's hills of heath,
Salutations, clear and cheerful,
Resound across the ocean;
And Celts, in might increasing,
With patriot emotion,
Vow in their souls unceasing:
" We'll avenge thee, Mother Tearful!"

———o———

"STAMPING OUT."

BY GEN. CHARLES G. HALPINE (" Miles O'Reilly").

" We must stamp out the fires of this Fenian insurrection and quench its embers in the blood of the wretches who are its promoters."—*London Times.*

Ay, stamp away! Can you stamp it out—
This quenchless fire of a nation's freedom?
Your feet are broad and your legs are stout,
But stouter for this you'll need 'em!
You have stamped away for six hundred years,
But again and again the Old Cause rallies,
Pikes gleam in the hands of our mountaineers,
And with scythes come the men from our valleys;

The steel-clad Norman as he roams,
  Is faced by our naked gallowglasses,
We lost the plains and our pleasant homes,
  But we held the hills and passes!
    And still the beltane fires at night,
      "If not a man were left to feed 'em—
    By widows' hands piled high and bright,
      Flashed far the flame of Freedom!

Ay, stamp away! Can you stamp it out,
  Or how have your brutal arts been baffled?
You have wielded the power of rope and knot,
  Fire, dungeon, sword and scaffold.
But still, as from each martyr's hand
  The Fiery Cross fell down in fighting,
A thousand sprang to seize the brand,
  Our beltane fires relighting!
And once again through Irish nights,
  O'er every dark hill redly streaming,
And numerous as the heavenly lights
  Our rebel fires were gleaming!
    And though again might fail that flame,
      Quenched in the blood of its devoted,
    Fresh chieftains 'rose, fresh clansmen came,
      And again the Old Flag floated!

That fire will burn, that flag will float,
  By Virtue nursed, by Valor tended—
Till with one fierce clutch upon your throat
  Your Moloch reign is ended!
It may be now, or it may be then,
  That the hour will come we have hoped for ages—
But, failing and failing, we try again,
  And again the conflict rages.
Our hate though hot is a patient hate,
  Deadly and patient to catch you tripping—
And your years are many, your crimes are great,
  And the scepter is from you slipping.
    But stamp away with your brutal hoof,
      While the fires to scorch you are upward cleaving,
    For, with bloody shuttles, the warp and woof
      Of your shroud the Fates are weaving!

THE DYING GIRL.

BY R. D. WILLIAMS.

FROM a Munster vale they brought her,
  From the pure and balmy air,
An Ormond peasant's daughter,
  With blue eyes and golden hair.
They brought her to the city,
  And she faded slowly there,
Consumption has no pity
  For the blue eyes and golden hair.

When I saw her first reclining,
  Her lips were moved in prayer,
And the setting sun was shining
  Oh her loosened golden hair.

When our kindly glances met her,
  Deadly brilliant was her eye,
And she said that she was better,
  While we knew that she must die.

She speaks of Munster valleys,
  The patron, dance and fair,
And her thin hand feebly dallies
  With her scattered golden hair.
When silently we listened
  To her breath with quiet care,
Her eyes with wonder glistened,
  And she asked us what was there.

The poor thing smiled to ask it,
　And her pretty mouth laid bare,
Like gems within a casket,
　A string of pearlets rare.
We said that we were trying
　By the gushing of her blood,
And the time she took in sighing,
　To know if she were good.

Well, she smil'd and chatted gayly,
　Tho' we saw in mute despair
The hectic brighter daily,
　And the death-dew on her hair.
And oft her wasted fingers
　Beating time upon the bed,
O'er some old tune she lingers,
　And she bows her golden head.

At length the harp is broken
　And the spirit in its strings,

As the last decree is spoken,
　To its source exulting springs.
Descending swiftly from the skies,
　Her guardian angel came,
He struck God's lightning from her eyes,
　And bore him back the flame.

Before the sun had risen
　Thro' the lark-loved morning air,
Her young soul left its prison,
　Undefiled by sin or care.
I stood beside the couch in tears
　Where pale and calm she slept,
And tho' I've gazed on death for years,
　I blush not that I wept.
I check'd with effort pity's sighs,
　And left the matron there,
To close the curtains of her eyes,
　And bind her golden hair.

DREAMS.

BY JOSEPH C. CLARKE.

Sweet kissings of the lips of night,
　What moves your eerie springs?
And whence troop out your angels white,
　Fair dreams, on lily wings?

Deep from the sleep-masked soul a ray
　Steals forth of buried times,
And blurred by changings of to-day,
　Pale Mem'ry wakes her chimes.

They sound with silver voices sweet,
　And all her dim-browed throng
Moves softly and with soundless feet
　Their olden paths along.

Adown dead faces course hot tears
　That burn upon the cheek,
And, brimming with the loss of years,
　Their lips all trembling speak.

Till fair and light will Fancy sweep,
　With thousand sprites and wiles,
That, mingling, twirl in magic leap
　Thro' Memory's grove defiles.

Flow'rs bloom supernal 'neath their tread,
　Lute tinklings fill the trees,
The gorgeous sun shines golden red,
　And perfumes clasp the breeze.

Then passion, with her blazing mien,
　And earnest, panting crew,
Step in and dance the lines between,
　And pulse the heart-string through.

When 'mid its laden, shadow-bliss,
　A shroud o'er all's unfurled,
And time, with envious, serpent hiss,
　Awakes us to the world.

And are these unrealities—
　Each form and lucent beam
That fled but as existence flees?
　Are these or life—a dream?

For is't not even thus as sweeps
　Life's ship o'er waters blind?
That passion glares and mem'ry weeps
　'Mid fancy's sons of wind?

What then's this spirit-life that flies,
　While visioned phantasms roll?
Sees it but as thro' others' eyes?
　Is it a deeper soul?

We'll know not till uplifts the dark,
　And life and dreams shall flee;
For kindred waves float each frail bark—
　Passion, fancy, memory.

THE WIDOW'S MESSAGE TO HER SON.

BY ELLEN FORRESTER.

" Remember, Denis, all I bade you say;
　Tell him we're well and happy, thank the Lord,

But of our troubles, since he went away,
   You'll mind, avick, and never say a word;
      Of cares and troubles, sure, we've all our share,
      The finest summer isn't always fair.

"Tell him the spotted heifer calved in May,
   She died, poor thing; but that you needn't mind;
Nor how the constant rain destroyed the hay;
   But tell him God to us was ever kind.
      And when the fever spread the country o'er,
      His mercy kept the 'sickness' from our door.

"Be sure you tell him how the neighbors came
   And cut the corn and stored it in the barn;
'Twould be as well to mention them by name—
   Pat Murphy, Ned M'Cabe, and James M'Carn,
      And big Tim Daly from behind the hill;
      But say, agra—Oh, say I missed him still.

"They came with ready hands our toil to share—
   'Twas then I missed him most—my own right hand;
I felt, although kind hearts were 'round me there,
   The kindest heart beat in a foreign land.
      Strong hand! brave heart! oh, severed far from me,
      By many a weary league of shore and sea.

"And tell him she was with us—he'll know who;
   Mavourneen, hasn't she the winsome eyes,
The darkest, deepest, brightest, bonniest blue
   I ever saw except in summer skies.
      And such black hair! It is the blackest hair
      That ever rippled o'er neck so fair.

"Tell him old Pincher fretted many a day,
   And moped, poor dog, 'twas well he didn't die,
Crouched by the road-side how he watched the way,
   And sniffed the travelers as they passed him by—
      Hail, rain, or sunshine, sure, 'twas all the same,
      He listened for the foot that never came.

"Tell him the house is lonesome-like and cold,
   The fire itself seems robbed of half its light;
But, maybe 'tis my eyes are growing old,
   And things look dim before my failing sight.
      For all that tell him 'twas my self that spun
      The shirts you bring, and stitched them every one.

"Give him my blessing, morning, noon and night,
   Tell him my prayers are offered for his good,
That he may keep his Maker still in sight,
   And firmly stand as his brave father stood,
      True to his name, his country, and his God,
      Faithful at home, and steadfast still abroad."

—————o—————

"PERSEVERE."

BY JOHN BROUGHAM.

ROBERT, the Bruce, in the dungeon stood,
  Waiting the hour of doom;
Behind him the Palace of Holyrood,
  Before him, a nameless tomb.
And the foam on his lip was flecked with red,
As away to the past his memory sped,
Upcalling the day of his great renown
When he won and he wore the Scottish
    crown;
  Yet come there shadow, or come there
    shine,
  The spider is spinning his thread so fine.

"I have sat on the royal seat of Scone,"
  He muttered, below his breath;
"It's a luckless change, from a kingly throne
  To a felon's shameful death."
And he clenched his hand in his despair,
And he struck at the shapes that were gath-
    ering there,
Pacing his cell in impatient rage,
As a new-caught lion paces his cage;
  But come there shadow, or come there
    shine,
  The spider is spinning his web so fine.

"Oh, were it my fate to yield up my life
  At the head of my liegemen all,
In the foremost shock of the battle-strife
  Breaking my country's thrall,
I'd welcome death from the foeman's steel,
Breathing a prayer for old Scotland's weal;
But here, where no pitying heart is nigh,
By a loathsome hand, it is hard to die;"
  Yet come there shadow, or come there
    shine,
  The spider is spinning his thread so fine.

"Time and again have I fronted the pride
  Of the tyrant's vast array.
But only to see, on the crimson tide,
  My hopes swept far away.

Now a landless chief, and a crownless king,
On the broad—broad earth, not a living thing
To keep me court, save yon insect small
Striving to reach from wall to wall;"
  For come there shadow, or come there
    shine,
  The spider is spinning his thread so fine.

"Work—work as a fool, as I have done,
  To the loss of your time and pain—
The space is too wide to be bridged across,
  You but waste your strength in vain."
And Bruce, for the moment, forgot his grief,
His soul now filled with the same belief,
That howsoever the issue went,
For evil or good was the omen sent;
  And come there shadow or come there
    shine,
  The spider is spinning his thread so fine.

As a gambler watches his turning card
  On which his all is staked;
As a mother waits for the hopeful word
  For which her soul has ached;
It was thus Bruce watched, with every sense
Centered alone in that look intense;
All rigid he stood with unuttered breath,
Now white, now red, but still as death;
  Yet come there shadow, or come there
    shine,
  The spider is spinning his thread so fine.

Six several times the creature tried,
  When at the seventh: "See—see!
He has spanned it over," the captive cried,
  "Lo! a bridge of hope to me;
Thee, God, I thank, for this lesson here
Has tutored my soul to Persevere!"
And it served him well, for ere long he wore
In freedom the Scottish crown once more;
  And come there shadow, or come there
    shine,
  The spider is spinning his thread so fine.

---o---

PASTHEEN FION.

(*From the Irish.*)

BY SAMUEL FERGUSON.

[In Hardiman's "Irish Minstrelsy" there is a note upon the original of *Pastheen Fion.* The name may be translated either fair youth or fair maiden, and the writer supposes it to have a political meaning, and to refer to the son of James II. Whatever may have been the intention of the author, it is, on the surface, an exquisite love song, and as such we have retained it.]

OH, my fair Pastheen is my heart's delight;
Her gay heart laughs in her blue eye bright;
Like the apple blossom her bosom white,
And her neck like the swan's on a March morn bright!

Then, Oro, come with me—come with me—come with me!
Oro, come with me! brown girl, sweet!
And, oh, I would go through snow and sleet,
If you would come with me, my brown girl, sweet!

Love of my heart, my fair Pastheen!
Her cheeks are as red as the rose's sheen,
But my lips have tasted no more, I ween,
Than the glass I drank to the health of my queen!
    Then, Oro, come with me—come with me—come with me!
    Oro, come with me! brown girl, sweet!
    And oh! I would go through snow and sleet
    If you would come with me, my brown girl, sweet!

Were I in the town, where's mirth and glee,
Or 'twixt two barrels of barley bree,
With my fair Pastheen upon my knee,
'Tis I would drink to her pleasantly!
    Then, Oro, come with me—come with me—come with me!
    Oro, come with me! brown girl, sweet!
    And, oh, I would go through snow and sleet
    If you would come with me, my brown girl, sweet!

Nine nights I lay in longing and pain,
Betwixt two bushes, beneath the rain,
Thinking to see you, love, once again;
But whistle and call were all in vain!
    Then, Oro, come with me—come with me—come with me!
    Oro, come with me! brown girl, sweet!
    And oh, I would go through snow and sleet
    If you would come with me, my brown girl, sweet!

I'll leave my people, both friend and foe;
From all the girls in the world I'll go;
But from you, sweetheart, oh, never, oh, no!
Till I lie in the coffin stretched, cold and low!
    Then, Oro, come with me—come with me—come with me!
    Oro, come with me! brown girl, sweet!
    And, oh, I would go through the snow and sleet
    If you would come with me, my brown girl, sweet!

———o———

PATER NOSTER.

BY M. J. HEFFERNAN.

FATHER of all! who reign'st supreme
  Beyond yon blue, o'er-arching sphere,
As Thy forever glorious name
  Is hallow'd there, so be it here;
Grant that our numbered hours may be
  So many hymns of praise to Thee!

"Thy kingdom come!" ah, yes, my God!
  That hope is sweet, indeed, to those
Who, in this cold world, feel the rod
  Of deep affliction, and the throes
Of pain: blest are they when the tomb
  Receives them; "oh, Thy kingdom come!"

Yet, Father! shouldst Thou deem it right
  To shower on me from year to year
Those miseries which crush and blight
  Young hope, no murmurs shalt Thou hear
From me, for I will utter none:
No—then as now—"Thy will be done!"

"Give us this day our daily bread!"
  That thus our hearts be always free
From sordid cares; and so be led
  To think more on Thy works and Thee.
Lord! keep our souls fed constantly
  With Faith, and Hope, and Charity.

If there be those who would me wrong
  In thought, or wish, or deed, or word,
Let their crimes be the first among
  Those that Thou'lt forgive; and grant, oh,
    Lord!
That I, too, may be forgiven
  For all my crimes 'gainst man and Heaven!

Thou knowest an inheritance
  Of frailty's ours, since first were driven
Our common parents from the once
  Elysian path that led to Heaven;
Then save us, Lord, from evil when
  Temptation spreads her lures.   Amen!

----o----

THE MOORE CENTENNIAL.

1879.

BY B. DORAN KILLIAN.

Long, long had Banba lain
  Within the circling main,
A lost Atlantis to her sister lands,
  Dumb with exceeding woe and voiceless
    pain:
  Her broken Harp, beside,
  Swayed in the songless tide,
That rose and fell, and rose and fell, in
    vain:
  'Till those who sailed her seas
  Said, sorrowing, words like these;
" Alas, poor Banba's hive of honey-bees
  Will never swarm again."

Not that her soul was old—
  Not that her clime was cold—
Or bosky fields and thymy woods were bare,
  Exhaust of juicy branch or pregnant
    mold;
  No! but that Hate and Feud
  Left her no calm to brood,
And none could sing who would, or could,
    would dare—
  The Themes of Hearth and Wold—
  Fame's Hesper fruits of gold—
That hung, in wealth untold,
  Yet turned to ashes there.

This—but not this alone—
  With a high pride unknown
To baser soils and less heroic mood,
  She sought the cause of every Fated One;
  Bared her breast to Bigot Zeal,
  Racked her arms on Change's wheel,
And held the Old and Leal, the Only Good;
  Then, with long suffering worn,
  Of all but Honor shorn,
In proud reserve of scorn,
  Scarce knew herself undone.

Who, the all-gifted one
  To loose her stricken tongue?
Whose, the all-potent hand to lead her
    forth—
  Roll back the gathered clouds and show
    the sun?
  Restring her ancient lyre—
  Restore her native fire—

And send her Song and Story 'round the
    Earth—
  So all who heard should say,
  " The Dead, but yesterday,
Is heard, again, in Freedom's choir
  And still has heart for Mirth."

O! who but you, Tom Moore,
  Made her New Life secure,
In pierceless panoply of deathless words—
  Whose burning luster blinds who would
    obscure;
  Soothed, to a sober heat,
  Her heart's convulsive beat,
And stilled the bigot strain that jarred its
    chords;
  Dowered her long-wasted strength,
  With Grecian grace, at length,
And quickening every power to feel,
  Gave hardness to endure.

Blessed be your natal day!
  Praised be your name alway!
Of Iber's later stock the first in fame,
  For Fancy-soaring Song and Freedom-
    saving Lay;
  And, O, while Banba's fields
  A single songster yields,
Be yours the name most green, and yours
    the grave most gay
  With all the gifts of spring
  That poet art can bring
To show, what else takes wing,
  God's Genius comes to stay.

Nor in your motherland
  Be the sole homage planned—
Where Hudson pours the exile-greeting
    wave,
Let sculpture sketch the frieze, and Ariel
    wave the wand—
  Where Northern Cedars grow,
  Let your immortelles blow,
And to the Schuylkill's flow, your name roll
    grand;
  Incorporate with the clime,
  And blending—dream divine!—
Hy-Braisil's bloom and Eman's prime
  From ocean strand to strand,

In mild Bermuda's groves,
 When Summer, sauntering, roves
Through languid airs and arbors breathing
        balm,
 To songs of yours, let Cupid yoke his
        doves,
   And Samos—sacred isle!—
   Forget her loss and smile—
In you, Anacreon lives and Sappho loves;
  Through you the Persian's shrines
  With Banba's Baal-fire shines,
While Iran's God inclines,
   And all the world approves!

O, Bard of every race!
  O, Song of seraph grace!
While bosoms glow or valor nerves an arm,
  Our heart's most sacred core shall be your
        place.
    Our Land, our cause, and you
    Shall kindred thoughts renew,
While Truth has words to please or voice to
        charm.
    But most to woman's call,
    At home-like hearth or hall,
To Irish Music's swooning fall,
   We'll pledge you, hand in hand.

———o———

IN THE PRISON CELL.

BY MRS. MARY J. O'DONOVAN ROSSA.

[Written after a visit to her husband in Portland Prison, in 1866.]

WITHIN the precincts of the prison bound,
 Treading the sunlit courtyard to a hall
Roomy and unadorned, where the light
 Through screenless windows glaringly did
        fall.

Within the precincts of the prison walls,
 With rushing memories and bated breath—
With heart elate, and light, swift step that
        smote
 Faint echoes in this house of living death,

Midway I stood in bright expectancy—
 Tightly I clasped my babe—my eager
        sight
Hungrily glancing down the long, low room,
 To where a door bedimmed the wall's pure
        white.

They moved—the noiseless locks! The
        portal fell
 With clank of chain wide open, and the
        room
Held him, my wedded love—my heart stood
        still
 With sudden shock—with sudden sense of
        doom.

Oh! for a moment's twilight that might hide
 The harsh, tanned features, once so soft
        and fair!
The shrunken eyes that with a feeble flash
 Smiled on my presence and his infant's
        there!

Oh! for a shadow on the cruel sun
 That mocked thy father, baby, with its
        glare!
Oh! for the night of nothingness, or death,
 Ere thou, my love, this felon's garb should
        wear!

My heart that had with glad, impatient
        bounds
 Counted the moments ere he should
        appear,
Drew back at sight so changed, and,
        shivering, waited,
 Pulselessly waited, while his step drew
        near!

My heart stood still, that had with gladsome
        bounds
 Marked the slow moments ere he should
        appear—
My heart stood still and waited while his
        voice—
 His voice, though altered, smote my quiet
        ear.

It needed not, my Love, those pain-wrung
        words,
 Falling with sad distinctness from thy lips,
To tell a tale of insult, abject toil,
 And day-long labor, hewing Portland
        steeps.

It needed not, my Love, this anguished
        glance,
 This fading fire within thy gentle eyes,
To rouse the torpid voices of my heart,
 Till all the sleeping Heavens shall hear
        their cries.

Yet must we cry: "How long, oh Lord—
        how long?"
 For seven red centuries a country's woe
Has wept the prayer in tears of blood; and
        still
 Our tears to-night for fresher victims flow!

REVELRY OF THE DYING.

[When it is remembered that the author of the following extraordinary stanzas was stricken down soon after they were written, they will present to the reader a flash of ghastly wit seldom exceeded in grimness. They were written, we believe, by an Irish officer of the Anglo-East-Indian army during the reign of a fearful pestilence.

WE meet 'neath the sounding rafter,
  And the walls around are bare;
As they shout to our peals of laughter
  It seems that the dead are there.
But stand to your glasses, steady!
  We drink to your comrades' eyes.
Quaff a glass to the dead already;
  And hurrah! for the next that dies.

Not here are the goblets flowing;
  Not here is the vintage sweet;
'Tis cold, as our hearts are growing,
  And dark as the doom we meet.
But stand to your glasses, steady!
  And soon shall our pulses rise,
A cup to the dead already;
  Hurrah! for the next that dies.

Not a sigh for the lot that darkles;
  Not a tear for the friends that sink;
We'll fall 'midst the wine-cup's sparkles
  As mute as the wine we drink.
So stand to your glasses, steady!
  'Tis this that the respite buys;
One cup to the dead already;
  Hurrah! for the next that dies.

Time was when we frowned at others;
  We thought we were wiser then.
Ha—ha! let them think of their mothers
  Who hope to see them again.
So stand to your glasses, steady!
  The thoughtless are here the wise;
A cup to the dead already;
  Hurrah! for the next that dies.

There's many a hand that's shaking;
  There's many a cheek that's sunk;
But soon, though our hearts are break-
    ing,
  They'll burn with the wine we've
    drunk.
So stand to your glasses, steady!
  'Tis here the revival lies;
A cup to the dead already;
  Hurrah! for the next that dies.

There's a mist on the glass congealing;
  'Tis the hurricane's fiery breath;
And thus does the warmth of feeling
  Turn ice in the grasp of death.
Ho! stand to your glasses, steady!
  For a moment the vapor flies;
A cup to the dead already;
  Hurrah! for the next that dies.

Who dreads to the dust returning?
  Who shrinks from the sable shore,
Where the high and haughty yearning
  Of the soul shall sing no more?
Ho! stand to your glasses, steady!
  The world is a world of lies;
A cup to the dead already;
  Hurrah! for the next that dies.

Cut off from the land that bore us,
  Betrayed by the land we find,
Where the brightest have gone before
    us,
  And the dullest remain behind.
Stand!—stand to your glasses, steady!
  'Tis all we have left to prize;
A cup to the dead already;
  And hurrah! for the next that dies.

MUSINGS.

BY J. E. FITZGERALD.

MUSING, ever musing, on the glories fled and past,
Thinking, ever thinking, if the gloom will always last,
Dreaming, ever dreaming, of a morning yet to come,
When motherland shall rise again triumphant from the tomb.

Reading, ever reading, o'er her history's crimson page,
'Till I lay the volume by me with very hate and rage,
And wish the strength of millions were centered all in me,
To wrench the Gordian knot, my motherland, from thee.

Praying, ever praying, with all a patriot's zeal,
  With all the fire and fervor that vengeance dire can feel,

That he who guides the destinies of nations here below,
Would send some angel of his wrath to strike the tyrant low.

Longing, weary longing, for the dawn of freedom's day,
For the cannon and the lances, and the men in strong array,
And the battle field all crimsoned with tyrant blood accursed,
And the rag of Saxon tyranny forever in the dust.

———o———

AN EXILE'S WOOING.

BY M. HIGGINS.

COME—come to me, love, I am lonely—
  I'm lonely and lowly and sad;
Come, darling, with you, and you only,
  Can pleasure or solace be had.
Tho' bright be the smiles of the many
  Who carol around me to-night,
The shade of your absence, dear Annie,
  Is hiding my heart from their light.

I'm cased in no mail of moroseness,
  I nurse no aversion to joy,
Yet all their good-humor seems grossness,
  Their kindness contrived to annoy.
Their music is rolling and bounding,
  Their laughter chimes cheery and free,
A tenebræ, dolefully sounding,
  Might wake as much mirth within me.

I wish to their songs you were listening
  And lending the sweetness they lack;
I wish that your blue eyes were glistening
  On mine, giving fond gazes back;
I wish that your fay foot was mingling
  In dances I coldly evade—
Ah! soon would be burning and tingling
  The pulse now so icy and staid.

I wish the next home-wending steamer,
  Which trails her long plumes thro' the
    gale,
Could carry your sorrowing dreamer
  Back—back to beloved Innisfail.
What joy ere the sunny June days slip
  Away like gold beads from life's threads,
To wander once more around Leixlip
  And drive thro' the strawberry beds.

With mountain-dew elixir gargle
  The throat that grows sore from my sighs,
Have a walk by your side through the
    Dargle,
  On Saggard's green slades cool my eyes;

Pass o'er every path where the plodder
  Each Sabbath seeks, seldom in vain,
Fair scenes and fresh air by the Dodder,
  To winnow all care from his brain.

I'd wish to go fish every nook a
  Fat trout loves to haunt in Loch Bray;
And be blest if I felt Poul-o-Phuca,
  Baptize me anew in her spray.
Faith the wag and the wit of these revels,
  Who haply see only in me
Some tethered ass owned by blue devils,
  Would gape at the madcap I'd be.

But the gruff voice of power prohibits
  My own land again to be mine,
Every right save to jails and to gibbets
  Must we who love Erin resign.
'Tis true that the prison and halter
  Might leave us unlodged or unstrung,
If we learn to truckle and palter
  With servile demeanor and tongue.

'Tis true, if we chose to go limping
  And crouching to life's latest goal,
Some gold might be twined with the
    gimping,
  Which bound us fast body and soul.
But better, far better to molder,
  'Neath hill-ferns gracing a grave,
Than thus with bowed head and crook'd
    shoulder,
  Conserve the vile shape of a slave.

In the land where no fetters can gall us
  We live with a vow to return,
When freedom and vengeance recall us,
  And beacons of hope for us burn.
Then come to me, love, I am lonely,
  'Mid mirth's pealing pipes a poor drone—
Come, darling, with you, and you only,
  Can pleasure and solace be known.

———o———

KATE OF KILLASHEE.

BY WILLIAM COLLINS.

BRIGHT are the heath-blossoms on Beara's mountain brown,
And bright the waves of Camolin that roll past Longford town;

But brighter still than flower or rill, and lovelier far is she,
The pride and boast of Longford, fair Kate of Killashee.

Sweet is the rippling laughter, the music of the tongue,
Like some old Irish melody by siren played or sung;
And like the sunny waters that go dancing to the sea,
In light and beauty beaming, is Kate of Killashee.

How bright her blushing glances of love whene'er we met,
Like rainbow tints upon the rose with dew of morning wet,
And bright the love-light shining from her eyes of hazel brown—
Oh! she's the star of Leinster, the pride of Longford town.

Fair Kate, 'tis mine to wander afar from Erin's strand—
Alone beside the Hudson's wave, within the strangers' land;
But backward ever flies my heart to home and love and thee—
To Longford's pleasant valleys and the Rose of Killashee.

---o---

A BROTHER'S CONSOLATION.

BY MICHAEL CAVANAGH.

They buried him on the "Rock" at the foot of the "Round Tower."—LETTER FROM HOME

SEARCH every fane the island 'round,
  Where rest the sainted and the brave,
Thou'lt never view more hallowed ground
  Than thy young baby's grave.

No king who ruled on Erin's throne,
  No chief who glory o'er her shed,
A nobler monument doth own
  Than that which marks his bed.

On "Patrick's Holy Rock" he sleeps,
  Where kings stood fenced by heroes' spears;
The "Tower" that o'er him vigil keeps,
  Stands there two thousand years.

The bones of prelates canonized
  Lie thick beneath those ruins grey;
The blood of martyrs fertilized
  That consecrated clay.

That grave is his by "right divine"—
  His sires ruled Munster's hills and plains;
The blood of Cormac's royal line
  Ran red within his veins.

A scion of that noble stock
  Which never flinched from friend or foe,
Has claims on his ancestral rock
  'Twere treason to forego.

In kindred dust his body lies,
  Where Erin's best through ages trod:
With kindred angels in the skies,
  His soul adores its God.

Then, though maternal tears you weep,
  While Nature's grief your bosom wrings,
Look up! Thank God, your boy's asleep,
  In "Cashel of the Kings!"

---o---

GATHERING THE CLANS.

BY RICHARD OULAHAN.

FROM Dublin gates to Galway, and up from Derry walls,
Through fierce Red Owen's tribe-lands, the rallying cry appals!
Kildare and Kerry, Clare and Cork, the gathering clans prepare:
And they ne'er will furl the old Green Flag till Freedom perches there!

A few days' earnest work would arm full fifty thousand more,
Whose hearts throb wildly for the fray, by Liffey, Boyne and Nore—
Each rifle true and dollar sent, before our Flag's unfurled,
Give heart and hope to fatherland, and joy to all the world!

The Irish army laugh to scorn Bull's coward, brutal boast,
To "stamp out," like his plague-struck Gods, Green Erin's Fenian Host—
Such bugbear threats advance the claim of outraged manhood's cause;
But the soldiers of the Sunburst accept reprisal laws.

He knows his bloated lords would hang—his cities light the sky;
And leave a wilderness of walls where Leeds and London lie!
For Freedom's boon—for land and life—our patriot-brothers smite,
And they ne'er will furl the old Green Flag till vict'ry ends the fight.

Shall those brave fellows "in the gap" call madly, but in vain,
For arms and aid, too long delayed through discord's fatal bane?
By martyrs' graves and prison-braves! the living and the dead!
We must not let the old Green Flag go down below the Red!

———o———

LOUGH INE.*

BY FITZJAMES O'BRIEN.

I KNOW a lake where the cool waves break,
  And softly sink on the silver sand!
No steps intrude on that solitude,
  And no voice save mine disturbs the
    strand.

There a mountain bold, like a giant of old,
  Turned to stone by some magic spell,
Uprears in might his misty hight,
  Like a warder watching o'er flood and fell.

In the midst doth smile a little isle,
  Whose verdure shames the emerald's
    green;
On its grassy side, in ruin'd pride,
  A castle of old is darkling seen!

On the lofty crest, the wild cranes nest:
  In its halls the sheep good shelter find;
And the ivy shades where a hundred-blades
  Were hung when their owners in sleep
    reclin'd.

That chieftain of old, could he now behold
  His lordly tower a shepherd's pen,
His corse long dead, from its narrow bed
  Would start with anger and shame again!

It is sweet to gaze, when the sun's bright
    rays
  Are cooling themselves in the trembling
    wave;
But 'tis sweeter far when the evening star
  Shines like a smile o'er Friendship's grave.

Then the hollow shells, through their
    wreathed cells,
  Make music on the silent shore,
As the summer breeze, through the distant
    trees,
  Murmurs in fragant breathings o'er.

And the sea-weed shines like the hidden
    mines
  Of the fairy cities beneath the sea;
And the wave washed stones are as bright
    as the thrones
  Of the ancient kings of Araby!

Oh! were it my lot in that fairy spot
  To live forever, and dream 'twere mine;
Courts might woo, and kings pursue,
  Ere I would leave thee—loved Lough Ine!

*A beautiful salt-water lake in the County of Cork.

———o———

AWAKE, MY DEAR COUNTRY.

(*Lines written on reading:* "*Oh! Blame Not The Bard.*")

BY THOMAS P. MASTERSON.

AWAKE, my dear country, and dry up thy tears,
  Deep grief unavailing too long has been thine;
Oh! heed not the minstrel that fosters thy fears,
  And bids thee the dream of thy freedom resign.
Look 'round on thy children who secretly sigh,
  Tho' treason's their love they await but the day
When 'neath thy green banner they'll throng at thy cry,
  For oh! there are men who've not learnt to betray.

Then rouse to the struggle, we'll shame not our sires,
   Nor yet undistinguished shall we pass away;
Nor need we the torch from the funeral pyres
   Of our country to light us thro' dignity's way.
We seek not the honors injustice bestows,
   We scorn the distinction by treachery bought;
And the beacon that lights us to liberty throws
   No reflection of shame on the path we have sought.

Awake, dearest Ireland! thy pride has not fled,
   Nor broken's the spirit inflamed thee of yore;
Nor dimmed are the rays of the glory that shed
   Its brightest effulgence for aye on thy shore.
Unfading's our hope for the land that we love,
   Our complainings no more shall be heard o'er the earth,
And our harp shall but tell of how nobly we strove
   To rescue dear Ireland, the land of our birth.

Then think not the tyrant who rivets thy chains
   Can weep for the captive his cruelty binds—
The captive who still her despoiler disdains,
   She asks not his pity and scorns his designs.
Then cease thy lamenting, that hour is now past,
   Like men, let us true to our purpose abide;
The tried and the trusted have gathered at last,
   Then on for dear Ireland! we've God on our side.

---o---

THE EXILE.

BY JOHN WALSH.

To Erin with a blessing,
   So far—so far away,
Do I send my heart's caressing,
   This merry Christmas day.
Far beyond the gliding waves,
   Where the wild winds moan above,
Raving thro' the rushing waters,
   Do I speed my meed of love,
Till it light within the glen,
   On my happy boyhood's home—
Oh, to Erin, with a blessing,
   My heart to-day will roam.

Oh, long since we have parted—
   The green old land and I,
Since, crushed and broken-hearted,
   From her bright face did I fly;
For I could not bear to think
   That the tyrant's grasp would hold,

And I tried to burst her bondage,
   With my brother exiles bold.
We failed—mavrone, how sadly
   Did I leave my boyhood's home—
Oh, to Erin, with a blessing,
   My heart to-day will roam.

Shall I live to see you, darling?
   Shall we meet for evermore?
For I dream from night till morning
   Of your green and sunny shore.
Thro' the golden summer sheen,
   Thro' the frosty winter's haze,
Thro' the midnight's dancing shadows
   And the noontide's fervid blaze,
My thoughts are ever turning
   To my happy boyhood's home—
Oh, to Erin, with a blessing,
   My heart to-day will roam.

---o---

MY NOBLE IRISH GIRL.

BY DR. L. REYNOLDS.

I LOVE thee—oh, that word is tame
   To tell how dear thou art;
No seraph feels a holier flame
   Than that which thrills my heart.

How mild and innocent the brow,
   Where thy dark ringlets curl,
Thy soul is pure as virgin dawn,
   My noble Irish girl.

I love to gaze upon thy smile,
  Thine eyes so bright and gay;
For there's no stain of art or guile
  In aught you think or say.
The happiest hour that e'er I knew,
  Though it my peace may peril,
Is when thee to my heart I drew,
  My noble Irish girl.

I need not in the herald's book
  My loved one's lineage trace—
I read her lineage in her look,
  Her record in her face;

I hear it in each touching tone
  That floats thro' rows of pearl;
Thou art my queen—my heart's thy throne,
  My noble Irish girl.

I feel the impress of thy worth,
  And strive to be like thee;
Thou art to me what Heaven's to earth,
  What sunshine's to the sea;
And if from me some luster beam,
  'Mid sin and passion's whirl,
'Tis thy light shines on my life's stream,
  My noble Irish girl.

ARTHUR M'COY.

BY PONTIAC.

WHILE the snow-flakes of winter are
    falling
On mountain, and housetop, and tree,
Come olden weird voices recalling
  The homes of Hy-Faly to me;
The ramble by river and wild wood,
  The legends of mountain and glen,
When the bright, magic mirror of childhood
  Made heroes and giants of men.

Then I had my dreamings ideal,
  My prophets and heroes sublime,
Yet I found one, true, living, and real,
  Surpass all the fictions of time:
Whose voice thrilled my heart to its center,
  Whose form tranced my soul and my eye;
A temple no treason could enter;
  My hero was Arthur M'Coy.

For Arthur M'Coy was no bragger,
  No bibber, nor blustering clown,
'Fore the club of an alehouse to swagger,
  Or drag his coat-tail through the town;
But a veteran, stern and steady,
  Who felt for his land and her ills;
In the hour of her need ever ready
  To shoulder a pike for the hills.

As the strong mountain tower spreads its
    arms,
  Dark, shadowy, silent, and tall,
In our tithe-raids and midnight alarms,
  His bosom gave refuge to all—
If a mind, clear, and calm, and expanded,
  A soul ever soaring and high,
'Mid a host—gave a right to command it—
  A hero was Arthur M'Coy.

While he knelt, with a Christian demeanor,
  To his priest, or his Maker alone,

He scorned the vile slave, or retainer,
  That crouched 'round the castle, or throne;
The Tudor—The Guelph, The Pretender,
  Were tyrants, alike, branch and stem;
But who'd free our fair land, and defend her,
  A nation, were monarchs to him.

And this faith in good works he attested,
  When Tone linked the true hearts, and
    brave,
Every billow of danger he breasted—
  His sword-flash, the crest of its wave;
A standard he captured in Gorey,
  A sword-cut and ball through the thigh
Were among the mementoes of glory
  Recorded of Arthur M'Coy.

Long the *quest* of the law and its beagles,
  His covert the cave and the tree;
Though his home was the home of the
    eagles,
  His soul was the soul of the free.
No toil, no defeat could enslave it,
  Nor franchise, nor "Amnesty Bill"—
No lord, but the Maker who gave it,
  Could curb the high pride of his will.

With the gloom of defeat ever laden—
  Seldom seen at the hurling or dance,
Where through blushes, the eye of the
    maiden
  Looks out for her lover's advance;
And whenever he stood to behold it,
  A curl of the lip or a sigh,
Was the silent reproach that unfolded
  The feelings of Arthur M'Coy.

For it told him of freedom o'ershaded—
  That the iron had entered their veins—
When beauty bears manhood degraded,
  And manhood's contented in chains,

Yet he loved that fair race as a martyr,
  And if his own death could recall
The blessings of liberty's charter,
  His bosom had bled for them all.

And he died for his love—I remember,
  On a mound by the Shannon's blue wave,

On a dark snowy eve in December,
  I knelt at the patriot's grave.

The aged were all heavy-hearted—
  No cheek in the churchyard was dry;
The sun of our hills had departed—
  God rest you, old Arthur M'Coy!

————o————

THE MOUNTAIN FORGE.

BY T. IRWIN.

In the gloomy mountain's lap
  Lies the village dark and quiet;
All have passed their labor-nap,
  And the peasant, half-awaking,
  A blind, yawning stretch is taking,
Ere he turns to rest again;
  There is not a sound of riot,
Not a sound save that of pain,
  Where some aged bones are aching;
Lo! the moon is in the wane—
  Even the moon a drowso is taking.

By the blossomed sycamore,
  Filled with bees when day is o'er it,
Stands the Forge, with smoky door;
  Idle chimney, blackened shed—
  All its merry din is dead;
Broken shaft and wheel disused
  Strew the umbered ground before it,
And the streamlet's voice is fused
  Faintly with the cricket's *chirrup*,
As it tinkles clear and small
  'Round the glooming hearth and wall,
  Hung with rusty shoe and stirrup.

Yes, the moon is in the wane;
  Hark! the sound of horses tramping
Down the road with might and main;
  Through the slaty runnels crumbling,
  Comes a carriage swinging, rumbling;
'Round the steep quick corner turning,
  Plunge the horses, puff'd and champing;
  Like the eyes of weary ghosts,
The red lamps are dimly burning.
  Now 'tis stopt—and one springs down,
  And cries unto the sleeping town—
"Ho! for a blacksmith—ho! awake!
Bring him who will his fortune make—
  The best—the best the village boasts!"

Up springs the brawny blacksmith now,
  And rubs his eyes, and brushes off
The iron'd sweat upon his brow,
  Hurries his clothes and apron on,
  And calls his wife and wakes his son,
And opens the door to the night air,
  And gives a husky cough;

Then hastens to the horses standing
  With drooping heads and hotly steaming,
And sees a dark-eyed youth out-handing
  A sweet maiden, light and beaming.

He strikes a lusty shoulder-blow;
  "Four shoes," he cries, "are quickly
    wanting;"
His face is in an eager glow.
  "Take my purse and all that's in its
  Heart, if you in twenty minutes
Fit us for the road." The smith
  Looks at the wearied horses panting,
  Then at the clustering gold;
  And thinks, as he falls to his work,
  He dreams—a mind-dream, rusty murk,
That this is but a fairy myth,
  A tale to-morrow to be told.

But now the forge fire spirts alive
  To the old bellows softly purring,
In the red dot the irons dive;
  Brighter and broader it is glowing,
  Stronger and stronger swells the blowing,
The bare armed men stand 'round and
    mutter
  Lowly while the cinders stirring—
Ho! out it flames 'mid sparkles dropping,
Spitting, glittering, flying, hopping;
Heavily now the hammers batter,
All is glaring din and clatter.

In the cottage dimly lighted
  By the taper's drowsy glare,
Stands the gentle girl benighted;
  By her side forever hovers
  That dark youth, O, best of lovers!
  Daring all that love will dare
With an aspect firm and gay;
  Now the moon seems shining clearer.
  Hark! a sound seems swooping nearer
From the heathy hills; the maid
  Lists with ear acute, and while
  One there with brave, assuring smile,
Smooths her forehead's chestnut braid,
  The danger softly dies away.

Now the forge is in a glow,
　Bellows roaring, irons ringing;
Three are made, and blow on blow
　Sets the patient anvil singing;
." Another shoe—another, hark ye,"
　Ra-ra—ra-ra—ra-ra-rap;
Split the ruddy sheddings sparky,
　Ra-ra—ra-ra—ra-ra-rap;
　　Strikes the quick and lifted hammer
On the anvil bright and worn;
　While amid the midnight there,
　Beyond the noisy streaming glare,
　　With a yellow misty glamor,
Looks the moon upon the corn.

On the hill-road moving nigher,
　Hurries something dimly shooting,
Glances from two eyes of fire;
　" Haste, O, haste!" they're working steady;
　Cries the blacksmith: "Now they're ready."
Pats the pawing horses, testing
　On the ground their iron footing;
Helps the lady, lightly-resting

On his black arm up the carriage;
Takes the gold with doubt and wonder—
　And as o'er the stones and gorses
　Tramp the hot pursuing horses,
Cries with voice of jolly thunder—
　" Trust me, *they* won't stop the marriage!"

Scarce a minute's past away
　When, O, magic scene! the village
Lies asleep all hushed and grey;
　But hark! who throng again the street
　With roaring voices, brows of heat?
Come they here the town to pillage?
　No. Across the road, o'erthrown,
　Carriage creaks and horses moan;
　" Blacksmith, ho!" the travelers cry—
　Not a taper cheers the eye;
While a-top a distant hill
　Flushed with dawn-light's silent warning,
　Speed the lovers toward the morning
With a rapid right good will;
　While behind that father fretting,
　The pale night-sick moon is setting.

———o———

IRELAND'S WELCOME TO THE DISCHARGED BRITISH SOLDIER OF IRISH BIRTH.

(*Woking Prison*, 1870.)

RICKARD O'S. BURKE.

[Written in reply to the suggestion of the *Pall Mall Gazette*, in the columns of which journal a paragraph appeared, advising the government to dishonorably discharge all Irishmen from Her Majesty's land service, on account of their long recognized disloyalty. The paragraph in question stated that the matter was about to receive Parliamentary action, which is supposed completed, and the soldiers of Irish birth discharged.]

AND Shamus, allhay, is it thrue, what they say, this news from the Parliament,
That all of my boys, my sojer boys, back home are to be sent?
Back home are to be sent, allhay, in shame and black disgrace,
For having, inside their scarlet coats, the heart of their grand old race?

Chorus.

From my heart I say, God bless this day,
　My bouchal bawn machree;
Without penny or pack to tack to your back,
　Your welcome home to me.

They'll be sorry and sore when you're not to the fore these dangerous coming years,
Oh, I forget, they're bairns yet, nusha, see their volunteers;
And whin those bairns meet the foe, faith vict'ries will be scant,
'Tis right enough, you're not the stuff, 'tis min wid legs they'll want.
　　　　　　　　　　　　　　　　　From my heart I say, etc.

Whin you, like a thraveling killin' machine, o'er land and say did roam,
Did it ever inther your mind at all, you'd have work to do at home?
You'd have work to do at home, allhay, of the easiest, quarriest kind,
Allana machree, come hither to me—there's somethin' in the wind.
　　　　　　　　　　　　　　　　　From my heart I say, etc.

In dark and in dawn, na bouchaleen bawn, they thried to coax you away,
Wid bounties, and medals, and dhrums, and fifes, and ribbons so bright and gay;

Machree, I knew to me you'd be thrue, through thick and thin aich day;
For heart so brave never beat in the slave who'd fight for nothing but pay.
> From my heart I say, etc.

The shan van vacht is goin' 'round and saying things mighty quaire,
Alanna machree, come hither to me—she has a word for you're air,
There's something in the wind, allhay, there's strange things going on,
And maybe the union jack won't go—where union jacks have gone.
> From my heart I say, etc.

Did these wholesale despots think, allhay, they bought you out and out
Whin they gave you a rag to cover your back, and a bit to put in your mouth?
They thought you'd forget, allanna machree, for they spoke so smooth and fair,
How they rooted you out of house and home and left you starving and bare.
> From my heart I say, etc.

The old home is in ruins now, 'twas the peelers, sure, pulled it down,
And mother and Eileen they died that night in the snow going into the town;
In the old grave yard they are lying, allhay, above them the night wind moans,
Alanna machree, sure you'll thry to free the sod that covers their bones?
> From my heart I say, etc.

In life there's nothing nobler than revenge for our martyr'd dead;
To lighten the load of the hand oppressed, to give the hungry bread;
To strive for the poor, the plundered poor, with a brother's strong, true hand,
To march to the grand old music still, for God and our mother land,
> From my heart I say, etc.

---o---

THE RETURNING JANIZARY.

BY FRANCIS BROWN.

THERE came a youth at dawn of day
From the Golden Gate of the proud Serai;
He came with no gifts of warrior pride
But the gleam of the good sword by his side,
And an arm that well could wield;
But he came with a form of matchless
    mould—
Like that by the Delphian shrine of old—
And an eye in whose depth of brightness
    shone
The light by the Grecian sunset thrown
On the dying Spartan's shield;
For the days of his boyhood's bonds were
    o'er,
And he stood as a free-born Greek once
    more!

They brought him robes of the richest dyes,
And a shield like the moon in autumn skies,
A steed that grew by the Prophet's tomb,
And a helmet crown'd with a heron's plume,
    And the world's strong tempter, Gold;
And they said: "Since thou turnest from
    the towers
Of honor's path and pleasure's bowers,
Go forth in the Saphi's conquering march—
And gold and glory requite thy search,
    Till a warrior's death unfold
For thee the gates of Paradise,
And thy welcome beam'd by the Houris'
    eyes."

"And where will the yearning memories
    sleep,
That have fill'd mine exiled years
With a voice of winds in the forest free,
With the sound of the old Ægean sea,
Through echoing grove and green defile,
On the shores of that unforgotten Isle
Which still the light of my mother's smile
    To her wanderer's memory wears—
And the voices ever sounding back
From my country's old triumphal track?
The faith that clings with a deathless hold
To the freedom and the fame of old,
Will they rest in a stranger's banner-shade,
    Though a conquering flag it be?
Will they joy with its myriad hosts to tread
    On a land that once was free?
Take back your gifts," the wanderer said—
    "And leave at last to me,
That far land's love—for ye cannot part
    His country from the Exile's heart!"

They said—"Thine isle is a land of slaves;
It gives no galley to the waves—
No cry with the battle's onset blent—
No banner broad on its breezes sent—
    No name to the lists of fame;
Thy home still stands by its winding shore,
But thy place by the hearth is known no
    more;
The evening fire on that hearth shines on,

But the light of thy mother's smile is gone—
  For a stranger bears her name—
And, bright though her smile and glance
    may be,
They're not like those that grew dim for
    thee."

"I know that my country's fame hath found
  No rest by her storied streams—
For cold is the chain for ages borne,
And deep is the track its weight hath worn!
The serf hath stood, in his fetters bound,
On hills that were freedom's battle-ground;
And my name is a long-forgotten sound
  In the home of my thousand dreams;
For change hath passed o'er each household
    face,
And my mother's heart hath a resting place
Where the years of her weary watch are
    past
For the step that so vainly comes at last.
But far there shines through the shadowy
    green
Of the laurels bending there,
One beckoning light—'tis the glancing sheen
Of a Grecian maiden's hair;
Alas, for the clouds that rose between
My gaze and one so fair!
Alas! for many a morning ray
That passed from life's misty hills away!"

So spake the Greek, but the tempter said—
"Why seek'st thou the flowers of summer
    fled?
The years that have made thy kindred
    strange

Have they not breathed with the breath of
    change
  On thine early chosen, too?
They have bound the wealth of that flowing
    hair—
They have crossed the brow with a shade of
    care;
For thy young and thy glad of heart hath
    grown
A matron saddened in glance and tone—
  From whose undreaming view
Life's early lights have fallen—and thou
Art a long forgotten vision now."

There rose a cloud in his clear dark eye,
  Like the mist of coming tears—
Yet it passed in silence, and there came
No after-voice from that perished dream
But he said—"Is it so, my land? Thou hast
No gift for thy wanderer but the past,
And a dream of a gathering trumpet's blast
  And a charge of Grecian spears!
That bright dream's promise ne'er may be—
But the earth hath banners broad and free;
There are gallant barks on the western
    wave—
And fields where a Greek may find a grave;
With a fearless arm, with a stainless brand,
  With a young brow I depart
To seek the hosts of some Christian land—
  But I go with an Exile's heart.
Yet, oft when the stranger's fight is done,
And their shouts arise for the battle won,
This heart will dream what its joy might be
Were it won but for Greece and Liberty!"

---o---

INNISHOWEN.

BY CHARLES GAVAN DUFFY, M. P.

[Innishowen (pronounced Innishone) is a wild and picturesque district in the county Donegal, inhabited chiefly by the descendants of the Irish clans, permitted to remain in Ulster after the plantation of James I. The native language, and the songs and legends of the country, are as universal as the people. One of the most familiar of these legends is, that a troop of Hugh O'Neill's horse lies in magic sleep in a cave under the hill of Aileach, where the princes of the country were formerly installed. These bold troopers only wait to have the spell removed to rush to the aid of their country; and a man (says the legend) who wandered accidentally into the cave, found them lying beside their horses, fully armed, and holding the bridles in their hands. One of them lifted his head, and asked: "Is the time come?" and when he received no answer—for the intruder was too much frightened to reply—dropped back into his lethargy. Some of the old folk consider the story an allegory, and interpret it as they desire.]

God bless the grey mountains of dark Donegal,
God bless Royal Aileach, the pride of them all;
For she sits evermore like a Queen on her throne,
And smiles on the valleys of Green Innishowen.
    And fair are the valleys of Green Innishowen,
    And hardy the fishers that call them their own—
    A race that nor traitor nor coward have known
    Enjoy the fair valleys of Green Innishowen.

O! simple and bold are the bosoms they bear,
Like the hills that with silence and nature they share;

For our God, who hath planted their home near his own,
Breathed His spirit abroad upon fair Innishowen.
   Then praise to our Father for wild Innishowen,
   Where fiercely for ever the surges are thrown—
   Nor weather nor fortune a tempest hath blown
   Could shake the strong bosoms of brave Innishowen.

See the bountiful Couldah* careering along—
A type of their manhood so stately and strong—
On the weary for ever its tide is bestown,
So they share with the stranger in fair Innishowen.
   God guard the kind homesteads of fair Innishowen,
   Which manhood and virtue have chosen for their own;
   Not long shall that nation in slavery groan,
   That rears the tall peasants of fair Innishowen.

Like that oak of St. Bride which nor Devil nor Dane,
Nor Saxon nor Dutchman could rend from her fane,
They have clung by the creed and their cause of their own
Through the midnight of danger in true Innishowen.
   Then shout for the glories of old Innishowen,
   The stronghold that foeman have never o'erthrown—
   The soul and the spirit, the blood and the bone,
   That guard the green valleys of true Innishowen.

Nor purer of old was the tongue of the Gael,
When the charging *aboo* made the foreigner quail;
Than it gladdens the stranger in welcome's soft tone,
In the home-loving cabins of kind Innishowen.
   O! flourish, ye homesteads of kind Innishowen,
   Where seeds of a people's redemption are sown;
   Right soon shall the fruit of that sowing have grown,
   To bless the kind homesteads of green Innishowen.

When they tell us the tale of a spell-stricken band
All entranced, with their bridles and broadswords in hand,
Who await but the word to give Erin her own,
They can read you that riddle in proud Innishowen.
   Hurrah for the spaemen† of proud Innishowen!—
   Long live the wild Seers of stout Innishowen!—
   May Mary, our mother, be deaf to their moan
   Who love not the promise of proud Innishowen!

---

* The Couldah, or Culdaff, is the chief river in the Innishowen mountains.
† An Ulster and Scotch term signifying a person gifted with "second sight"—a prophet.

"THE BRIGADE" AT FONTENOY.

BY BARTHOLOMEW DOWLING.

By our camp fires 'rose a murmur
   At the dawning of the day,
And the tread of many footsteps
   Spoke the advent of a fray;
And as we took our places,
   Few and stern were our words,
While some were tightening horse-girths,
   And some were girding swords.

The trumpet blast has sounded
   Our footmen to array—
The willing steed has bounded,
   Impatient for the fray—
The green flag is unfolded,
   While arose the cry of joy—
"Heaven speed dear Ireland's banner
   To-day at Fontenoy."

We looked upon that banner,
  And the memory arose
Of our homes and perished kindred,
  Where the Lee or Shannon flows;
We looked upon that banner,
  And we swore to God on high,
To smite to-day the Saxon's might—
  To conquer or to die.

Loud swells the charging trumpet—
  'Tis a voice from our own land—
God of battles—God of vengeance,
  Guide to-day the patriots' band;
There are stains to wash away—
  There are memories to destroy,
In the best blood of the Briton
  To-day at Fontenoy.

Plunge deep the fiery rowels
  In a thousand reeking flanks—
Down, chivalry of Ireland,
  Down on the British ranks—
Now shall their serried columns
  Beneath our sabers reel—
Through their ranks, then, with the war-
    horse—
  Through their bosoms with the steel.

With one shout for good King Louis,
  And the fair land of the vine,
Like the wrathful Alpine tempest
  We swept upon their line—

Then rang along the battle-field
  Triumphant our hurrah,
And we smote them down still cheering
  "*Erin, slanthagal go bragh!*" *

As prized as is the blessing
  From an aged father's lip—
As welcome as the haven
  To the tempest-driven ship—'
As dear as to the lover,
  The smile of gentle maid—
Is this day of long-sought vengeance
  To the swords of the brigade.

See their shattered forces flying,
  A broken, routed line—
See England, what brave laurels
  For your brow to-day we twine.
Oh, thrice blessed the hour that witnessed
  The Briton turn to flee
From the chivalry of Erin,
  And France's "*fleur de lis.*"

As we lay beside our camp fires,
  When the sun had passed away,
And thought upon our brethren
  Who had perished in the fray—
We prayed to God to grant us,
  And then we'd die with joy,
One day upon our own dear land
  Like this of Fontenoy.

* Ireland, the bright toast forever!

THE IRISH-AMERICAN.

BY T. D. SULLIVAN.

COLUMBIA the free is the land of my birth,
And my paths have been all on American earth;
But my blood is as Irish as any can be,
And my heart is with Erin afar o'er the sea.

My father and mother, and friends all around,
Are daughters and sons of the sainted old ground—
They rambled its bright plains and mountains among,
And filled its fair valleys with laugh and with song.

But I sing their sweet music, and often they own,
It is true to old Ireland in style and in tone;
I dance their gay dances, and hear them with glee
Say each touch tells of Erin afar o'er the sea.

I have tufts of green shamrock in sods they brought o'er,
I have shells they picked up ere they stepped from the shore,
I have books that are treasures; the fondest I hold
Is " The Melodies," clasped and nigh covered with gold.

My pictures are pictures of scenes that are dear,
For the beauties they are, or the glories they were,

And of good men and great men whose merits shall be
Long the pride of green Erin afar o'er the sea.

If I were in beautiful Dublin to-day,
To the spots I hold sacred I'd soon find my way,
For I know where O'Connell and Curran are laid,
And where loved Robert Emmet sleeps cold " in the shade."

And if I were in Wexford—how fondly I'd trace
Each field I have marked on my maps of the place,
Where the brave Ninety-Eight men poured hotly and free
Their blood for dear Erin afar o'er the sea.

Dear home of my fathers! I'd hold thee to blame
And my cheeks would at times take the crimson of shame,
Did thy sad tale not show, in each sorrow-stained line,
That the might of thy tyrant was greater than thine.

But her soldiers are many, abroad and at home,
Her ships on all oceans are ploughing the foam,
And her wealth is untold—sure no equal was she,
For my poor plundered Erin afar o'er the sea.

Yet they tell me the strife is not yet given o'er—
That the gallant old island will try it once more;
And will call, with her harp, when her flag is unfurled,
Her sons, and *their* sons, from the ends of the world.

If so, I've a rifle that's true to a hair,
A brain that can plan and a hand that can dare;
And the summons will scarce have died out when I'll be
'Mid the green fields of Erin afar o'er the sea.

———o———

'TWAS A VISION, AND IT FADED.

BY MICHAEL SCANLAN.

'TWAS a vision, and it faded
  In a moment 'fore his eyes,
Yet his life seemed overshaded
  As it vanished down the skies.
For his soul in that blessed minute
  Saw its broad capacity—
All his years were mirrored in it,
  What might but would not be.

She whose presence fired his spirit,
  Till it 'rose on eagle wings—
Swept the fields it would inherit,
  In its dream of better things.
Knowing life was naught without her,
  Cold as virtue, passed from thence,
Drew her robes of light about her,
  And smote him with indifference.

She who came unto life's prison,
  Where his listless years had lain,
When his heart had grandly risen
  To the high degrees of pain:
With her brown eyes, bright and tender,
  And her sweet voice like the dove,
Chilled him with her icy splendor—
  And a freedom without love.

'Twas a vision, and it faded,
  Flashed and leaped into the night,
And his life was overshaded
  As it faded from his sight.
For his soul in that blessed minute
  Saw its broad capacity—
All his years seemed mirrored in it,
  What might but would not be!

———o———

THE HARP WITHOUT THE CROWN.

BY CARROLL MALONE.

OH! how she ploughed the ocean, the good ship *Castle Down*,
The day we hung our colors out, the Harp *without* the Crown!

A gallant bark, she topped the wave; and fearless hearts were we,
With guns, and pikes, and bayonets, a stalwart company.
'Twas sixteen years from Thurot;* and sweeping down the bay,
The " Siege of Carrickfergus" so merrily we did play;
By the old Castle's foot we went, with three right hearty cheers;
And waved our green cockades aloft, for we were Volunteers,
                    Volunteers,
Oh! we were in our prime that day, stout Irish Volunteers.
'Twas when we waved our anchor on the breast of smooth Garmoyle,
Our guns spoke out in thunder: "Adieu, sweet Irish soil!"
At Whiteabbey, and Greencastle, and Holywood so gay,
Were hundreds waving handkerchiefs, with many a loud huzza.
Our voices o'er the water went to the voices 'round; ·
Young Freedom struggling at her birth, might utter such a sound.
But one green slope beside Belfast, we cheered, and cheered it still;
The people had changed its name that year, and called it Bunker's Hill; +
                    Bunker's Hill,
Oh! that our hands, like our hearts, had been in the trench at Bunker's Hill!

Our ship cleared out for Quebec port; but thither little bent,
Up some New England river, to run her keel we meant.
We took our course due north as out 'round old Blackhead we steered,
Till Ireland bore southwest by south, and Fingal's rock appeared.
Then on the poop stood Webster, while the ship hung flutteringly,
About to take her tack across the wide, wide ocean sea.
He points to the Atlantic—" Yonder's no place for slaves:
Haul down these British badges; for Freedom rules the waves,
                    Rules the waves!"
Three hundred strong men answered, shouting: "Freedom rules the waves!"
Then altogether they arose, and brought the British ensign down;
And up we raised our island Green, without the British Crown;
Emblazoned there a golden harp, like maiden undefiled,
A shamrock wreath around its head, looked o'er the sea and smiled.
A hundred days, with adverse winds, we kept our course afar;
On the hundredth day, came bearing down, a British sloop-of-war.
When they spied our flag they fired a gun; but as they neared us fast,
Old Andrew Jackson went aloft, and nailed it to the mast,
                    To the mast.
A sailor was that old Jackson; he made our colors fast.
Patrick Henry was our captain, as brave as ever sailed;
"Now we must do or die," said he, "for our green flag is nailed."

Silently came the sloop along; and silently we lay
Till with ringing cheers and cannonade the foe began the fray;
Then, their boarders o'er the bulwarks, like shuttlecocks we cast,
One broadside volley from our guns swept down the tapering mast:—
" Now, British Tars! St. George's cross is trailing in the sea;
How·do you like the greeting, and the handsel of the Free?
                    Of the Free?
These are the terms and tokens of men who will be free."
They answered us with cannon, their honor to redeem,
To shoot away our Irish flag, each gunner took his aim;
They ripped it up in ribbons, till it fluttered in the air,
And filled with shot-holes, till no trace of golden Harp was there;

---

* The landing of Thurot at Carrickfergus, in 1760, was long used as an epoch by the people in the north, and is known to have occasioned the first formation of the Irish Volunteers.
+ Bunker's Hill, on the shore of Down, opposite Belfast, was so called in honor of the famous Hill at Boston.

But the ragged holes did glance and gleam, in the sun's golden light,
Even as the twinkling stars adorn God's unfurled flag at night.
With drooping fire, we sung: "Good-night, and fare-ye-well, brave Tars!"
Our Captain looked aloft: "By Heaven! the flag is stripes and stars,
    Stripes and stars."
Right into Boston port we sailed, below the Stripes and Stars.

———o———

THE MEMORY OF THE DEAD.

(ANONYMOUS.)

Who fears to speak of Ninety-Eight?
 Who blushes at the name?
When cowards mock the patriot's fate,
 Who hangs his head for shame?
He's all a knave or half a slave,
 Who slights his country thus;
But a true man, like you, man,
 Will fill your glass with us.

We drink the memory of the brave,
 The faithful and the few—
Some lie far off beyond the wave—
 Some sleep in Ireland, too;
All—all are gone—but still lives on
 The fame of those who died—
All true men, like you, men,
 Remember them with pride.

Some on the shores of distant lands
 Their weary hearts have laid,
And by the stranger's heedless hands
 Their lonely graves were made;
But, though their clay be far away
 Beyond the Atlantic foam—
In true men, like you, men,
 Their spirit's still at home.

The dust of some is Irish earth;
 Among their own they rest;
And the same land that gave them birth
 Has caught them to her breast;
And we will pray that from their clay
 Full many a race may start
Of true men, like you, men,
 To act as brave a part.

They 'rose in dark and evil days
 To right their native land:
They kindled here a living blaze
 That nothing shall withstand.
Alas! that Might can vanquish Right—
 They fell and passed away;
But true men, like you, men,
 Are plenty here to-day.

Then here's their memory—may be
 For us a guiding light,
To cheer our strife for liberty,
 And teach us to unite.
Through good and ill, be Ireland's still,
 Though sad as theirs your fate;
And true men, be you, men,
 Like those of Ninety-Eight.

———o———

EVENING BY THE HUDSON.

BY JOHN LOCKE.

Here I sit this silent even by the broad, blue Hudson's side,
While the flow'rets fondly drooping kiss the ripples on its tide;
All the clouds are blushing crimson, and the sunset's lingering ray
Lights the long, green maple woodland, stretching westward far away—
While the wind rolls up the vapors to the mountains of the west,
And the cloud with folded pinions, bears the round moon in its breast.

But to me those evening beauties bring no thoughts of joy or pride,
For my weary heart is wand'ring o'er the ocean's troubled tide,
To a valley in green Erin, where the streamlets sweetly sing—
Where the winds creep thro' the clover, and the clover blossoms swing,
Where the lilies shimmer over blue lagoons of sunny sheen,
And the poplar woodland shadows parkland, slope and pasture green—
Where the bright-eyed village maidens while away the Sabbath noon,
And my youthhood's years rolled over—years that rolled away too soon.

Oh! that happy time of boyhood, when the sunshine of the spring
Was not half so bright or glowing as my soul's imagining!
When my young heart filled with gladness, like a glade with summer flow'rs,
On the magic wings of Fancy roamed through Dreamland's rosy bow'rs,
Singing lays of love to Ireland, weaving sonnet-wreaths for May,
Twining garlands for my Kathleen till the summer passed away.

Now I welcome not the Maytime, for its winds chant in mine ears
Nought but weary, woe-filled dirges for the hopes of buried years;
Summer comes with fruit and blossom, but no garlands now I twine,
For a weary weight of sorrow and a broken heart are mine;
Still beside this western river, mem'ries of the olden days
Come at times like autumn sun-gleams struggling thro' the harvest haze.

Years have rolled since I and Kathleen roamed around the fairy rath;
Many shadows since have fallen on the exile's darkened path;
Ah, those cold—cold years of exile have been bitter years to me,
For where'er my footsteps turned still my heart strayed o'er the sea,—
Back again to those who loved me, to the maid who night and day
Ever sent her dearest blessings to the wand'rer far away.

Now blow soft ye winds of ocean, and bear tidings unto me,
Of the friends at home in Erin o'er the far Atlantic sea;
For tho' friends or home or country Fate may ne'er again restore,
'Round my heart their memories olden shall be twined for evermore.

------o------

ADIEU, MY OWN DEAR ERIN.

BY J. J. CALLANAN.

ADIEU, my own dear Erin,
  Receive my fond, my last adieu;
I go, but with me bearing
  A heart still fondly turn'd to you.

The charms that nature gave thee
  With lavish hand, shall cease to smile,
And the soul of friendship leave thee,
  E'er I forget my own green isle.

Ye fields where heroes bounded
  To meet the foes of liberty;
Ye hills that oft resounded
  The joyful shouts of victory.

Obscured is all your glory,
  Forgotten all your former fame,
And the minstrel's mournful story
  Now calls a tear at Erin's name.

But still the day may brighten
  When those tears shall cease to flow,
And the shout of freedom lighten
  Spirits now so drooping low.

Then should the glad breeze blowing
  Convey the echo o'er the sea,
My heart, with transport glowing,
  Shall bless the hand that made thee
    free.

------o------

THE PILLAR TOWERS OF IRELAND.

BY D. F. M'CARTHY.

THE pillar towers of Ireland, how wondrously they stand
By the lakes and rushing rivers, through the valleys of our land;
In mystic file, through the isle, they lift their heads sublime,
These grey old pillar temples, these conquerors of time.

Beside these grey old pillars, how perishing and weak,
The Roman's arch of triumph, and the temple of the Greek,
And the golden domes of Byzantium, and the pointed Gothic spires,
All are gone, one by one, but the temples of our sires.

The column, with its capital, is level with the dust,
And the proud halls of the mighty and the calm homes of the just;
For the proudest works of man, as certainly, but slower,
Pass like the grass at the sharp scythe of the mower.

But the grass grows again, when in majesty and mirth,
On the wing of the spring, comes the goddess of the earth;
But for man in this world no spring-tide e'er returns
To the labors of his hands or the ashes of his urns.

Two favorites hath Time—the pyramids of Nile,
And the old mystic temples of our own dear isle;
As the breeze o'er the seas, where the halcyon has its nest,
Thus Time o'er Egypt's tombs and the temples of the West!

The names of their founders have vanished in the gloom,
Like the dry branch in the fire or the body in the tomb;
But to-day, in the ray, their shadows still they cast—
These temples of forgotten Gods—these relics of the past!

Around these walls have wandered the Briton and the Dane—
The captives of Armorica, the cavaliers of Spain—
Phœnician and Milesian, and the plundering Norman Peers—
And the swordsmen of brave Brian, and the chief of later years!

How many different rites have these grey old temples known!
To the mind what dreams are written in these chronicles of stone!
What terror and what error, what gleams of love and truth,
Have flashed from these walls since the world was in its youth!

Here blazed the sacred fire, and, when the sun was gone,
As a star from afar to the traveler it shone;
And the warm blood of the victim have these grey old temples drunk,
And the death-song of the Druid and the matin of the Monk.

Here was placed the holy chalice that held the sacred wine,
And the gold cross from the altar, and the relics from the shrine,
And the mitre shining brighter with its diamonds than the East,
And the crozier of the pontiff, and the vestments of the priest.

Where blazed the sacred fire, rang out the vesper bell,
Where the fugitive found shelter, became the hermit's cell;
And hope hung out its symbol to the innocent and good,
For the cross o'er the moss of the pointed summit stood.

There may it stand forever, while this symbol doth impart
To the mind one glorious vision, or one proud throb to the heart;
While the breast needeth rest may these grey old temples last,
Bright prophets of the future, as preachers of the past.

———o———

THE WEARING OF THE GREEN.

BY HENRY GRATTAN CURRAN.

One blessing on my native isle!
  One curse upon her foes!
While yet her skies above me smile,
  Her breeze around me blows:
Now, never more my cheek be wet,
  Nor sigh, nor altered mien,
Tell the dark tyrant I regret
  The Wearing of the Green,

Sweet land! my parents loved you well!:
  They sleep within your breast;
With theirs—for love no words can tell—
  My bones must never rest,
And lonely must my true love stray,
  That was our village queen,
When I am banished far away,
  For the Wearing of the Green,

But, Mary, dry that bitter tear,
  'Twould break my heart to see;
And sweetly sleep my parents dear,
  That cannot weep for me.
I'll think not of my distant tomb,
  Nor seas rolled wide between,
But watch the hour that yet will come,
  For the Wearing of the Green.

Oh, I care not for the thistle,
  And I care not for the rose,
For when the cold winds whistle
  Neither down nor crimson shows;

But like hope to him that's friendless
  Where no gaudy flower is seen,
By our graves, with love that's endless,
  Waves our own true-hearted Green.

Oh, sure God's world was wide enough,
  And plentiful for all!
And ruined cabins were no stuff
  To build a lordly hall;
They might have let the poor man live,
  Yet all as lordly been;
But Heaven its own good time will give
  For the Wearing of the Green.

---o---

THE YOUNG ENTHUSIAST.

BY THOMAS FRANCIS MEAGHER.

THOUGH young that heart, though free each
    thought,
  Though free and wild each feeling;
And though with fire each dream be fraught
  Across those bright eyes stealing—

That heart is true, those thoughts are bold;
  And bold each feeling sweepeth;
There lies not there a bosom cold,
  A pulse that faintly sleepeth.

His dreams are idiot dreams, ye say,
  The dreams of fairy story;
Those dreams will burn in might some day
  And flood his path with glory!

Thou old dull vassal! fling thy sneer
Upon that young heart coldly,
  And laugh at deeds *thy* heart may fear,
Yet *he* will venture boldly.

Ay, fling thy sneer, while dull and slow
  Thy withered blood is creeping;

That heart will beat, *that* spirit glow,
  When thy tame pulse is sleeping.

Ay, laugh when o'er his country's ills
  With manly eye he weepeth:
Laugh, when his brave heart throbs and
    thrills,
  And thy cold bosom sleepeth.

Laugh, when he vows in Heaven's sight,
  Ne'er to flinch—ne'er to falter;
To toil and fight for a nation's right,
  And guard old Freedom's altar.

Ay, laugh, when on the fiery wing
  Of hero thought ascending,
To fame's bold cliff, with eagle spring,
  That young bright mind is tending.

He'll gain that cliff, he'll reach that throne,
  The throne where genius shineth,
When 'round and through thy nameless
    stone,
  The green weed thickly twineth.

---o---

SONGS OF OUR LAND.

AIR:—" *Old Langolee.* "

SONGS of our land, ye are with us forever;
  The power and the splendor of thrones passed away,
But yours is the might of some far flowing river,
  Through summer's bright roses, or autumn's decay.
Ye treasure each voice of the swift passing ages,
  And truth, which time writeth on leaves or on sand;
Ye bring us the bright thoughts of poets and sages,
  And keep them among us, old songs of our land,

The bards may go down to the place of their slumbers,
  The lyre of the charmer be hushed in the grave,
But far in the future the power of their numbers
  Shall kindle the hearts of our faithful and brave,

It will waken an echo in souls deep and lonely,
  Like voices of reeds by the summer breeze fanned;
It will call up a spirit of freedom, when only
  Her breathings are heard in the songs of our land.

For they keep a record of those, the true-hearted,
  Who fell with the cause they had vowed to maintain;
They show us bright shadows of glory departed,
  Of the love that grew cold, and the hope that was vain;
The page may be lost and the pen long forsaken,
  And when weeds may grow wild o'er the brave heart and hand;
But ye are still left when all else hath been taken,
  Like streams in the desert, sweet songs of our land.

Songs of our land, ye have followed the stranger,
  With power over ocean and desert afar,
Ye have gone with our wanderers through distance and danger,
  And gladdened their path like a home-guiding star;
With the breath of our mountains in summers long vanished,
  And visions that passed like a wave from our strand,
With hope for their country and joy from her banished,
  Ye come to us ever, sweet songs of our land.

The spring-time may come with the song of her glory,
  To bid the green heart of the forest rejoice;
But the pine of the mountain, though blasted and hoary,
  And rock in the desert can send forth a voice.
It is thus in their triumph for deep desolations.
  While ocean waves roll or the mountains shall stand,
Still hearts, that are bravest, and best of the nations,
  Shall glory and live in the songs of our land.

---o---

ANNIE, DEAR.

BY THOMAS DAVIS.

OUR mountain brooks were rushing,
              Annie, dear;
The autumn eve was flushing,
              Annie, dear;
But brighter was your blushing,
When first, your murmurs hushing,
I told my love outgushing,
              Annie, dear.

Ah! but our hopes were splendid,
              Annie, dear;
How sadly they have ended,
              Annie, dear;
The ring betwixt us broken,
When our vows of love were spoken,
Of your poor heart was a token,
              Annie, dear.

The primrose flow'rs were shining,
              Annie, dear,
When on my breast reclining,
              Annie, dear.

Began our Mi-na-Meala,
And many a month did follow
Of joy—but life is hollow,
              Annie, dear.

For once, when home returning,
              Annie, dear,
I found our cottage burning,
              Annie, dear;
Around it were the yeomen,
Of every ill and omen,
The country's bitter foemen,
              Annie, dear.

But why arose a morrow,
              Annie, dear?
Upon that night of sorrow,
              Annie, dear?
Far better, by thee lying,
Their bayonets defying,
Than live in exile sighing,
              Annie, dear.

THE SPIRIT BRIDE.

BY B. DORAN KILLIAN.

IN the deep'ning gloom of the forest eves
  A white face ever my soul descries,
And the lush—lush green of the locust leaves
  Is gemmed with the glow of two spirit
      eyes:—
Eyes of the deepest, haziest blue;
  Face like a moonlit waterfall's foam,
That evermore say: "I am waiting for you,
  So tarry not long, love, come, love, come!"

Sombrous aisles, where my lost one strays!
  Sacred shades, where my lost one roves!
I wander and watch in your deepest maze,
  In the heart and the hush of your darkest
      groves—
Groves, where the white face brightest
      gleams—
Groves where the blue eyes bluest grow,
Till I catch the light of the bright—bright
      beams,
  And the red—red lips I used to know.

An orange bloom in a cypress wreath
  My spirit bride her brow has on;
And she leans and leans till I feel her breath,
  And her drooping hair my cheek upon.
Oh! sweet, warm breath of the days gone by;
  Oh! soft—soft hair of the silver sheen,
You come for the kiss that may not cloy,
  And the closer clasps that should have
      been.

In the sapphire courts of the bright and
     blest
  She bides till the eve on the earth descends,
Then, all in her bridal garments drest,
  To our trysting-place in the woods she
      wends:
Bridal and burial garments white,
  Orange and rue on her veiled head!
True to the troth of her maiden plight,
  She hies to the joys of the nuptial bed.

Oh! mortal tongues may never disclose,
  And mortal eyes may nevermore see,

Such burning kisses my bride bestows,
  And warm embraces she gives to me;
Kisses full of Seraphic fire;
  Embraces such as the Cherubim know;
Free of the dross of earthly desire,
  We kiss and clasp, and glow and glow!

Have you seen the depths of a cross-girt
     spring
  When the sun a sidelong glance sends
     through?
Have you watched the vistas that lead and
     bring
  The eye to the skies divinest blue?
That spring is the type of her deep, pure
     truth,
  That vista its weird—weird story,
So saddened, and sunned, and circled with
     ruth,
  It shines with heavenly glory!

Betimes a grief all human will come
  Across our brightest trysting hour,
A grief all human, but such an one
  Of more than human power;
As angels feel who know their love
  For mortal form requited,
Yet know, their golden gates above
  Shut out the loved benighted.

Then sigh on sigh, and gaze on gaze,
  And tenderest drawings nearer;
Then all the thousand—thousand ways
  The dear one makes the dearer;
Ah! sorrow may come in many a guise,
  On ebon pinions moving,
But soonest it comes, and longest it lies,
  Where part the leal and loving!

Fall, shades of evening, gather and fall
  Fast and thick, 'mid the locust leaves;
Weave, funeral pines, your shadiest pall
  Where my Spirit Bride receives;
The pall will shift like a cloud eclipse
  When her white robe glints the air,
And Heaven break in while I press her lips,
  And toy with her silver hair!

----o----

WINTER.

BY MICHAEL J. HEFFERNAN.

CLOSE the shutters, bolt and bar the doors, the cheerless day is gone,
  And night, borne on the wintry blast, wraps all the earth in gloom;
Heap wood upon those dying sparks, and leave me to my own
  Silent broodings in my lonely little room.

What music do the wretched hear in every dismal sound
   That marks the gloomy tracks of Desolation and Despair?
How they love to brood upon the past when Horror reigns around!
   Calm sunshine the unhappy cannot bear.

Let others love the Springtime, or the Summer calm and bright,
   Or the golden Autumn twilight—sweetest season of the year,
But, ah! *I* always welcome the cold, joyless Winter night—
   Its wild howlings fall like music on my ear.

Yet I, too, had my *Spring-tide* joys, when in the flush of youth
   I plucked the modest daisy and the primrose from the sward,
To bring them to a little girl, the soul of Love and Truth,
   And snatched the kiss half granted in reward.

The attributes from angels beamed from out my Mary's face,
   Her smile would make a hermit's life one live-long Summer day;
Oh! who could look upon that form of light, unearthly grace,
   And think it was, or e'er could be—but clay?

Our youth—our Springtide—passed away one hallow'd blissful dream,
   The May-time came, and soon I called my Mary " little wife,"
And I took her to my cottage by the margin of a stream:
   Oh! then began the *Summer* of my life!

Sweet Mary! how thine image, clear and fresh as yesterday,
   Comes floating on my memory o'er the rapid stream of Time;
How my weary heart is yearning once again to fly away,
   Back to the golden sunshine of our prime!

Can'st thou, my sainted bride, now from thy new home in the skies,
   See the heart thou hast left desolate corroding with mute woe?
Can'st thou watch me in my broken sleep, and hear the unconscious sighs
   I offer to thy memory here below?

Can'st thou see our little cottage door, where oft thou'st watched for me
   At sunset; whilst the anxious tears into thine eyes would start,
If thou sawest me not coming at the wonted hour to thee,
   To calm the foolish throbbings of thy heart?

But, oh! never—never shall thy kiss of welcome greet me more;
   Cold are those rich, ripe lips, those love-lit eyes, that marble brow'
Drear loneliness remains for me; my summer days are o'er;
   This world has Winter only for me now!

Ah. well do I remember, love, the *Autumn* eve that found
   Thy fever'd cheek upon my breast; the golden sunset beamed
Thro' our chamber's half-closed window, throwing mellow light around,
   While the parting soul within thy blue eyes gleamed.

Methinks thou art before me now. The cold sweat mats thy hair;
   The death-smile quivers on thy lip; the flush has left thy cheek;
Thine eyes grow dim; thy spirit-sister angels fill the air;
   Thou sighest the farewell thou canst not speak.

Thou art gone. Thy saintly spirit with the angels wings her way
   To the blest home thy Creator hath prepared for thee above;
Leaving me but the cold semblance, in this pallid form of clay,
   Of the early, only object of my love.

And now, indeed, 'tis *Winter*, and no hopes for me remain
   In this cold and dreary vale of tears, of sorrow and of pain;

But to struggle on in Virtue's path, that I may soon again
  Meet thee where naught can enter with a stain.

Oh, once I loved the Spring-tide, and the Summer calm and bright,
  And the golden Autumn twilight— sweetest season of the year;
But now I always welcome the cold, joyless *Winter night,*
  Whose cold howlings fall like music on my ear.

———o———

O'DONNELL ABU.

BY M. J. M'CANN.

PROUDLY the note of the trumpet is
      sounding,
  Loudly the war-cries arise on the gale,
Fleetly the steed by Loc Suilig is bounding,
  To join the thick squadrons in Saimear's
      green vale.
        On, every mountaineer,
        Strangers to flight and fear;
    Rush to the standard of dauntless Red
      Hugh!
        Bonnought and Gallowglass
        Throng from each mountain pass!
  On for old Erin—O'Donnell abu!

Princely O'Neill to our aid is advancing,
  With many a chieftain and warrior-clan;
A thousand proud steeds in his vanguard are
      prancing,
  'Neath the borders brave from the banks
      of the Bann:
        Many a heart shall quail
        Under its coat of mail;
    Deeply the merciless tyrant shall rue,
        When on his ear shall ring,
        Borne on the breeze's wing,
    Tyrconnell's dread war-cry—O'Donnell
      abu!

Wildly o'er Desmond the war wolf is
      howling,
  Fearless the eagle sweeps over the plain,
The fox in the streets of the city is prowling,
  All—all who would scare them are
      banished or slain!
        Grasp, every stalwart hand,
        Hackbut and battle-brand—
    Pay them all back the deep debt so long
      due;
        Norris and Clifford well
        Can of Tir-Conaill tell—
  Onward to glory—O'Donnell abu!

Sacred the cause that Clan-Conaill's
      defending—
  The altars we kneel at and homes of our
      sires;
Ruthless the ruin the foe is extending—
  Midnight is red with the plunderer's fires!
        On with O'Domnall, then,
        Fight the old fight again,
    Sons of Tir-Conaill all valiant and true!
        Make the false Saxon feel
        Erin's avenging steel!
    Strike for your country!—O'Donnell
      abu!

———o———

HE SAID THAT HE WAS NOT OUR BROTHER.

BY JOHN BANIM.

HE said that he was not our brother—
  The mongrel! he said what we knew—
No, Eire! our dear Island-mother,
  He ne'er had his black blood from you!
And what though the milk of your bosom
  Gave vigor and health to his veins—
He was but a foul foreign blossom,
  Blown hither to poison our plains!

He said that the sword had enslaved us—
  That still at its point we must kneel,—
The liar!—though often it braved us,
  We crossed it with hardier steel!

This witness his Richard—our vassal!
  His Essex—whose plumes we trod down!
His Willy—whose peerless sword-tassel
  We tarnish'd at Limerick town!

No! falsehood and feud were our evils,
  While force not a fetter could twine—
Come, Northmen—come, Normans—come,
      Devils!
  We gave them our *Sparth* to the chine!
And if once again he would try us,
  To the music of trumpet and drum,
And no traitor among us or nigh us—
  Let him come, the Brigand! let him come!

AN EXILE'S DREAM.

BY JOSEPH BRENNAN.

I WILL go to holy Ireland,
  The land of Saint and Sage,
Where the pulse of boyhood's leaping
  In the shrunken form of Age;
Where the shadow of giant Hopes
  For evermore is cast,
And the wraiths of mighty chieftains
  Are looming through the Past.
From the cold land of the Stranger
  I will take my joyous flight,
To sit by my slumbering country,
  And watch her through the night;
When Spring is in the sky,
  And the flowers are on the land,
I will go to ancient Ireland,
  Of the open heart and hand.

I will go where the Galtees,
  Are rising bare and high,
With their haggard foreheads fronting
  The scowl of the clouded sky;
I will gaze adown on the valleys,
  And bless the teeming sod,
And commune with the mountains—
  "The Almoners of God;"
I will list to the murmurous song
  Which is rising from the river,
Which flows, crooning to the ocean,
  Forever and forever.
When the May month is come,
  When the year is fresh and young,
I will go to the home of my fathers—
  The land of sword and song.

I will go where Killarney
  Is sleeping in peaceful rest,
Unmoved, save when a falling leaf
  Ripples its placid breast;
Where the branches of oak and arbutus
  Are weaving a pleasant screen,
And the sunshine breaks in diamonds
  Through its tracery of green;
Where the mists, like fantastic specters,
  Forever rise and fall,
And the rainbow of the Covenant
  Is spanning the mountains tall.

When the wind blows from the west
  Across the deep Sea,
I will sail to my Innisfail—
  To the "Isle of Destiny."

I will go to beautiful Wicklow,
  The hunted outlaw's rest,
Which the tread of rebel and rapparee
  In many a struggle prest;
I will go to the lonely graveyard,
  Near the pleasant fields of Kildare,
And pray for my chief and my hero,
  Young Tone, who is sleeping there.
I will go to the gloomy Thomas street,
  Where gallant Robert died,
And to the grim St. Michan's,
  Where the "Brothers" lie side by side;
I will go to where the heroes
  Of the Celts are laid,
And chant a Miserere
  For the souls of the mighty Dead.

I will seize my pilgrim staff,
  And cheerily wander forth
From the face of the smiling South
  To the black frown of the North;
And in some hour of twilight
  I will mount the tall Slieve-Bloom,
And weave me a picture-vision
  In the evening's pleasant gloom;
I will call up the buried leaders
  Of the ancient Celtic race,
And gaze with a filial fondness
  On each sternly-noble face—
The masters of the mind,
  And the chieftains of the steel,
Young Carolan, and Grattan,
  The M'Caura, and O'Neill;
I will learn from their voices,
  With a student's love and pride,
To live as they lived,
  And to die as they died.
Oh, I will sail from the West,
  And never more will part
From the ancient home of my people—
  The land of the loving heart,

THE "HOLLY AND IVY" GIRL.

BY J. KEEGAN.

"COME, buy my nice, fresh Ivy, and my Holly sprigs so green;
I have the finest branches that ever yet were seen,
Come, buy from me, good Christians, and let me home, I pray,
And I'll wish you 'Merry Christmas Times, and a happy New Year's Day.'

"Ah! won't you take my ivy?—the loveliest ever seen!
Ah! won't you have my Holly boughs?—all you who love the Green!
Do!—take a little bunch of each, and on my knees I'll pray,
That God may bless your Christmas, and be with you New Year's Day.

" This wind is black and bitter, and the hail-stones do not spare
My shivering form, my bleeding feet, and stiff, entangled hair;
Then, when the skies are pitiless, be merciful, I say—
So Heaven will light your Christmas and the coming New Year's Day."

'Twas thus a dying maiden sung, while the cold hail rattled down,
And fierce winds whistled mournfully o'er Dublin's dreary town:—
One stiff hand clutched her Ivy sprigs and Holly Boughs so fair,
With the other she kept brushing the haildrops from her hair.

So grim and statue-like she seemed, 'twas evident that Death
Was lurking in her footsteps—while her hot, impeded breath
Too plainly told her early doom—though the burden of her lay
Was still of life and Christmas joys, and a Happy New Year's Day.

'Twas in that broad, bleak Thomas street, I heard the wanderer sing,
I stood a moment in the mire, beyond the ragged ring—
My heart felt cold and lonely, and my thoughts were far away,
Where I was many a Christmas-tide and Happy New Year's Day.

I dreamed of wanderings in the woods among the Holly Green:
I dreamed of my own native cot and porch with Ivy Screen;
I dreamed of lights forever dimm'd—of Hopes that can't return—
And dropped a tear on Christmas fires that never more can burn.

The ghost-like singer still sung on, but no one came to buy;
The hurrying crowd passed to and fro, but did not heed her cry;
She uttered one low, piercing moan—then cast her boughs away—
And smiling, cried—" I'll rest with God before the New Year's Day!"

    *   *   *   *   *   *

On New Year's Day I said my prayers above a new-made grave,
Dug decently in sacred soil, by Liffey's murmuring wave;
The Minstrel maid from Earth to Heaven has winged her happy way,
And now enjoys, with sister saints, an endless New Year's Day.

———o———

THE LADY OF THE EMERALD.

BY D. HOLLAND.

[In the East and in the West, in the olden days, the emerald was more highly valued than the diamond; and it was believed that certain mystic virtues, protecting the wearer against the wiles of evil men and evil spirits, lurked in the emerald that was pure in color and without a flaw.]

The queen of my love is fair and bright,
  With neck like the drifting snows;
And her shadowy eyes have a witching
    light
Like the starry gleam of the autumn night;
  But the hue of the summer rose
May not rival the virgin fires that beam
  On her blushing cheek, I trow;
And her brown hair shines with a sunny
    gleam;
But cold and dark as a winter's dream
  Is the shadow upon her brow,

In robe as green as the Dryad's vest
  My queenly love is dight;
A ruby glows on her snowy breast,
And the girdle that clasps her yielding
    waist
  With starry gems is bright,
But her foes have plundered her regal
    dower;
  She wears no longer now
(When shame and sorrow around her lower)
The mystic sign of her queenly power—
  The Emerald on her brow,

But I'll win back that gem for my bright
 lady,
The jewel of sea-bright green,
That bears a fairy potency,
For hearts that are brave and souls that are
 free,
In its mystic stainless sheen.

And her robes shall glitter with gems
 untold;
And her wasted cheek shall glow
With the roseate hue it wore of old;
And I'll circle her locks in a wreath of
 gold,
With the emerald on her brow

FILL HIGH TO-NIGHT.

BY WILLIAM PEMBROKE MULCHINOCK.

Fill high to-night, in our halls of light
 The toast on our lips shall be—
"The sinewy hand, the glittering brand,
 Our homes and our altars free."

Though the coward pale, like the girl may
 wail,
And sleep in his chains for years,
The sound of our mirth shall pass over earth
 With balm for a nation's tears.

A curse for the cold, a cup for the bold,
 A smile for the girls we love;
And for him who'd bleed, in his country's
 need,
 A home in the skies above.

We have asked the page of a former age
 For hope secure and bright,

And the spell it gave to the stricken slave
 Was in one strong word—"Unite."

Though the wind howl free o'er a simple
 tree
 Till it bends beneath its frown—
For many a day it will howl away
 Ere a forest be stricken down

By the martyr's dead, who for freedom bled,
 By all that man deems divine,
Our patriot band for a sainted land
 Like brothers shall all combine.

Then fill to-night, in our halls of light,
 The toast on our lips must be—
"The sinewy hand, the glittering brand,
 Our homes and our altars free."

THE MUNSTER WAR-SONG.

1190.

BY R. D. WILLIAMS.

[This ballad relates to the time when the Irish began to rally and unite against their invaders. The union was, alas! brief; but its effects were great. The troops of Connaught and Ulster, under Cathal Cruv deaҏg (Cathal O'Connor of the Red Hand), defeated and slew Armoric St. Laurence, and stripped De Courcy of half his conquests. But the ballad refers to Munster; and an extract from Moore's book will show that there was solid ground for triumph. "Among the chiefs who agreed at this crisis to postpone their mutual feuds and act in concert against the enemy, were O'Brian of Thomond, and Mac Carthy of Desmond, hereditary rulers of North and South Munster, and chiefs respectively of the two rival tribes, the Dalcassians and Eoganians. By a truce now formed between those princes, O'Brian was left free to direct his arms against the English; and having attacked their forces at Thurles, in Fogarty's country, gave them a complete overthrow, putting to the sword, adds the Munster Annals, a great number of knights."—History of Ireland, A. D. 1190.]

Can the depths of the ocean afford you not graves,
That you come thus to perish afar o'er the waves;
To redden and swell the wild torrents that flow,
Through the valley of vengeance, the dark Aharlow?*

The clangor of conflict o'erburdens the breeze,
From the stormy Slieve Bloom to the stately Galtees;
Your caverns and torrents are purple with gore,
Slievenamon, Glencoloc, and sublime Galtymore!

The Sun-burst that slumbered embalmed in our tears,
Tipperary! shall wave o'er thy tall mountaineers!
And the dark hill shall bristle with saber and spear,
While one tyrant remains to forge manacles here.

* Aharlow glen, County of Tipperary.

The riderless war-steed careers o'er the plain,
With a shaft in his flank and a blood-dripping mane,
His gallant breast labors, and glares his wild eyes;
He plunges in torture—falls—shivers—and dies.

Let the trumpets ring triumph! the tyrant is slain,
He reels o'er his charger deep-pierced through the brain;
And his myriads are flying like leaves on the gale,
But, who shall escape from our hills with the tale?

For the arrows of vengeance are show'ring like rain,
And choke the strong rivers with islands of slain,
Till thy waves, "lordly Shannon," all crimsonly flow,
Like the billows of hell with the blood of the foe.

Ay! the foemen are flying, but vainly they fly—
Revenge, with the fleetness of lightning, can vie;
And the septs of the mountains spring up from each rock,
And rush down the ravines like wolves on the flock.

And who shall pass over the stormy Slieve Bloom,
To tell the pale Saxon of tyranny's doom;
When, like tigers from ambush, our fierce mountaineers
Leap along from the crags with their death-dealing spears?

They came with high boasting to bind us as slaves,
But the glen and the torrent have yawned for their graves—
From the gloomy Ardfinnan to wild Templemore—
From the Suir to the Shannon—is red with their gore.

By the soul of Heremon! our warriors may smile,
To remember the march of the foe through our isle;
Their banners and harness were costly and gay,
And proudly they flash'd in the summer sun's ray.

The hilts of their falchions were crusted with gold,
And the gems of their helmets were bright to behold,
By Saint Bride of Kildare! but they moved in fair show—
To gorge the young eagles of dark Aharlow!

———o———

THE GROVES OF BLARNEY.

BY R. A. MILLIKEN.

THE groves of Blarney they look so
    charming,
  Down by the purling of sweet silent
    streams,
Being banked with posies that spontaneous
    grow there,
  Planted in order by the sweet rock close.
'Tis there the daisy and the sweet carnation,
  The blooming pink, and the rose so fair;
The daffydowndilly—likewise the lily,
  All flowers that scent the sweet fragrant
    air.

There's gravel walks there, for speculation,
  And conversation in sweet solitude.
'Tis there the lover may hear the dove, or
  The gentle plover in the afternoon;

And if a lady should be so engaging,
  As to walk alone in those shady bowers,
'Tis there the courtier he may transport
    her,
  Into some fort, or all under ground.

There is a stone there, that whoever kisses,
  Oh! he never misses to grow eloquent;
'Tis he may clamber to a lady's chamber,
  Or become a member of Parliament;
A clever spouter he'll soon turn out, or
  An out-and-outer, "to be left alone."
Don't hope to hinder him, or to bewilder
    him,
  Sure he's a pilgrim from the Blarney
    Stone.

THE EXILE OF ERIN.

BY G. A. REYNOLDS.

THERE came to the beach a poor exile of
    Erin,
  The dew on his raiment was heavy and
    chill;
For his country he sighed when at twilight
    repairing,
  To wander alone by the wind-beaten hill.
But the day star attracted his eyes' sad
    devotion,
For it rose o'er his own native isle of the
    ocean,
Where oft in the fire of his youthful emotion,
  He sang the bold anthem of ERIN GO
    BRAGH.

"Oh, sad is my fate," said the heart-broken
    stranger,
  "The wild deer and wolf to a covert can
    flee;
But I have no refuge from famine and
    danger,
  A home and a country remain not to me.
Ah! never again in the green sunny bowers,
Where my forefathers liv'd shall I spend the
    sweet hours,
Or cover my harp with the wild woven
    flowers,
  And strike to the numbers of ERIN GO
    BRAGH.

"Erin, my country, though sad and forsaken,
  In dreams I revisit thy sea-beaten shore,
But alas! in a far foreign land I awaken,
  And sigh for the friends who can meet me
    no more.

Oh! cruel fate, wilt thou never replace me
  In a mansion of peace where no perils can
    chase me?
Ah! never again shall my brothers embrace
    me—
  They died to defend me, or lived to deplore.

"Where is my cabin door, fast by the wild
    wood?
  Sisters and sires, did you weep for its fall?
Where is the mother that looked on my
    childhood?
  And where is the bosom friend dearer
    than all?
Oh! my sad heart, long abandoned by
    pleasure,
Why did it dote on a fast-fading treasure,
Tears like the rain-drop may fall without
    measure,
  But rapture and beauty they cannot recall.

"Yet all its sad recollections suppressing,
  One dying wish my lone bosom can draw—
Erin, an exile bequeaths thee his blessing,
  Land of my forefathers, ERIN GO BRAGH.
Buried and cold when my heart stills her
    motion,
Green be thy fields, sweetest Isle of the
    ocean,
And thy harp-striking bards sing aloud with
    emotion,
  ERIN, MAVOURNEEN! ERIN GO BRAGH!

---o---

ERIN, MY COUNTRY.

BY WM. M'COMB.

OH, Erin, my country! although thy harp slumbers,
  And lies in oblivion in Tara's old hall,
With scarce one kind hand to awaken its numbers,
  Or sound a lone dirge to the Son of Fingal;
The trophies of warfare may hang there neglected,
  For dead are the warriors to whom they were known;
But the harp of old Erin will still be respected,
  While there lives but one Bard to enliven its tone.

Oh, Erin, my country! I love thy green bowers,
  No music's to me like thy murmuring rills,
Thy shamrock to me is the fairest of flowers,
  And nought is more dear than thy daisy-clad hills;
Thy caves, whether used by thy warriors or sages,
  Are still sacred held in each Irishman's heart,
And thy ivy-crowned turrets, the pride of past ages,
  Though mouldering in ruins, do grandeur impart!

Britannia may vaunt of her lion and armor,
  And glory when she her old wooden walls views:
Caledonia may boast of her pibroch and claymore,
  And pride in her philabeg, kilt, and her hose:
But where is the nation to rival old Erin?
  Or where is the country such heroes can boast?
In battle they're brave as the tiger or lion,
  And bold as the eagle that flies 'round our coast!

The breezes oft shake both the rose and the thistle,
  While Erin's green shamrock lies hushed in the dale;
In safety it rests, while the stormy winds whistle,
  And grows undisturbed 'midst the moss of the vale;
Then, hail! fairest island in Neptune's old ocean!
  Thou land of Saint Patrick, my parent *agra!*
Cold—cold must the heart be, and void of emotion
  That loves not the music of " Erin-go-Bragh!"

MA CHREEVIN EVIN.

BY EDWARD WALSH.

AIR:—"*Mo Chraoivin Aovinn.*"

YE dark-haired youths and elders hoary,
  List to the wand'ring harper's song,
My *clairsheach* weeps my true love's story,
  In my true love's native tongue;
She's bound and bleeding 'neath the
    oppressor,
  Few her friends and fierce her foe,
And brave hearts cold who would redress
    her,
  Ma chreevin evin alga, oh!

My love had riches once and beauty,
  Till want and sorrow paled her cheek;
And stalwart hearts for honor's duty—
  They're crouching now, like cravens sleek.
Oh, Heaven! that e'er this day of rigor
  Saw sons of heroes, abject, low—
And blood and tears thy face disfigure,
  Ma chreevin evin alga, oh!

I see young virgins step the mountain
  As graceful as the bounding fawn,
With cheeks like heath-flow'r by the
    fountain,

  And breasts like downy *ceanaran.*
Shall bondsmen share those beauties ample?
  Shall their pure bosoms' current flow
To nurse new slaves for them that trample
  Ma chreevin evin alga, oh?

Around my *clairsheach's* speaking measures,
  Men, like their fathers tall, arise—
Their heart the same deep hatred treasures,
  I read it in their kindling eyes!
The same proud brow to frown at danger—
  The same long *coulin's* graceful flow—
The same dear tongue to curse the stranger—
  Ma chreevin evin alga, oh?

I'd sing ye more, but age is stealing
  Along my pulse and tuneful fires;
Far bolder woke my chord, appealing
  For craven *Sheamus* to your sires.
Arouse to vengeance, men of brav'ry,
  For broken oaths—for altars low—
For bonds that bind in bitter slav'ry—
  Ma chreevin evin alga, oh!

THE GREEN ABOVE THE RED.

BY THOMAS DAVIS.

AIR:—" *Irish Molly O!*"

FULL often when our fathers saw the Red above the Green,
They 'rose in rude but fierce array, with saber, pike, and skian,
And over many a noble town, and many a field of dead,
They proudly set the Irish Green above the English Red.

But in the end, throughout the land, the shameful sight was seen—
The English Red in triumph high above the Irish Green;
But well they died in breach and field, who, as their spirits fled,
Still saw the Green maintain its place above the English Red.

And they who saw, in after times, the Red above the Green,
Were withered as the grass that dies beneath a forest screen;
Yet often by this healthy hope their sinking hearts were fed,
That, in some day to come, the Green should flutter o'er the Red.

Sure 'twas for this Lord Edward died, and Wolfe Tone sunk serene—
Because they could not bear to leave the Red above the Green;
And 'twas for this that Owen fought, and Sarsfield nobly bled—
Because their eyes were hot to see the Green above the Red.

So, when the strife began again, our darling Irish Green
Was down upon the earth, while high the English Red was seen;
Yet still we held our fearless course, for something in us said:
" Before the strife is o'er you'll see the Green above the Red."

And 'tis for this we think and toil, and knowledge strive to glean,
That we may pull the English Red below the Irish Green,
And leave our sons sweet Liberty and smiling plenty spread,
Above the land once dark with blood—*the Green above the Red.*

The jealous English tyrant now has bann'd the Irish Green,
And forced us to conceal it like a something foul and mean;
But yet, by Heavens! he'll sooner raise his victims from the dead
Than force our hearts to leave the Green and cotton to the Red.

We'll trust ourselves, for God is good, and blesses those who lean
On their brave hearts, and not upon an earthly king or queen;
And, freely as we lift our hands, we vow our blood to shed
Once and for evermore to raise the Green above the Red.

————o————

ROVING BRIAN O'CONNELL.
BY ROBERT D. JOYCE.

"How do you like her for your wife,
Roving Brian O'Connell?
A loving mate and true for life,
Roving Brian O'Connell."
"She's as fit to be my wife
As my sword is for the strife,"
Said the Rapparee trooper,
Roving Brian O'Connell!

"Ne'er to Mabel prove untrue,
Roving Brian O'Connell,
For oh! she'd die for love of you,
Roving Brian O'Connell!"
"Oh! my wild heart never knew
A flame so constant, too,"
Said the Rapparee trooper,
Roving Brian O'Connell!

"Her father died as dies the brave,
Roving Brian O'Connell;
Beneath the blow the Saxon gave,
Roving Brian O'Connell."

"Next we'll meet the Saxon knave
He'll get pike and gun and glaive!"
Said the Rapparee trooper,
Roving Brian O'Connell.

"How will you your young bride keep,
Roving Brian O'Connell?
The foeman's bands are ne'er asleep,
Roving Brian O'Connell."
"In our hold by Conail's steep
Who dare make my Mabel weep?"
Said the Rapparee trooper,
Roving Brian O'Connell.

"This day in ruined church you stand,
Roving Brian O'Connell;
To take your young bride's priceless hand,
Roving Brian O'Connell."
"Oh, my heart, my arm, my brand,
Are for her and our dear land!"
Said the Rapparee trooper,
Roving Brian O'Connell.

KILLARNEY.

BY M. W. BALFE.

By Killarney's lakes and fells,
  Emerald isles and winding bays,
Mountain paths, and woodland dells,
  Memory ever fondly strays.
Bounteous nature loves all lands,
  Beauty wanders everywhere,
Footprints leaves on many strands,
  But her home is surely there.
    Angels fold their wings and rest
    In that Eden of the west,
    Beauty's home, Killarney,
    Heaven's reflex, Killarney.

Innisfallen's ruin'd shrine
  May suggest a passing sigh,
But man's faith can ne'er decline
  Such God's wonders floating by
Castle Lough and Glena Bay,
  Mountains Tore and Eagle's nest,
Still at Muckross you must pray,
  Though the monks are now at rest.
    Angels wonder not that man
    There would fain prolong life's span,
    Beauty's home, etc.

No place else can charm the eye
  With such bright and varied tints,
Every rock that you pass by
  Verdure borders or besprints.
Virgin there the green grass grows,
  Every morn Spring's natal day,
Bright hued berries daff the snows,
  Smiling winter's frown away.
    Angels often pausing there,
    Doubt if Eden were more fair,
    Beauty's home, etc.

Music there for echo dwells,
  Makes each sound a harmony,
Many voic'd the chorus swells,
  Till it faints in ecstasy.
With the charmful tints below
  Seems the Heaven above to vie,
All rich colors that we know
  Tinge the cloud wreaths in that sky.
    Wings of angels so might shine,
    Glancing back soft light divine,
    Beauty's home, etc.

THE IRISHMAN.

BY JAMES ORR.

[A United Irishman of 1798, and fought at Antrim.]

THE savage loves his native shore,
  Though rude the soil and chill the air;
Then well may Erin's sons adore
  Their isle which nature formed so fair.
What flood reflects a shore so sweet
  As Shannon sweet or pastoral Baun?
Or who a friend or foe can meet
  So generous as an Irishman?

His hand is rash, his heart is warm,
  But honesty is still his guide;
None more repents a deed of harm,
  And none forgives with nobler pride;
He may be duped, but won't be dared—
  More fit to practice than to plan;
He dearly earns his poor reward,
  And spends it like an Irishman.

If strange or poor, for you he'll pay,
  And guide to where you safe may be;
If you're his guest, while e'er you stay,
  His cottage holds a jubilee.

His inmost soul he will unlock,
  And if he may your secrets scan,
Your confidence he scorns to mock,
  For faithful is an Irishman.

By honor bound in woe or weal,
  Whate'er she bids he dares to do;
Try him with bribes—they won't prev
  Prove him in fire—you'll find him tr
He seeks not safety, let his post
  Be where it ought in danger's van;
And if the field of fame be lost,
  It won't be by an Irishman.

Erin, loved land, from age to age,
  Be thou more great, more famed and
May peace be thine, or, shouldst thou v
  Defensive war—cheap victory.
May plenty bloom in every field,
  Which gentle breezes softly fan,
And cheerful smiles serenely gild
  The home of every Irishman.

THE OLD CHURCH.

BY TYRONE POWER, (*Irish Comedian.*)

THOU art crumbling to the dust, old pile!
  Thou art hastening to thy fall,
And 'round thee in thy loneliness
  Clings the Ivy to the wall.
The worshipers are scattered now
  Who knelt before thy shrine,
And silence reigns where anthems rose
  In days of " Auld Lang Syne."

And sadly sighs the wandering wind,
  Where oft, in years gone by,
Prayers rose from many hearts to Him,
  The Highest of the High;
The tramp of many a busy foot
  That sought thy aisles, is o'er,
And many a weary heart around
  It still forever more.

How doth Ambition's hope take wing,
  How droops the spirit now,
We hear the distant city's din,
  The dead are mute below;
The sun that shone upon their paths
  Now gilds their lonely graves,
The zephyrs which once fanned their
    brows,
  The grass above them waves.

Oh! could we call the many back
  Who've gathered here in vain,
Who've careless roved where we do now,
  Who'll never meet again;
How would our very soul be stirred,
  To meet the earnest gaze
Of the lovely and the beautiful,
  The lights of other days.

---o---

CELTS AND SAXONS.

BY THOMAS DAVIS.

WE hate the Saxon and the Dane,
  We hate the Norman men;
We cursed their greed for blood and gain,
  We curse them now again.
Yet start not, Irish born man,
  If you're to Ireland true.
We heed not blood, nor creed, nor clan—
  We have no curse for you.

We have no curse for you or yours,
  But Friendship's ready grasp,
And faith to stand by you and yours
  Unto our latest gasp;
To stand by you against all foes,
  Howe'er or whence they come,
With traitor arts, or bribes, or blows,
  From England, France or Rome.

What matter that at different shrines
  We pray unto one God;
What matter that at different times
  Our fathers won this sod—
In fortune and in name we're bound
  By stronger links than steel;
And neither can be safe nor sound
  But in the other's weal.

As Nubian rocks, and Ethiop sand
  Long drifting down the Nile,
Built up old Egypt's fertile land
  For many a hundred mile.
So Pagan clans to Ireland came,
  And clans of Christendom,
Yet joined their wisdom and their fame
  To build a nation from.

Here came the brown Phœnician,
  The man of trade and toil—
Here came the proud Milesian,
  Ahungering for spoil.
And the Firbolg and the Cymry,
  And the hard, enduring Dane,
And the iron Lords of Normandy,
  With the Saxons in their train.

And, oh, it were a gallant deed
  To show before mankind,
How every race and every creed
  Might be by love combined;
Might be combined, yet not forget
  The fountain whence they rose,
As, filled by many a rivulet
  The stately Shannon flows.

Nor would we wreak our ancient feud
  On Belgian or on Dane,
Nor visit in a hostile mood
  The hearths of Gaul or Spain;
But long as on our country lies
  The Anglo-Norman yoke,
Their tyranny we'll signalize,
  And God's revenge invoke.

We do not hate, we never cursed,
  Nor spoke a foeman's word
Against a man in Ireland nursed,
  Howe'er we thought he erred;
So start not, Irish born man,
  If you're to Ireland true.
We heed not race, nor creed, nor clan,
  We've hearts and hands for you.

THE DYING PATRIOT.

BY CHRISTOPHER M. O'KEEFE.

THE warrior's face, as he calmly lay,
Extended mute on the gory clay,
Was pale and dim as the wintry light,
That heralds the fall of a stormy night—
When the sun is rebuked by some gloomy
    power
And abashed by its menace app'rs to cower.
From his wounded side in a purple flood
Was silently welling the warrior's blood.
While kneeling beside him, his brother
    tried
To stop the rush of that vital tide.
But vain were the efforts of love to stay
The streamlet of agony ebbing away.
His gasping breath and his broken sigh,
And the film of death on his fading eye,
O'erwhelm the Gilly with black despair,
Who sees him with horror beyond his care.
The heaving, at length, of the heart is o'er,

And the pulse of the valiant will throb no
    more.
Then wild with his terrors—distressed and
    pale,
The Gilly in agony utters a wail.
Apparently waked by those mournful cries,
The perishing warrior turns his eyes.
Through the mist of death he essays to scan
The hueless face of the desolate man,
Perusing that visage disfigured with care,
He dimly descries that his brother is there.
"Ah! why do I see thee lingering here,
When the tumult of battle is echoing near?
Can this be the place ,for a patriot knight,
Whom the cry of a nation would summon to
    fight?
The land of our birth is more helpless than
    I—
Away to the battle, and leave me to die."

SHAMUS O'BRIEN, THE BOLD BOY OF GLINGALL.

A Tale of 'Ninety-Eight.

BY SAMUEL LOVER.

JIST afther the war, in the year '98,
As soon as the boys wor all scattered and bate,
'Twas the custom, whenever a peasant was got,
To hang him by thrial—barrin' sich as was shot.
There was trial by jury goin' on by daylight,
And the martial-law hangin' the lavins by night;
It's them was hard times for an honest gossoon,
If he missed in the judges—he'd meet a dragoon;
An' whether the sodgers or judges gev sentence,
The divil a much time they allowed for repentance;
An' it's many's the fine boy was then on his keepin'
Wid small share iv restin', or aitin', or sleepin',
An' because they loved Erin, an' scorned to sell it,
A prey for the bloodhound, a mark for the bullet.
Unsheltered by night, and unrested by day,
With the heath for their barracks, revenge for their pay;
An' the bravest an' hardiest boy iv them all
Was Shamus O'Brien, from the town of Glingall.
His limbs were well set, an' his body was light,
And the keen-fanged hound had not teeth half so white;
But his face was as pale as the face of the dead,
An' his cheek never warmed with the blush of the red;
An' for all that he was an ugly young b'y,
For the divil himself couldn't blaze with his eye,
So droll an' so wicked, so dark an' so bright,
Like a fire flash that crossed the depths of the night!
An' he was the best mower that ever has been,
An' the illigantest hurler that ever was seen,
An' his dancin' was sich that the men used to stare,
An' the women turn crazy, he done it so quare,
An' by gorra, the whole world gev it into him there,
An' it's he was the b'y that was hard to be caught,

An' it's often he run, an' it's often he fought,
An' it's many the one can remember right well
The quare things he done; and it's oft I heard tell
How he lathered the yeomen, himself agin' four,
An' stretched the two strongest on old Galtimore.
 But the fox must sleep sometimes, the wild deer must rest,
An' treachery prey on the blood iv the best;
Afther many a brave action of power and pride,
An' many a hard night on the mountain's bleak side,
An' a thousand great dangers and toils overpast,
In the darkness of night he was taken at last.
Now, Shamus, look back on the beautiful moon,
For the door of the prison must close on you soon,
An' take your last look at her dim lovely light,
That falls on the mountain and valley this night;
One look at the village, one look at the flood,
An' one at the sheltering, far distant wood;
Farewell to the forest, farewell to the hill,
An' farewell to the friends that will think of you still;
Farewell to the pathern, the hurlin' an' wake,
An' farewell to the girl that would die for your sake.
An' twelve sodgers brought him to Maryborough jail,
An' the turnkey resaved him, refusin' all bail;
The fleet limbs wor chained, an' the strong hands wor bound,
An' he laid down his length on the cowld prison ground;
An' the dreams of his childhood came over him there
As gentle an' soft as the sweet summer air,
An' happy remembrances crowding on ever,
As fast as the foam-flakes dhrift down on the river,
Bringing fresh to his heart merry days long gone by,
Till the tears gathered heavy and thick in his eye.
But the tears didn't fall, for the pride of his heart
Would not suffer one drop down his pale cheek to start;
An' he sprung to his feet in his dark prison cave,
An' swore with the fierceness that misery gave,
By the hopes of the good, an' the cause of the brave,
That when he was mouldering in the cold grave
His enemies should never have it to boast
His scorn of their vengeance one moment was lost;
His bosom might bleed, but his cheek would be dhry;
For undaunted he lived, and undaunted he'd die.
Well, as soon as a few weeks were over and gone,
The terrible day iv the thrial kem on;
There was sich a crowd there was scarce room to stand,
An' sodgers on guard, and dhragoons sword-in-hand
An' the court-house so full that the people were bothered,
An' attorneys an' criers on the point iv bein' smothered;
An' counsellors almost gev over for dead,
An' the jury sittin' up in their box overhead;
An' the judge settled out so detarmined and big,
With his gown on his back, and an illegant new wig;
An' silence was called, an' the minute it was said,
The court was as still as the heart of the dead,
An' they heard but the openin' of one prison lock,
An' Shamus O'Brien came into the dock.
For one minute he turned his eye 'round on the throng,
An' he looked at the bars so firm and strong,
An' he saw that he had not a hope nor a friend,
A chance to escape, nor a word to defend,
An' he folded his arms as he stood there alone,
As calm an' as cold as a statue of stone;
An' they read a big writin', a yard long at laste,

An' Jim didn't understand it, or mind it a taste,
An' the judge took a big pinch iv snuff, an' he says,
"Are you guilty or not, Jim O'Brien, av you pl'ase?"
An' all held their breath in the silence of dhread,
An' Shamus O'Brien made answer and said:
"My lord, if you ask me if in my life-time
I thought any treason, or did any crime
That should call to my cheek, as I stand alone here,
The hot blush of shame or coldness of fear,
Though I stood by the grave to receive my death-blow,
Before God and the world I would answer you, no!
But if you would ask me, as I think it like,
If in the rebellion I carried a pike,
An' fought for ould Ireland from the first to the close,
An' shed the heart's blood of her bitterest foes,
I answer you, yes, and I tell you again,
Though I stand here to perish, it's my glory that then
In her cause I was willing that my veins should run dry,
An' now for her sake I am ready to die."
Then the silence was great, and the jury smiled bright,
An' the judge wasn't sorry the job was made light;
By my sowl, it's himself was the crabbed ould chap!
In a twinklin' he pulled on his ugly black cap.
Then Shamus' mother in the crowd standin' by,
Called out to the judge with a pitiful cry:
"O, judge, darlin', don't, O, don't say the word!
The crathur is young, have mercy, my lord,
He was foolish, he didn't know what he was doin';
You don't know him, my lord—O, don't give him to ruin;
He's the kindliest crathur, the tendherest-hearted,
Don't part us forever, we that's so long parted.
Judge, mavourneen, forgive him, forgive him, my lord,
An' God will forgive you—O, don't say the word!"
That was the first minute that O'Brien was shaken,
When he saw that he was not quite forgot or forsaken;
An' down his pale cheeks, at the words of his mother,
The big tears wor runnin' fast, one after th' other;
An' two or three times he endeavored to spake,
But the sthrong manly voice used to falther and break;
But at last by the strength of his high mounted pride,
He conquered and masthered his grief's swelling tide;
"An'" said he, "mother, darlin', don't break your poor heart,
For, sooner or later, the dearest must part;
An' God knows it's betther than wandering in fear
On the bleak, trackless mountain, among the wild deer,
To lie in the grave, where the head, heart and breast,
From thought, labor, and sorrow, forever shall rest.
Then, mother, my darlin', don't cry any more,
Don't make me seem broken in this, my last hour;
For I wish, when my head's lying undher the raven,
No thrue man can say I died like a craven!"
Then towards the judge Shamus bent down his head,
An' that minute the solemn death-sentence was said.
The mornin' was bright, an' the mists rose on high,
An' the lark whistled merrily in the clear sky;
But why are the men standin' idle so late?
An' why do the crowds gather so fast in the strate?
What come they to talk of? What come they to see?
An' why does the long rope hang from the tree?
O, Shamus O'Brien! pray fervent and fast,
May the Saints take your soul, for this day is your last;
Pray fast an' pray sthrong, for the moment is nigh

When, strong, proud an' great as you are, you must die.
An' fasther an' fasther, the crowd gathered there,
Boys, horses an' gingerbread, just like a fair;
An' whiskey was sellin', and cussamuck, too,
An' ould men and young women enjoying the view,
An' ould Tim Mulvany, he med the remark,
There wasn't sich a sight since the time of Noah's ark;
An' begorry 'twas thrue for him, for divil sich a scruge,
Sich divarshin an' crowds, was known since the deluge;
For thousands were gathered there, if there was one,
Waitin' till sich time as the hangin' id come on.
At last they threw open the big prison gate,
An' out came the sheriffs an' sodgers in state,
An' a cart in the middle, an' Shamus was in it,
Not paler, but prouder than ever that minute.
An' as soon as the people saw Shamus O'Brien,
Wid prayin' an' blessin', and all the girls cryin',
A wild, wailin' sound kem on by degrees,
Like the sound of the lonesome wind blowin' through trees.
On—on to the gallows the sheriffs are gone,
An' the cart an' the sodgers go steadily on;
An' at every side swellin' around of the cart,
A wild, sorrowful sound that id open your heart;
Now undher the gallows the cart takes its stand,
An' the hangman gets up wid the rope in his hand;
An' the priest havin' blessed, goes down on the ground,
An' Shamus O'Brien throws one last look around.
Then the hangman dhrew near, an' the people grew still,
Young faces turned sickly, and warm hearts turn chill;
An' the rope bein' ready, his neck was made bare,
For the gripe iv the life-strangling cord to prepare;
An' the good priest has left him, havin' said his last prayer.
But the good priest done more, for his hands he unbound,
And with one daring spring Jim has leaped on the ground;
Bang—bang! go the carbines, and clash! go the sabers;
He's not down! he's alive still! now stand to him, neighbors!
Through the smoke and the horses he's into the crowd,
By the Heavens he's free!—then thunder, more loud,
By one shout from the people the Heavens are shaken,
One shout from the world that the dead might awaken.
The sodgers ran this way, the sheriffs ran that,
An' Father Malone lost his new Sunday hat;
To-night he'll be sleepin' in Aherloe Glin,
And the divil's in the dice if you catch him ag'in.
Your swords they may glitter, your carbines go bang,
But if you want hangin', it's yourself you must hang.
He has mounted his horse, and soon he will be
In America, darlint, the land of the free.

———o———

THE HERMIT.

BY OLIVER GOLDSMITH.

"TURN, gentle hermit of the dale,
  And guide my lonely way,
To where yon taper cheers the vale
  With hospitable ray;

" For here, forlorn and lost, I tread
  With fainting steps and slow—

Where wilds, immeasurably spread,
  Seem lengthening as I go."

" Forbear, my son," the hermit cries,
  " To tempt the dangerous gloom;
For yonder faithless phantom flies
  To lure thee to thy doom,

"Here, to the houseless child of want
　My door is open still;
And, though my portion is but scant,
　I give it with good will.

"Then turn, to-night, and freely share
　Whate'er my cell bestows—
My rushy couch and frugal fare,
　My blessing and repose.

"No flocks that range the valley free
　To slaughter I condemn—
Taught by that power that pities me,
　I learn to pity them.

"But, from the mountain's grassy side
　A guiltless feast I bring—
A scrip with herbs and fruits supplied,
　And water from the spring.

"Then, pilgrim, turn, thy cares forego;
　All earth-born cares are wrong;
Man wants but little here below,
　Nor wants that little long."

Soft as the dew from Heaven descends,
　His gentle accents fell;
The modest stranger slowly bends,
　And follows to the cell.

Far, in a wilderness obscure,
　The lonely mansion lay;
A refuge to the neighboring poor,
　And strangers led astray.

No stores beneath its humble thatch
　Requir'd a master's care;
The wicket, opening with a latch,
　Receiv'd the harmless pair.

And now, when busy crowds retire
　To take their evening rest,
The hermit trimm'd his little fire,
　And cheer'd his pensive guest;

And spread his vegetable store,
　And gayly press'd and smil'd;
And, skill'd in legendary lore,
　The lingering hours beguil'd.

Around in sympathetic mirth,
　Its tricks the kitten tries—
The cricket chirrups on the hearth,
　The crackling fagot flies;

But, nothing could a charm impart
　To soothe the stranger's woe—
For grief was heavy at his heart,
　And tears began to flow.

His rising cares the hermit spied—
　With answering care oppress'd;
"And whence, unhappy youth," he cried,
　"The sorrows of thy breast?

"From better habitations spurn'd,
　Reluctant dost thou rove?
Or grieve for friendship unreturn'd,
　Or unregarded love?

"Alas! the joys that fortune brings
　Are trifling, and decay—
And those who prize the paltry things
　More trifling still than they.

"And what is friendship but a name,
　A charm that lulls to sleep—
A shade that follows wealth or fame,
　But leaves the wretch to weep?

"And love is still an emptier sound—
　The modern fair-one's jest;
On earth unseen, or only found,
　To warm the turtle's nest.

"For shame, fond youth, thy sorrows
　　hush—
And spurn the sex," he said;
But while he spoke, a rising blush
　His lovelorn guest betray'd;

Surpris'd, he sees new beauties rise,
　Swift mantling to the view—
Like colors o'er the morning skies,
　As bright, as transient too.

The bashful look, the rising breast,
　Alternate spread alarms;
The lovely stranger stands confess'd,
　A maid in all her charms.

"And, ah! forgive a stranger rude,
　A wretch forlorn," she cried—
"Whose feet unhallowed thus intrude
　Where Heaven and you reside;

"But let a maid thy pity share,
　Whom love has taught to stray—
Who seeks for rest, but finds despair
　Companion of her way.

"My father liv'd beside the Tyne—
　A wealthy lord was he;
And all his wealth was mark'd as mine;
　He had but only me.

"To win me from his tender arms
　Unnumber'd suitors came;
Who prais'd me for imputed charms,
　And felt or feigned a flame.

"Each hour, a mercenary crowd
  With richest proffers strove;
Among the rest young Edwin bow'd—
  But never talked of love.

"In humble, simplest habit clad,
  No wealth nor power had he;
Wisdom and worth were all he had—
  But these were all to me.

"And when, beside me in the dale,
  He carol'd lays of love,
His breath lent fragrance to the gale,
  And music to the grove.

"The blossoms opening to the day,
  The dews of Heaven refined,
Could nought of purity display
  To emulate his mind.

"The dew, the blossom on the tree,
  With charms inconstant shine;
Their charms were his; but, woe to me,
  Their constancy was mine.

"For still I tried each fickle art,
  Importunate and vain;
And while his passion touched my heart,
  I triumph'd in his pain.

"Till, quite dejected with my scorn,
  He left me to my pride,

And sought a solitude forlorn,
  In secret, where he died.

"But mine the sorrow, mine the fault,
  And well my life shall pay:
I'll seek the solitude he sought,
  And stretch me where he lay.

"And there, forlorn, despairing, hid—
  I'll lay me down and die;
'Twas so for me that Edwin died,
  And so for him will I."

"Forbid it, Heaven!" the hermit cried,
  And clasp'd her to his breast;
The wondering fair one turned to chide,
  'Twas Edwin's self that press'd.

"Turn, Angelina! ever dear—
  My charmer, turn to see
Thy own, thy long-lost Edwin here,
  Restor'd to love and thee.

"Thus let me hold thee to my heart,
  And every care resign;
And shall we never—never part,
  My life—my all that's mine?

"No; never from this hour to part,
  We'll live and love so true;
The sigh that rends thy constant heart
  Shall break thy Edwin's too."

———o———

THE TOAST.

BY COL. MICHAEL DOHENY.

AIR:—"*Garryowen.*"

A BUMPER, my comrades, fill—fill to the brim,
With our hearts flushing in it we drink it to him
To whose steel in the clash of the hot battle's glow
Shall first gush the red blood from the heart of the foe.
  The day is nearing bright and fast,
  The long, lone, starless night is passed,
  And you will win our own at last,
On the fields of our dear native island.
A bumper, my comrades, fill—fill to the brim,
With our hearts flushing in it, we drink it to him
To whose steel in the first clash of hot battle's glow
Shall first gush the blood from the heart of the foe.

Another, my comrades, the toast of all toasts,
Let us drink with a cheer that will ring through the hosts—
Here's to him who first leaps on the green island's shore,
And first hallows its tear-watered soil with his gore.
  The youthful hearts swell proudly there,
  They hug dear vengeance, and prepare
  To drive the tiger from his lair,
O'er the hills of our dear native island,

Another, my comrades, the toast of all toasts,
Let us drink with a cheer that will ring through the hosts,
Here's to him who first leaps on the green island's shore,
And first hallows its tear-watered soil with his gore.

Let us drink once again, boys! before we depart,
With a will that betokens the fire of the heart;
Let us drink—up uncovered—the valorous band
That will fling to the sky first the flag of our land.
        Their eager eyes are straining far,
        For this long-looked-for glorious star;
        Oh! who such holy hopes would mar,
    In the brightening heart of our island?
Let us drink once again, boys! before we depart,
With a will that betokens the fire of the heart;
Let us drink—up uncovered—the valorous band
That will fling to the sky first the flag of our land.

Crown another, and oh, may it be, boys, the last
We will drink on this earth—may dishonor be cast
On our corses unburied, and memories of shame,
If we shrink from redeeming the green island's name.
        Be this our latest night of cheer—
        Then onward on our high career,
        To chase the churls like frighted deer,
    O'er the hills of our dear native island.
Crown another, and oh, may it be, boys, the last
We will drink on this earth—may dishonor be cast
On our corses unburied, and memories of shame,
If we shrink from redeeming the green island's name.

———o———

OLD LAND MARKS ON THE SHANNON.

BY JOHN F. O'DONNELL.

We stand by the bridge, in the level morning,
    And the saffron water below us flows—
Saffron save where, in yon eastern inlet,
    The light has deepened its bloom to rose.
There is the city, good Master Leonard,
    Tailor and poet, sir, as you are,
And here am I with my heart to bursting,
    Gossiping under that huge bright star;
There is the city with roof and casement,
    Belfry and steeple, of which we sung,
When we were boys in St. Michael's parish;
    Then was the time for a man to be young.

Then the city—I still keep thinking—
    Looked gayer, grander, fairer than now,
You say it didn't: "Not half as splendid."
    And I object with my next best bow.
Hark! 'tis the bell of St. Dominic ringing,
    Ah, weary music that bell to me;
For I remember another music
    In days that I never again shall see.
Heavy—heavy monotonous tolling
    Out from the belfry this morning's rung;
I can recall when the saint kept singing:
    Now is the time for a man to be young.

Oh, the delight of the Sunday mornings,
    And the country folks at the chapel door;
And the golden blaze from the lofty
        windows
    That slanted in on the crowded floor.
Far off the altar, the priests, the incense—
    The sound of the gong, the sigh of the soul,
And over the heads of the congregation
    The curtained organ's terrible roll.
The green leaves danced on the yellow
        casement,
    Each separate leaf like a narrow tongue;
And the old roof branded in restless shadow;
    That was the time for a man to be young.

I'm not pious, and not affected;
    I like the life of a true, straight man,
I strike the world whenever it strikes me,
    And do my duty as best I can.
But, Master Leonard, you will believe me,
    I'd give the best fame that the world has
        made,
Throw fortune in with a: "God go with
        you,"
    To pray one prayer now as then I prayed.

Somehow the years draw out the distance
  'Twixt us and the space where the stars
    are hung,
On tiptoe then I could look into Heaven;
  That was the time for a man to be young.

Mark you the ridge in the midnight torrent,
  'Tis sixty miles from that to the sea;
Whenever the spring-tide soars across it
  The water is brackish as salt can be.
There's the old mill in the frothing currents,
  And the thin bridge spanning the void to
    land;
The mealy windows, the straight, buff gable,
  And the wheel-arch choking with weed
    and sand;
The wheel spins merrily this fair morning
  A ballad that better were left unsung,
Once it was: "Little Boy, God hears both of
    us!"
  Ah! 'twas the time for a man to be young.

Come down the quay, as the day increases,
  Oh, silent river—oh, naked slips!
Where are the sunburnt, bearded sailors,
  The masts, and yards, and the sails of the
    ships;
The gaunt, black sides of the barks, the
    rigging,
  The mermaids, sidelong on every prow,
With painted vestures, and gilded ankles,
  And Psyche, blossomed on breast and
    brow?
'Round the world as the world advances
  Newer girdles of commerce are flung;
But I remember the port twice-masted—
  That was the time for a man to be young.

In the old days you heard strange voices,
  Scented of foreign region and sea;
Saw merchandise of the lands remotest
  Chartered and piled on this mighty quay.
Now the sign of life on the river
  (Which you and I saw this morning blush)
Is the emigrant ship, with its thrice-cursed
    trimness,
  The brown boat hailing from near Kilrush.
No more the craft with the brazen bottom,
  To which the shells of the deep sea clung;

It rested once by these limestone bulwarks—
  Days, indeed, for a man to be young.

Have they gone for good? have they gone
    forever?
  Well, God and the Future only know.
I tell you, Leonard, amid this ruin,
  My heart beats sickened, and thick and
    slow.
Man has his future, and man his past, too,
  And hope fulfilled is their common crown;
What is our hope? what is our fulfilment?
  A city of graves, and a perishing town!
The doom is written, the doom is spoken,
  The knell of death is solemnly rung;
Shame on these days of woe and
    bereavement—
  These are not days for a man to be young.

Ere I depart, and the grim cathedral
  Fades in the glare of the evening heat,
Leonard, good Christian, just come with me
  A little journey up Catherine street.
There, o'er a wall, between two tall houses,
  A noble chestnut gallantly blew,
In the olden time, when Doonas was distant,
  And the Heavens were closer to me and
    you.
How the great pods fell in the precious sea-
    son,
  And the lark at the basket-maker's sung,
As we paused from school, in song and in
    shadow—
  Ah! those were the days for a man to be
    young.

Have mercy, Lord! lo! the Heavens are
    lighting,
  A torrent of fire through a sea of blue,
The hills are giants of flame, as falling
  The sun reels over remote Tervoe;
And the river writhes in increasing splen-
    dor,
  The hooker glows in the luminous track;
Forest gives forest, and mountain mountain,
  The face of the god and his glory back.
I go, while the chimes of the steepled city
  In clashing discords abroad are flung;
God bring thee back, town of my fathers,
  The golden days for a man to be young.

————o————

THE CALM AVONREE.

BY JOHN LOCKE.

BRIGHT home of my youth, my own sorrowing sireland,
  My fond heart o'erflows and the tears dim mine eyes,
When I think of thee, far-distant, beautiful Ireland,
  And the dark seas between me and you, my heart's prize.
Oft—oft do I sigh for the days of my childhood,
  When I plucked the wild flow'rs on the fair upland lea,

Or roamed the long day thro' the sweet, shady wildwood,
    On the green, grassy banks of the calm Avonree.

Ah, me! could I fly o'er the dark, swelling ocean,
    To the home of my heart, to the land of my love,
I'd be up on the wings with an exile's devotion,
    And dare every danger the dark seas above.
Again would I roam thro' the fair, leafy bowers,
    Where the boys used to drill ere I first crossed the sea;
And I'd weave for my Kathleen a garland of flowers,
    On the green, grassy banks of the calm Avonree.

Again would I hear the wild thrush in his bower,
    The loud-singing lark o'er the deep, mossy dell,
And the blackird's soft song on the tall, wild tower
    That shadows the clear-springing, sweet "Abbey well."
Once more would I hear the wild cuckoo's notes swelling,
    Along the rich valley, o'er moorland and lea,
And the blithe sparrows chirp 'round my own peaceful dwelling,
    On the green, grassy banks of the calm Avonree.

But the day may yet come when I'll see thee soft smiling,
    And gaze on thee fondly, fair, beautiful land;
I may yet live to see thro' thy narrow glens filing,
    The exiles now cast on a far, foreign strand.
I may fight for thee, too, ere the trees again blossom,
    And see thee, my Erin, yet happy and free;
And my heart may yet rest on thy soft, dewy bosom,
    In a green, grassy grave by the calm Avonree.

————o————

MOTHERLAND.

BY JOHN LOCKE.

Over many a field our fathers
    Led the lilied flag of France,
And Europe's proudest veterans
    Knew and feared their fierce advance;
Their lightning swords struck terror
    Into many a valiant band—
God of Heaven! had those weapons
    Been but swung for Motherland!
        For suffering Motherland, boys—
        For bleeding Motherland,
        All the clanking chains had fallen
        From our captive Motherland!

Our Nugent led the Austrian
    Through many a red campaign,
Full many a victor garland
    Our O'Donnells won for Spain.
But what are all the victories
    Gained on a foreign strand
To a triumph won for freedom
    And the cause of Motherland?
        The cause of Motherland, boys,
        The cause of Motherland;
        True hero he who battles
        In the cause of Motherland.

For the glorious land of Washington
    Our blood has flowed like rain;
Oft our foes had cause to mutter:
    "There's that damned green flag again!"
For victory loved to hover
    Where the wind her tatters fanned,
But when next the green flag flutters
    It shall be for Motherland.
        It must be for Motherland, boys,
        Long-trodden Motherland;
        When next the green flag flutters
        It shall be for Motherland.

Too long the crimson current
    Of our generous Celtic blood
Has flowed in foreign valleys—
    Has been shed for others' good;
Now we swear its rich libation
    Shall bedew no foreign strand
Till the flashing light of freedom
    Shall illume our Motherland.
        Our grand old Motherland, boys,
        Our brave old Motherland,
        Till the flashing light of freedom
        Shall illume our Motherland.

————o————

THE KNIGHT OF THE SHAMROCK.

BY J. FRAZER.

My Lady-love, hadst thou not broken
  The spirit of thy sacred vow,
The burning words would be unspoken,
  That scar thy guilty bosom now.
In fealty, faith—and hope, I followed
  Wooed—waited—watched thy steps for
    years;
At last, my very heart was hollowed
  By scorching thoughts and scalding tears.

My fortunes by thy house were blighted—
  And full revenge I ne'er forgot;
Until thy queenly word was plighted
  To love me—why redeem it not?
It waked a passion that betrayed me
  From vengeance, till the chance was gone,
Thy truth itself had scarce repaid me—
  Thy falsehood left me more undone.

Wert thou of cold, repelling nature—
  Unkind to suitors, one and all—
I could forgive thee, heartless creature,
  Who recked not for my rise, or fall;
But I for scoff and scorn was singled;
  And all the treacheries of thy race,
In thy deceitful smile were mingled,
  To ruin—wrong me—and debase.

Thy quarrel found me ever ready—
  Thy bidding set my lance in rest—
My arm and heart, how strong and steady,
  Thy friends and foes have both confess'd.
And if, as oft, in general gladness
  My prowess was forgotten—then
It was my strange escape from sadness,
  To dare, and do, for thee again.

————o————

LISTENING FOR THE FOOTFALLS.

BY STEPHEN J. MEANY.

ALONE in the autumn twilight,
  In the evening's gathering gloom,
She sat, that Irish peasant wife,
  In the porch of her cottage home.
Her woman's work around her—
  Her busy hands at play—
And in tune her voice kept crooning
  Some old-time Irish lay.

But hark! in the distance a rustling
  The shadowy leaves among—
And the welcoming chirping of children—
  And she stops both work and song.
And she lovingly listens the coming
  Of the pride of her happy life—
The husband and little ones home again,
  To cheer the heart of that Irish wife.

————o————

ACUSHLA GAL MACHREE.

BY MICHAEL DOHENY.

THE long-long wished for hour has come,
  But come, asthore, in vain,
And left thee but the wailing hum
  Of sorrow and of pain;
My light of life, my only love,
  Thy portion sure must be
Man's scorn below, God's wrath above—
  Acushla gal machree.

'Twas told of thee the world around,
  Was hoped for thee by all,
That with one gallant sunward bound
  'Thou'd burst long ages' thrall;
Thy fate was tried, alas! and those
  Who perilled all for thee
Were cursed and branded as thy foes,
  Acushla gal machree.

What fate is thine, unhappy isle,
  That e'en the trusted few
Should pay thee back with fraud and guile
  When most they should be true?
'Twas not thy strength or courage failed
  Nor those whose souls were free;
By moral force wert thou betrayed,
  Acushla gal machree.

I've given thee my youth and prime,
  And manhood's waning years;
I've blest thee in thy sunniest time,
  And shed for thee my tears;
And mother, tho' thou'st cast away
  The child who'd die for thee,
My fondest wish is still to pray—
  For Cushla gal machree.

I've tracked for thee the mountain sides
  And slept within the brake,
More lonely than the swan that glides
  On Lua's fairy lake;
The rich have spurned me from their door
  Because I'd set thee free,
Yet do I love thee more and more—
  Acushla gal machree.

I've run the outlaw's bold career,
  And borne his load of ill,
His troubled rest and waking fear
  With fixed, sustaining will;
And should his last dread chance befall,
  E'en that should welcome be.
In Death, I'll love thee more than all—
  Acushla gal machree.

MOTHER, HE'S GOING AWAY.

BY SAMUEL LOVER.

Mother.

Now what are you crying for, Nelly?
  Don't be blubbering there like a fool;
With the weight o' the grief, faith, I tell
    you
You'll break down the three-legged stool.
I suppose now you're crying for Barney,
  But don't b'lieve a word that he'd say,
He tells nothing but big lies and blarney—
  Sure you know how he served poor Kate
    Karney.

Daughter. But, mother!
Mother. Oh, bother.
Daughter. Oh, mother, he's going away,
    And I dreamt the other night
    Of his ghost—*all in white!*
[*Mother speaks in an undertone.*] The
  dirty blackguard!
Daughter. Oh, mother, he's going away.

Mother.

If he's going away, all the betther—
  Blessed hour when he's out of your sight!
There's one comfort—you can't get a
    letther—
For yiz neither can read nor can write.
Sure 'twas only last week you protested,
  Since he courted fat Jinney M'Cray,
That the sight o' the scamp you detested—
  With abuse sure your tongue never
    rested—

Daughter. But, mother!
Mother. Oh, bother!
Daughter. Oh, mother, he's going away.
[*Mother speaking again with peculiar parental piety.*] May he never come back!
Daughter. And I dream of his ghost,
    Walking round my bedpost—
  Oh, mother, he's going away.

THE SONG OF THE COSSACK.

(*From the French of Beranger.*)

BY THE REV. F. MAHONY ("FATHER PROUT.")

[The original of the following stanzas was written by Beranger—who, as our readers are aware, was a French compound of Burns, Moore and Swift—shortly after the restoration of the Bourbons, consequent upon the first downfall of Napoleon. How it must have fired the blood of Republican France and whetted the steel of the worshiping legions of *le petit corporal* on his return from Elba!]

COME arouse thee up, my gallant horse, and hear thy rider on!
The comrade thou, and the friend, I trow, of the dweller on "the Don."
Pillage and death have spread their wings!—'tis the hour to hie thee forth,
And with thy hoofs an echo make to the trumpets of the North!
Nor gun, nor gold, do men behold upon thy saddle-tree;
But earth affords the wealth of lords for thy master and for thee;
Then fiercely neigh, my charger grey! O, thy chest is proud and ample;
And thy hoofs shall prance o'er the fields of France, and the pride of her heroes trample.

Europe is weak—she hath grown old; her bulwarks are laid low;
She is loth to hear the blast of war—she shrinketh from a foe!
Come, in our turn, let us sojourn, in her goodly haunts of joy—
In the pillar'd porch to wave the torch, and her palaces destroy!
Proud as when first thou slak'dst thy thirst in the flow of conquer'd Seine,
Ay, shalt thou lave, within that wave, thy blood-red flanks again.

Then fiercely neigh, my gallant grey! O, thy chest is strong and ample;
And thy hoofs shall prance o'er the fields of France, and the pride of our heroes trample.

Kings are beleaguer'd on their thrones by their own vassal crew;
And in their den quake noblemen, and priests are bearded, too;
And loud they yelp for the Cossack's help to keep their bondsmen down,
And they think it meet, while they kiss our feet, to wear a tyrant's crown!
The scepter now to my lance shall bow, and the crosier and the cross,
All shall bend alike, when I lift my pike, and aloft that scepter toss!
Then proudly neigh, my gallant grey! O, thy chest is broad and ample;
And thy hoofs shall prance o'er the fields of France, and the pride of her heroes trample.

In a night of storm I have seen a form! and the figure was a giant,
And his eye was bent on the Cossack's tent, and his look was all defiant;
Kingly his crest—and toward the West with his battle-ax he pointed,
And the "form" I saw was Attila, of this earth the scourge anointed.
From the Cossack's camp let the horseman's tramp the coming crash announce;
Let the vulture whet his beak sharp-set, on the carrion field to pounce!
Then proudly neigh, my gallant grey! O, thy chest is broad and ample;
And thy hoofs shall prance o'er the fields of France, and the pride of heroes trample.

What boots old Europe's boasted fame, on which she builds reliance,
When the North shall launch its avalanche on her works of art and science?
Hath she not wept her cities swept by our hordes of trampling stallions?
And tower and arch crush'd in the march of our barbarous battalions?
Can we not wield our fathers' shield? the same war-hatchet handle?
Do our blades want length, or the reapers strength, for the harvest of the Vandal?
Then proudly neigh, my gallant grey! O, thy chest is strong and ample;
And thy hoofs shall prance o'er the fields of France, and the pride of our heroes trample.

———o———

SUBLIME WAS THE WARNING.

BY THOMAS MOORE.

AIR:—"*The Black Joke.*"

SUBLIME was the warning which Liberty spoke,
And grand was the moment when Spaniards awoke
  Into life and revenge from the Conqueror's chain!
Oh, Liberty! let not this spirit have rest
Till it move, like a breeze, o'er the waves of the west;
Give the light of your look to each sorrowing spot,
Nor, oh! be the shamrock of Erin forgot,
  While you add to your garland the olive of Spain!

If the fame of our fathers, bequeath'd with their rights,
Give to country its charms, and to home its delights;
  If deceit be a wound, and suspicion a stain;
Then, ye men of Iberia! our cause is the same—
And, oh! may his tomb want a tear and a name,
Who would ask for a nobler, a holier death,
Than to turn his last sigh into Victory's breath
  For the shamrock of Erin and olive of Spain!

Ye Blakes and O'Donnels, whose fathers resign'd
The green hills of their youth, among strangers to find
  That repose which, at home, they had sigh'd for in vain,
Breathe a hope that the magical flame, which you light,
May be felt yet in Erin, as calm and as bright;
And forgive even Albion, while, blushing, she draws,
Like a truant, her sword, in the long-slighted cause
  Of the shamrock of Erin and olive of Spain!

———o———

THE FELON'S LOVE.

BY J. K. CASEY.

"GRACIE O'DONNELL—oh! why sit you there,
Twining so calmly your bright yellow hair,
Wait you a lover to come from Knockbwee,
When the brown moon arises on mountain and sea?

"You have eyes like the starlight on Nephin's gray peak,
There is bloom on your lips—why the snow on your cheek?
The smile on thy face, gentle maiden, is gone,
And the touch of your fingers is cold as the stone."

"I wait not a lover to come from Knockbwee,
My lover's in chains on the wide swelling sea,
O, Willie *mavourneen*, when traitors stood high,
The foe felt the glance of your clear flashing eye.

"You loved me, *asthore*, and your heart broke across,
When you thought of the parting, the sorrow and loss,
But you knew your own Gracie would wither in shame,
If the brand of a traitor was placed on your name.

"They called you a *felon*—they chained you as one—
And made you the brother of Emmet and Tone;
Oh! princes might envy that title to-day,
For the sake of the hearts lying down in the clay.

"Yes, a traitor to England—a foe of its race,
You proudly looked up to the black tyrant's face;
'Twas the crime of our fathers—their sons stand up now,
With *that* mark of a traitor stamped plain on each brow.

"The last kiss I've pressed on your lips and your cheek,
The last word you've heard for your Gracie to speak;
The last time I've looked on my brave Willie's face,
And felt the wild clasp of a felon's embrace.

"I am twining my hair, for a bridal is near,
By the walls of Kilkeevan they'll carry a bier,
For the felon's true love could not live while the brand
Was not flashing on high in the grasp of his hand."

———o———

THE IRISH RAPPAREES.

A Peasant Ballad of 1691.

BY CHARLES GAVAN DUFFY, M. P.

[When Limerick was surrendered, and the bulk of the Irish army took service with Louis XIV., a multitude of the old soldiers of the Boyne, Aughrim, and Limerick, preferred remaining in the country at the risk of fighting for their daily bread; and with them some gentlemen, loth to part with their estates or their sweethearts, among whom Redmond O'Hanlon is perhaps the most memorable. The English army and the English law drove them by degrees to the hills, where they were long a terror to the new and old settlers from England, and a secret pride and comfort to the trampled peasantry who loved them even for their excesses. It was all they had left to take pride in.]

RIGH SHEMUS* he has gone to France, and left his crown behind—
Ill luck be theirs, both day and night, put runnin' in his mind!
Lord Lucan† followed after, with his Slashers brave and true,

---

* *Righ Shemus.*—King James II.
† After the Treaty of Limerick, Patrick Sarsfield, Lord Lucan, sailed with the brigade to France, and was killed while leading his countrymen to victory at the battle of Landen, in the Low Countries, on 29th July, 1693.

And now the doleful keen is raised: "What will poor Ireland do?
What must poor Ireland do?
Our luck," they say, "has gone to France—what *can* poor Ireland do?"

Oh, never fear for Ireland, for she has so'gers still,
For Rory's boys are in the wood, and Remy's on the hill;
And never had poor Ireland more loyal hearts than these—
May God be kind and good to them, the faithful Rapparees!
The fearless Rapparees!
The jewel were you, Rory, with your Irish Rapparees!

Oh, black's your heart, Clan Oliver, and colder than the clay!
Oh, high's your head, Clan Sassenach, since Sarsfield's gone away!
It's little love you bear to us, for sake of long ago,
But how'd your hand, for Ireland still can strike a deadly blow—
Can strike a mortal blow—
Och! *dhar-a-Chreesth!* 'tis she that still could strike the deadly blow!

The Master's bawn, the Master's seat, a surly *bodagh** fills;
The Master's son, an outlawed man, is riding on the hills.
But, God be praised, that 'round him throng, as thick as summer bees,
The swords that guarded Limerick wall—his loyal Rapparees!
His lovin' Rapparees!
Who dare say *no* to Rory Oge, with all his Rapparees?

Black Billy Grimes of Latnamard, he racked us long and sore—
God rest the faithful hearts he broke—we'll never see them more!
But I'll go bail he'll break no more, while Truagh has gallows-trees,
For why?—he met, one lonesome night, the fearless Rapparees!
The angry Rapparees!
They never sin no more, my boys, who cross the Rapparees!

Now, Sassenach and Cromweller, take heed of what I say—
Keep down your black and angry looks, that scorn us night and day,
For there's a just and wrathful Judge, that every action sees,
And He'll make strong, to right our wrong, the faithful Rapparees!
The fearless Rapparees!
The men that rode at Sarsfield's side, the roving Rapparees!

* *Bodagh.*—A severe and inhospitable man.

———o———

THE CHURCHYARD BRIDE.

BY WILLIAM CARLETON.

The bride she bound her golden hair—
Killeevy, oh, Killeevy!
And her step was light as the breezy air,
When it bends the morning flowers so fair,
By the bonnie green woods of Killeevy.

And oh, but her eyes they danced so bright,
Killeevy, oh, Killeevy!
As she longed for the dawn of to-morrow's light,
Her bridal vows of love to plight,
By the bonnie green woods of Killeevy.

The bridegroom is come with youthful brow,
Killeevy, oh, Killeevy!
To receive from his Eva her virgin vow;
"Why tarries the bride of my bosom now,
By the bonnie green woods of Killeevy?"

A cry—a cry! 'twas her maiden spoke,
Killeevy, oh, Killeevy!
"Your bride is asleep—she has not awoke:
And the sleep she sleeps will be never broke,
By the bonnie green woods of Killeevy."

Sir Turlough sank down with a heavy moan,
Killeevy, oh, Killeevy!
And his cheek became like the marble stone—
"Oh, the pulse of my heart is forever gone!
By the bonnie green woods of Killeevy."

The keen is loud, it comes again,
Killeevy, oh, Killeevy!
And rises sad from the funeral train,
As in sorrow it winds along the plain
By the bonnie green woods of Killeevy.

And, oh, but the plumes of white were fair,
    Killeevy, oh, Killeevy!
When they flutter'd all mournful in the air,
As rose the hymn of the requiem prayer,
    By the bonnie green woods of Killeevy.

There is a voice that but one can hear,
    Killeevy, oh, Killeevy!
And it softly pours, from behind the bier,
Its note of death on Sir Turlough's ear,
    By the bonnie green woods of Killeevy.

The keen is loud, but that voice is low,
    Killeevy, oh, Killeevy!
And it sings its song of sorrow slow,
And names young Turlough's name with
    woe,
    By the bonnie green woods of Killeevy.

Now the grave is closed, and the mass is
    said,
    Killeevy, oh, Killeevy!
And the bride she sleeps in her lonely bed,
The fairest corpse among the dead,
    By the bonnie green woods of Killeevy.

The wreaths of virgin white are laid,
    Killeevy, oh, Killeevy!
By virgin hands o'er the spotless maid;
And the flowers are strewn, but they soon
    will fade
    By the bonnie green woods of Killeevy.

"Oh, go not yet—nor yet away,
    Killeevy, oh, Killeevy!
Let us feel that *life* is near our clay,"
The long departed seem to say,
    By the bonnie green woods of Killeevy.

But the tramp and the voices of *life* are
    gone,
    Killeevy, oh, Killeevy!
And beneath each cold forgotten stone,
The mouldering dead sleep all alone,
    By the bonnie green woods of Killeevy.

But who is he who lingereth yet?
    Killeevy, oh, Killeevy!
The fresh green sod with his tears is wet,
And his heart in the bridal grave is set,
    By the bonnie green woods of Killeevy.

O, who but Sir Turlough, the young and
    brave,
    Killeevy, oh, Killeevy!
Should bend him o'er that bridal grave,
And to his death-bound Eva rave,
    By the bonnie green woods of Killeevy.

"Weep not—weep not," said a lady fair,
    Killeevy, oh, Killeevy!
"Should youth and valor thus despair,
And pour their vows to the empty air,
    By the bonnie green woods of Killeevy?"

There's charmed music upon her tongue,
    Killeevy, oh, Killeevy!
Such beauty—bright, and warm, and
    young—
Was never seen the maids among,
    By the bonnie green woods of Killeevy.

A laughing light, a tender grace,
    Killeevy, oh, Killeevy!
Sparkled in beauty around her face,
That grief from mortal heart might chase,
    By the bonnie green woods of Killeevy.

"The maid for whom thy salt tears fall,
    Killeevy, oh, Killeevy!
Thy grief or love can ne'er recall;
She rests beneath that grassy pall,
    By the bonnie green woods of Killeevy.

"My heart it strangely cleaves to thee,
    Killeevy, oh, Killeevy!
And now that thy plighted love is free,
Give its unbroken pledge to me,
    By the bonnie green woods of Killeevy."

The charm is strong upon Turlough's eye,
    Killeevy, oh, Killeevy!
His faithless tears are already dry,
And his yielding heart has ceased to sigh,
    By the bonnie green woods of Killeevy.

"To thee," the charmed chief replied,
    Killeevy, oh, Killeevy!
"I pledge that love o'er my buried bride;
O! come, and in Turlough's hall abide,
    By the bonnie green woods of Killeevy."

Again the funeral voice came o'er,
    Killeevy, oh, Killeevy!
The passing breeze, as it wailed before,
And streams of mournful music bore,
    By the bonnie green woods of Killeevy.

"If I to thy youthful heart am dear,
    Killeevy, oh, Killeevy!
One month from hence thou wilt meet me
    here,
Where lay thy bridal, Eva's bier,
    By the bonnie green woods of Killeevy."

He pressed her lips as the words were
    spoken,
    Killeevy, oh, Killeevy!
And his *banshee's* wail—now far and
    broken—
Murmured: "Death," as he gave the token,
    By the bonnie green woods of Killeevy.

"Adieu—adieu!" said the lady bright,
    Killeevy, oh, Killeevy!
And she slowly passed like a thing of light,
Or a morning cloud, from Sir Turlough's
    sight,
    By the bonnie green woods of Killeevy.

Now Sir Turlough has death in every vein,
Killeevy, oh, Killeevy!
And there's fear and grief o'er his wide
domain,
And gold for those who will calm his brain,
By the bonnie green woods of Killeevy.

"Come, haste thee, leech, right swiftly ride,
Killeevy, oh, Killeevy!
Sir Turlough the brave, Green Truagha's
pride,
Has pledged his love to the churchyard
bride,
By the bonnie green woods of Killeevy."

The leech groaned loud: "Come tell me this,
Killeevy, oh, Killeevy!
By all thy hopes of weal and bliss,
Has Sir Turlough given the fatal kiss,
By the bonnie green woods of Killeevy?"

"The banshee's cry is loud and long,
Killeevy, oh, Killeevy!
At eve she weeps her funeral song,
And it floats on the twilight breeze along,
By the bonnie green woods of Killeevy.

"Then the fatal kiss is given—the last,
Killeevy, oh, Killeevy!
Of Turlough's race and name is past,
His doom is seal'd, his die is cast,
By the bonnie green woods of Killeevy.

"Leech, say not that thy skill is vain,
Killeevy, oh, Killeevy!
Oh, calm the power of his frenzied brain,
And half his lands thou shalt retain,
By the bonnie green woods of Killeevy."

The leech has failed, and the hoary priest, .
Killeevy, oh, Killeevy!
With pious shrift his soul released,
And the smoke is high of his funeral feast,
By the bonnie green woods of Killeevy.

The *shanachies* now assembled all,
Killeevy, oh, Killeevy!
And the songs of praise in Sir Turlough's
hall,
To the sorrowing harp's dark music fall,
By the bonnie green woods of Killeevy.

And there is trophy, banner, and plume,
Killeevy, oh, Killeevy!
And the pomp of death with its darkest
gloom,
O'ershadows the Irish chieftain's tomb,
By the bonnie green woods of Killeevy!

The month is closed, and Green Truagha's
pride,
Killeevy, oh, Killeevy!
Is married to death—and, side by side,
He slumbers now with his churchyard bride,
By the bonnie green woods of Killeevy.

———o———

BINGEN ON THE RHINE.

BY THE HON. MRS. NORTON.

A SOLDIER of the Legion lay dying in Algiers,
There was lack of woman's nursing, there was dearth of woman's tears;
But a comrade stood beside him, while his life-blood ebbed away,
And bent with pitying glances, to hear what he might say.
The dying soldier faltered, as he took that comrade's hand,
And he said: "I never more shall see my own, my native land;
Take a message and a token to some distant friends of mine,
For I was born at Bingen—at Bingen on the Rhine.

"Tell my brothers and companions, when they meet and crowd around,
To hear my mournful story in the pleasant vineyard ground,
That we fought the battle bravely, and when the day was done,
Full many a corpse lay ghastly pale beneath the setting sun.
And amidst the dead and dying were some grown old in wars,
The death-wound on their gallant breasts, the last of many scars;
And some were young—and suddenly beheld life's morn decline;
And one had come from Bingen—fair Bingen on the Rhine.

"Tell my mother that her other sons shall comfort her old age,
And I was but a truant bird, that thought my home a cage;
For my father was a soldier, and even as a child,
My heart leaped forth to hear him tell of struggles fierce and wild;
And when he died, and left us to divide his scanty hoard,
I let them take whate'er they would, but kept my father's sword;

And with boyish love I hung it where the bright light used to shine
On the cottage wall at Bingen—calm Bingen on the Rhine!

" Tell my sister not to weep for me, and sob with drooping head,
When the troops are marching home again, with glad and gallant tread;
But to look upon them proudly, with a calm and steadfast eye,
For her brother was a soldier, too, and not afraid to die.
And if a comrade seek her love, I ask her in my name,
To listen to him kindly, without regret or shame;
And to hang the old sword in its place (my father's sword and mine)—
For the honor of old Bingen—dear Bingen on the Rhine!

" There's another—not my sister; in the happy days gone by,
You'd have known her by the merriment that sparkled in her eye;
Too innocent for coquetry—too fond for idle scorning—
O, friend! I fear the lightest heart makes sometimes heaviest mourning;
Tell her the last night of my life (for ere the moon be risen,
My body will be out of pain—my soul be out of prison)
I dreamed I stood with *her*, and saw the yellow sunlight shine
On the vine-clad hills of Bingen—fair Bingen on the Rhine!

" I saw the blue Rhine sweep along—I heard, or seemed to hear,
The German songs we used to sing, in chorus sweet and clear;
And down the pleasant river, and up the slanting hill,
The echoing chorus sounding through the evening calm and still;
And her glad blue eye was on me as we passed with friendly talk
Down many a path beloved of yore, and well-remembered walk,
And her little hand lay lightly, confidingly in mine,
But we'll meet no more at Bingen—loved Bingen on the Rhine."

His voice grew faint and hoarser—his grasp was childish weak—
His eyes put on a dying look—he sighed and ceased to speak;
His comrade bent to lift him, but the spark of life had fled—
The soldier of the Legion, in a foreign land—was dead!
And the soft moon rose up slowly, and calmly she looked down
On the red sand of the battle field, with bloody corpses strewn;
Yea, calmly on that dreadful scene her pale light seemed to shine,
As it shone on distant Bingen—fair Bingen on the Rhine.

———o———

FAREWELL! BUT WHENEVER YOU WELCOME THE HOUR.

BY THOMAS MOORE.

AIR:—" *Moll Roone.*"

FAREWELL! but, whenever you welcome the hour
That awakens the night song of mirth in your bower,
Then think of the friend who once welcom'd it too,
And forgot his own griefs to be happy with you.
His griefs may return—not a hope may remain
Of the few that have brightened his pathway of pain;
But he never will forget the short vision, that threw
Its enchantment around him while lingering with you!

And still, on that evening, when pleasure fills up
To the highest top sparkle each heart and each cup,
Where'er my path lies, be it gloomy or bright,
My soul, happy friends! shall be with you that night;

Shall join in your revels, your sports and your wiles,
And return to me, beaming all o'er with your smiles!
Too blest, if it tells me that, 'mid the gay cheer,
Some kind voice had murmur'd: "I wish he were here!"

Let Fate do her worst, there are relics of joy,
Bright dreams of the past which she cannot destroy—
Which come, in the night-time of sorrow and care,
And bring back the features that Joy us'd to wear;
Long—long be my heart with such memories filled
Like the vase, in which roses have once been distilled—
You may break, you may ruin the vase, if you will,
But the scent of the roses will hang 'round it still.

———o———

THE BEAR OF THE STRONG LEFT HAND.

BY DENNIS O'SULLIVAN.

"To horse! to horse!" The bugle blast rang out upon the plain,
And the shrilly neigh of the startled steed sends back a wild refrain;
Then hurrying here and rushing there the drowsy troopers glide,
While the carbines' ring and the saddles' fling denote a hasty ride.

"Mount, and away!" ere break of day—'tis many a mile away;
We were on the trail of the Spotted Tail, who was out on a bold foray;
And ere the sun in the meridian sent down its dazzling light,
We had caught the Sioux, and whipped them, too, in an open prairie fight.

One of the captives in the fray, and the boldest of the band,
Was a brave who hailed among his tribe as the Bear of the Strong Left Hand,
And a nobler face or a manlier form ne'er graced a royal throne,
While a courage high that could not die from out the dark eye shone.

With folded arms, and clouded brow, and ever-silent tongue,
The captive Bear met the ruthless jeers that the thoughtless troopers flung;
And though wounded sore, and the crimson gore his buffalo robe had dyed,
No plaint nor moan, no sigh nor groan, betrayed his stoic pride.

The life of our troop was an Irishman—a rollicking lad from Clare—
Who was ever ready for frolic and fun—a regular devil-may-care;
And many a humorous trick he played on stranger, friend and foe,
And 'tis little he recked of the danger entailed, nor cared he for word or blow.

The Spirit of Mischief never sleeps, it stalks in camp and court;
The wise and the brave, as well as the fool, are ever at its sport;
And now the Bear of the Strong Left Hand, the red man sad and sore,
Must bear a share, for Jack O'Hare was at his pranks once more.

We camped that night, and all was quiet, save the sentry's guarded cry,
Or a howl that arose from the prowling wolves that ever hovered nigh;
Then Jack O'Hare stole through the camp to where the Strong Hand lay,
Dreaming, maybe, of brighter days, and of dear ones far away.

Like a crafty fox Jack stole along, so silent and so sly,
A roguish smile was on his face, there was mischief in his eye;
And as he passed by the burning pile he stooped and raised a brand,
'Twas then we knew, the favored few, he was after the Strong Left Hand

Yes, Jack had spotted the silent brave, and he swore he'd break the spell,
Or, in his own expressive words: "He'd raise particular h—ll;"
And all the day we heard him say, and he muttered it o'er and o'er:
"I'll set a trap for that dummy chap—I'll make the Strong Bear roar."

The men who ride in the western land soon cruel and callous grow,
And no gleam of pity enters the heart for the treacherous dusky foe;
The reeking scalps, the burning camps, the torture horrid and slow,
Has made them feel that the bullet and steel is the only mercy to show.

Now Jack bent o'er the fallen foe, and down went the blazing stick,
Deep into the flesh of the sleeping brave, till it burnt him to the quick;
And then such a wail as rose on the gale, such a yell of rage and pain,
'Twas enough to make the stoutest quake, as it swept o'er the silent plain.

With a lightning bound and a fierce look 'round, up sprang the madden'd Bear,
But no form met his sight in the clear moonlight, nor man nor beast seemed there;
One glance he cast on the smould'ring brand, as his quivering flesh did quail,
And then, in the ancient Celtic tongue, he shouted out: "Hanna mon dheil!"*

"By the powers above!" cried Jack O'Hare, as he sprang from his hiding-place,
"Those words never fell from a cursed Sioux—he's one of my own old race;
What in the devil drove you here, in the red man's feathers and paint,
And fighting, too, with this Indian crew?—Oh, Lord, the poor fellow is faint!

"Run, Harry, run, bid the doctor come; you, Barney, fly to the tent;
Bring me the flask, quick, do what I ask—his life is nearly spent;
You great fool there, what makes you stare—why can't you give me a band?
He's no red thief at all, but white, like us all—a boy from my own old land!"

With scowling brows and ominous vows, the troopers thronged the glade,
While one old scout, with a vengeful shout, cried: "Death to the Renegade!"
"Ay, string him up, the mongrel pup!" yelled roaring Barney Shaw,
"No quarter for those who join our foes.   Hurrah for the Border Law!"

"I don't care a straw for your Border Law," cried out bold Jack O'Hare;
"Nay—nay, don't frown—the man is down, and—touch him if you dare!
I can feel Death now on his clammy brow: don't you see the staring eye?
For the sake of Him who forgives all sin, let us leave him in peace to die.

"And how do you know what bitter woe, what luckless stroke of Fate
Has made him roam from friends and home, in this forlorn state?
Perchance, even now, as his death you vow, a mother or wife may mourn,
And be praying to God, on the dear old sod, for the wanderer's safe return."

The troopers rough felt Jack's rebuff, and old Flint-eye, the guide,
Was the first to cry, with a moistened eye: " Let the derned galloot just slide."
Even Barney Shaw felt his rough heart thaw, and he muttered to Dan the Rake,
"As sure as a gun, we've missed our fun—let's give him a rousing wake."

We bore the Bear to the nearest tent, and then the surgeon came.
He felt the pulse of the weary man, and gazed on the stalwart frame;
One silent shake of the old man's head, and not a signal more—
We could almost hear Death drawing near—the warrior's pains were o'er.

A long-drawn sigh, some muttered words, an anxious look around.
A hand thrust near the manly breast, and a packet falls to the ground;
Then a gleam of hope, and rest and peace o'er those sad features stole,
As the penitent words 'scaped from his lips—"God's mercy on my soul!"

With a heartfelt sigh, and a tearful eye, Jack knelt by the lifeless clay,
And offered up a fervent prayer for the soul that had passed away;
While the troopers there, with heads all bare, gazed silently on the dead,
And one would know, in a whisper low: " If the paper couldn't be read?"

* Your soul to the devil.

By the light of the blazing pine, in a voice that was solemn and slow,
The surgeon read to the wondering group the following tale of woe;
While now and then, as the words came forth, strong Jack O'Hare would sigh,
And clasping the hand of the silent dead, would utter a piteous cry.

" 'Tis many a day and far away, in that Isle of sorrow and glee,
Since Pat and I, 'neath old Lordon's eye, propounded our A B C;
And ever since then, as boys and men, in pleasure, or peril, or pain,
He was more to me than a brother could be—I'll ne'er meet his like again.

" In boyhood we strayed o'er hill and glade, singing lays of our native land,
While in after days, 'neath the twilight rays, we danced with the village bard;
And my own colleen, with the bright blue e'en, ne'er grudged O'Neill a kiss,
Yet so clear to me was his loyalty, I ne'er took the joke amiss.

" In the goal-field strife, when blows were rife, and each one battled to win,
My generous Pat—I'll e'er mind that—never belted me on the shin;
When the murderous pack were on our track, athirsting for our blood,
In the lonely glen, as two to ten, for life and land we stood.

" And in the great strife for this nation's life, through many a rough campaign,
Side by side, in love and pride, we trudged in the sun and the rain;
When in the fight on Fredericksburg Height, a bullet struck me down,
Who bore me away from deadly fray, but the friend from our own old town!

"Away from the din, the crime and sin, and the city's feverish toil,
We strove to win, for our kith and kin, a home on Iowa's soil;
And 'twas pleasant to see the plenty and glee that reigned in our teeming vale:
Woe—woe to think we were on the brink—but list to my harrowing tale.

" 'Twas Christmas time, and the joyous chime rang out o'er the prairie clear,
And the merry sleigh-bells and the winsome belles came in chorus from far and near;
'Neath the holy sign of a love Divine young and old knelt down to pray,
And peace and good will did each bosom fill on that blessed Christ-born day.

" Like a horrid dream the rest did seem, but no dream e'er caused such blight,
For—curse the hand that raised the brand—I killed my friend that night!
He was stiff and cold, when the neighbors told we had fought with clubs and knives,
And the fight began, so the story ran, o'er a game of Forty-Fives.

" Oh, God! to think that the cursed drink, and the still more cursed play,
Should cause such woe and overthrow the peace of that happy day!
I had killed my friend, my generous friend—I had hacked his kindly face—
Whose only crime, through a long life-time, was *robbing without the ace.*

" As I could not face the dark disgrace, like a haunted being I fled,
With little care, in this world drear, where I laid my weary head;
When a roving band from the Indian land o'ertook me, famished and sore,
I had little fear that death seemed near—I had prayed for it evermore.

" And time and again, in the conflict's din, have I sought, and sought in vain
For the bullet or steel to strike and heal my soul-eating anguish and pain;
And 'tis little they knew, the savage crew, that, though ever in danger's van,
I ne'er struck a blow, drew trigger or bow, 'gainst the life of a fellow man.

"When this is read, the Bear will be dead, and you may know the name
He had borne before the blight came o'er, and the country from whence he came;
Near a thriving town of old renown, on the fertile plains of Clare,
Where, pure and young, he danced and sung, he was known as James O'Hare."

·———

Still, by the light of the blazing pine, we stared on the living and dead,
For Jack O'Hare was crouching there, caressing the lifeless head;
And not an eye in that tent was dry, and not a word was said,
But we stayed, and Jack pray'd by his brother's corpse until the East grew red.

In a sheltered glade a grave we made; we dug it wide and deep,
And there we laid the lifeless clay of James O'Hare to sleep;
But since that night no merry light, no touch of the devil-may-care,
No wit nor glee could the troopers see in grief-stricken Jack O'Hare.

———o———

THE BURIAL OF SIR JOHN MOORE.

BY REV. CHARLES WOLFE.

NOT a drum was heard, not a funeral note,
  As his corse to the rampart we hurried;
Not a soldier discharged his farewell shot
  O'er the grave where our hero we buried.

We buried him darkly at dead of night,
  The sods with our bayonets turning,
By the struggling moonbeams' misty light,
  And the lantern dimly burning.

No useless coffin enclosed his breast,
  Not in sheet nor in shroud we wound him;
But he lay like a warrior taking his rest,
  With his martial cloak around him.

Few and short were the prayers we said,
  And we spoke not a word of sorrow;
But we steadfastly gazed on the face that was
      dead,
  And we bitterly thought of the morrow.

We thought, as we hollow'd his narrow bed,
  And smoothed down his lonely pillow,
That the foe and the stranger would tread
      o'er his head,
  And we far away on the billow!

Lightly they'll talk of the spirit that's gone,
  And o'er his cold ashes upbraid him,
But little he'll reck, if they'll let him sleep
      on
  In the grave where a Briton has laid him.

But half of our heavy task was done,
  When the clock struck the hour for retir-
      ing;
And we heard the distant and random gun
  That the foe was sullenly firing.

Slowly and sadly we laid him down,
  From the field of his fame, fresh and gory,
We carved not a line, we raised not a stone;
  But we left him alone in his glory!

———o———

HAD I A HEART FOR FALSEHOOD FRAMED.

BY RICHARD BRINSLEY SHERIDAN.

HAD I a heart for falsehood framed,
  I ne'er could injure you,
For, tho' your tongue no promise claim'd,
  Your charms would make me true;
Then, lady, dread not here deceit,
  Nor fear to suffer wrong,
For friends in all the aged you'll meet,
  And lovers in the young.

But when they find that you have bless'd
  Another with your heart,
They'll bid aspiring passion rest,
  And act a brother's part.
Then, lady, dread not here deceit,
  Nor fear to suffer wrong,
For friends in all the aged you'll meet,
  And brothers in the young.

———o———

TWENTY GOLDEN YEARS AGO.

BY JAMES CLARENCE MANGAN.

Oh, the rain, the weary, dreary rain,
 How it plashes on the window-sill!
Night, I guess, too, must be on the wane,
 Strass and Gass* around are grown so still.
Here I sit, with coffee in my cup—
 Ah! 'twas rarely I beheld it flow
In the tavern where I loved to sup
 Twenty golden years ago!

Twenty years ago, alas!—but stay—
 On my life, 'tis half-past twelve o'clock!
After all, the hours *do* slip away—
 Come, here goes to burn another block!
For the night, or morn, is wet and cold,
 And my fire is dwindling rather low;—
I had fire enough, when young and bold,
 Twenty golden years ago.

Dear! I don't feel well at all, somehow;
 Few in Weimar dream how bad I am;
Floods of tears grow common with me now,
 High-Dutch floods, that reason cannot
 dam.
Doctors think I'll neither live nor thrive
 If I mope at home so;—I don't know—
Am I living *now?* I *was* alive
 Twenty golden years ago.

Wifeless, friendless, flagonless, alone,
 Not quite bookless, though, unless I
 choose,
Left with nought to do, except to groan,
 Not a soul to woo, except the muse—
Oh! this is hard for *me* to bear,
 Me, who whilom lived so much *en haut*,
Me, who broke all hearts like china-ware,
 Twenty golden years ago.

Perhaps 'tis better;—time's defacing waves
 Long have quench'd the radiance of my
 brow—

They who curse me nightly from their
 graves,
 Scarce could love me were they living
 now;
But my loneliness hath darker ills—
 Such duns as Conscience, Thought and Co.,
Awful Gorgons! worse than tailors' bills
 Twenty golden years ago!

Did I paint a fifth of what I feel,
 Oh, how plaintive you would ween I was!
But I won't, albeit I have a deal
 More to wail about than Kerner has!
Kerner's tears are wept for wither'd flowers,
 Mine for wither'd hopes; my scroll of woe
Dates, alas! from youth's deserted bowers,
 Twenty golden years ago!

Yet may Deutschland's bardlings flourish
 long;
 Me, I tweak no beak among them; hawks
Must not pounce on hawks; besides, in song
 I could once beat all of them by chalks.
Though you find me, as I near my jail,
 Sentimentalizing like Rousseau,
Oh! I had a grand Byronian soul
 Twenty golden years ago!

Tick-tick, tick-tick! not a sound save Time's
 And the wind-gust as it drives the rain—
Tortured torturer of reluctant rhymes,
 Go to bed, and rest thine aching brain!
Sleep! no more the dupe of hopes or schemes;
 Soon thou sleepest where the thistles
 blow—
Curious anticlimax to thy dreams
 Twenty golden years ago!

* Street and lane.

---o---

FLAG OF OUR LAND.

BY FATHER A. J. RYAN.

Flag of our Land, that oft has streamed through battle's lurid blaze and smoke,
When the long ranks were wrapped in flame, and in the shock the legions broke,
Flag of our Land! for you, for us they say the sun of hope has set,
We give them back the craven lie! we're shattered, but not beaten yet.

The Norman trampled on your folds, the Norman trampled on us, too;
And Saxon hate and native guile did all the wreck that Hell could do.
Not coward-like, but wild for fight, have we and they in conflict met,
We've borne the loss for centuries; repulsed, but never beaten yet.

This isle is ours, its plains and hills, from center to the utmost sea,
We tread its soil, we speak its tongue, we dearly pray to see it free.
Patience and faith shall do the work, and earnestness shall win the debt;
Hark you who still have hearts to toil; we're scattered, but not beaten yet.

While in this Irish Land their lives the spirit of an Irish race,
The pluck that smiles at worst reverse and meets disaster face to face,
By Heaven and all the shining stars, around the throne of Godhead set,
The future teems with hope for us; we're watchful, but not beaten yet.

"Perish the past!" the patriot cried; ay, let the mournful ages go,
With bitter feud, the curse of hate, they've made our heritage of woe.
Into the darkness of our doom a ray of nobler glory let;
Seize fast the present; years to come they'll swear we were not beaten yet.

Down with the feuds of vanished years, they waste our breath, they break our strength;
A nobler creed, a nobler life, 'tis ours to preach and fill at length.
Flag of our Land, float high and fair; they lie who say our sun has set;
God and the future still are ours; we live, and are not beaten yet.

———o———

PRIEZ POUR LE MALHEUREUX.*

BY JOHN SAVAGE.

Ah! once an aged friend I had,
  When I was very young;
His head was white, his mouth was sad,
  He spoke a foreign tongue;
Whose waning eye and withered cheek
  Said: "Here misfortune grew;"
And his words were—when'er he'd speak—
  "*Priez Pour le Malheureux.*"

I, wistful, wondered what they meant,
  And viewed his weary look,
As by his bending breast I leant
  Beside a babbling brook;
A holy well they said it was—
  An old cross stood there, too,
And heard, with many a tearful pause:
  "*Priez Pour le Malheureux.*"

The tears would often, streaming down
  His cheeks, my young heart melt;
And then he'd look a kindly frown
  To check the grief I felt.
But thoughts that would not quiet keep
  My yearning heart-strings drew—
'Tis sad to see an old man weep;
  "*Priez Pour le Malheureux.*"

Days swelled to months, which bloomed in
    years;
  Years pass'd too swiftly o'er,
And still the brook, the cross and tear
  Were blended as before;

He was the same, though graver grown,
  And I, as childhood flew,
The better learnt to feel his moan:
  "*Priez Pour le Malheureux.*"

Oh! wonder-building days of joy,
  Through which the child is led,
Which seem ne'er coming to the boy
  Till they are felt and fled.
Ye now are here—my feelings start
  With prayers my childhood knew;
Thank God I've not outgrown my heart!
  "*Priez Pour le Malheureux.*"

And thus he grew down to the grave,
  And I grew stout of limb;
Like shoots that grow trees, ere they have
  To be cut down like him.
He fell back into nature's womb
  As into cowslips dew,
And lonely I sobbed o'er his tomb:
  "*Priez Pour le Malheureux.*"

The old man gone, I daily trod
  The wild but hallowed spot
Where oft he had commun'd with God,
  To soothe his weary lot;
And while through summer sang the birds,
  And nature Heavenly grew,
I carved upon the cross his words:
  "*Priez Pour le Malheureux.*"

*Pray for the unfortunate.

My hope—entrancing boyhood sped,
　The boy a student grown,
The meaning of the words I read
　I'd carved upon the stone:
Oh, pray for the unfortunate!
Now seemed my sense to view
Why cried my friend importunate:
　"*Priez Pour le Malheureux.*"

Now fancy told me sorrows keen
　Had crush'd, not killed, his truth;
That Fate had set its "might have been"
　On life, and love, and youth—
Had worn the cheek and dimmed the eye,
　Had spoke the words I knew,
And led him from his home to die:
　"*Priez Pour le Malheureux.*"

THE BIVOUAC.

BY CHARLES LEVER.

AIR:—"*Garryowen.*"

Now that we've pledged each eye of blue,
And every maiden fair and true,
And our green island home—to you
　The ocean's wave adorning,
Let's give one hip—hip—hip, hurra!
And drink e'en to the coming day,
　When squadron square
　We'll all be there!
To meet the French in the morning.

May his bright laurels never fade,
Who leads our fighting fifth brigade,
Those lads so true in heart and blade,
　And famed for danger scorning;

So join me in one hip, hurra!
And drink e'en to the coming day,
　When squadron square
　We'll all be there!
To meet the French in the morning.

And when with years and honors crown'd,
You sit some homeward hearth around,
And hear no more the stirring sound
　That spoke the trumpet's warning;
You fill, and drink, one hip, hurra!
And pledge the memory of the day,
　When squadron square
　They all were there
To meet the French in the morning.

O, SAY, MY BROWN DRIMIN.

BY J. J. CALLANAN.

[Drimin is the favorite name of a cow, by which Ireland is here allegorically denoted. The five ends of Erin are the five kingdoms—Munster, Leinster, Ulster, Connaught, and Meath—into which the island was divided under the Milesian dynasty.]

O, SAY, my brown Drimin, thou silk of the kine,
Where—where are thy strong ones, last hope of thy line?
Too deep and too long is the slumber they take;
At the loud call of freedom why don't they awake?

My strong ones have fallen—from the bright eye of day,
All darkly they sleep in their dwelling of clay;
The cold turf is o'er them—they hear not my cries,
And since Louis no aid gives, I cannot arise.

Oh! where art thou, Louis? Our eyes are on thee;
Are thy lofty ships walking in strength on the sea?
In freedom's last strife if you linger or quail,
No morn e'er shall break on the night of the Gael.

But should the king's son, now bereft of his right,
Come proud in his strength for his country to fight,
Like leaves on the trees will new people arise,
And deep from their mountains shout back to my cries.

When the prince, now an exile, shall come for his own,
The isles of his father, his rights, and his throne,
My people in battle the Saxons will meet,
And kick them before like old shoes from their feet.

O'er mountains and valleys they'll press on their route,
The five ends of Erin shall ring to their shout;
My sons all united, shall bless the glad day
When the flint-hearted Saxons they've chased far away.

———o———

WIDOW MALONE.

BY CHARLES LEVER.

Did you hear of the Widow Malone,
    Ohone!
Who lived in the town of Athlone?
    Ohone!
 Oh, she melted the hearts
 Of the swains in them parts,
So lovely the Widow Malone,
    Ohone!
So lovely the Widow Malone.

Of lovers she had a full score,
    Or more,
And fortunes they all had galore,
    In store;
 From the minister down
 To the clerk of the crown,
All were courting the Widow Malone,
    Ohone!
All were courting the Widow Malone.

But so modest was Mistress Malone,
    'Twas known,
That no one could see her alone,
    Ohone!
 Let them ogle and sigh,
 They could ne'er catch her eye,
So bashful the Widow Malone,
    Ohone!
So bashful the Widow Malone.

'Till one Mister O'Brien, from Clare—
    How quare!
It's little for blushing they care
    Down there,
 Put his arm 'round her waist—
 Gave ten kisses at laste—
"Oh," says he, "you're my Molly Malone,
    My own!
"Oh," says he, "you're my Molly Malone."

And the widow they all thought so shy,
    My eye!
Ne'er thought of a simper or sigh,
    For why?
 But, "Lucius," says she,
 "Since you've now made so free,
You may marry your Mary Malone,
    Ohone!
You may marry your Mary Malone."

There's a moral contained in my song,
    Not wrong,
And one comfort it's not very long,
    But strong—
 If for widows you die,
 Learn to kiss, not to sigh,
For they're all like sweet Mistress Malone,
    Ohone!
Oh, they're all like sweet Mistress Malone.

———o———

RORY O'MORE; OR, GOOD OMENS.

BY SAMUEL LOVER.

Young Rory O'More courted Kathleen Bawn,
He was bold as a hawk, she as soft as the dawn;
He wish'd in his heart pretty Kathleen to please,
And he thought the best way to do *that* was to tease.
"Now, Rory be aisy," sweet Kathleen would cry,
(Reproof on her lip, but a smile in her eye,)
"With your tricks I don't know, in troth, what I'm about;
Faith you've teased till I've put on my cloak inside out."
"Oh! jewel," says Rory, "that same is the way
You've thrated my heart this many a day;
And 'tis plazed that I am, and why not, to be sure?
For 'tis all for good luck," says bold Rory O'More.

"Indeed, then," says Kathleen, "don't think of the like,
For I half gave a promise to *soothering* Mike:
The ground that I walk on he loves, I'll be bound."
"Faith," says Rory, "I'd rather love *you* than the ground."

"Now, Rory, I'll cry if you don't let me go;
Sure I drame ev'ry night that I'm hating you so!"
"Oh," says Rory, "that same I'm delighted to hear,
For *drames* always go by *conthrairies*, my dear;
Oh! jewel, keep draming that same till you die,
And bright morning will give dirty night the black lie!
And 'tis plazed that I am, and why not, to be sure?
Since 'tis all for good luck," says bold Rory O'More.

"Arrah, Kathleen, my darlint, you've teased me enough,
Sure I've thrash'd for your sake Dinny Grimes and Jim Duff;
And I've made myself, drinking your health, quite a *baste*,
So I think after that, I may *talk to the praste.*"*
Then Rory the rogue, stole his arm 'round her neck,
So soft and so white, without freckle or speck,
And he looked in her eyes that were beaming with light,
And he kissed her sweet lips;—don't you think he was right?
"Now, Rory, leave off, sir; you'll hug me no more,
That's eight times to-day you've kiss'd me before."
"Then here goes another," says he, "to make sure,
For there's luck in odd numbers," says Rory O'More.

*Paddy's mode of asking a girl to name the day.

BAD LUCK TO THIS MARCHING.

BY CHARLES LEVER.

BAD luck to this marching,
Pipeclaying and starching;
How neat one must be to be kill'd by the
French!
I'm sick of parading,
Through wet and cold wading,
Or standing all night to be shot in a trench.
To the tune of a fife
They dispose of your life,
You surrender your soul to some illigant lilt;
Now I like "Garryowen"
When I hear it at home,
But it's not half so sweet when you're going
to be kilt.

Then, though up late and early,
Our pay comes so rarely,
The devil a farthing we've ever to spare;
They say some disaster
Befell the paymaster;
On my conscience I think that the money's
not there.
And, just think, what a blunder,
They won't let us plunder,

While the convents invite us to rob them,
'tis clear;
Though there isn't a village
But cries: "Come and pillage!"
Yet we leave all the mutton behind for
Monseer.

Like a sailor that's nigh land,
I long for that Island
Where even the kisses we steal if we please;
Where it is no disgrace
If you don't wash your face,
And you've nothing to do but to stand at
your ease.
With no sergeant to abuse us,
We fight to amuse us,
Sure it's better beat Christians than kick a
baboon;
How I'd dance like a fairy
To see old Dunleary,
And think twice ere I'd leave it to be a
dragoon!

THE WEARING OF THE GREEN.

BY DION BOUCICAULT.

Oh, Paddy dear, an' did you hear the news that's going 'round?
The shamrock is forbid, by law, to grow on Irish ground!
No more St. Patrick's day we'll keep, his color can't be seen;
For there's a bloody law ag'in the Wearing of the Green!

Oh, I met with Napper Tandy, and he took me by the hand,
And he says: How's poor Ould Ireland, and how does she stand?
She's the most distressed country that ever I have seen;
For they're hanging men and women for the Wearing of the Green!

And since the color we must wear is England's cruel red,
Ould Ireland's sons will ne'er forget the blood that they have shed;
Then take the shamrock from your hat, and cast it on the sod—
It will take root and flourish still, tho' under foot 'tis trod.

When the law can stop the blades of grass from growing as they grow,
And when the leaves in summer time their verdure do not show;
Then I will change the color I wear in my caubeen—
But, 'till that day, plaze God! I'll stick to the Wearing of the Green!

But if, at last, her colors should be torn from Ireland's heart—
Her sons, with shame and sorrow, from the dear old soil will part;
I've heard whispers of a country that lies far beyond the sae,
Where rich and poor stand equal, in the light of Freedom's day!

Oh, Erin! must we leave you? driven by the tyrant's hand;
Must we ask a mother's blessing, in a strange, but happy land?
Where the cruel Cross of England's thraldom's never to be seen—
But where, thank God! we'll live and die, still Wearing of the Green!

————o————

THE MUSTER OF THE GAEL.

BY T. O'D. O'CALLAGHAN.

LIST—list! the world is all astir from both poles to Equator,
Upheaving like a wind-tossed sea, Ætna's fiery crater.
While yet the molten lava tide adown its side comes rolling
With force which evermore may mock all human powers controlling.
Yes—yes, old Earth is all ablazing with sights and sounds all-thrilling,
And oh, this wild commotion is with joy my bosom filling!
For I have pined this many a day in dark despair and sadness,
Without a throb of painless joy, without a ray of gladness,
To pierce the gloom which filled my soul at seeing the olden glory
Departing from the Isle of Saints, old land of song and story—
At seeing our ancient Gaelic race wide scattered o'er the world;
Oh, I have waited long to see the Green once more unfurled—
To view our scattered race come forth in strong embattled legions,
From torrid zone and temp'rate climes, and frigid Northern regions,
Where they have wandered lone and long, with hearts dark draped in sorrow,
Still watching for the promised dawn of that grand and glorious morrow
Which golden prophets had foretold, in words of inspiration,
When Freedom's sun should gild once more the banner of our nation,
As in the golden days of yore, ere Strongbow crossed the water,
And stained our country's emerald soil with crimson hue of slaughter.

Hark! 'tis the trumpet's martial blast, through many a fair land ringing,
And faith and hope and joy once more to Celtic bosoms bringing—
To million bosoms of our race in alien climes sojourning,
Through all the years, in all the lands, for vengeance ever burning,
See—see, those ships in many a bay, with winged canvas spreading!
The anchor now is weighed, and now for Ireland's shore they're heading;
God speed them in their gallant course far o'er old ocean foaming,
How glorious in the captive land to watch those fleets a-coming!
To hear the joyous cheers roll out, like pealing thunder bursting
From million hearts on Ireland's shore for Saxon blood a-thirsting!

Thrice glorious 'twere, in faith, to list that glad and thunderous greeting,
And see our scattered race once more beneath the Sunburst meeting,
From far Australia's friendly shores a galiant host is coming,
For lo! high o'er the Pacific that war-cloud darkly looming;
And see! on broad Atlantic's breast full many a flag unfurled
O'er that great host which saileth from the mighty Western world.
From east and west, from north and south, the Gael are homeward sailing,
Dark vengeance throned in every heart, and fealty unfailing;
Since first old ocean's circling waves from bonds of chaos sallied,
Ne'er host so vast, on sea or shore, 'round Freedom's banner rallied.
O, Erin old! thine exiled sons have heard thy trumpet sounding,
And now, as sprang thy wolf-dog erst, their gallant ships are bounding
On to thy shores, and many a heart is throbbing with emotion,
And eyes are strained on all thy hills to scan the misty ocean.

They land! they land! the cheering news o'er all the Isle is winging;
To arms! to arms! is the cry o'er mount and valley ringing;
And bonfires blaze on all the hills, and chapel bells are tolling,
And Heaven's blue vault is rent with cheers in mighty chorus rolling;
And prison chains are burst in twain, and freedom's 'fulgent sunlight
Streams in on noble spirits there, erst wrapped in dungeon's dun light:
And gladness spreads o'er all the land, and rusted swords are brightened,
While war-steeds prance impatiently, as saddle-girths are tightened;
Heavens! 'tis a glorious sight—those green flags proudly streaming—
Bright, vengeful pikes and flashing swords in serried phalanx gleaming—
The vast, embattled host its march o'er plain and valley wending,
While roll of drum and trumpet bray with clank of steel are blending.
Now, men of Ireland, halt!—array your lines in battle column!
See! yonder gleams the Saxon steel!—the hour is grand and solemn!
Your country's wrongs for vengeance call!—fling out your bold defiance!
On Heaven and Right, on gun and steel, this day be your reliance!

Ho comes the foe—his scarlet lines in War's proud pomp advancing:
His banners wave right jauntily, his bayonets are glancing
Bright in the golden noonday sun, while fife and drum are sounding,
And battle-steeds, caparisoned right pompously are bounding.
They've met, and pike and bayonet in deadly strife are clashing;
In vain the column of the foe 'gainst Freedom's host are dashing;
Their ranks are broke from rear to van, their banners rent and torn,
While high o'er all, in Victory's light, the Green is proudly borne.
'Tis sunset now—the field is won—the beaten foe is flying!
Of that proud host not one remains, save captured, dead and dying;
The clash of steel is heard no more—hushed is the cannon's thunder;
Thank God! the chains of centuried thrall at last are rent asunder!
Strike, strike the harp of Innisfail to martial strains of gladness!
No more, no more awake its voice in slavish tones of sadness!
Old Freedom's regal scepter hence shall rule the plains of Sireland,
Till Doomsday's fire may wrap in flame the hills of rescued Ireland.

———o———

. THE SPRING TIME.

BY WILLIAM GEOGHEGAN.

REGRETS! the troubles of this lower world
    Fall from my mind, as from the new-clad Earth
Fades out the memory of the dead leaves twirl'd
    About her Autumns past. This glorious birth
Of buds and grasses, and the scented air,
Make one forget all things that are less fair.

Eternal Spring-tide! for it is eternal—
  'Tis we who pass out of it, in the shade
Of youth's eclipse; but it has regions vernal
  And haunting odors that die, not fade;
Or else why should we look so fondly back,
And through the years still scent its flowery track?

Years after we have mouldered into dust
  Young hearts shall feel what ours feel to-day;
Yet in the fairer Home there surely must
  Be joys before which this shall pale its ray.
Death is so near in sunshine, and my mood
Would take it as a step to greater good.

'Twould not be hard to die 'neath this new sun;
  'Twere better, perhaps, than waiting till it set
In winter glooms that tinge the soul with dun,
  And mar its vision with a vain regret.
Heaven is so near. Oh, ærial maids, take me!
I should not fear to die and soar with ye.

Strange that the earth, the fairer that it grows,
  Should make one sit more lightly to it, than
When from the pale north sky fall fast the snows,
  And babbling brooks, ice-bound, no longer ran;
We had no restless longings in those days—
We sat contented in the wintry rays.

Like children quiet, in an alien place,
  Forgetful or unheeding, 'mid their toys,
Until some semblance of their mother's face,
  With longing grief their little hearts annoy,
And all's forgotten, all things lose their charms,
Poor comforters, for lack of mother's loving arms.

Dear mother nature, but one glance from thee
  Is Spring for us; a smile, and Summer blooms;
A passing frown, and Autumn from the tree
  Scatters the leaves; then Winter quick entombs
The earth, and it, like buried Lazarus, sleeps,
Nor wakes till o'er it tender April weeps.

O, SONS OF ERIN.

BY REV. WILLIAM J. M'CLURE.

O, sons of Erin, brave and strong,
  Upon your prostrate mother gaze;
Her sorrows have been overlong,
  'Tis time her beauteous face to raise.
When tyranny usurps the right,
  And chivalry pines in the jail,
There's deep revenge in Freedom's fight—
  'Tis life to win, 'tis death to fail!

The power of monarchy is steel,
  And crushing, soul-subduing laws,
Whose weight alone the toilers feel,
  And murmur oft, and know the cause.

And battle oft the despot's might,
  And scorning torture and the jail,
Seek swift revenge in Freedom's fight—
  'Tis life to win, 'tis death to fail!

Wild—wild's the night e'er freedom's sun
  Lights up the ramparts of the free;
It rolls away, the battle's won,
  And sounds a glorious reveille—
A reveille of hearts full light,
  Uncrushed by slavery and the jail,
It echoed down the Alpine hight,
  'Twill glad the hills of Inisfail!

THE SHAMROCK AND THE LILY.

BY JOHN BANIM.

Sir Shamrock, sitting drinking,
  At close of day—at close of day,
Saw Orange Lily, thinking,
  Come by that way—come by that way;
With can in hand we hail'd him,
  And jovial din—and jovial din;
The Lily's drought ne'er fail'd him—
  So he stept in—so he stept in.

At first they talk'd together,
  Reserved and flat—reserved and flat,
About the crops, the weather,
  And this and that—and this and that—
But, as the glass moved quicker,
  To make amends—to make amends,
They spoke—though somewhat thicker—
  Yet more like friends—yet more like
    friends.

" Why not call long before, man,
  To try a glass—to try a glass?"
Quoth Lily—" People told me
  You'd let me pass—you'd let me pass—
Nay, and they whisper'd, too, man,
  Death in the pot—death in the pot,
Slipt in for me by you, man—
  Though I hope not—though I hope not."

" Oh, foolish—foolish Lily!
  Good drink to miss—good drink to miss,
For gossip all so silly,
  And false as this—and false as this;
And 'tis the very way, man,
  With such bald chat—with such bald chat,
You're losing, day by day, man,
  Much more than that—much more than
    that.

" Here, in this land of mine, man,
  Good friends with me—good friends with
    me,
A life almost divine, man,
  Your life might be—your life might be.
But—jars for you! till, in man,
  My smiling land—my smiling land,
You bilious grow, and thin, man,
  As you can stand—as you can stand.

" Now, if 'tis no affront, man,
  On you I call—on you I call,
To tell me what you want, man,
  At-all-at-all—at-all-at-all;

Come let us have in season,
  A word or two—a word or two;
For there's neither rhyme nor reason
  In your hubbubboo—your hubbubboo!

" With you I'll give and take, man,
  A foe to cares—a foe to cares,
Just asking, for God's sake, man,
  To say my prayers—to say my prayers.
And, like an honest fellow,
  To take my drop—to take my drop,
In reason, till I'm mellow,
  And then to stop—and then to stop.

" And why should not things be so,
  Between us both—between us both?
You're so afraid of me? Pho!
  All fudge and froth—all fudge and froth.
Or why, for little Willy,
  So much ado—so much ado?
What is he, silly Lily,
  To me or you—to me or you?

" Can he, for all you shout, man,
  Back to us come—back to us come,
Our devils to cast out, man,
  And strike them dumb—and strike them
    dumb?
Or breezes mild make blow, man,
  In summer-peace—in summer-peace,
Until the land o'erflow, man,
  With God's increase—with God's
    increase?"

" What you do say, Sir Shamrock,"
  The Lily cried—the Lily cried,
" I'll think of, my old game-cock,
  And more beside—and more beside.
One thing is certain, brother—
  I'm free to say—I'm free to say,
We should be more together,
  Just in this way—just in this way."

" Well—top your glass, Sir Lily,
  Our parting one—our parting one—
A bumper and a *tilly*,
  To past and gone—to past and gone—
And to the future day, lad,
  That ye may see—that ye may see,
Good humor and fair play, lad,
  'Twixt you and me—'twixt you and me!"

THE RIVER OF TIME.

BY T. O'D. O'CALLAGHAN.

Oh, River of Time! the long ago thou wert but a rippling rill,
And the dulcet rhyme of thy crystal flow was sweet as wind-harp's trill;
That song of joy like a lullaby on the air 'rose soft and low,
As thy ripples sped from their fountain-head and flashed in the morning's glow;
While Earth's fair queen, in radiant sheen, flower-crowned by angel hands,
The beauteous grace of her mirror'd face oft scann'd in thy golden sands;
And the dreamy moon, in night's mystic noon, when her full, round orb shone bright,
Gazed down with pride on thy silvery tide, pale shimmering in her light,
While the primal stars in their gilded cars rolled on through the azure hight—
Fair, glittering gems, bright diadems high set on the brow of Night.

Oh, River of Time! thy stream has swelled thro' the centuried lapse of years—
Has grown and swelled since of old it welled from its fount 'mid the starry spheres,
Till now, broad and deep, with majestic sweep, like the roll of an inland sea,
That stream, erst a rill, turns God's mighty mill on its course to eternity!
Oh, methinks I hear, rising high and clear on the ghostly midnight wind,
The surge and the roar of thy waves evermore and the rush of the flood behind,
And the shrieks of the lost on thy bosom tossed, like wrecks on the ocean waves,
Drifting out to sea, oh, River, with thee, far away from the land of graves!

Oh, River of Time! from the days of yore flowing on to the billowy sea,
Bring us back once more from the silent shore the friends who have flown with thee,
The myriad host of the loved and lost—the hearts that were fond—ah, me!—
The beauty and bloom in the grave's dark womb—the spirits that wander free
From sin's dark slime in that wondrous clime—bright land of the ransomed souls,
Where Death's cold shadow never falls, nor death-bell sadly tolls.
Ah! in vain we crave, for thy ebbless wave, when it passeth the grave's dark bourne,
With its freight of souls, as it seaward rolls, never can nor will return!

Oh, River of Time! flowing slowly on, with the wrecks of our hopes and dreams—
On, evermore on to the great Unknown, where the rapturing vision gleams,
And the white souls float in space, as the mote on summer's irradiant beams—
Oh! swollen thy flood with the priceless blood·which ever and ay doth well
From human souls slain on Life's battle-plain by the ambushed hosts of hell;
Sin's juggernaut rolls over prostrate souls thick strewn on the field of strife,
While thy mystic tide with their blood is dyed—red blood from the battle of life!

Oh, River of Time! in the dim, dark past, full many and many a year,
Thou'st left thy fount on that sacred mount, long lost to both "sage" and "seer;"
No human eye, as the years sped by, has ever beheld, I ween,
That mystic mount, or that crystal fount, all bright in its virgin sheen,
Since the first twain fell 'neath the tempter's spell, amid Eden's flowery bowers,
When earth was young, ere yet upsprung the thorns among the flowers;
When thy limpid stream in the morning gleam reflected the Heavenly towers,
And Paradise rang with the silvery clang of the harps of seraphic powers;
For Earth, at its birth, in its child-like mirth, flower-gemmed and green and fair,
Careering through space, in emulous race with the stars and the spirits of air,
Was nigher, I ween, to the angelic scene, than this Earth of ours to-day,
With its deep, dark crime, oh, River of Time—in sorrow and sin grown grey!

———o———

GOOD-NIGHT.

MILES O'REILLY.

GOOD-NIGHT; I have to say good-night
To such a host of peerless things;
Good-night unto that fragile hand,
All queenly with its weight of rings;
Good-night to fond, uplifted eyes,
Good-night unto the perfect mouth,
And all the sweetness nestled there—
The snowy hand detains me, then
I'll have to say good-night again.

But there will come a time, my love,
When, if I read our stars aright,
I shall not linger by this porch
With my adieus. Till then, good-night!
You wish the time were now? And I.
You do not blush to wish it so?
You would have blushed yourself to death
To own so much a year ago—
What, both these snowy hands? Ah, then
I'll have to say good-night again.

————o————

THE BOYS OF WEXFORD.

BY ROBERT DWYER JOYCE, M. D.

IN comes the captain's daughter,
The captain of the Yeos,
Saying: "Brave United men,
We'll ne'er again be foes.
A thousand pounds I'll give you,
And fly from home with thee,
And dress myself in man's attire,
And fight for liberty!"
    We are the boys of Wexford,
    Who fought with heart and hand
    To burst in twain the galling chain,
    And free our native land!

And when we left our cabins, boys,
We left with right good will,
To see our friends and neighbors
That were at Vinegar Hill.
A young man from our ranks,
A cannon he let go;
He slapped it into Lord Mountjoy—
A tyrant he laid low.
    We are the boys of Wexford,
    We fought with heart and hand
    To burst in twain the galling chain,
    And free our native land.

We bravely fought and conquered
At Ross and Wexford town;
And, if we failed to keep them,
'Twas drink that brought us down.
We had no drink beside us
On Tubber'neering's day,

Depending on the long bright pike,
And well it worked its way!
    We are the boys of Wexford,
    Who fought with heart and hand
    To burst in twain the galling chain,
    And free our native land!

They came into the country
Our blood to waste and spill;
But let them weep for Wexford,
And think of Oulart Hill!
'Twas drink that still betrayed us—
Of them we had no fear;
For every man could do his part
Like Forth and Shelmalier!
    We are the boys of Wexford,
    Who fought with heart and hand
    To burst in twain the galling chain,
    And free our native land!

My curse upon all drinking,
It made our hearts full sore;
For bravery won each battle,
But drink lost ever more;
And if, for want of leaders,
We lost at Vinegar Hill,
We're ready for another fight,
And love our country still!
    We are the boys of Wexford,
    Who fought with heart and hand
    To burst in twain the galling chain,
    And free our native land!

————o————

LIMERICK TOWN.

BY JOHN F. O'DONNELL ("CAVIARE").

HERE I've got you, Philip Desmond, standing in the market-place,
'Mid the farmers and the corn-sacks, and the hay in either space,
Near the fruit-stalls, and the woman knitting socks and selling lace,

There is High street, up the hill-side, twenty shops on either side,
Queer, old-fashioned, dusky High street—here so narrow, there so wide,
Whips and harness, saddles, signboards, hanging out in quiet pride.

Up and down the noisy highway, how the market people go!
Country girls in Turkey kerchiefs—poppies moving to and fro—
Frieze-clad fathers, great in buttons, brass and watch-seals, all a show.

Merry—merry are their voices, Philip Desmond, unto me,
Dear the mellow Munster accent, with its intermittent glee;
Dear the blue cloaks and the grey coats, things I long have longed to see.

E'en the curses, adjurations, in my senses sound like rhyme,
And the great rough-throated laughter of that peasant, in his prime,
Winking from the grass-bound cart-shaft, brings me back the other time.

Not a soul, observe you, knows me, not a friend a hand will yield,
Would they know, if to the land-marks all around them I appealed?
Know me! If I died this minute—dig for me the Potter's field.

Bricks wax grey, and memories greyer, and our faces somehow pass
Like reflections from the surface of a sudden-darkened glass.
Live you do, but as a unit of the undistinguished mass.

" Pshaw! you're prosy." Am I prosy? Mark you then this sunward flight:
" I have seen this street and roof-tops ambered in the morning's light,
Golden in the deep of noonday, crimson on the marge of night.

" Continents of gorgeous cloud-land, argosies of blue and flame,
With the sea-wind's even pressure o'er this roaring fabourg came."
This is fine supernal nonsense. Look, it puts my cheek to shame.

Come, I want a storm of gossip, pleasant jests and ancient chat;
At that dusky doorway yonder my grandfather smoked and sat,
Tendrils of the wind-blown clover sticking in his broad-leafed hat.

There he sat and read the paper. Fancy I recall him now!
All the shadow of the front-house slanting up from knee to brow;
Critic he of far convulsions, keen-eyed judge of sheep and cow.

Now he lives in GOD's good judgments. Simon, much he thought of me,
Laughing gravely at my questions, as I sat upon his knee—
As I trifled with his watch-seal, red carbuncle fair to see.

Ancient house that held my father, all are gone beyond recall,
There's where Uncle Michael painted flower-pots on the parlor wall,
There's where Nannie, best of she-goats, munched her hay and had her stall.

Many a night from race and market down this street six brothers strode,
Finer, blither, truer fellows never barred a country road,
Shouting, wheeling, fighting, scorning watchman's law and borough code.

Hither, with my hand in her hand, came my mother many a day,
She, the old man's pet and darling, at his side or far away,
And her chair was near the window, half in square and half in bay.

Oh, my mother, my pure-hearted, dear to me as child and wife,
Ever earnest, ever toilsome in this quick, unresting strife,
Ever working out the mission of a silent, noble life.

Do I love you? Can you ask me? Do I love you, mother mine?
Love you! Yes, while GOD exists and while His sun and moon shall shine,
I was yours, O. sweet. bright darling, in the Heavens I shall be thine.

If I write this rhyming gossip, all about the ancient street,
'Tis because the very footpaths were made blessed by your feet;
Dear, pale mother! writing of you, how my heart and pulses beat!

Beat and beat with warm convulsions, and my eyes are thick with tears,
And your low song by my cradle sounds again within mine ears;
Here's the highway which you trod once, I thrice filled with childish fears.

Rolled the wagons, swore the carters outside in the crowded street,
Horses reared, and cattle stumbled, dogs barked high from loads of wheat,
But inside the room was pleasant, and the air with thyme was sweet.

Others now are in their places, honest folk who know us not,
Do I chafe at the transition? Philip, 'tis the common lot;
Do your duty, live your lifetime, say your prayers, and be forgot.

---o---

SARSFIELD'S RIDE; OR, THE AMBUSH OF SLIAV BLOOM.

BY R. D. JOYCE, M. D.

[The generally received historical acount of the exploit related in the following ballad differs in several points from the traditionary version. And yet the latter should not be despised, for the peasantry of Limerick and Tipperary have stories of the incident, all agreeing with regard to the ride of Galloping O'Hogan. The songs also of the time preserve the name of that celebrated horseman and outlaw in connection with the affair. For instance, after mentioning the way in which the outlawed inhabitants of the surrounding country hung on the track of King William's convoy, one of these old songs represents O'Hogan as saying:

"We marched with bold Lord Lucan before the break of day,
  Until we came to Kinmagoun where the artilery lay;
  Then God He cleared the firmament, the moon and stars gave light, ·
  And for the Battle of the Boyne we had revenge that night!"

It may be also stated that in every song and story of the time, King William is always nicknamed "Dutch Bill," a cognomen by which he is even to the present day remembered in many parts of Munster.]

PART THE FIRST.

"Come up to the hill, Johnnie Moran, and the de'il's in the sight you will see,
The men of Dutch Bill in the lowlands are marching o'er valley and lea;
Brave cannon they bring for their warfare, good powder and bullets *go leor*,
To batter the grey walls of Limerick adown by the deep Shannon shore!"

They girded their corselets and sabers that morning so glorious and still,
They leapt like good men to their saddles, and took the lone path to the hill;
And deftly they handled their bridles as they rode thro' each green, fairy coom,
Each woodland, and broad rocky valley, till they came to the crest of Sliav Bloom!

"Look down to the east, Johnnie Moran, where the wings of the morning are spread,
Each basnet you see in the sunlight it gleams on an enemy's head;
Look down on their long line of baggage, their huge guns of iron and brass,
That, as sure as my name is O'Hogan, will ne'er to the Williamites pass!

"Spur, then, to the green shores of Brosna—see Ned of the Hills on your way—
Have all the brave boys at the muster by Brosna at close of the day;
I'll ride off for Sarsfield to Lim'rick, and tell what I've seen from the hill—
If Sarsfield won't capture their cannon, by the Cross of Kildare, but we will!"

Away to the north went young Johnnie, like an arbalast bolt in his speed,
Away to the west brave O'Hogan gives bridle and spur to his steed;
Through the fierce highland torrent he dashes, through copse and down greenwood full
    fain,
Till he biddeth farewell to the mountains, and sweeps o'er the flat lowland plain:

You'd search from the grey Rocks of Cashel each side to the blue ocean's rim,
Through green dale, and hamlet, and city, but you'd ne'er find a horseman like him;
With his foot, as if grown to the stirrup, his knee, with its rooted hold ta'en,
With his seat in the saddle so graceful, and his sure hand so light on the rein!

As the cloud-shadow skims o'er the meadows, when the fleet-winged summer winds blow,
By war-wasted castle and village, and streamlet and crag doth he go;
The foam-flakes drop quick from his charger, yet never a bridle draws he,
Till he baits in the hot, blazing noontide by the cool fairy well of Lisbui!

He rubbed down his charger full fondly, the dry grass he heaped for its food,
He ate of the green cress and shamrock, and drank of the sweet crystal flood;
He's up in his saddle and flying o'er wood-track and broad heath once more,
Till the sand 'neath the hoofs of his charger is crunch'd by the wide Shannon's shore!

For never a ford did he linger, but swam his good charger across—
It clomb the steep bank like a wolf-dog—then dashed over moorland and moss.
The shepherds who looked from the highland, they crossed themselves thrice as he passed,
And they said 'twas a sprite from Crag Aeivil, went by on the wings of the blast.

PART THE SECOND.

Dutch Bill sent a summons to Limerick—a summons to open their gate,
Their fortress and stores to surrender, else the pike and the gun were their fate.
Brave Sarsfield he answered the summons: "Though all holy Ireland in flames
Blazed up to the skies to consume us, we'll hold the good town for King James."

Dutch Bill, when he listed the answer, he stamped, and he vowed, and he swore
That he'd bury the town, ere he'd leave it, in grim fiery ruin and gore;
From black Ireton's Fort with his cannon he hammered it well all the day,
And he wished for his huge guns to back him that were yet o'er the hills far away.

The soft curfew bell from Saint Mary's tolled out in the calm sunset air,
And Sarsfield stood high on the rampart and looked o'er the green fields of Clare;
And anon from the copses of Cratloe a flash to his keen eyes there came,
'Twas the spike of O'Hogan's bright basnet glist'ning forth in the red sunset flame!

Then down came the galloping horseman with the speed of a culverin ball,
And he reined up his foam-flecked charger with a gallant gambade by the wall;
And his keen eye searched tower, fosse and rampart—they lay all securely and still—
And then to the bold Lord of Lucan he told what he'd seen from the hill!

The good steed he rests in the stable, the bold rider feasts at the board,
But the gay, laughing revel once ended, he'll soon have a feast for his sword;
And now he looks out at the window, where the moonbeams flash pale on the square,
For Sarsfield, full dight in his harness, with five hundred bold troopers is there!

He's mounted his steed in the moonlight, and away from the North Gate they go,
Where the woods cast their black spectral shadows, and the streams with their lone voices
   flow;
The peasants awoke from their slumbers, and prayed as they swept through the glen,
For they thought 'twas the great Garodh Earla,* that thundered adown with his men!

The grey, ghastly midnight was 'round them, the banks they were rocky and steep;
The hills with one sullen roar echoed, for the huge stream was angry and deep;
But the bold Lord of Lucan he cared not, he asked for no light save the moon's,
And he's forded the broad, lordly Shannon, with his galloping guide and dragoons.

---

* Garrett, the great Earl of Desmond, who is still believed by the peasantry to arise from
his enchanted cave beside Lough Gur in Limerick, on the St. John's night of every seventh year, and
sweep, at the head of his mail-clad barons and knights, through the surrounding country.

the star of the morning out glimmered, as fast by Lisearly they rode;
As they swept round the base of Comailta the sun on their bright helmets glowed.
Now the steeds in the valley are grazing, and the horsemen crouch down in the broom, .
And Sarsfield peers out like an eagle on the low-lying plains from Sliav Bloom.

PART THE THIRD.

O'Hogan is down in the valleys, a watch on the track of the foe,
Johnnie Moran from Brosna is marching, that his men be in time for a blow.
All day from the bright blooming heather the tall Lord of Lucan looks down
On the roads, where the train of Dutch Billy on its slow march of danger is bowne.

The red sunset died in the heavens; night fell over mountain and shore;
The moon shed her light on the valleys, and the stars glimmered brightly once more;
Then Sarsfield sprang up from the heather, for a horse tramp he heard on the waste,
'Twas O'Hogan, the black mountain sweeping, like a specter of night, in his haste.'

"Lord Lucan, they've camped in the forest that skirts Ballyneety's grey tower,
I've found out the path to fall on them and slay in the dread midnight hour;
They have powder, pontoons, and great cannons—Dhar Dhia! but their long tubes are
     bright!
They have treasure *go leor* for the taking, and their watchword is 'Sarsfield!' to-night."

The star of the midnight was shining when the gallant dragoons got the word,
Each sprang with one bound to his saddle, and looked to his pistols and sword ▸
And away down Comailta's deep valleys the guide and bold Sarsfield are gone,
While the long stream of helmets behind them in the cold moonlight glimmered and shone.

They stayed not for loud brawling river, they looked not for togher or path,
They tore up the long street of Cullen with the speed of the storm in its wrath;
When on old Ballyneety they thundered, the sentinel's challenge rang clear—
"Ho! Sarsfield's the word," cried Lord Lucan, " and you'll soon find that Sarsfield is here!"

He clove through the sentinel's basnet, he rushed by the side of the glen,
And down on the enemy's convoy, where they stood to their cannons like men;
His troopers with pistol and saber, through the camp like a whirlwind they tore,
With a crash and a loud-ringing war-cry, and a plashing and stamping in gore!

The red-coated convoy they've sabered, Dutch Bill's mighty guns they have ta'en,
And they laugh as they look on their capture, for they'll ne'er see such wonders again;
Those guns, with one loud-roaring volley, might batter a strong mountain down,
Wirristhru for its gallant defenders if they e'er came to Limerick town!

They filled them and rammed them with powder, they turned down their mouths to the
     clay.
The dry casks they piled all around them, the baggage above did they lay;
A mine train they laid to the powder, afar to the greenwood out thrown—
" Now, give us the match!" cried Lord Lucan, "and an earthquake we'll have of our own!

O'Hogan the quick fuse he lighted—it whizzed—then a flash and a glare
Of broad blinding brightness infernal burst out in the calm midnight air;
A hoarse crash of thunder volcanic roared up to the bright stars on high,
And the splinters of guns and of baggage showered flaming around through the sky!

The firm earth it rocked and it trembled, the camp showed its red pools of gore,
And old Ballyneety's grey castle came down with a crash and a roar;*
The fierce sound o'er highland and lowland rolled on like the dread earthquake's tramp,
And it wakened Dutch Bill from his slumbers and gay dreams that night in his camp!

+ The ancient castle of Ballyneety was rent asunder by the shock of the explosion, half of it falling
with a loud crash that added not a little to the horror of the scene.

Lord Lucan dashed back o'er the Shannon ere the bright star of morning ar—,
With his men through the North Gate he clattered, unhurt and unseen by his foes;
Johnny Moran rushed down from Comailta—not a foe was alive for his blade,
But his men searched the black gory ruins, and the deil's in the spoil that they made!

———o———

SWEET SIBYL.

BY CHARLES GAVAN DUFFY, M. P.

My Love is as fresh as the morning sky,
  My Love is as soft as the summer air,
My Love is as true as the saints on high,
  And never was saint so fair!
    O, glad is my heart when I name her
      name,
    For it sounds like a song to me—
    I'll love you, it sings, nor heed their
      blame,
    For you love me, *Astore Machree!*

Sweet Sibyl—sweet Sibyl! my heart is wild
  With the fairy spell that her eyes have lit;
I sit in a dream where my Love has smil'd—
  I kiss where her name is writ!
    O, darling, I fly like a dreamy boy;
      The toil that is joy to the strong and
        true,
    The life that the brave for their land
    ·   employ,
    I squander in dreams of you.

The face of my Love has the changeful light
That gladdens the sparkling sky of spring;

The voice of my Love is a strange delight,
  As when birds in the May-time sing.
    O, hope of my heart! O, light of my
      life!
    O, come to me, darling, with peace
      and rest?
    O, come like the Summer, my own
      sweet wife,
    To your home in my longing breast!

Be blessed with the home sweet Sibyl will
  sway
  With the glance of her soft and queenly
    eyes;
O! happy the love young Sibyl will pay
  With the breath of her tender sighs.
    That home is the hope of my waking
      dreams—
    That love fills my eyes with pride—
    There's light in their glance, there's
      joy in their beams,
    When I think of my own young
      bride.

———o———

MY OWN.

(*From the Irish.*)

BY EVA. (MISS MARY EVA KELLY.)

By the strange beating of my heart,
  Finding no place for all its joy—
By those soft tears that wet my cheek,
  Like dews from Summer sky—
By this wild rush through every vein—
  This chok'd and trembling tone,
Surcharg'd with bliss it cannot tell—
  I feel thou art my own.

And yet it cannot all be true,
  I've dream'd a thousand wilder dreams;
But this is brighter, wilder far,
  Than even the wildest seems.

I've dreamed of wonders, spirit-climes,
  Of glories and of blisses won;
But ne'er before did vision come,
  To say thou wert my own!

My own—my own! thus gazing on,
  My life-breath seems to ebb away;
And o'er and o'er, and still again,
  The same dear words I say!
I know—I know it must be true,
  And here, with Heaven and Love alone,
I hold thee next my heart of hearts!
  For thou art all my own!

———o———

WHEAT-GRAINS.

BY JOHN BOYLE O'REILLY.

As grains from chaff, I sift these worldly
rules,
Kernels of wisdom, from the husks of
schools:

Benevolence fits the wisest mind;
But he who has not studied to be kind,
Who grants for asking, gives without a rule,
Hurts whom he helps, and proves himself a
fool.

The wise man is sincere; but he who tries
To be sincere, hap-hazard, is not wise.

Knowledge is gold to him who can discern
That he who loves to know must love to learn.

Straightforward speech is very certain good;
But he who has not learned its rule is rude.

Boldness and firmness, these are virtues
each,
Noble in action, excellent in speech.
But who is bold, without considerate skill,
Rashly rebels, and has no law but will;
While he called firm, illiterate and crass,
With mulish stubborness obstructs the pass.

The mean of soul are sure their faults to
gloss,
And find a secret gain in other's loss.

Applause the bold man wins, respect the
grave;
Some, only being *not* modest, think they're
brave.

The petty wrong-doer may escape unseen;
But what from sight the moon eclipsed shall
screen?
Superior minds must err in sight of men,
Their eclipse o'er, they rule the world again.

Temptation waits for all, and ill will come;
But some go out and ask the devil home.

"I love God," said the saint. God spake
above,
"Who loveth me must love those whom I
love."
"I scourge myself," the hermit cried. God
spake:
"Kindness is prayer; but not a self-made
ache."

---o---

THE RISING OF THE MOON.

BY JOHN K. CASEY.

" 'Oh, then tell me, Shawn O'Ferrall,
Tell me why you hurry so?'
'Hush, ma bouchal, hush and listen;'
And his cheeks were all aglow.
'I bear ordhers from the captain,
Get you ready quick and soon;
For the pikes must be together
At the risin' of the moon.'

" 'Oh, then tell me, Shawn O'Ferrall,
Where the gatherin' is to be?'
'In the ould spot by the river,
Right well known to you and me.
One word more—for signal token,
Whistle up the marchin' tune,
With your pike upon your shoulder
By the risin' of the moon.'

" Out from many a mud-wall cabin
Eyes were watching through that
night,
Many a manly chest was throbbing
For the blessed warning light.

Murmurs passed along the valley,
Like the banshee's lonely croon,
And a thousand blades were flashing
At the risin' of the moon.

" There beside the singing river
That dark mass of men was seen,
Far above the shining weapons
Hung their own beloved green.
'Death to every foe and traitor,
Forward, strike the marchin' tune,
And hurrah, my boys, for Freedom!
'Tis the risin' of the moon.'

" Well they fought for poor old Ireland
And full bitter was their fate.
(Oh, what glorious pride and sorrow
Fill the name of Ninety-eight!)
Yet, thank God, e'en still are beating
Hearts in manhood's burning noon,
Who would follow in their footsteps,
At the risin' of the moon."

---o---

THE MAN OF THE NORTH COUNTRIE.

BY T. D. M'GEE.

HE came from the North, and his words
    were few,
But his voice was kind and his heart was
    true,
And I knew by his eyes no guile had he,
So I married the man of the North Countrie.

O! Garryowen may be more gay,
Than this quiet street of Ballibay;
And I know the sun shines softly down
On the river that passes my native town.

But there's not—I say it with joy and pride—
Better man than mine in Munster wide;
And Limerick Town has no happier hearth
Than mine has been with my Man of the
    North.

I wish that in Munster they only knew
The kind—kind neighbors I came unto:
Small hate or scorn would ever be
Between the South and the North Countrie.

——o——

MY FIRST PAIR OF BOOTS.

(1829—1879.)

BY RICHARD OULAHAN.

'TWAS the vigil of Christmas, away in the past,
    When a loving young mother, of rich raven locks,
Plagued with coaxing and teasing, had promis'd, at last,
    That the "gift" to her boy should be no baby's box;
Full of hopes for the morrow, Queen Mab spun a dream
    About candy-framed pictures, and fairest of fruits,
Till my eyelids unlock'd, in the morning's first gleam,
    And I found, on the pillow, my first pair of boots!

Oh, the joy of that waking!—Now fifty long years
    Since I kiss'd their red tops with uproarious glee;
And, in free dishabille, amid laughter and cheers,
    Hugg'd the old mastiff, Wolf, barking "encore!" at me.
When the red-leggin'd jack-daw, so humanly vain,
    Struts about, like a fop, and exultingly hoots,
I can fancy a fat little coxcomb again,
    To his fellows displaying his first pair of boots.

In my waterproof armor, right up to the knees,
    How I daringly dash'd where the boys fear'd to go,
Making light of the warning that "somebody'll freeze,"
    As I plung'd through a miniature mountain of snow;
If these memories sadden, I'm glad when they come
    To attest that the heart is still fresh at the roots,
And remembers each scene 'round its infancy's home,
    Where my last Christmas box was my first pair of boots.

As we jostle along o'er the rocks of Life's track—
    In the dim distance leaving the schoolhouse and play,
From the brain-busy Present we seldom look back
    'Till the tablets of childhood are lost on the way—
Let the soldier have trophies, the poet green bays,
    And the soul-troubled Shylock, his golden pursuits;
Heaven's angel of Happiness lovingly plays
    With the boisterous boy in his first pair of boots.

——o——

ROBERT EMMET.

[Written on the occasion of his Centennial, March 4, 1878.]

BY WM. GEOGHEGAN.

THOUGH over your ashes the grave grass
    tangles,
  And night winds moan 'round your clayey
    bed,
Yet a voice sounds forth in the silent
    watches—
  "O, martyred Emmet, thou art not dead!"
Not in the land that you loved and cherished,
  Not in the hearts of the Celtic race,
For whose rights you strove, till the blood-
    marked pillars
  Of tyranny shook, to their bone-made base!

Death may come with his somber vestment
  To hide such hearts from our earthly ken;
But the spirit within, no death nor darkness
  Can ever conceal from the gaze of men.
To the doomful gibbet the tyrant led thee,
  And quenched life's flame in its lucent
    prime;
But no tyrant *ever* can dim the halo
  That rings thy name for all future time.

Over thy urn no white shaft rises,
  No pompous mark of the sculptor's art;
But thy glorious name and thy grand
    achievements
  Are graven forever on Ireland's heart!

There alone let them stand recorded,
  Till vict'ry comes on the battle's flood
To the deathless cause that was consecrated
  In the holy font of thy generous blood!

O, Spirit that soared upon eagle pinions,
  And lived and died for a grand design,
There's a radiant wreath in the future
    waiting
  The land that nurtured such soul as thine;
O'er the weary years and the anxious vigils
  The Day of Deliverance yet will rise,
And the hills shall echo a grand *Te Deum*
  For her martyrs' pray'rs and her exiles'
    sighs.

Then with her chainless hand she'll fashion
  A garland meet for her martyr's tomb,
And where now the graveyard nettle is
    trailing
  The tended lily shall sweetly bloom;
And the pilgrim over thy green grave
    bending
  Shall murmur soft as his pray'r is done—
"It wasn't in vain you died, oh, Emmet,
  For the cause you championed at last is
    won!"

———o———

A WANDERER'S MUSINGS.

BY WM. GEOGHEGAN.

THOU art far away, my mother, far o'er the mighty sea,
Yet flies my lonely spirit on wings of love to thee;
And in the hours of silence, when darkness veils the earth,
In fancy I revisit the land that gave me birth.

I meet the smiling welcome—thy lips I fondly press,
Oh! is there aught more holy—a mother's pure caress?
I feel the gentle presence of thy soft hand in mine,
I see the beaming love-light in those dear eyes of thine.

And memory sweetly pictures the scenes of childhood fair,
The cottage in the valley, the Inny flowing there;
The paddock and the woodland, the orchard and the glade,
Where oft in boyhood's freedom my careless footsteps stray'd.

Oh! Columbia's scenes of beauty do charm the traveler's eye,
When Nature's bloom and verdure in rich profusion lie;
Where Art with magic fingers hath reared her lofty dome,
Yet still to me is fairer my own, my childhood's home.

God bless thee, gentle mother; may he thy spirit cheer,
May His abundant mercy dry every falling tear;
And when thou meekly kneelest in solitude to pray,
Think of the lonely wanderer in distant lands away.

——o——

THE CHRISTMASTIDE OF OLD.

BY WM. GEOGHEGAN.

ONCE more the bells of Christmas
  Send their chimes across the snow;
And the holly branches glisten
  In the firelight's ruddy glow;
Glad voices give me greeting
  In the old accustomed way—
"I wish you a merry Christmas
  And a happy New Year's Day!"
But the tender words and wishes
  Leave me lorn and pensive-souled,
For my thoughts go bounding backward
  To the Christmas Days of old.

From the mirth-resounding circles
  That I loved in boyhood's days,
And whose songs and lightsome laughter
  Crackled like the yule-log's blaze—
Many a friendly face has vanished,
  Many a form is lying low
Where the Inny's dancing waters
  To Lough Ree's bright bosom flow;
Others walk the path of exile,
  And the hearthstone now is cold
Where they loved and danced and feasted
  In the Christmastide of old.

As I sit within my chamber
  Listening to the night-wind's moan,
I mark two empty places
  By this fireside of my own.
Two vacant chairs are standing,
  Where, in other days for me
Two loved ones laughed and prattled,
  Or contended for my knee!
Ah, it's hard to think they're lying
  'Neath the heavy churchyard mould,
Whose presence lent such luster
  To the Christmas Days of old!

God be with them. They are happy;
  And for us who yet remain
In this vale of mortal sorrow
  'Tis not fitting to complain.
Ring out, sweet bells of Christmas,
  Across December's snow,
You mind us of another land
  Where flow'rs immortal blow,
Where the loved ones never leave us
  To commingle with the mould,
Where the nightless years are brighter
  Than our Christmas Days of old.

THE END.